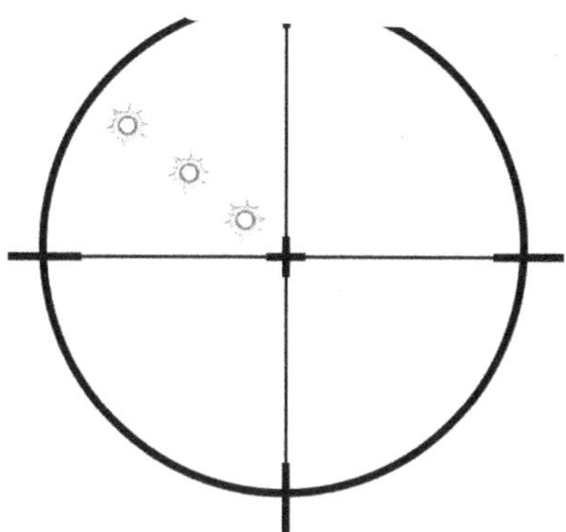

Samir's Revenge

(A novel)

Other books by Dave Admire:

Terror in Paris

Forthcoming:

The Korean Connection

Samir's Revenge

(A novel)

Dave Admire

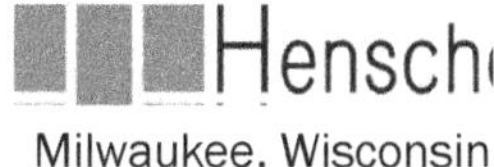

Milwaukee, Wisconsin

Published by Three Towers Press,
An imprint of HenschelHAUS Publishing, Inc.
www.henschelHAUSbooks.com

ISBN (Paperback): 978159598-680-1
ISBN (Hardcover): 978159598-681-8
E-ISBN: 978159598-682-5
LCCN: 2018963145

Cover design by Ryan Allen

This book is dedicated to my children La, Ryan, DJ and Kyle,
who have and continue to brighten my life in all aspects.

Cast of Characters

The Professor's Group
DJ Anderson – Professor
Sandy Anderson
  Jill – daughter
Mac MacDonald – Retired Professor
Ann MacDonald
Ty Smith – Professor
Leanne Smith
  Clint – son
  Julie – daughter-in-law
  Kelsey – granddaughter
Derek - former student

The Government Group
John Bradford – President

Federal Bureau of Investigation
Richard Jackson – Director
Sam Wyman – Director, Counterterrorism
Art Rheingold – Special Agent in Charge
Stu Williams – agent
Jake Sanders – agent
Ethan Clark – agent
Sherry Webster – agent
Jeff Turner – agent

The Coast Guard
LTJG Amanda Wakefield
Chief Petty Officer Kyle Burke
Seaman Rod Jamison
Petty Officer Jake Milam
Seaman Tom Jayson

Border Patrol – El Paso
Art McCall – supervising agent
Bill Jackson – agent
Jean Jackson – ex-wife
  Hannah Jackson – daughter
  Sarah Jackson – daughter
Jeanette Hauser – agent
Jared Isom – agent
Jason Crow – agent

Police
Chief Brian Martin
Jolene – dispatcher

Other Americans
Jack – University President
Renee – pole dancer
Michaela Clarkson – receptionist at the Wynn
Frank Jordan – helicopter pilot
Blaine Jones – helicopter pilot
Don Martin – Vietnam vet
Jaron Reese – medic
Dick Jensen – New Year's Eve celebrant
Toni Jensen – New Year's Eve celebrant
  Michelle Jensen – daughter
  Jordan Jensen – daughter
Ed Smith – trooper
Pete Wilson– New Year's Eve celebrant
Victoria Walker – New Year's Eve celebrant

Saudi Students
Hadi
Riaz

French Officials
Pierre Belcher – Director, Counter Terrorism
Mael Couseau – Deputy Director, Counter Terrorism
President
Prime Minister

Terrorists

Samir's Unit
Chuck James – RV driver
Samantha James – RV driver
Omar Abbas
Saad Darosa
Nasser Maj
Abdullah
Karim
Khalid
Rashid
Mustafa

Kamil's Unit
George Smithson – RV driver
Molly Smithson – RV driver
Majid
Moiz
Asad
Ali
Jawad
Hossien
Yaser
Mohammed

Mohammed's Unit
Will Jacobson – RV driver
Brianne Jacobson – RV driver
Abdul
Bakir
Jalal
Fahd
Talib

Others
Ahmed – assistant leader
Zuni – computer specialist
Salah – Samir's friend, deceased

American Conspirators
Stan – assassin
Tommy – American kidnapper
Phil – American kidnapper
Gary Bell – Las Vegas contact for Samir
"Janet Jackson" – contract criminal

Cartel Members
Pedro– driver/recruiter
Enrique Hernandez – recruiter
Juan – crossing leader
Javier – member

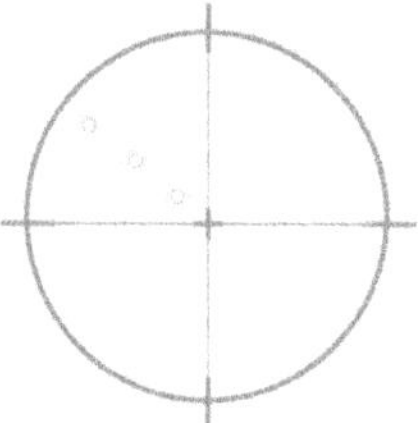

Prologue

In late September, Mac, Ty, and I returned to the U.S. with 17 students from a study-abroad program in Paris. During that time, we were caught in a coordinated terrorist attack that had brought Paris to its knees. Unfortunately, our hotel was one of many that were attacked. But because Mac and Ty were retired police officers, we were not the normal victims caught in a terrorist rampage. With a great deal of luck and some intense planning, we were able to defend ourselves and our students from increasingly heavy attacks the terrorists threw at us. Three of our students were killed and others injured, but most of us were able to escape to safety and to the protection of the French military. During the last attack, a terrorist voice came over the radio. It was the leader of the attack, a man named Samir. We had killed his best friend, Salah, and many of his men.

And, now, he is coming for us.

Book One

The Beginning

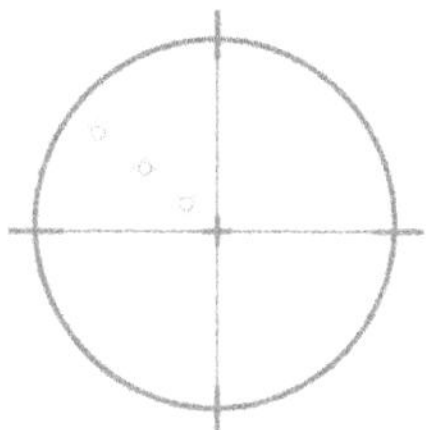

Chapter 1

Mac, Ty, and I were sitting on the patio of Mac's house having a hot toddy and catching up as our wives finished preparations for an early dinner. My cell phone rang. The call was unexpected, and I wasn't going to answer it. However, Mac indicated we had plenty of time to take the call before dinner. I got up and stepped away, "Hello?"

"Professor?"

I responded, "Who's this?"

There was a pause and then I heard, "This is Samir."

I quickly put the phone on speaker mode and waited for Mac's and Ty's attention before responding, "Who?" In my heart, I knew the person on the other end.

"You killed many of my men in Paris and my best friend, Salah. I just wanted to let you know that I'm coming for all of you now." The phone went dead.

The shocked look on their faces mirrored the words of both Mac and Ty, who exclaimed, "Holy shit!"

My mind was abuzz. I felt a combination of both fear and anger. Fear at what might happen and anger that we might have to go through this again. Mac was clearly agitated, but with a gleam in his eye that said, "Bring it on." Ty, on the other hand, was more reserved as he contemplated what was to come.

To say we were shocked was an understatement. Thoughts of the three students who had not come home ran through my mind. I had thought that the incident with the terrorists was behind us.

Mac regained his composure and smiled, "Well, what do we do now, Daddy?" He had used that term for me since I became the department chair and nominal leader of our study abroad trip.

"Can't you give that damned thing up?"

"Why should I, DJ? I get your goat every time I say it." With his flippant wit, Mac had diffused the tension in the room.

Ty just sat there, shaking his head and laughing at both of us. Then he turned serious and stated, "We need to talk about what just happened. He sounded serious to me. Maybe it's his way of getting back at us. You know, he may not really mean it, but he wants us to think about the possibility of his coming after us, which, frankly, scares the hell out of me."

"Wait a minute," I responded. "How did he get my cell number?"

"It doesn't matter, DJ," Mac commented. "He did."

I switched my attention to Ty. "It sounded like a pretty damned serious threat to me. I don't think it's something we can ignore, but the bigger question remains, what can we do? Shit, I can't believe this is happening."

I could see the concern begin to form on Mac's face. The lines that walked across his forehead seemed to deepen as he considered the content of the phone call. He tilted his head and looked at me, then switched his attention to Ty. "Do you really think he would attack us again?"

Ty did not wait long to respond. "Given what he did in Paris, I have no doubt that if he wanted to get us, he could. I'm not sure there's any other way we can take it, but seriously. If we do nothing, and he comes, we're dead men. If we develop a plan to deal with this, we might have a chance of not being dead men. This is a hell of a way to start our Christmas vacation."

As professors at the local university, Ty and I had just finished our fall semester and were scheduled to begin classes just after the New Year.

I responded next. "I agree with Ty. We can't do nothing given this guy's history; to do that would be incredibly stupid and puts our families at risk."

Mac stood up and stretched. With his hands on his hips, he said, "Well, for the first time in a long time, I think both you guys are right. That means we need to start putting together a plan of action to protect our families and ourselves. Frankly, I think we should do that sooner than later."

The door opened, and we turned to see Mac's wife, Ann, standing in the doorway. She smiled at us and announced, "Dinner is ready, big guys. Why don't you come and get it?"

As we headed for the door, Mac whispered to us, "Let's not say anything about the call until we have had a chance to talk about our options."

Both Ty and I mouthed, "Okay."

The table had been set and the aroma of barbecued ribs and sweet potatoes almost made us forget the threat. I sat at one end of the table with Mac at the other. Mac was 55 and carried his 185 pounds in a tall, lean body. He had served more than 20 years in police operations. Mac's time as a police office had provided him with a vast array of stories, and he shared these stories without being asked. I do believe that at least a small portion of his stories were actually true. His hair and beard were white and he joked that he wasn't sure whether that had been caused by his wife or his job. He had retired from the university the year before and had promised me that he would participate in the study abroad to Paris.

On my right was Ty. He had retired from the Metro Police Department in Las Vegas after serving 22 years. His hair was prematurely gray and of medium length, typical of a retired police officer. He was quick to laugh at himself and his eyes sparkled when he did so. Ty brought his experience as a police officer into his classroom and kept his students enthralled as he brought criminal justice to life. I knew he would become one of the students' favorite professors.

To his right sat his wife, Leanne. She was quite a few years younger than Ty, which allowed us to make many jokes at his expense. Leanne was petite with brown hair, green eyes and a sprinkling of freckles across her nose. She, like Ty, was slim and her expressive face lit up when she smiled. Leanne had met Ty at a friend's wedding. They had hit it off immediately and had become inseparable ever since.

Ann, seated to Mac's left, and like Mac, was fit from the morning walks they took together. She had light brown hair that fell to her shoulders and was a perfect height for him. She could hold her own with Mac's quick wit and knew how to put him in his place when necessary. We all smiled when she gave him "the look." He often said there were times when it was best to give in if one hoped to get lucky that night. She also reminded him of that fact when necessary.

My wife, Sandy, sat to my left. Sandy and I had been married for 25 years and were perfect partners. We complemented each other's strengths and weaknesses, which made each of us better. She came up to my shoulders and had soft, light blonde hair, cut short. She had retired a few years before that, and she jokes that I had now become her full-time job.

My name is DJ Anderson and I am a retired judge. As the department chair, I am Ty's boss and used to be Mac's also. Although I am not sure that Mac can really ever be bossed. He is, however, my best friend with Ty running a close second. At 5 foot 10, I am probably a bit overweight from sitting all the time. As a lawyer, I tend to come down on the side of protecting rights while Mac and Ty believe it is best to lock them up first and worry about technicalities later. As different as the three of us are, we are close friends who enjoy each other's company.

Ann interrupted my thoughts. "What were you guys talking about when I came to get you for dinner?"

I looked at Mac questioningly and saw Ty do the same. "Nothing, honey, don't worry about it."

She gave him a sweet smile and looked deeply his eyes. "Don't give me that 'honey' shit, honey. Tell me what's going on. The look on the three of your faces said that something had come up. So spill the beans or sleep in the other bedroom tonight."

Sandy stated, "No, no beans please!"

In spite of herself, even Ann laughed.

Mac looked at me, his eyes begging for help. I tried, "You sure are suspicious today, Ann. Has he been trying to pull the wool over your eyes on something?"

She looked at me smiling and with a hard look in her eyes, and said, "So you're going to try to play dumb, too? Do you guys think we're stupid?"

The three of us looked at each other and realized this was not a place we wanted to go. I continued, "I have called Mac 'stupid' many times but never you. If I did, I know that you carry a handgun and I probably wouldn't make it out of here alive. So I refused to entertain any further questions on the ground of self-incrimination, which may lead to my death." I crossed my arms on my chest and sat back, determined not to say another word.

Ann looked at Ty next. "Are you going to play dumb and stupid, too? Or are you going to be smart and tell us the whole story?"

"I also am taking the fifth and will say nothing further." He also crossed his arms on his chest and sat back, smiling at Mac.

Mac looked at each one of us with hurt in his eyes. "You two are the biggest chicken shits I've ever seen. Aren't you going to support me?" Both Ty and I looked at each other, nodded, and in perfect harmony, placed our thumbs and index fingers on one corner of our mouths and drew them across to the far corner, indicating absolute silence.

"You know that I carry a weapon also. Right?"

Ty and I both looked toward the ceiling and didn't respond.

Sandy poked me in the arm to get my attention. "Just tell us what is going on."

I looked at her and waited for a moment. "This is Mac's house and I defer to him."

Ty spoke up immediately. "I couldn't agree with DJ more. Mac is more than capable of answering any questions his mom—I mean wife—asks him."

All eyes turned to Mac. "Assholes! If someone had ever suggested to me that these two strong and capable men would become shrinking violets in front of my wife, I would have struck them down. Absolutely incredible, chicken shits galore. Okay, I'll tell you what's going on. DJ just received a phone call from Samir."

"*The* Samir?" exclaimed Ann.

"Would you be quiet and let me tell my story? You're the one who's demanded it, so let me tell it. Yes, Samir, the leader of the terrorist group that attacked Paris while we were there."

Sandy responded with, "What the hell?! You guys were trying to hide this from us?"

Leanne followed with, "Ty, you'd better have a good excuse for this. If you don't, you may not get lucky for a long, long, long time. So spit it out."

We both looked at Mac and nodded. "If you guys will just let me finish. I will tell you everything, but you have to promise not to interrupt me until I have finished the story." He looked at the three women and slowly each of them nodded their agreement. "We weren't going to tell you about the call until we had a plan worked out. Samir identified himself to us and told us that we had killed his best friend and several of his men. He said he was coming for us. We had just begun to talk about what we needed to do when Ann came out. That's it, that's the whole story."

Sandy and Leanne exploded with cries of alarm based on the fear that rose in their throats.

Ann, with a concerned look, asked. "So, what are you going to do?"

Mac answered, "We haven't got there yet. After dinner, we were going to spend some time figuring out what we should do. Until then, I have nothing else to tell you."

"All three of us will be included. Right, ladies?" Sandy and Leanne nodded their agreement. "Now that that simple question has been answered, let's drink and then eat."

"Right now, drinking sounds great," Leanne whispered.

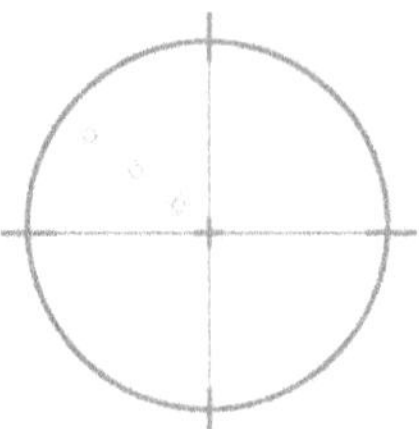

Chapter 2

Samir smiled as he imagined the fear that now flowed through the Americans as a result of his call. Since speed was important right now, he followed protocol by taking the battery out of the phone he had used to make the call. He motioned for one of his men to come to him from across the room. "Take this phone out, smash it, and get rid of it. Do not try to use it. Remember, the Americans have ways of tracing any phone we use. If you do anything but what I tell you, you may find an American missile coming down on your head. Now get going."

Since the attack they had carried out in Paris, he had moved from one apartment building to another. For the moment, he felt it was safe to stay in his current location. It was a nondescript, dirty white building, reminiscent of buildings all over Paris, six stories high with only four apartments on each floor. Over the past months, he and his people had been able to rent each of the apartments on the top floor. This area of Paris was predominantly Muslim and the remainder of the tenants in the building were of his faith. As a result, he believed the likelihood of his being discovered was less likely. Still, he insisted that security protocols be maintained at all times. The French were leaving no stone unturned as they searched for him and his people.

Of the four apartments on the top floor, three were occupied by him and his compatriots, Ahmed and Kamil. The fourth apartment was the command center where much of their work was done. He saw Ahmed, who had been with him for some time now, and Kamil, who had proved his value many times over. Both were huddled over a desk and speaking in low tones so as not to be heard by anyone else in the room. Samir had come to trust them implicitly, but no one would ever be able to attain the level of trust that he had shared with his departed friend, Salah.

Samir was still bitter over the mistake he had made during the attack on Paris. Those damned Americans infidels in the hotel had held off the first two attacks he had sent against them. Then, without examining the potential consequences, he had sent a large force led by Salah to wipe them out. Somehow, the Americans fought off that attack as well and escaped the destruction he had planned for them. And even worse, during the attack, Salah had been killed. There had been no real need to send Salah to lead the attack because other men were available to him. Every time he thought of the error he had made by sending Salah, he was filled with great sadness. But with that sadness came a grim determination to cause the deaths of those who had killed his friend. He knew that Ahmed and Kamil were concerned that his drive for revenge would hinder his ability to spread terror among the Americans in the United States, a plan they were working on now. He tried to hide the depth of his feelings about the loss of Salah, but there burned deep within him a fire that demanded that he kill these three Americans. The time for revenge would come, of that he was sure.

After working for an hour, he walked over to the desk where Ahmed and Kamil were sitting. They looked up at him as he approached. He smiled and said, "I'm going to my apartment to rest for a few moments. I will return shortly."

After Samir left, Ahmed glanced at Kamil. "Does he seem any better to you?"

Kamil shook his head. "I think he needs more time to adjust to the death of Salah. He will come around. We must continue to be the ones he can rely on as we plan our operations in America."

At the end of the hallway, Samir entered his dingy apartment but left the lights off as the dusky light of the day still lit the room. Samir walked his lanky 6' 3" frame into the bathroom, looked at himself in the mirror and saw the deep sadness clouding his eyes. He turned the water on and splashed his face with the cold liquid, hoping it would bring him energy. Again, looking into the mirror, he was surprised at the gauntness of his face and the dullness that had become his eyes. Samir turned, walked to his bed, lay down, and stared at the ceiling. After a few deep breaths, his eyes slowly closed, giving him some peace. He drifted off to sleep, letting the exhaustion seep out of him.

After a short hour of rest, Samir's mind became active once again. He was in that place between being asleep and being awake. While his body seemed to have rejuvenated, his mind took him into the past, to places he did not wish to go. He was first filled with great happiness as he spoke with Salah about the plans they had been making. Samir's mind thought of the various attacks they had planned and carried out in Paris. The success of those attacks had been unparalleled and cause for great joy. But his mind quickly changed with the vision of the three professors who had survived his attacks and killed Salah. Their photographs had been carried in all the Paris newspapers. His happiness was quickly replaced by a great anger as he envisioned Salah lying face down in his own blood. Samir's state of sleep left him immediately as he sat up in his bed. He could hear his heart beating and feel the sweat flowing down his face. Every day since Salah's death, his attempt to sleep had ended in the same way. The terrorist leader knew in the depth of his being that he would not have a restful night's sleep until he carried out his revenge.

Samir rose from his bed and walked to the shower, determined to cleanse himself of these feelings of failure. He knew he must refocus his energies to lead his men in the attack against America. With that promise to himself, he stepped into the shower and tried to wash away his guilt.

He stayed in the shower for nearly 20 minutes, letting the water flow over him. Samir turned the shower off, reached for a towel and dried himself. Samir stepped into his bedroom and put on the clean clothes he had laid out. The shower had done its job; he felt energized, refreshed, and able to continue.

He left his apartment and entered the command center, determined and refocused. Both Ahmed and Kamil were surprised to see that he had returned so soon; he seemed refreshed and ready to continue their planning.

Samir sat on the sofa and motioned for the two of them to join him. As they took their seats, he began, "I think it is time that we begin the concrete planning necessary to carry out our next attacks. We have discussed this many times hypothetically, but now we need to decide our best course of action. I've asked each of you to use your creative genius to develop a foolproof plan. I've tried to stay out of your way so that your work would not be hindered by my views." He looked at each man, assessing what their reactions to his words might be. "So, now, it is your time to explain to me what actions you believe we should take in the name of Allah."

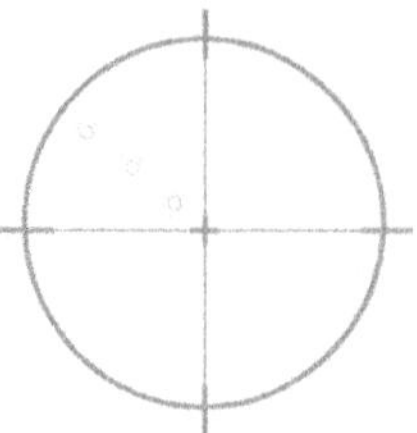

Chapter 3

After dinner, we bundled up and joined Mac on the patio around the fire pit. Even though it was December, it was surprisingly mild. Still, Mac prepared a warm grog for each of us to sip on to keep the coming winter chill at bay. We had not discussed Samir's threat during dinner but rather enjoyed the company of close friends. As we got settled in our chairs, Mac looked at me. "DJ?"

"Okay. Frankly, I think we are in a world of hurt. As I see it, we could be attacked anytime, anyplace, anywhere. How do we defend against that? My initial thoughts are that we have to inform the various government agencies about what is going on."

Leanne spoke up first. "You know, this is all bullshit. I mean, how can this happen in this country?" We could see that she was on the verge of tears.

Ty reached over and put his arm around her shoulder. "Don't worry, honey, we'll figure this out. We're not just going to stand here and take it."

Ann stood up and looked at all of us. "No shit, Sherlock. We are not going to take this lying down. We will come up with a plan and we'll execute it! And we will kill these SOBs should they ever approach us! But we can't wallow in self-pity. We need to move and move fast. So let's start listing what needs to be done and decide who's going to do it."

Mac put his hand in the air and Ann gave him a high five. "That's my wife! Ever since I've known her, she's been ready to kick ass and take names. And she is right, so let's make a list of things that need to be done. I also agree with DJ. We need to start with the appropriate government officials." Mac got up and walked into the house. A moment later, he returned with a marker and a legal pad. "Let's brainstorm this. I'll write it down so DJ, with his advanced age, will remember."

In response, I gave him the finger.

"I'm ready to start the list," Ty stated. "First, we need to contact the FBI, Homeland Security, local police and government officials, the state police and the governor's office." As Ty spoke, Mac furiously scribbled down every suggestion. Ty continued, "And those are just the obvious agencies we need to contact. Any other suggestions?"

I responded, "If they're gonna come after us, they have to come into the country somehow. Therefore, we should notify the border patrol, TSA, and the National Security Agency. But the real problem is that we need all of these agencies to work together. So the question becomes, do we notify them individually or do we ask for someone to coordinate the entire response?"

Mac looked at our list. "We need to get some political pull on our side, also. We should inform our senators and representatives that there is a clear and direct threat to their constituents. Maybe that will help get a coordinated response from the government."

Sandy, who had not said a word during this discussion, spoke up forcefully. "I think you guys are trying to reinvent the wheel. The government is supposed to know how to handle this stuff, not us. We simply need to inform the government of what's going on and let them do what they're trained to do. So, my suggestion is that DJ, Mac and Ty go to the FBI tomorrow and lay it all out for them. Then we need to get out of their way and let them do their job. That gives us the opportunity to decide how we can protect ourselves."

Leanne gave Sandy a thumbs up. "Sandy is absolutely correct. We need to come up with a plan to protect us; let the government decide how to protect the country." Ty started to interrupt and Leanne cut him off. "This is not a time for you dingdongs to let your testosterone get in the way of your good sense." She was trying not to laugh and not being entirely successful.

Ty, who was facing the house and across the fire pit from me, rose and looked at Leanne. "I'm going to take my testosterone-filled body to the bathroom to take a leak." As he turned toward the door, he suddenly spun to the ground, groaning. That was followed immediately by the muffled sound of a gunshot. I saw blood seeping from the back of his upper arm. The window behind me shattered and the glass clattered to the ground.

Mac yelled, "Everybody down!" Each of us leapt out of our chairs and fell to the ground. Just as I dropped, my chair was knocked backwards and fell against the wall. I glanced at the chair and noticed a hole in the back at a level where my heart would have been.

We were fortunate because Mac had built a small wall approximately two feet high separating the patio from the grass. As long as we stayed below the height of the wall, we should be safe from further gunfire. Mac looked at the women and yelled, "Stay down and crawl into the house. Get to a safe place inside where the shooter can't see you and turn off the lights." Mac and I crawled toward Ty. He was lying on his back and blood was flowing away from his arm. Ty's face was contorted in pain. Mac was lying on his belly next to Ty. He moved Ty's arm to see where he been shot. "Ty, you've been hit in the back of your arm. It's through and through."

"It may be through and through," Ty responded through gritted teeth, "but it hurts like a son of a bitch."

I looked at Mac and pointed toward the door. "Let's get him out of the line of fire and stop the bleeding!" I looked at Ty, "Do you think you can crawl to the door?"

"I don't think so. I don't think I can use my arm. Shit, it hurts."

"Stop being a baby, Ty." Mac smiled.

"Asshole."

"Mac, let's just drag him in the house." We grabbed his shirt, then crawled and pulled him along the ground into the house, and behind the kitchen island, which shielded us from the shooter. Mac opened a drawer, pulled out some kitchen towels and proceeded to wrap them tightly around Ty's arm. He put pressure on the entry and exit wounds where the bullet had passed through. The blood began to soak through the towel and I looked at Mac questioningly.

Mac smiled at me. "He's going to be okay. The bleeding is already slowing. DJ, keep pressure on his arm, I'm going to see what's happening outside. Ann, are you guys okay?"

"Yes, and I've called 911. The deputies are on their way. I told them a man had been shot, and they said an ambulance would be here shortly."

Mac crawled to the back bedroom. He opened the shades sufficiently to scan the fields adjacent to the back of his property line approximately 500 yards away. Initially, he saw nothing, but then he observed a man carrying a rifle and running in a crouched position toward the road that ran along the back of his land. Mac could see that the man was headed for a car parked on the side of the road. He quickly ran back to Ty and me.

"Ann, get over here." As she rounded the corner, Mac pointed at Ty. "Take care of him. DJ and I are going after the shooter."

"We are?"

"Yes, the son of a bitch is trying to get away." He glanced at Ann, "Do you have your weapon?"

"Of course," she replied. "Go get that bastard."

As a retired police officer, Mac always carried a weapon. I followed him as he ran through the front door to his truck. He jumped in the driver's side and started the vehicle. I climbed in the passenger side as he backed out of the driveway. Mac pointed toward the glovebox. "There's a weapon in there."

I pulled out a 9-mm Glock and made sure it was loaded. By this time, Mac was flying down the dirt road that led to the entrance of his ranch. He slid around the corner through the open gate and drove toward where he had seen the shooter's car. I glanced at Mac and said, "I assume you have a plan when we catch up to the son of a bitch?"

He smiled at me with a gleam in his eye and responded, "I'm going to kill the bastard before the police get here. Do you have a problem with that?"

The edge in his voice and the look in his eye sent a chill down my spine. It was clear that no one should attempt to stop him. "Nope, just wondering."

"Good!"

When we arrived at the spot where Mac had seen the man with the rifle, there was no sign of the car or the shooter. Mac decided to drive towards town, thinking the man would travel in that direction. As we passed a side street, Mac pulled his truck to the side of the road. Jerking his hand back over his shoulder, he said, "I think I saw the shooter's vehicle parked on the side of the road about 200 feet down the street. Stay here, I'll be right back." With that, he opened the door and ran toward the street behind us. I turned, looked back and in a few moments saw him running back toward the truck. He jumped in and looked at me. "I'm almost sure that that's the shooter. We'll go around the block and come at him head on."

Mac drove quickly around the block and, as we turned toward what Mac thought was the shooter's vehicle, I could see someone in the driver's seat who appeared to be talking on a cell phone. Mac drove at a normal speed toward the vehicle but stopped suddenly when they were side by side. Mac's window was down and he brought his Glock up, aiming it at the man in the car. Shock crossed the man's face and he quickly raised his own gun. Mac shot twice, striking the man in the forehead. The man slumped over the console.

I jumped out of the truck and ran to the shooter, who was obviously dead. Mac, who had also exited his truck, reached through the window and grabbed the cell phone resting on the man's lap. He picked it up and put it on speaker. I heard a voice yelling, "What's going on? Stan, answer me!"

Mac growled, "Who the hell is this?"

The man on the phone responded, "This is Samir. Who am I talking to?"

Mac answered, "Samir, you old piece of pig shit. I just killed Stan. Is he another one of your inept followers?"

Samir responded, "Make no mistake about it, I am coming and I will kill you!"

Mac started laughing. "You and what army?

I could hear the anger in Samir's voice. "You're a dead man. All of you are dead men."

Mac sounded as if he had no worries. "Bring it on, asshole. We will be waiting for you."

Before Samir disconnected the call, he said, "You won't see me coming, but you'll regret everything you said." The call ended abruptly.

I stared at Mac and shook my head. "I think you pissed him off."

"Good. If he's pissed off, he'll make mistakes. That's good for us. Let's head back to the house. We can tell the deputies where to find this guy and what happened. But first, as the lawyer, don't you think you should read Stan his rights?"

I smiled at Mac. "I think you're absolutely right. Stan, you have the right to be dead. You have the right to remain silent, but if you do speak, it will surprise the shit out of us. Finally, you have the right to an attorney. He or she can help bury your sorry ass."

I looked at Mac and he gave me a thumbs up. Upon completion of our legal duty, we headed back to Mac's house.

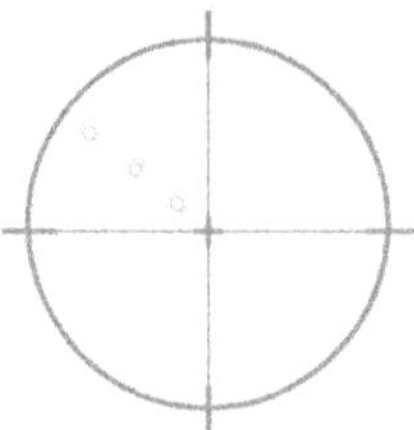

Chapter 4

Bill Jackson was sitting in his too-small office. His home away from home was about ten feet by ten feet. This bothered Bill a lot, since after all, he was a senior border patrol agent. He knew people in his building who had offices much larger than his. Bill also knew that the work they did shriveled in responsibility compared to his job.

As he sat there with his feet on his desk, he studied the photo that graced the wall, showing the President of the United States standing next to him. The previous President had been touring various border patrol offices and happened to stop by his. Bill didn't necessarily care for the President's policies, but he did value the photo and the value he believed it gave him. As he looked at the photo, he could see his stomach, like the President's, hanging over his belt. His hand moved unconsciously from his chair to his stomach, which still draped over his belt. Regardless of his attempts at dieting and exercise, he simply couldn't lose any weight. At 45, Bill was at that stage of life where keeping in shape had become more difficult. Part of the problem he knew was that his job required him to be sitting in a vehicle or at his desk most of the day. Both of these actions were the cause of his seeming inability to get consistent exercise. He was a short 5 foot 10 and weighed about 220 pounds, give or take. His face was tan from the sun, but had the white circles around his eyes that told everyone he wore sunglasses.

Bill lived in a small apartment not far from his office. He had been there since he and his wife, Jean, divorced a year ago. Bill had two daughters, ages four and seven, and was paying child support for the children and alimony to his ex-wife. Bill had to work a lot of overtime in order to meet his financial obligations, and it also reduced the time he could spend with his children. That was what was difficult for him to understand. The court had ordered that he pay child support and alimony. The court also gave him visitation rights. However, because the amounts he was required to pay for child support and alimony were so high, he was unable to exercise his visitation consistently because he had to work so much overtime. In essence, the court was forcing him to look for alternative means of income.

After work, Bill stopped at a bar about a mile from his office. When he walked in, he could see that it was like every other bar in his town. It was dark and filled with smoke. Texas didn't care about secondhand smoke. Two guys were playing pool and another was waiting to take on the winner. Bill walked over to the bar, sat down and ordered a beer. He was still dressed in his border patrol uniform. As he glanced around the bar, he did not recognize a single person. Anyone could see that he was just a lonely guy enjoying a beer and who had no better place to be.

After three beers in an hour, Bill was feeling pretty good. A young man of about 30 came out of the bathroom and walked over and sat on the stool next to him. The young man looked over and said, "How's it going?"

Bill smiled and responded, "Not bad. You?"

"Good, very good indeed!" The smile on his face confirmed his feelings.

Bill could see the man's eyes light up. "Why are you so good?" The young man reached into his pocket and pulled out a wad of bills and smiled.

The man pointed at Bill's uniform. "I can't tell you; you work for the man. You think I'm crazy?"

Bill looked at his uniform and responded, "I may be a border patrol agent, but I really don't give a shit what you're doing. As far as I'm concerned, anybody who can pick up a little extra cash is lucky."

"Why do you say that, man?"

Bill glanced around the bar before he responded. "I mean, I may work for the government, but the government has screwed me over big time, and I don't have time to see my kids because of it. I got divorced a while ago, and I have to pay child support which I don't mind, but I also have to pay alimony. I have to bust my butt while my ex-wife sits on her ass while she should be out working. The result is, I have to work mucho overtime to pay her. It ain't fair, but you know the whole system is rigged for the woman. We guys just get screwed."

Bill's whole demeanor changed as he spoke. His body tensed and his eyes flared. As he finished speaking, his hand crashed down on the bar, almost breaking the beer glass in his hand. He took a deep breath to calm himself. "Sorry about the outburst. By the way, my name is Bill."

"Not a problem, Bill. I'm Pedro." He looked around the bar to see if anybody was paying attention to them. Seeing nothing out of the ordinary, Pedro continued, "Listen, Bill, I feel for the position you're in, and I may be able to help you in some way. I know how you can make some extra cash, good cash, on the side. Are you interested?"

"I may be. What's the deal?"

"You saw that thousand dollars I showed you from my pocket? Just ask what I did to earn it."

"I don't have a clue. Did you rob somebody?"

Pedro responded, "Nothing like that, man. I probably shouldn't tell you this, but you told me about your financial problems. I work with a guy who leads Mexican illegal immigrants across the border. Many of them are just women and children. He hands them off to me and I drive them to a warehouse not too far from here. It takes me about two hours from the time I leave home until I drop them off, and I get a grand, each trip. Safe and easy money. I can introduce you to him if you want. However, my guess is he will be very suspicious of you since you are a border patrol agent. I will tell you one thing, though, you don't want to screw with these guys. They mean business."

Bill wasn't sure that he had heard Pedro correctly. After all, he had just finished his fourth beer, and everything was a little blurry. "I'm not sure I can do that, but the money sounds awfully good. I need to think about it overnight. Can we meet here tomorrow? Here's my cell phone number if you need it."

Pedro eyed Bill closely. "Okay, same time tomorrow. But Bill, don't mess with me and try to set me up for the cops. I'm trusting you on this." With that, Pedro walked out of the bar.

Bill followed shortly thereafter. He had a lot to think about.

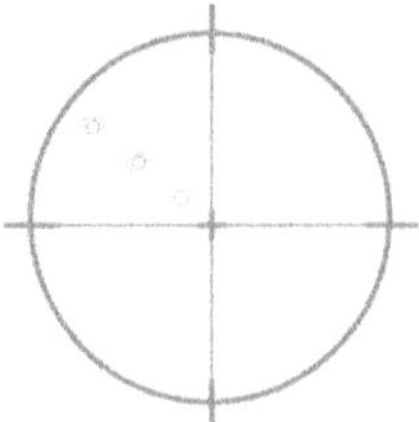

Chapter 5

Mac, Ty, and I were on our way to visit the local FBI office. Mac was driving his old 1984 Ford pickup, which by some miracle was still running. He had taken good care of his truck and put well over 200,000 miles on it. I was sitting on the right side of the bench seat, and I pounded the dashboard with the palm of my hand. "Damn it, Mac, when are you going to get rid of this old beater and buy something new?"

"Well, DJ, this sweetheart is like an old girlfriend. She gets warmed up easily, moves with a sway that brings a smile to your face, and never talks back to me. So, why should I get rid of her?"

"You're comparing this old, broken-down truck to an old girlfriend? Mac, you're worse off than I thought. I mean, you should get something more like your wife. Hot, fast, and purrs like a kitten."

Ty, who was sitting between the two, started laughing. "Don't make me laugh, my arm still hurts."

"Stop being a baby, Ty. My God, you only got shot."

"You're not the one who got shot, asshole," Ty responded.

Mac smiled at Ty and stated, "I've gone out with women who hurt me more than just a little bullet." At that point, Mac turned right into a parking lot. He found an open space and pulled in. Pointing straight at the entrance to the building, Mac said, "I do believe that the FBI's offices are through those doors. Let's go see what they have to say about our little phone call and visitor."

As we walked into the FBI office, we were met by a rather stern receptionist. I smiled at her and said, "We have an appointment to meet with Agent Rheingold at 11 AM. I know we're a little early."

"And your name is?"

"I'm sorry. I am DJ Anderson, and these are my two friends Mac MacDonald and Ty Smith."

"Thank you. If you will be seated, I'll contact Agent Rheingold." With that, she turned her back to us and picked up the phone.

Mac, Ty, and I sat down in chairs facing the receptionist. The reception area was typical of a government office. The furniture was practical and inexpensive. The art on the wall followed in the same style. After waiting a few minutes, a tall, broad-shouldered man emerged from the back-office area. He seemed to be about 50 and his time in the FBI was evidenced by the seriousness of his facial expression. The man was wearing a light blue dress shirt set off with a dark blue tie. He walked up to us and stated, "I'm Agent Rheingold. Which one of you is Anderson?"

I stood and replied, "I am, and these are my friends Mac MacDonald and Ty Smith." I reached out and shook his hand, as did Mac and Ty.

"Nice to meet each of you. Why don't we go back to my office?" We followed him into the inner sanctum of the FBI offices and to an office in the corner of the building. He motioned for each of us to sit down. "Now, as I understand it from talking to DJ on the phone, you believe that a terrorist attack is coming. Am I correct?"

"If I can, let me explain," I answered. "A few months ago, we were involved in the terrorist attack that occurred in Paris. We were leading a group of students..."

Rheingold interrupted me before I could finish my sentence. "Wait a minute. You're the three professors with the students who fought off the terrorists in your hotel?"

"Yes, and evidently the fight that occurred there is not over."

Rheingold looked at the three of us and chuckled. "Well, now I know you're not like the ordinary nuts who come into this office with outrageous stories. From what I read in the papers, it sounded like you guys had a hell of a battle against determined fanatics. Sometime we'll have to talk about your experiences there. I don't have a lot of time before my next appointment. Why don't you tell me why you're here?"

"Well, it's pretty simple. Yesterday, the three of us were having dinner with our wives. I received a phone call from an individual who identified himself as Samir, who we know to be the leader of the terrorist group in Paris. He said that we had killed a lot of his men and his best friend, Salah. He wanted us to know that he was coming for us next. Then he hung up. A few hours later, someone began shooting at all of us and that's when Ty got shot. There is not much more to the incident than that except that we caught up to the shooter and killed him."

Rheingold's expression didn't change.

Ty spoke up. "Calling it an incident makes it sound so dry and impersonal since my arm still hurts."

Mac added, "Ty's been whining about that ever since. But to go on, all three of us heard Samir. There was no question in my mind that he meant it. The local police investigated the shooting at my house and informed us that the shooter was a known hitman."

Before Mac could say anything further, Ty jumped in. "So, what do we do?"

Rheingold looked at the three of us and shook his head. "Well, initially, I'm not sure. I have to run this up the chain of command, which means Homeland Security will become involved. The more I think about it, there will probably be a lot of agencies involved to some degree or other. Let me ask you a couple questions. First, do you think this Samir is capable of coming to this country and mounting an operation against you? Second, what do you think the Bureau should do?" Once again, he looked at the three of us for an answer.

"I heard the tone of Samir's voice. It was clear that he is very angry," Ty answered. "I do not take it as an idle threat. In fact, my immediate concern is the safety of my family. I'm not afraid to admit that a chill went down my spine when I heard what he had to say. And, given what happened at the ranch, it seems clear to me that he is deadly serious about coming after us."

I saw Mac nodding in agreement. I started to speak, but Mac held up his hand and stated, "I agree completely with Ty. When you look at what this guy did in Paris, I don't think idle threats are part of his vocabulary. We saw the terror in Paris with our own eyes, and you've probably seen the reports of the damage that was caused. It was one of the most well-coordinated attacks I have ever seen. How they could keep the breadth of those attacks secret is beyond me. Do I think he could come over here and kill us? Absolutely I do."

Mac took a deep breath and continued, "What I would be concerned about, if I were you, is what other attacks he has planned while he is here. He must have incredible resources available to him if you look at the scope of the attacks in Paris. I don't think he would come here just to kill us; well, I suppose he might, but this man thinks big. I don't think we are that big, but merely an additional item to be checked off his list. Since he hired a professional hitman, I don't think he cares necessarily about doing the job himself. I don't know about DJ and Ty, but I would like the government to provide some form of protection for me and my family. Also, I would like any suggestions that you or anyone else has on how we can protect ourselves."

I found myself nodding my agreement. "I agree with everything Ty and Mac said. We need a lot of help. None of us asked for this."

Rheingold leaned back in his chair and looked out his window. He was quiet for several moments as he pondered what he had heard. Finally, he turned toward us. "Well, at this point, there's no information I can give you. I understand your concern and what it's based on. I'll talk with my superiors, get their take on it, and then get back in touch with you. Do you have cards with your contact information?"

Each of us placed a business card on his desk. He then rose, signaling that the meeting was over, before walking around his desk and shaking each of our hands. "Thanks for coming in. The information that you provided is important and distressing. Hopefully, we will be able to put together an action plan that works for all of us. I'll be in touch." He opened the door and we walked out, the door closing behind us.

Mac spoke first. "Well, that was interesting. Did we get the brush-off or was he serious?"

I responded, "I think he saw the seriousness of the situation and your comments about other potential attacks certainly grabbed his attention. I guess we just wait until we hear from him. In the meantime, there are some other things we need to take care of. I think our next meeting has to be with the president of the university. What do you guys think?"

"I agree," Ty responded. "We have to let the university know what the threat is. If we don't inform them, and Samir comes onto the campus and kills students, how could we live with ourselves? We probably should do that sooner than later."

I looked at Mac and he nodded his agreement. "Okay, I'll call and see if the president is available today and whether we can meet with him this afternoon." We climbed back into Mac's truck and headed toward the university which was about an hour away. "Mac, it wouldn't look good for us to be killed in this beater truck you have. You need to get something new."

"Are you nuts? If I get a new truck and your brains gets sprayed all over it, I don't think my insurance would cover it. For a lawyer, you're not very smart." Both he and Ty had a good laugh at my expense.

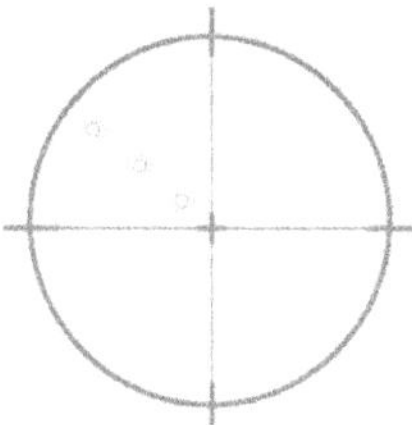

Chapter 6

Samir had been listening to Ahmed for several minutes, but he watched him closely also. He understood that while Ahmed's words set forth the actions that he was promoting, his body language would indicate how strongly he believed in what he said. Ahmed was taller than most Saudis. His hair was a glossy black, as was the beard that covered his face. He possessed an inquisitive mind that helped him as he considered potential plans. As opposed to the seriousness of many freedom fighters, he had a keen sense of humor and a quick smile that lit up his face.

When Ahmed had completed his suggestions, Samir looked at Kamil and nodded for him to continue. Kamil immediately began to describe the options that he believed should be considered. Samir listened intently as he laid out his plans. Kamil had a slender and muscular frame. Typical of many Saudi's, he had dark shiny hair, which he kept cropped short. He, too, had a full beard that covered his face. His most striking feature were the dark, serious eyes that seemed to pierce one's soul when he spoke. Unlike Ahmed's easy-going manner, Kamil had a quick temper. Those who worked for him knew that to invoke his temper risked retaliation and they certainly wished to avoid that. After a few minutes, Kamil concluded his presentation.

Samir looked at both of them and smiled. "I like your suggestions, but I have a few questions. First, have you given any thought as to exactly how we're going to be able to enter the United States? I don't believe we're on their no-fly list, but I don't want to take the chance of entering their country openly."

Kamil responded initially. "We have contacts in one of the Mexican cartels. I've made inquiries with them, and I believe we can be smuggled into the U. S. with one of their drug couriers. While there is always a possibility that we could be intercepted, they do this regularly enough that I believe the risks are small. We would just have to determine when and where we wanted to cross the border. There obviously would be a cost that would need to be paid, but it would not be extravagant."

"You have looked into this closely? This, I believe, could very well be the most dangerous part of our entire operation," Samir asked.

"Yes, I have. However, before we embark on this operation, I would examine it again to discover if there are unforeseen problems that I had not detected previously. As you know, many of these cartels have connections with the Afghan opium dealers. I would not say that we could trust them, but I would make it very clear that if there are any surprises, they should expect serious and deadly reprisals."

Samir continued, "My second concern is how we get our supplies into the U.S."

Ahmed responded to Samir's question. "We've looked at various options while addressing this issue. First, since we'll have many people involved in our operations, each could carry explosives with them as they crossed over the border. These explosives can be easily purchased in Mexico. As a backup, we have shipped explosives to the U.S. in cargo containers. They are at warehouses we have previously leased. As you know, we previously shipped these items because we knew we would be attacking America.

"Is it a risk that those explosives will be found? Obviously, the customs agents certainly could have discovered them. However, it wouldn't be likely because they simply do not have sufficient resources to check each and every container that comes into the country. There are hundreds of thousands of shipping containers that come through U.S. ports every year. Our main objective was to disguise the explosives in a way that would avoid detection from dogs or other means. I will check with our contacts to see if the containers did in fact arrive."

Kamil looked at Samir. "Do you believe we have sufficient financial resources to carry out the operations we have described?"

Samir had not shared with Kamil nor Ahmed any information regarding how he obtained the funds required to carry out their operations. Only Salah had been privy to that information prior to Paris. "Yes, I assure you, our financial resources are virtually unlimited. In time, I will share that information with you, but I have another concern. What you have presented to me has very little information on how we're going to kill the three professors."

Kamil and Ahmed looked at each other hesitantly. Kamil took a deep breath and answered. "It seemed to us that the killing of the three Americans was secondary to our goal of attacking America." Kamil saw Samir's eyes flash from the building anger he felt. Kamil hurried on. "So that took most of our initial planning. The actions we discussed previously are substantially more complex than the simple assassination of three individuals. We can easily develop a plan for the assassination."

Samir looked from one to the other, bottling the anger within him. "Let there be no mistake as to my desire to eliminate these people. This is not a secondary objective, nor should it be overlooked in any way. The failure of the assassin we hired merely hardens my belief that we need to carefully plan their deaths. Do I make myself clear?"

Ahmed looked at Kamil before he responded. "Samir, both of us understand your feelings in this matter. We also know how difficult Salah's death has been for you. As you've told us many times, our focus should always remain on hurting the Great Satan as much as we can. This attack on the professors, while important, does not, it seems to us, fall into the primary category you've always impressed upon us. Our loyalty to you demands that we bring this question to you. Obviously, we will follow your orders."

Samir tried to control his emotions. However, it was difficult to do so, for the pain of Salah's death and his loss radiated throughout his very being. He understood Kamil and Ahmed's concern. Samir also appreciated their courage in voicing their concerns. Samir sat back in his chair and looked at the ceiling as he tried to calm the fury he felt. Finally, in control of himself, he looked at the two of them. "Thank you for bringing this matter to my attention. I know it was not easy for you. You are correct that our focus should always be on America, but we will plan the attack on the three professors with the same seriousness we plan all of our attacks. I will not let my anger at the Americans and my desire for revenge disturb the success of our other plans. I promise you that only after the primary attacks have concluded will we change our focus to the three Americans. Does that relieve any concerns you may have?" Both Ahmed and Kamil nodded their heads.

"Okay, now that that has been resolved, what are the next steps we need to take?"

Kamil took a deep breath before he responded. "If you'll give us your approval for the plans we have laid out, we will begin implementing them."

Samir smiled. "You have my approval."

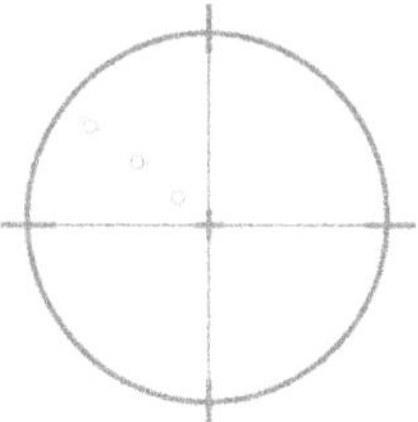

Chapter 7

Since it was late in the afternoon, Mac had no trouble finding a parking spot near the president's office. After we left the FBI's office, I had called the university president's office and was able to set up an appointment. As we walked toward the magnificent old building where the office was located, I stated, "I don't know about you guys, but I love this old, ivy-covered edifice. It reminds me of all the struggles that the people of this town went through to establish this university. It is amazing to me that people took out second mortgages so that this institution could be built."

Mac answered, "I agree. Sometimes I think that the generations that came before us sacrificed much more than those that followed. I wonder if those coming after us will say the same things about us."

The three of us walked up the stairs and entered the building. The president's office was on the second floor and we were soon standing before the student receptionist. I smiled at her. "I'm DJ Anderson and the three of us have an appointment with the president."

"I know who you guys are! The whole university knows who you are. One of my best friends was on your trip to Paris with you. She told me everything that happened. What an amazing story. I don't think I could've been as brave as your students were."

"Who is your friend?" I asked.

"Sheila Smith."

"Sheila was an important part of the group and I'm glad she was with us."

The receptionist smiled at me and picked up the phone. She spoke briefly to the person on the receiving end of her call and said, "The president can see you now."

We walked into the president's office and saw him sitting at his desk. He rose and came to greet us, shaking each of our hands, before motioning to the conference table. We sat down across from him. The disagreements we had with the president during our time in Paris had been long forgotten. When we returned from Paris, we had cleared the air. The president spoke first. "Guys, we need to quit meeting like this," he chuckled. "So, what's up?"

I looked at Mac and Ty to see if they wanted to begin this conversation. Mac simply nodded to me.

"We have some information we need to bring to your attention."

"Am I going to like this information or should I simply show you to the door now?" He smiled.

I returned his smile, "Well, we can leave now if you want. However, I know you're not one to put your head in the sand to avoid difficult situations. The gist of the matter is simple. I received a phone call a couple of days ago from Samir who, if you remember, was the leader of the terrorist group in Paris."

"He called you directly? I mean, how would he even know your phone number?"

"I can't answer that, but he obviously found my number some way." I explained the gist of the conversation. "A couple of hours later, a man shot at us while we were at Mac's house." I further explained to the president how we caught up and killed the shooter.

"Well, I'll be damned. That obviously raises a whole bunch of issues for us and for you. Do you think he'll come here to get you?"

"We met with the FBI today and that was the first question the agent asked."

Mac interrupted before I could respond further. "There's no question in my mind that he was serious. I don't believe he's the type to make idle threats, especially since he already sent an assassin to take care of us. Obviously, we felt it was very important to bring you into the loop. We informed the FBI of this incident and expect that our conversation with the agent will generate a lot of activity from the feds. The agent was unable to tell us anything specific at this time, but I imagine he has had discussions with his superiors already."

Ty leaned forward and spoke directly to the president. "We also asked the agent what suggestions he would have for what we could do to protect ourselves. Who would've thought that a simple study-abroad trip would bring these consequences?"

The president leaned back in his chair and pondered the information that had been given to him. "It seems to me that there are several issues that need to be discussed. I need to report this to the Board of Trustees and the Regents. We obviously will need to heighten security here at the university. Our main concern has to be the safety of our students. Wow, the more I think about this, the greater the ramifications I see for the university and for you guys."

Ty raised the question we all were thinking. "What exactly, besides our safety, are the ramifications you see for us?"

"Well, frankly, I can tell you that the first question both the regents and the trustees will ask is whether you should continue being on the university grounds. Their concerns, I believe, will be that if you continue to be present at the university, our students would be in jeopardy. We're going to have to figure out a way around that. I will need some time to discuss it with them. They will not want to station armed guards around the university. That may very well scare away our students."

I was shocked to hear what he was saying. "Are you saying that Ty and I could be fired? I mean, considering how we handled the situation in Paris that would be a strange way of saying thank you."

The president shook his head. "I don't mean being fired, but rather more like a leave of absence. I'm just talking off the top of my head here. First, there isn't anyone who respects and appreciates the work you did for us in Paris more than I do. You can be sure that I will always do what

I can to protect you. But before we go off half-cocked, let me discuss this with my staff, the trustees, and the regents. I need to find out what our options are." He smiled at the three of us. "The next time you come to my office, I hope it's for a nice lunch or maybe a round of golf."

I rose to leave and looked at him. "I know that these problems we bring you are trivial in nature," I smiled at him, "but that's what you get paid the big bucks for."

He rolled his eyes at me. "You know, you are full of it."

Mac started laughing, "I tell him that all the time, but he just doesn't seem to get it. Thanks for meeting with us, Jack."

"I'll be in touch with you just as soon as I can."

After the obligatory handshakes, the three of us walked out the door and waved at the receptionist as we headed down the stairs. Each of us was lost in our own thoughts as we walked toward Mac's truck. Just before we got in, Mac turned toward Ty and me. "Even though I don't work here anymore, I think he's right about the two of you being on campus. Your presence here simply puts the students at risk."

"I know you're right, Mac, but at least I hope we get paid," Ty said as he opened the door to the truck and got in.

"Well, from my perspective," Mac said, "you're probably not worth what they pay you anyway."

"Go to hell, Mac."

I jumped in, "I agree with Ty, asshole."

Mac looked at each of us with a big smile on his face and gave us the finger. So ended our conversation for the time being.

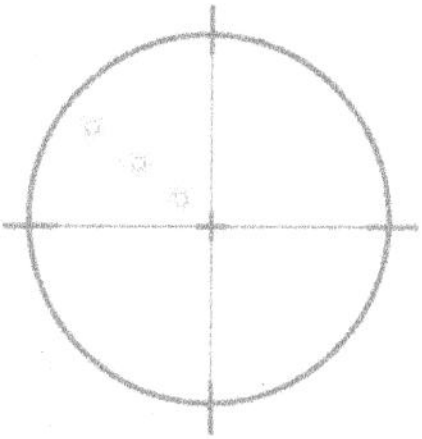

Chapter 8

Agent Rheingold waited patiently for Sam Wyman, the FBI's Director of Counterterrorism, to answer his phone. He had worked with Wyman early in his career when they were both stationed at the same FBI field office in Dallas. Wyman was a smart and dedicated member of the Bureau. He was interested to see how Sam would react to the information he was about to give him.

Suddenly the phone erupted. "Art, you old sonofabitch. How the hell are you?"

Rheingold responded, "Sam, I'm good but the real question is, are you as ugly as the last time I saw you?"

Wyman's deep laugh came through the phone. "Well, my wife tells me it depends on the day of the week. What's up with you?"

"I have some business for you. It's about a potential terrorist attack that may occur in my area."

"You have my attention. What do you know?

Rheingold could hear the change in the tone of Wyman's voice. "Remember those three professors and the students who became targets of the terrorist attack in Paris a few months back?"

"Of course, it was a national story for a while. What's up with them?"

"They came into my office today to warn me of a potential attack. If you remember, the leader of the terrorist group in Paris was a man named Samir. Well, Samir called one of the professors to tell him that he was coming to get him and his two fellow professors. After that conversation, within an hour or so, a shooter tried to take them out. Two of the three professors chased the guy and ended up killing him.

He was a known assassin. The assassin was talking on his cell phone with this Samir when the two professors got to him. One of the two picked up the phone, and Samir said he was coming to kill them. I asked the professors if they believed he was serious and capable of carrying out such an attack. Both indicated that Samir certainly was capable of such an attack given what he accomplished in Paris and the recent assassin's attack. They also did not believe he was a man to make idle threats. It is clear they are worried that he is coming for them. One of them also stated that given the resources the terrorist had, we should expect additional terrorist attacks to the country if they get here."

Wyman, who was nearing the end of his career in the FBI, swiveled his chair to look out his window to consider what he just heard. Wyman was a tall man and kept himself in good shape with a regular workout schedule. His silver hair was thinning but it still responded to a comb. "Art, when I read the news accounts, I was concerned that some retaliatory action might be taken against those gentlemen. There was simply too much news coverage about them to allow them to escape into obscurity. What have you told them that the Bureau would do?"

"Nothing. I told them I'd have to bring the situation to the higher-ups in the Bureau. I can tell you they are concerned for the safety of their families. They asked for any suggestions we might have as to what they can do to protect themselves. I would like to help them if we can. What do you think?" Art asked.

"My initial thoughts would be that there is not a whole lot we can do to protect them. I mean we can't give three people 24-hour protection for an undetermined amount of time. I'm going to have to give this some thought. The problem with these open-ended threats is that there simply is very little information to go on. We can let people in the system know that we have received this threat. Unfortunately, we receive such threats all the time, and people don't give them much thought anymore," Sam said in his gravelly voice.

"In this instance, I suspect we can assume that the terrorists have not yet entered the country. We can certainly inform the customs officials to be on the lookout for Middle Easterners flying into the country. We also have to put the word out to the border agents to be on the lookout for Arabs trying to enter the country. Do you have any other ideas, Art?"

"No, not really. What do you suggest I tell them, Sam?"

"I would be very upfront with the professors about the challenges posed by such threats. We don't want to give them false hope that we can provide something we can't. You know, if we gave them 24-hour protection, the terrorists would probably identify our agents. I'm sure they would try to keep those guys under some kind of observation before planning and initiating their attack. If they saw our guys, they'd just wait until we got bored and gave up.

"However, there is another possibility we could consider. Instead of protecting them, we could keep them under observation and perhaps discover any terrorists watching the guys. If we could find them, we could take them into custody and see what they know. If the terrorists were planning additional attacks, perhaps we could head those off," Sam said.

Rheingold interrupted Wyman before he could go on. "Wouldn't that depend on whether the attacks were planned before or after the attack on the professors? I mean if the attacks on other targets occurred before the attack on the professors, we wouldn't have any advance warning."

Sam growled into the phone, "That certainly is possible, but if the bad guys are just doing a reconnaissance of the professors, we might be able to get lucky and interrupt an attack that hasn't taken place yet. For us, it would be better if they plan to attack the professors first and carry out the other attacks after that. Obviously, we simply wouldn't know. And unfortunately for us, it's the nature of this business."

"If we put the professors under observation, would we want to notify them of that fact?" Art asked.

Wyman paused a moment before answering. "I don't think that would be a good idea. They could give away the fact that we were there, which would defeat the whole purpose. No, we would want the professors to just act fat, dumb, and stupid. In that way, we might get lucky and nab one of the terrorists. I think that's the way we should handle this. Do you have any problems with that, Art?"

"No, not really. So basically, we're using them as bait," Rheingold said.

"That's about the size of it. I am sorry we might have to sacrifice them to get at the terrorists, but sometimes that has to be done. I will get a team set up to keep them under observation. I'll have our guys report to you when they arrive and you can coordinate their actions with me. Does that work for you, Art?"

"That works for me, Sam. Let's have dinner when I get back to D.C."

"I look forward to that." Sam hung up his phone and returned to his computer. Before resuming typing, he paused for a moment. Sam disliked the idea of using the professors as bait but saw no other option. He looked at his computer screen and initiated the plan to send his agents as observers.

After he hung up the call with Sam Wyman, Art Rheingold pondered the professors' dilemma. He, too, disliked using DJ, Mac, and Ty in this manner and could only hope that this decision didn't result in their deaths. With an anxious sigh, he reached for his phone and dialed DJ's number to give him the news.

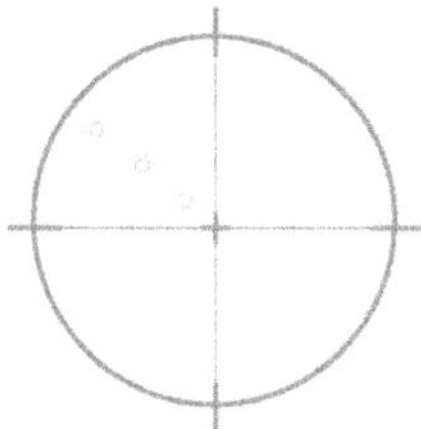

Chapter 9

Bill was standing outside the bar where he had met Pedro initially. Earlier in the day, Pedro had called him to arrange a meeting and said that he would pick Bill up outside the bar at 8 PM sharp. Bill glanced at his watch and saw that it was 7:50 PM. He did not want to be late for this meeting.

After talking with Pedro in the bar, Bill had given a lot of thought to what the other man had proposed. The border patrol agent knew that it was a potential source of grave danger to him. If he chose to go forward, he could end up in prison. But as Pedro had explained the work to him, it seemed like there was very little chance for him to be caught. The more he thought about his financial difficulties, the more this opportunity seemed to be the answer. As a result, he now stood before the bar, waiting to take that next step into financial security.

At the end of the block, Pedro sat in the driver's seat of a rented Toyota Camry. Next to him sat Enrique Hernandez. They had arrived at their location an hour earlier. Before meeting with Bill, Enrique wanted to make sure that the agent was not setting them up with the feds. Each man had binoculars and had been watching the cars and buildings around the bar. To this point, they had seen nothing out of the ordinary or anything that would make them suspicious. Now they were watching Bill. He seemed a little nervous but that was normal, nothing to cause any concern. At 8:05 PM, Enrique said, "Let's go get him."

Bill was getting a little worried because Pedro had said 8 PM sharp. He began to wonder if the meeting was still on. He glanced to his left and saw a vehicle approaching the bar. As it got closer, he recognized

Pedro as the driver. Bill breathed a sigh of relief as the Camry pulled up. Another man, who was in the passenger seat, rolled down his window and told Bill to get in the back seat. Bill pulled open the door and climbed in the car. Without another word, the car sped off.

"Hi," Bill opened up.

The man in the passenger seat turned and looked at Bill. "Please be quiet until we reach our destination." Bill nodded and sat back in the seat. The car drove for about 30 minutes before it pulled into a restaurant parking lot. The three men got out and walked into the restaurant.

Pedro asked Bill to go with him to the bathroom. Once there, Pedro said, "I need to search you." Finding nothing, the two men returned to the booth. Pedro nodded to Enrique, "No wires."

Bill sat there a bit surprised though he knew he shouldn't be.

Across the street, two men sat in another vehicle watching to see if anyone had followed the Camry. One of the men exited the vehicle, walked over to the restaurant and entered. He moved slowly toward the rear of the dingy dining room, where the three men were seated at a booth in the corner. Enrique looked at him and the man gave him a thumbs up. Enrique knew that it was safe to continue.

After they ordered drinks, Enrique begin the conversation. "Bill, I understand you might be open to earning some extra cash. Is that correct?"

"Yes, I've given it a lot of thought. Pedro told me that he picks people up and takes them to a warehouse. Is that what I would be doing?"

"Yes, for the most part. However, given your position with the border patrol, we might schedule crossings when you're working. You would be paid for simply letting these people pass. In other words, we could move people across the border with much less risk of detection if you were there. How does that sound to you?"

"Would you just call me and tell me when I would be looking the other way?"

Enrique continued, "Yes, we would provide a phone for you to use. Obviously, you would give us your schedule beforehand so that we could arrange crossings at the appropriate times."

"I understand from Pedro that he is paid $1,000 each time he takes people to the warehouse. Would I be paid the same amount for doing that work? Also, when I'm just looking the other way, what would I be paid for that?" Bill waited for the man's answer.

"You would receive the same fee that Pedro does for his work. However, we realize that looking the other way certainly carries more danger to you. Therefore, we are prepared to pay you $2,500 each time. How does that sound to you?"

Bill felt a thrill pass through his body; he was very excited about the money he could earn. Dollar signs spun before his eyes. "That sounds great to me. When do we begin?"

"Well, I just want to make sure you were good with all of this. If we believe you have involved the police or any federal agencies in our financial arrangement, we would be very unhappy. In fact, you will be killed. Do you understand that?"

Bill felt a lump in his throat as he heard this very direct threat to his well-being. However, he had listened to the warning Pedro had given him previously, and he was not really surprised that it was mentioned. Even so, hearing it from Enrique made it all too real. He knew that he had crossed the line into criminal behavior and there would be no going back. He looked at Enrique and stated, "I understand completely. You don't have to worry about me. I need the money, and I've been screwed by the government more times than I care to think about. In fact, I am open to any other suggestions on how you can use me."

Enrique looked at him closely for several moments. "I expect we will begin working together shortly. I want you to meet Pedro at the bar tomorrow at 7 PM. He will give you your phone and we will contact you when we are in need of your services. If you take people to the warehouse, you'll be paid at the warehouse. When you look the other way, Pedro will have your money at the bar the next day. Any questions?"

"No, I'm good to go."

Enrique got up and shook Bill's hand. "Pedro will take you back to the bar. You'll hear from us soon." Enrique walked to the door and pushed the glass door open.

Pedro smiled at Bill, "You're all set, my man. Let's grab a beer at the bar." The two men walked out of the restaurant. Enrique had disappeared.

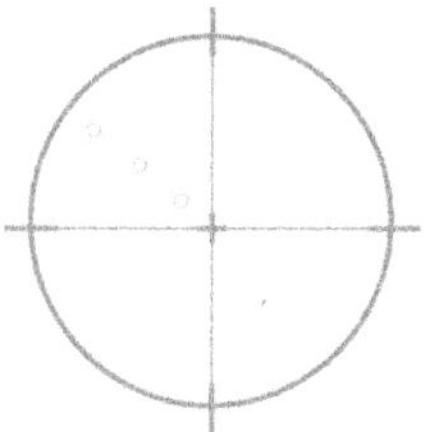

Chapter 10

A black Peugeot pulled up to the gate of the French government building. A young soldier walked up to the car to determine if he was going to allow the vehicle to enter. He looked in the driver's door window, recognized the driver and glancing in the back seat, he saw Pierre Belcher nodding at him. The soldier opened the gate and allowed the car holding the Director of Counterterrorism for the French government to drive into the inner courtyard.

The driver exited the car and opened the door for Pierre. The director climbed out and walked into the building. A few moments later, Pierre walked into his office suite and nodded to his receptionist. Pierre opened the door to his office, walked in, took off his dark blue suit coat, and draped it over the back of his leather chair.

After making an espresso from a machine located on the small table near the door, he returned to his desk and sat down. Pierre leaned back, closed his eyes and began to think about the meeting he had just left. Since the massive terrorist attack on Paris previously, the people of France were demanding not only action against the terrorists, but were also seeking someone to blame. Given his position, he was a prime target. The meeting, held in the president's conference room, was attended by most of the government leaders and the heads of the various political parties in France. The meeting had been held to determine who had been at fault for the successful terrorist attack.

When he had initially entered the conference room, Pierre believed his head was on the chopping block. The President began the meeting with an overview of the attack and its consequences. The cost to repair the damages was in the billions of Euros. Following this discussion, the

President stated his belief that someone was at fault for allowing this attack to occur. He then turned to Pierre. "Pierre, as the Director of Counterterrorism, it would seem that you bear the brunt of criticism for failing to foresee and prevent this attack." Pierre observed the Prime Minister nodding his head in agreement. During the attack, the Prime Minister had placed the blame squarely on Pierre. The President continued, "Do you have some defense you can raise on your behalf?"

Pierre began, "Thank you, Mister President, for this opportunity to discuss this matter. I should start by saying that my department had no actionable intelligence that would have led us to conclude that an attack was imminent. As you can imagine, my staff and I examined the intelligence we were able to obtain. This included electronic surveillance, reports from our informants, and the work of all of our agents. At no time did we receive any information that would indicate that an attack was being planned or close to being carried out. I want you to know that I believe that this has nothing to do with the capabilities of the people working in my department. And I will address why I believe that shortly.

"As all of you know, this was a massive and well-coordinated attack. The scope of the attack was so large that one would believe operational secrecy of the terrorists would have been breached. In other words, you would think that someone involved in the attack would have talked about it. We detected nothing of the sort. Does that mean that there were not breaches of operational secrecy? We simply do not know if in fact they had occurred. That does not, however, mean failure on our part.

"I can say with confidence that we would've discovered those breaches if our ability to detect potential terrorist attacks had not been severely compromised. By that, I mean the Prime Minister has, for the last three years, reduced my department's budget by an average of 10% per year. As a result of those cuts, I've had to reduce the number of agents and support staff whose work directly affects our ability to deter potential terrorist attacks."

The Prime Minister slammed his fist down onto the table, startling everyone in attendance. "I find it outrageous that the Director is now trying to avoid responsibility for these attacks."

The President held up his hand to quiet the Prime Minister. "Please be quiet and let the Director complete his remarks." The President nodded to Pierre. "Please continue."

"Thank you, Mister President. As I was saying, before I was interrupted, our budget has been cut by nearly 30% over the last three years. That has a direct impact on our ability to obtain information and, ultimately, deter terrorist attacks. I have here in my briefcase a series of emails and letters to the Prime Minister asking him to reinstate the funds he cut from our budget. These letters also indicate quite clearly the impact that these cuts have had on our ability to protect France." Pierre then opened his briefcase and took out a sheaf of paper. "I have copies of these documents for you." Pierre then passed the documents around the table.

Once attention returned to him, Pierre continued. "There is another factor that hindered our ability to perform our duties appropriately. The Prime Minister on numerous occasions interfered with our ability to obtain the necessary intelligence. He believed that our efforts should be directed toward electronic communications, and that we should cut our expenditures on human intelligence, which is the prime work of our agents and informants. In essence, the Prime Minister was trying to run my department, even though he lacked the minimal experience in intelligence operations required to make these kinds of determinations." Pierre pulled additional documents from his briefcase. "I'm now going to hand around to each of you copies of documents detailing the Prime Minister's interference in my ability to efficiently and appropriately run my department. After you've had a chance to review these documents, I will entertain any questions you may have."

Pierre watched the others as they reviewed the documents. This took nearly 30 minutes before the participants in the meeting were ready to proceed. The President then opened the discussion. "Mister Prime Minister, do you deny that these documents are authentic?"

"I have barely had time to review these papers, so I am unable to answer your question."

The President responded, "Do you believe these documents set forth your position fairly?"

"As I indicated to you previously, I cannot answer the question."

There was a loud murmuring of voices as the participants listened to the Prime Minister's response. Pierre watched the reactions to the Prime Minister's statement; he perceived a certain disbelief among these individuals.

The President addressed the Prime Minister once again. "The Director of Counterterrorism has stated his belief that you are responsible for his department's failure to detect and deter the terrorist attack that ravaged Paris. What would you like to say in your defense?"

"It is simply unbelievable that Mr. Belcher would try to shift blame for his failure to defend our country and place the blame on me. As you well know, we have competing priorities for the limited funds we have available to us. It is my responsibility to allocate funds as I believe is necessary. I did not order Mr. Belcher to spend his allocated funds in any way. I did make suggestions that would give us the best intelligence given the funds available, but it was his choice on whether to follow them. This is a witch hunt trying to find a scapegoat. Frankly, I do not wish to take part in this charade any further."

"Mister Prime Minister," the President stated. "You knew the purpose of this meeting today. I've heard you say, since the attack, that you believed Mr. Belcher should be removed from his position. My question is, why were you not prepared to address what you had to know would be his defense?"

"Because I did not believe that anyone would take his defense seriously. I am a patriot of France, yet here, I am made to feel that I'm responsible for the acts of these terrorists. I have nothing further to say."

The President pointed to Belcher and then turned a stiff index finger toward Prime Minister. "Gentlemen, would you wait outside while we discuss this matter?" Both men left the room.

The discussion among those remaining did not last long, and within minutes, the two gentlemen were brought back into the room. The President continued, "After a thorough discussion of this matter, it is our belief that the Prime Minister should resign his position. Mr. Belcher, you may leave this meeting and continue the good work you've done." Pierre rose, gave a small nod, and left. He heard the Prime Minister arguing his position once again, trying to get the participants to reverse their decision. A few steps later, Pierre was out of earshot, but knew that someone would tell him what had occurred.

As Pierre continued to drink his coffee and reflect on the meeting, there was a sharp knock at the door. "Come in." The door opened and Mael Couseau entered the office.

Mael, a former field agent and currently the deputy director of the agency, spoke. "Well, are we all fired?"

"You may wish you could get out of your difficult job that easily," replied Pierre with a grin. "I am happy to inform you that we have not been fired, but rather, the Prime Minister has."

"It couldn't have happened to a nicer guy." Pierre could see the smile light up Mael's face. "Damn, I would like to have observed that meeting." Mael watched the director smile. He saw that this man of nearly 60, slender of build and a man of high intelligence, just had a huge weight lifted from him. Pierre's forehead seemed to be less deeply furrowed than previously. Mael also knew that those furrows would return because of the heavy responsibilities that Pierre shouldered.

Pierre watched Mael as he spoke. Mael had black hair, stood 4 inches above 6 foot and his frame carried 250 pounds of solid muscle. Even though his position would normally require him to wear a suit, today he was dressed in dark slacks and an open-collared blue shirt. Pierre appreciated Mael's loyalty to him and to the department, but most of all he appreciated his determination to protect France from enemies both within and without. "Do you have any new intelligence you would like to share with me, Mael?"

"Actually, I have some information I think we should share with the U.S."

Pierre's eyebrows rose in surprise. "Please explain."

"Some of my agents on the street are picking up some interesting information. While it's not absolutely clear, we hear that some terrorists are planning to enter America for attacks there. It's not anything concrete, just rumors, but I would like to inform the Americans so they might have some advanced information as to a potential attack. What do you think?"

"It's pretty thin information, don't you think?"

"It definitely is. However, if we had had this type of information before the attack on Paris, perhaps the result would've been different. I don't think people are laughing about this being trivial information anymore. It seems to me the countries now would prefer any advance warning they can get, trivial or not. If you have no objection, I'll share this information with my contacts in the U.S."

"Please do and let me know what their responses are."

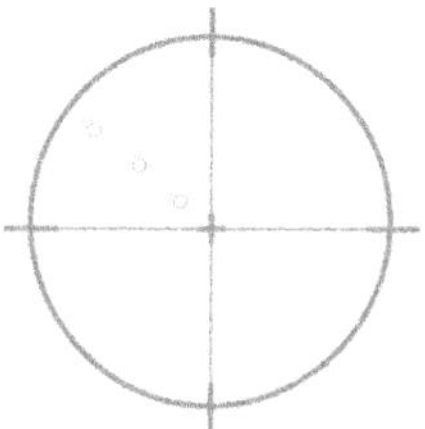

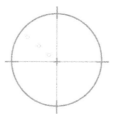

Chapter 11

Samir, Ahmed, and Kamil had just finished reviewing their plan. All three sat at the table in the command center. Their faces indicated they were quite pleased and excited. Samir continued their conversation. "The last thing I would like to discuss now is how we move our 21 operatives and us to the staging area in Mexico?"

Ahmed provided the answer. "Well, as you know, we have split them into five-man teams. Those teams will be further divided into groups of two and three. We spent a lot of time reviewing what would be appropriate airline flights for these groups. We had some initial rules that we developed that guided this process. First, we would have no more than three individuals on any single flight. This reduces our risk of being stopped by limiting the number of men of Middle Eastern decent on a plane. Second, we decided that some would travel directly from Paris to Mexico City and others would make stops in between. Those with stops in between will spend at least a day at their intermediate stop and then fly the next day on a different airline to Mexico City. These groups would fly over a three-day period, which we hope will disrupt any pattern the authorities might be looking for. Third, all tickets will be round-trip, again, to avoid any potential risks.

"We also instructed all of our operatives to be clean-shaven and well-groomed by the time of their departure. We have provided them with passports from various countries and complete background stories of their lives."

Kamil interrupted Ahmed. "I have been working with each of our operatives on his background information. Each has a firm grasp of his family and work history. If the men are stopped for any reason, they should be fine as long as they keep to their stories."

Ahmed continued once more. "As you know, all of our people speak English. Aside from the three of us, none of them are fluent in Spanish, but that should not be a problem because the people they will be dealing with in Mexico City should speak English. We have reservations at a number of different hotels for everyone in Mexico City. They will be provided with sufficient funds to pay for their expenses, plus the credit cards that we arranged for them. We also will have someone meet each group as it arrives; they will take the men from the airport to their hotels. Transport has also been arranged for everyone from Mexico City to Juarez. From there, we will travel with our guide across the border."

Samir held his hand up to stop Ahmed from continuing. "What about the guns and other armaments we need?"

"That is my responsibility," Kamil replied. "I have worked with a well-known arms dealer to provide us with the necessary armaments, which will be placed in storage at a warehouse outside of Mexico City. Just to be safe, I have also contracted with a second arms dealer to provide that same equipment to be stored at a different warehouse in Mexico City. We will have sufficient handguns and AK-47s to equip everyone and a large amount of C4, all of which will be packed in such a manner as to be easily movable across the border by our men. I'm confident these plans will work for us."

Samir nodded his agreement. "Well, we know what day we wish to strike America. That being the case, when should we cross from Mexico into the U.S.?"

"We've given much thought to that question," stated Ahmed. "Our conclusion was that given all things concerned, we should cross into America on Christmas Eve. This is a time when most Americans begin their Christmas holiday. It will give us sufficient time to travel to our first destination. Furthermore, it gives us additional time to look around the city and to see if there are any reasons why we should not carry out the attack on the day planned. I think it is a good timetable."

"Kamil, do you agree with Ahmed that this is a good timetable?" Samir queried, eyebrows raised. Kamil simply nodded his head in agreement. "Okay, that's how we will do it."

Just then, the three men were interrupted by a fourth man who entered the room. He bent over and spoke quietly into Kamil's ear.

Kamil looked at Samir and said, "We may have a problem. It seems that one of our younger men is talking when he shouldn't. Evidently, he has been bragging about going to America. How do you want to handle this, Samir?"

"Bring him to me immediately." Kamil looked at the man who had brought him the news and nodded. The man left the room.

A few moments later, the door opened again and the messenger and a frightened young man of eighteen entered. Samir smiled and asked," Do you know why you've been brought here to talk to me?"

"I'm not sure," the young man replied, "but they told me I did something stupid."

"Tell me what you think you have done that was stupid."

"I don't know, I really don't."

Kamil stood and walked over to the young man. "I've been informed that you were in a coffee shop bragging to some of your friends that you are going to America. Is that correct?"

"Yes, I did mention that to some of my friends. I don't see what's wrong with that."

The young man could see the fire in Kamil's eyes as he spoke. "How many times have I instructed you in our operational security?"

The young man answered. "I don't see if..."

"Don't interrupt me when I'm speaking. I have told you since you joined our group that you are never to discuss any of our plans or your part in them with anyone. Yet, now I have learned that you have been shooting your mouth off to your supposed friends."

The young man quickly understood that he was in serious trouble. "Apparently I made a serious mistake. It never occurred to me that merely saying I was going to America would put any of us in jeopardy. I'm so sorry."

Samir looked at the young man and asked, "Do you still wish to remain a member of our group?"

"Yes, of course I do. I want this chance to serve Allah."

Samir replied, "I have decided to give you one more chance to be a faithful member of our team. Kamil is going to take you to a house we have in the country where you will stay for one week. During that time, I want you to think about the error you have committed. At the end of those seven days, you'll be brought back before me for another discussion. Do you have any questions?"

"No, sir. Thank you for giving me another opportunity to serve Allah."

"Wait outside for Kamil. He will be with you as soon as we complete our meeting." The slender young man bowed and walked out the door. Samir looked at Kamil. "Now back to business. When do we initiate the transfer of our men to Mexico City?"

Ahmed responded, "The first group will leave in two days. I'll give you a complete schedule by tomorrow. The three of us will leave together after the last group arrives in Mexico City. That will allow us to reschedule should there be any problems in Mexico."

Samir nodded his approval. "Well, I think that's all we need to decide today. Kamil, can you return here in about two hours? You know what to do."

Kahlil nodded and left.

A little over two hours later, he returned and found Samir working at the table. As he approached, Samir turned to face him. "Well, tell me what happened."

"I drove out into the woods and we got out of the car. He told me he didn't see a house. When I pulled my gun out, he fell to his knees begging for his life to be spared. He asked for another chance to serve Allah. I then shot him twice in the head and buried him in a shallow grave."

Samir smiled and said, "Good." Then he turned back to the table to continue working.

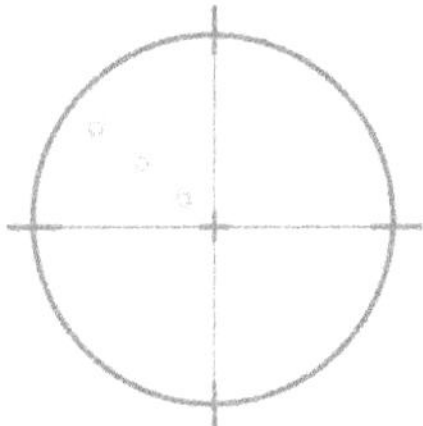

Chapter 12

The weather was beginning to cool as I drove down the hill from my house. Even though winter was nearly upon us, the blue sky and bright sunshine reminded me of summer. Our first snowfall had come in November. This area is blessed with 300+ days of sunshine each year. Typically, we could receive six inches of snow and within two hours, the sun was back in the sky. I would never go back to the Northwest where the sun teased you most of the year while the clouds and rain were a constant part of your life.

I pulled into the parking lot surrounding our local Starbucks. As I entered the store, I saw Ty and Mac had already arrived and were sipping their beverages of choice. I approached their table. "Hey guys, what's up?"

Mac responded, "Not much except that this drink has nothing in it to put a warm glow in my stomach."

"Well, it is only 10 AM. Give it a least another half hour, don't you think? You have the whole day in front of you."

"I am retired and don't have to think of such things. Since the university has put you on leave, I suggest that you use this time to see what retired life is like. I mean, DJ, you're retiring at the end of this year, aren't you? Ty, how much more time do you have left before you retire?"

"Mac, I do expect to retire at the end of this school year if we can put Samir behind us."

"Oh, hell, Mac," Ty answered, "I still have another 10 to 15 years, I expect. It doesn't really matter now since I enjoy what I do. Don't you miss your interactions with the students?"

Mac smiled at Ty. "Not like I thought I would. I love working with the students who put in the effort, but there were too few of them. You know what it's like. Too many students believe they should get good grades without even trying to learn the material. I leave them to you."

I turned and headed for the order line. Over my shoulder, I said, "I'm going to get some coffee and will be back in a minute." I could hear Mac and Ty continue their discussion of the students. I ordered my drink from the barista. A few moments later, I was holding a latte and heading back to my friends. I sat in the free chair and began our conversation. "So, what do we need to do? You guys have a lot more experience in this field than I do, so I'll just follow your lead."

Ty looked at me. "I know that you used a weapon in Paris, but do you have any formal training or knowledge about firearms?"

"Not much really. Probably 20 years ago, I received some training with a handgun. I was threatened by this guy, so the police suggested that I take a firearms class and arm myself for any potentiality that might occur."

Ty continued, "Well, Leanne has never even fired a weapon. Does Sandy have any training?" I shook my head in the negative. "It seems to me then that we need to bring you guys up to speed. That should be easy enough to do. Mac?"

"That shouldn't be a problem for Sandy and Leanne. But this dumb shit over here," he said pointing at me, "that may take a year or so."

Ty started chuckling when he saw me flip Mac off. I responded, "You seem to forget that I saved your silly ass in Paris."

Mac sat up in his chair. "You did what?"

"How quickly you forget, but given your age, I understand. If you'll recall, just before the RPG that injured me exploded, I told you to get your ass back. You jumped back behind the corner all safe and sound. Yes, I saved your sorry ass." I gave him my best sarcastic smile.

"Once again, you use your lawyer skills to write revisionist history. You forget, I'm the one who came back and hauled your butt to safety."

"As I recall, Mac, you were overwhelmed with guilt for leaving me there in the first place."

"You are so full of shit, DJ. I'm sure you forgot the fact that you told me to leave. Now I'm beginning to think that I made a mistake coming back."

I tried not to laugh. "If you had done that, then who would be here to give you grief?"

Ty raised both of his hands in the air. "Do you guys always give each other so much shit? I'm being kind here, mind you. Both of you sound like a couple of old women. Can we get back to the issue at hand because if we can't, I want a stiff shot of scotch just to put up with you?" He looked at both of us and waited for a response.

"Absolutely, let's get back to how we're going to protect ourselves. Should we write it down? I mean, Mac has a hard time remembering anything these days." I couldn't resist one more jab.

Mac returned my smile and said, "For a lawyer, you don't have much of a sense of humor. I would've thought you'd have tried to say something funny. Oh, well, let's continue. Who knows, maybe DJ will think of something funny later. Okay, so we're going to set up weapons training for Sandy and Leanne. I have some books with pictures for DJ."

Ty was staring at the ceiling. "Are you guys done?"

Mac and I nodded.

"Mac, what weapons do we need to get?" I asked.

"Well, we probably need to determine what we have already. I have two AR 15 semi-automatics and probably five 12-gauge shotguns. I also have several 1911 handguns. What about you, Ty?"

"I still have my service revolver, but that's about it."

"And you, DJ?"

"I have nothing to add to our arsenal, except that Sandy has some cast-iron skillets and a scrub brush."

Mac ignored the comment. "I would suggest that each person be armed with an AR 15, one handgun and a tactical knife. Everyone will need an assault vest and a go bag."

I interrupted Mac and said, "What is a 'go bag'?"

"It's a bag that's packed and ready to go. Duh. It contains magazines for each weapon, an assault vest, a small flashlight, and a first-aid kit with large bandages and tourniquets. That way, we will have everything we need in one place and will be ready to go."

"We should probably have a thousand rounds each, don't you think, Mac?" Ty asked.

"Yeah, I think that should be sufficient. DJ, will you and Ty buy the ammo and load the magazines? I have enough handguns for all of us. Obviously, we will need some additional AR 15s and tactical knives. Can either of you think of anything else?"

"You two are the experts. I'm relying on your opinion," I responded.

Ty answered Mac's question, "I think that'll do it, Mac. DJ and I will go buy what we don't have now. We'll also need to set up a time for training on the use of these firearms. I suggest that we do it sooner than later. Are you guys free tomorrow?"

I responded first. "That will work for Sandy and me. Mac?"

"That's okay for Ann and me. How about 1 PM?" He looked at both of us and we nodded our agreement. "Ty, how about you and Ann work with Sandy and Leanne? There is a separate place in the range I can take DJ with a 5-foot high concrete wall I can stand behind when he is shooting."

"Mac, there is no wall high enough that will protect you when I start shooting."

Mac smiled and stated, "I know. That's what I'm afraid of."

With that, we strode out of the coffee shop. Ty looked back and said, "Did you see the look on that guy's face? Do you think he realized we were only joking?"

"Who's joking?" I responded with a smile.

Book Two
Preparations

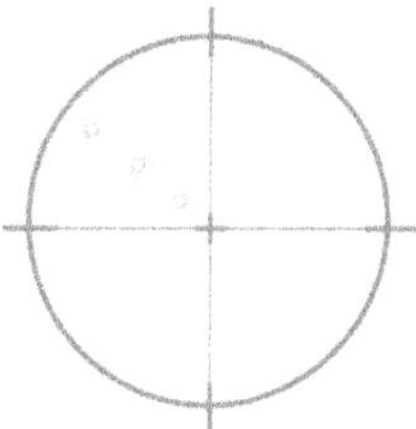

Chapter 13

The trip from Paris to Mexico City was a long one. Samir was traveling as a business executive, and therefore, sat in first class. Ahmad and Kamil were both traveling as business reps for a French marketing company. They sat together in the economy class near the front of the airplane.

Samir glanced out the window and saw what he believed was the Mexico City International Airport several miles away. He had turned off his computer already, placed it in its travel bag, and put it under the seat in front of him. Samir listened as the attendant announced the gate they would be arriving at. He had not been able to sleep during the flight because of the adrenaline coursing through his system, but he did not feel tired in the least. Samir realized that this day had been a long time in coming, and he understood that they had moved from the planning phase to the execution phase.

During the flight, Samir had mentally reviewed every part of their planned operations. No part caused him any undue concern. He also knew that the best-laid plans often went awry. Something totally unconnected with their operation could materialize and interrupt their plans. While they had explored and tried to plan for every potentiality, Samir knew that they would need to be flexible to avoid being brought down by the unexpected. He was confident that Ahmed and Kamil could adjust their plans as needed if something surprising happened.

The sudden bump of the airplane touching down chased his concerns away. He would have time to deal with them again in the not-too-distant future. Samir looked out the window and watched as the plane engaged its reverse thrusters, which reduced its speed quickly. In short order, the plane arrived at the gate. There was a minor wait for the gate attendant to arrive. Once the jet way gently touched the skin of the airplane, the attendant opened the door. As was normal, the first-class passengers began the deplaning process. As Samir walked toward the door, he observed both Ahmed and Kamil standing and holding their carry-on luggage. Samir walked out the door and passed the passengers waiting to board the plane for a return trip to Paris.

Ahmed and Kamil soon exited the plane and followed a short distance behind Samir as he walked toward baggage claim and customs. They decided before leaving Paris that it was important for Samir to stay separated from Ahmed and Kamil until they arrived at the hotel.

After passing through customs and having his passport checked, Samir headed toward baggage claim. It took but a few moments before Samir's suitcase appeared and made its way to where he was standing. He hauled the brown Samsonite case off the rotating carousel, and went through customs and immediately exited, following the signs to the taxi stand.

Several people were in line ahead of him waiting for transportation. This gave him time to turn and scan the people coming in and out of the doors leading to the baggage claim area. There was no reason for him to believe that he may be under surveillance, but he slowly and carefully let his eyes wander over the crowd. He saw Ahmed and Kamil standing in line for a taxi as well.

As Samir glanced about, he was certain that no one had any interest in him or his two associates. Soon, it was his turn to enter a cab and he did so. He gave the driver the address of a small hotel on the outskirts of the city. Unlike his other men, he, Ahmed and Kamil would take taxis to their hotel. To keep their identities secret, no one would be there to transport them.

It took 45 minutes to arrive at the hotel. The driver demanded what Samir was sure was an inflated fare. He did not want to raise any concern, so he simply paid the price the driver quoted. He walked into the small hotel and approached the reception desk. Samir told the clerk he was unsure how many days he would be staying and registered under the name contained in his travel documents. Samir would be known as Antoine Grenier while in Mexico. All of his travel documents, including several credit cards, were in that name.

The bored clerk gave him his room key and directed him to the elevator. As Samir walked to the elevator, he observed Ahmed and Kamil entering the building. Samir turned and looked at the clerk and said, "Room 314, is that correct?" The hotel clerk simply nodded. Samir had stated his question loud enough for both Ahmed and Kamil to have heard it. Then he turned and entered the elevator.

Thirty minutes later, Samir was seated on the sofa of his mini-suite. It was a plain room with functional furniture, the kind of room a business executive watching his pennies would find. Samir wanted to keep a low profile, but one that supported the role he was playing. A sharp knock at the door interrupted his thoughts. He walked to the door and looked through the peep hole. Samir opened the door and Ahmed and Kamil strode quickly into the room.

"Did you have any trouble at the airport or getting here?" Samir asked.

Kamil smiled at Samir. "Everything went very smoothly. Absolutely no problems at all. Both of us kept our eyes on the people around us. We saw no one showing any interest in us. I think we have entered the country undetected."

"Good. Tomorrow, I want both of you to call and check in with our various groups. If everything has gone according to plan and you have discovered no problems, we will leave for Juarez the day after tomorrow. Ahmed, you should organize the transfer of our armaments and explosives to Juarez. As I recall, you've previously arranged for that. Is that correct?"

"Yes, that has already been arranged. I just need to give them the order to head for Juarez. It should not be a problem."

"Have you had anything to eat since we left Paris?" Samir asked. Both men shook their heads in the negative. "I want each of you to go have dinner and return here tomorrow at noon. We will review your progress at that time and make any corrections that are necessary. Any questions?"

Kamil, who had been in Mexico previously, spoke up, "I have had Mexican food before and it is not something I look forward to now. Let's hope our move across the border goes smoothly. I wouldn't want to be subjected to the Mexican food for too long." With that, the two men left Samir's room.

Samir waited for half an hour before exiting the hotel in search of his own dinner.

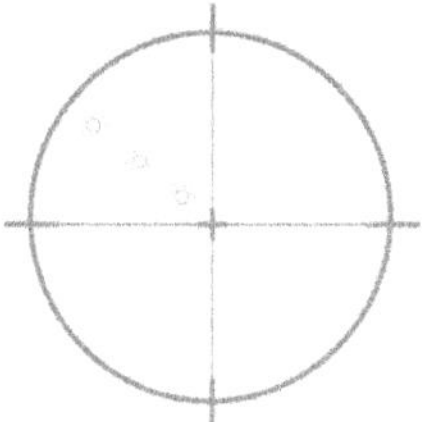

Chapter 14

Mael walked into the director's office suite and saw Pierre's assistant typing away on her computer. She looked up at him and smiled, "Hello, Mael. I haven't seen you for a while. Have you been out of town?"

"Yes, I spent the last few days in Marseille checking out some leads. Is the boss in?"

"He is and he's expecting you. Go on in."

Mael walked to the door of the director's office, knocked lightly, and opened the door. He saw Pierre sitting at his desk reading some document on his computer. "Good morning, Pierre. Is this a bad time to chat?"

"This is as good a time as any." Pierre stood and walked around his desk to shake hands with Mael. "Did you learn anything while you were in Marseille? Is there anything brewing down there?"

The director's handshake was as firm as ever. "No, nothing of significance. The information from our informant in Marseille, while accurate, did not lead to the results we hoped for. Our people down there will continue to monitor the situation." The director motioned to one of the chairs in front of his desk and Mael seated himself. Pierre returned to his own chair and leaned back, folding his hands over his stomach and peering at Mael with anticipation.

Mael continued, "I wanted to brief you on my conversations with our American counterparts. I passed on the information we've been receiving of potential terrorists heading to the U.S. The Americans indicated that they had received similar information. They questioned me about the details, and I gave them everything we had, which, as you know, is not much. The information they received matched ours. As you know, our information came from more than one informant. Their information, however, came from electronic sources. There is no one better than the Americans in capturing electronic information."

Pierre smiled and nodded. "I often wonder what secrets they have obtained about us through their electronic surveillance. Did they give you any idea about how they are planning to proceed?"

"Not really. By that I mean, there really is no actionable intelligence. They did tell me that they have put their border guards on high alert. TSA has also been informed. The U.S. has, and will, step up its scrutiny of Middle Eastern males entering the United States. They have decided not to increase the terror alert because the information they have is so vague. Frankly, I'm not sure what else they can do. I can tell you that they were very appreciative of having received our information and assistance. The Americans will keep me informed of anything they learn and asked us to forward to them whatever relevant material comes into our hands. I agreed to do so."

Pierre leaned back in his chair, turned slightly and gazed out the window. "That's the difficulty of this damned job. We rarely receive concrete information that we can act on. It seems that the information we do get is either vague or merely a small piece of a puzzle we have to put together. More often than not, we just need to be lucky to stop a terrorist attack."

Mael understood exactly what the director meant. "Do you have any more information about the attack on Paris?"

"Very little, if any. The forensic work at the various attack sites continues. We're fortunate that so many different countries have sent forensic experts to assist us. We have received DNA results that have led to the identity of some of the suicide attackers. One specifically was the man your informant brought to our attention. He evidently drove one of the trucks that attacked the Eiffel Tower. However, most of the DNA recovered has not been matched to any individual. The only reason we have identified some people with DNA matches is because they were previously involved in criminal activity here in France. I'm not sure we will ever be able to ID all of the attackers. So far, the ones who have been identified have not led us to the leaders of their group."

Mael was not surprised at the director's conclusions. The attack had been very well planned. Operational security was so high and effective that it continued to hinder their attempts to determine who was behind the attacks. "Have we made any strides in determining who Samir is?"

The director shook his head back and forth before speaking. "Samir seems to have dropped off the face of the earth. The problem is that the only information that we have on this individual comes from the American professors. And that was through a radio communication they heard. We don't even know if that's his real name. The police have talked to a farmer who lives outside of Paris. He approached them to explain a conversation he had with some Middle Eastern gentlemen. Evidently there is a house bordering his farm that was usually vacant. The farmer saw some activity at that house and decided to check it out. When he approached the house and knocked on the door, he found four Middle Eastern men. They said they were from Paris and had come to the house, which they had previously rented, to get away for some peace and quiet. They invited him in to have a beer."

Mael raised his bushy eyebrows. "Muslims drinking beer? I've seen it happen before but not often."

"The farmer actually inquired about that and one of the Middle Easterners told him that they were not strict Muslims and mentioned that they would be back in a couple of weeks. The old man actually invited them to join him at his house when they returned. They readily agreed to do so. No one has returned to the house since the attack on Paris.

"The police looked into the situation. The house was evidently rented by a sham company that we have learned doesn't exist. These men may have been involved in the attack, but that's conjecture. Interestingly though, the house had been wiped clean of any fingerprints.

The police will continue looking into this potential lead and keep us informed. Do you have anything else for me, Mael?"

"Not at this time, but you will be the first to know if I learn anything."

"Good, keep me advised as always."

Mael nodded his assent as he rose to leave. Pierre stood heavily and walked to the window, gazing out at gray roofs of Paris. Once again, he was struck by the lack of the Eiffel Tower rising to the sky. The director wondered what else would happen to his beloved city.

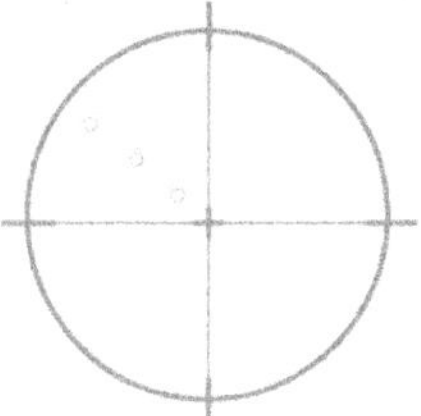

Chapter 15

It was 2:30 PM when Sandy and I pulled into the local Denny's and parked. As we entered the restaurant, I saw Mac and Ann sitting in a round corner booth in the back. When the waitress approached us, I pointed to the booth and said we were joining our friends. Just as we sat down, Mac pointed toward the door through which Ty and Leanne had entered. Soon the six of us were seated together. We ordered coffee, while our wives ordered iced tea.

Mac began the conversation. "Why has our fearless leader called us together?"

"Well," I began, "it obviously isn't because I missed your company. Actually, there is some interesting news."

Mac interrupted me. "No offense, but if I wanted news, I would read the paper. I was just getting ready to take my afternoon nap...with my wife." The smile on his face spoke volumes and in response to that smile, Ann poked him with her elbow sharply enough to make him groan, which brought chuckles from around the table.

Ty broke in, "So you were thinking you were going to get lucky this afternoon, huh? Make sure you let us know how that goes."

"Perhaps it would be safer if we started our discussion of Samir," I suggested. "One of the most difficult issues we have to confront is that we have no idea when he may strike, if at all. What I wanted to talk about is a new development that may help us with that issue. There's a young Saudi student I have come to know. We ran into each other at Walmart yesterday. He asked me why I was not teaching next semester, and I explained to him what was going on."

"Do you think that was smart?" Ty said with a concerned look on his face. "I mean the Saudi students tend to stick together."

"I think he'll be okay. I've known him for over a year now. He seems like a straight shooter and is actually a member of the royal family in some way. He made it very clear to me previously, and yesterday, that he is not a supporter of terrorism in any manner. When I talked to him about it before, the student told me there were some Saudi students who may have sympathy with the terrorists' goals. It was clear to me he was not one of them."

Leanne spoke up. "Aside from the fact that he's not a terrorist, why is this good news for us?"

"In our discussion yesterday, the student asked if there was anything he could do to help us. I told him it was difficult for us to plan any defensive measures since we do not know when or if Samir would strike. I asked him if there was any way he would know if Samir or his people were here. The student knows all the Saudis on campus and was sure he could tell if any new Saudi men arrived in the area. The young man also promised that if he heard anything about terrorist activities or if new Saudis showed up, he would contact me immediately. I think potentially that gives us a leg up on the terrorists. It's certainly more than we have now. Also, if the terrorists do come and the student learns about it, we may have the means to feed them false information."

Everyone around the table seemed lost in thought as they considered what I had said. Finally, Ty broke the silence. "Well, that certainly could provide information we wouldn't necessarily have otherwise. Obviously, the first question that comes to me is, can we trust him? Listening to you, it seems like you have a positive connection with the guy."

"I do trust him and do so for several reasons. First, in our discussions, the young man has had a visceral negative reaction to terrorists. Second, he is a very good student who works hard and has a good mind. Third, while being a member of the royal family does not guarantee that you are not a terrorist, it does seem that supporting any terrorist activity is not in their best interest. Fourth, it seems that the Saudi government is grooming him for law school. I think they want him to attend an American law school, which will give them a check on the advice they receive from American law firms they hire. So, yes, I do believe we can trust him."

Sandy continued the conversation. "DJ told me about this young man before all this business with Samir came up. He was impressed with the student and clearly still is. I think we should work with him."

I spoke up again. "While it may be taking a chance, I'm not sure we have any other options. If so, let me hear it."

When no one spoke up, Ann continued, "This may be our best chance to potentially have a heads up if and when an attack may come."

Looking around the table and everyone seemed to agree. "Okay, I will keep in contact with him and let you know if anything comes up. Also, don't speak about this with anyone. We don't want to put him in danger."

I leaned over and whispered to Mac. "Do you want me to say anything to Ann to help you get back into her good graces?" His only response was flashing his middle finger at me.

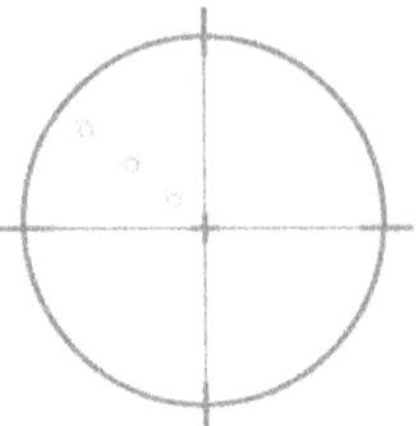

Chapter 16

Samir sat in the front passenger seat of the Toyota Camry. Juan, a member of the cartel the terrorists were working with, was driving and two other operatives were in the backseat. It had taken two days for Ahmed to rent a 24-foot truck and pick up the weapons and explosives stashed in various warehouses around Mexico City, along with the various other supplies they would need. Ahmed was driving the truck, following Samir's Toyota. Kamil had led most of the other operatives to Ciudad Juarez the previous day, where they were currently waiting in a small warehouse on the western outskirts. Samir and his men simply referred to it as Juarez. During the 20-hour drive from Mexico City to Juarez, they had seen no police officials of any kind.

This part of their journey was dangerous because if the truck was stopped and searched, they would have no option but to fight their way out. Juan had explained that this was unlikely because the police officials had been bribed to look the other way. Regardless of the assurances given by the cartel, Samir was nervous and on edge as they approached Juarez. Whenever Samir raised the issue of their security with Juan, the young man assured him that there would be no problems. He indicated that he had made this run numerous times and never experienced any trouble. Even so, Samir's eyes darted about as they continued down the road.

Within an hour, Juan had traveled down several dusty roads on the outskirts of the city until he pulled up in front of a small warehouse. The building was located at the end of a small street, the nearest structure several hundred yards away. Juan stepped out of his vehicle and walked a few feet to the small door leading into the warehouse. He pushed a button next to the door and shortly, a middle-aged Hispanic man appeared and invited him in. Within a minute, the large metal door began to roll upward. Juan walked out of the warehouse through the large door, climbed back in the Toyota, and drove into the warehouse. Ahmed followed the Toyota into the building. As Samir stepped out of the Toyota, the heavy door began to roll down.

Kamil appeared and shook Samir's hand. "Everything is ready and we are on the verge of entering the United States." Samir observed the large smile on Kamil's face and the excitement in his eyes. Kamil continued, "All of our planning is coming to fruition; it is so amazing. I can admit now that, at times, I wondered whether we would truly reach this point."

Samir gazed around the warehouse and saw his men sitting at various tables, talking among themselves. A few had come over to investigate the new arrivals. "Kamil, have you experienced any problems of any kind?"

"None. That is what is so amazing. From the time we landed in Mexico City, things have gone according to plan. Our long trip to Juarez was easy. As you can see, the cartel has provided sleeping bags and mattresses so that we can stay here tonight. All we have left to do prior to leaving tomorrow is distribute the weapons and explosives among the men. You do not need to be bothered with that. I will take care of it."

"Who is in charge of the warehouse?"

"The old man over there." Kamil nodded toward the gentleman who had answered the door for Juan. "Aside from us, he is the only person here except for your driver. His name is Javier. Do you wish to meet him?"

"No, I don't believe that's necessary. You can work with him if our needs require it. Have you met the person who's going to lead us across the border?"

"It is my understanding that the person who drove you here will also take us into the U.S. From what you have said, I assume he did not give you that information."

Samir turned and motioned for Juan to join him and Kamil. As Juan approached, Samir asked, "Is it true, Juan, that you are going to guide us over the border?"

"Yes, sir, that is correct."

Samir eyed him closely. "Why didn't you tell me that previously?"

"You did not ask me, and I've been instructed not to say anything about this venture to anyone. I am sorry if that is concerning to you. My superiors were very adamant about the secrecy required for this mission."

Samir watched him for a minute and then replied, "I'm not concerned, but just had a question about it. You have followed your superior's instructions very well. I wish my men were as conscientious as you are." Juan beamed at the compliment. "Can you tell me what your plan is for our crossing into the U.S.?"

"As I understand, you and my superiors have agreed to the following. If that is not correct, please let me know now. Since it will be dark shortly and you have much to prepare before we leave, I think it is best to wait to begin our journey until tomorrow night. I suggest we plan to leave here by 10 PM. We will travel to a point approximately two miles from the actual border, and then we will cross to meet one of our men inside the U.S. There are fences covering certain parts of the border, but not where we will cross. Our journey from the time we leave here until we meet our man in the U.S. will take several hours. It may seem like a long time, but we will be extremely cautious as we cross the border. There will be times when we may need to simply wait and see how the situation develops. But, again, you should not worry about this portion of the trip. I've done it several times without any problems. I shall exercise great caution to assure that your crossing goes smoothly."

Samir nodded his understanding. "How will we travel from here to the point where we will begin to walk across the border?"

"Four pickup trucks will arrive here just after dark. That should be sufficient for all of your men and their equipment. Once they drop us off, three of the trucks will leave. One truck will be left for me to drive back to the warehouse after I've returned."

"What about the Rio Grande?"

"As you shall see, it will not be a problem."

"I've only been given a brief outline of what to expect once we get into the U.S. Please explain what the plan is once we meet your man on the other side of the border," Samir said.

"I do not know all of the details since I normally return to Mexico once I have dropped off the people I'm escorting. However, this is what I have been told will occur. The man we will meet will be approximately three miles past the border along the trail I've used many times. The man who will meet us is named Pedro, not his real name; he is a cousin of mine. He has a large box truck that your entire group can ride in. He will drive you to a warehouse on the outskirts of El Paso. You will stay there that night and then you'll take a bus to your final destination. No one has told me what your destination in the U.S. is. I think my cousin made all the arrangements. Was that your understanding of what would happen?"

Samir nodded his agreement. "Thank you, Juan." Ahmed joined Kamil and Samir, and the latter explained to Ahmed that they would leave the next evening. They had until that time to prepare themselves. "Ahmed, how are the men doing?"

"They're excited and energized. Everyone is looking forward to our crossing tomorrow and the successful completion of our mission. Their morale is very high."

"That is good to hear. Let's take the time tonight to get everything packed and ready to go. Do we have the packs we wanted?"

"Yes, the cartel provided us with brand-new hiking packs from a company called REI. They should have sufficient room for everything we'll need. However, there's one thing that does not make sense to me."

"What's that?"

"While the men understand that we can fill our packs with explosives and handguns, they are questioning how are we going to take rifles on the bus?"

"As you know, I never intended to take a bus and certainly would not tell the cartel where or how we are going. We do not want anyone outside of our group to know anything of our plans. Kamil, tell Ahmed what our actual travel plans are."

"We're going to travel like Americans. I've made arrangements to rent three large RVs. Do you know what they are?"

Ahmed responded, "Yes, I've seen some of those in France. But are they large enough to carry our supplies and our men?"

"Yes, it should not be a problem. Also, they will be driven by some of our people who have lived in the U.S. for a long time. Like us, they are true believers." Kamil smiled at Ahmed. "Just think, Ahmed, we're going to cross America in one of their favorite modes of vacation travel."

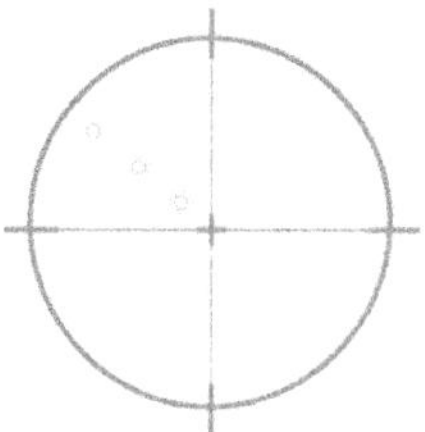

Chapter 17

The week before Christmas was cold and overcast. I was waiting for Mac to pick me up for our meeting with the police chief, who had called me earlier to say he needed to talk to the three of us. When I asked what the meeting was for, he said he wanted to learn more about the shooting in which the shooter had been killed. I talked with both Mac and Ty about his request and each was willing to meet with Chief Brian Martin.

Wearing my lawyer hat, I told them that this meeting had red flags all over it. While I believed the killing of the shooter had certainly been justified, since he was raising his pistol to fire at us, not everyone might agree with Mac's decision to fire. It was not impossible that both Mac and I could be charged with some form of homicide. I discussed this matter with both Ty and Mac. As retired police officers, they certainly understood the potential ramifications.

Driving his old pickup, Mac pulled up in front of my house. I walked out, approached his truck, and clambered in. I said, "You still haven't taken my advice to buy a new truck."

Mac started laughing. "You and Ty simply don't understand. This truck runs like a finely tuned machine. There aren't too many bumps and bruises on it. Most importantly, it is part of me. So get over it."

"I'm just trying to bring you into the 21st century. You don't even use a smart phone."

"I appreciate your concern. However, what does a smart phone give me that I don't already have?"

"Well, for one thing, you'd have the Internet at your fingertips. Just having Google readily available to answer questions is amazing. Now that I think about it, you are a techno-dinosaur. If you lived in the 1920s, you probably would've believed that the automobile would never replace a horse. I'm sure you would've questioned why people would ever listen to the radio or watch TV."

Mac smiled at me and responded, "That's what's wrong with you, DJ. You don't appreciate the good old days?"

"That's because the old days were never that good." Mac chuckled, put the truck in gear, and we headed for Ty's house, a short five-minute drive away. Ty was sitting on the porch waiting for us. He had a pensive look on his face as he approached the truck.

"Climb on in, Ty, and enjoy your ride in this vintage vehicle. Why the sour look?" Mac asked.

"Frankly, I'm concerned about this meeting. Do you think we need an attorney?"

"Listen, Ty, you have nothing to worry about. You didn't do anything that could put you in legal trouble. You weren't even at the scene of the shooting. Mac could be culpable because he pulled the trigger. Me, less so, but I was there."

"I agree with DJ," Mac stated. "But think about it. Do you really believe that the prosecutor would file charges against us because we knocked off a known hitman? I don't think so. There is no reason for them to waste their time trying that type of case. Just stick to the truth and answer the man's questions. Hell, I bet the chief is just going through the motions. If we need any legal help, we have DJ with us."

"I can't represent you, Mac. It would be a hell of a conflict of interest."

Mac started laughing again. "Don't go all legal on me, DJ. You know what I mean. If the conversation doesn't go the way I think it will, just interrupt and say we need an attorney. Okay?"

I looked at Mac and understood what he was saying. "If we get into a place that I'm concerned about during this conversation with Chief Martin, I'll just end the meeting." As I finished speaking, Mac pulled into the parking lot. "Let's do this."

All of us got out of the truck and headed toward the door of the police department. The receptionist greeted us with a friendly smile and asked what she could do for us. "We have an appointment with the chief. Is he available now?" I asked.

"And you are?"

Mac reached over and tapped my forehead. "DJ, where are your manners? You can tell Chief Martin that the three professors are here at his request." She pushed some buttons and a moment later, the chief came walking out of his office.

"Hi, guys. I'm glad you could come. Let's go into my office." The three of us followed him in and sat in the three chairs facing his desk. I glanced around; the office appeared to be more functional than impressive. On his wall were various photos of Chief Martin and various city officials. Behind him, bookshelves were filled with various binders, most of them budget-related, based on their spines.

Mac spoke first. "Well, chief, why are these two sorry asses and me sitting before you?" Ty and I immediately looked at him. "I'm sorry. These two distinguished gentleman and me."

Looking at both Ty and me, Chief Martin stated, "You know he is just this side of crazy, don't you?"

Before Ty had a chance to say anything, I answered. "Yes, we know that, but he is relatively harmless. We always have him under observation except when we take him home and lock him in his room. So, Chief, why are we here?"

"I need to talk about what happened at the shooting."

Mac replied, "I've gone over that with your detective more than once. Do you have a concern about whether it was a good shoot? I guess the real question is, do I need an attorney?"

Martin shook his head back and forth. "No, you misunderstand me. I think it was a clear case of self-defense. I know you informed me earlier about this Samir character and his threats to you. Are you sure the guy who shot at you is connected with Samir?"

"Absolutely," I answered, "Mac talked to Samir on the guy's phone. He again reiterated his threats against us. My take is that he hired this guy so he didn't have to come and personally carry out his threats. Now I believe he will be coming."

The chief looked at me for a moment. "That's what I was afraid of. My concern, as you can guess, is whether there's going to be more violence in my town. From what you told me, it appears to me that it is a good possibility. What are you going to do and how can I help you?"

The three of us filled him in on the various meetings we'd had; the actions we had taken and I told him what we were looking to do in the future. He sat listening quietly, then said, "From my perspective, it seems to me that you have more than just a difficult task ahead. They could attack you anytime, anyplace. If he attacks you individually, your ability to defend yourselves is reduced dramatically. Gentlemen, I fear for your lives. We will obviously do whatever we can to assist you, but my resources are limited. It's clear you were really lucky that the shooter failed in his attack."

Ty spoke up, "How can you consider it a failure, given that he shot me?"

"There he goes, whining again," Mac responded.

When the laughter died out, Chief Martin continued, "Seriously, I'm not sure how long your luck can continue. Do you have any idea when he might strike?"

Ty answered, "We really don't know. It could be today or six months from now."

"Based on your experience with Samir in Paris and here, can you make an educated guess about when an attack might come?" All three of us shook our heads. "Would you like me to assign one of my men to coordinate with you on what we might be able to put together?"

"That would be great," I responded.

"Let me tell you the huge concern I have," Mac said. "Even if we were all together when they strike, we will be at a severe disadvantage. I am confident they will have automatic weapons and we will have to face them with our semi-automatics. My guess is that they will also have hand grenades and other types of explosives. We need to find a way to even the odds. As you well know, Chief, it is against the law for us to have automatics in our possession. It is also against the law for us to have grenades or other explosives. Do you have any suggestions on how we might be able to make the fight more even?"

The chief peered over his broad wooden desk with understanding in his eyes. He looked down while his fingers drummed a steady beat. He sat there for several minutes without saying a word. When he spoke up, there was a knowing grin on his face. "There may be a way to help you out or at least some of you. Mac, you and Ty are retired police officers, correct?" Both men nodded their agreement. "As you know, police officers are not under the same restrictions as citizens. We can use different weapons based on the situation confronting us. What if I made both of you reserve officers in the department? You would then be able to use weapons that are available to us. I can justify that, given the situation and your prior training. That would not, however, apply to DJ or your wives. What do you think of that?"

I looked at Ty and Mac for a response. Ty had a grin spread across his face and Mac was nodding his head. Mac responded, "I think that's a great idea. That would help even the odds a bit."

"I couldn't agree more," Ty stated.

The chief then looked at me. "Now, DJ, I cannot in good conscience make you a reserve officer." I nodded my understanding. "However, if you happen to use one of the weapons assigned to Mac or Ty during an attack, there is not much I can do about it. In any event, I can't imagine any prosecutor being concerned with the weapons you use should you be confronted."

He continued. "Mac, being the experienced officer you are, I assume both you and Ty will want more than one automatic rifle. I mean, we all want to have a backup with us. So I need to know the type and number of weapons you would like issued to you, and I'll will try to make them available to you. Also, should you need any safety gear or other material, please let me know what that might be. Any questions?"

Mac responded for us. "I think that covers about everything. Chief, you're a giant among men and you do have our deepest appreciation and respect. Thanks again."

"Think nothing of it. I'm just a small-town police chief trying to do his duty." The chief winked at Mac and rose to show us out. "Good luck, guys. I'll help you as much as I can."

Nobody said anything as we walked to Mac's truck. Ty was the first one to speak. "I'll be damned. I wasn't expecting that."

I shook my head. "Me neither. Actually, I'm quite astonished."

Mac let out a belly laugh. "I told you guys we didn't need a lawyer."

Ty sighed, "Well, maybe we have a chance now."

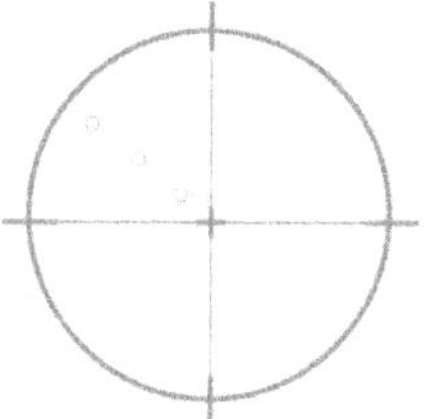

Chapter 18

Samir was in the passenger seat of the lead vehicle. Juan, who was driving, maintained a safe and deliberate speed as he guided the vehicle down the rutted dirt road. Samir glanced back at the three following trucks. He knew that Ahmed was in the truck directly behind him and Kamil was in the vehicle behind Ahmed. They had been traveling now for approximately an hour and a half at speeds that would not attract attention. Even though the trucks had their headlights on, it was dark enough that Samir could see very little outside his door window. Samir looked at Juan, whose face reflected the light coming from the instrument panel. "How much longer before we begin our walk across the border?"

Juan kept his concentration on the road ahead and did not look at Samir. "Not far, maybe another five minutes."

"Is there a marker or something?"

Samir could see the smile on Juan's face when he replied, "No, we do not want to give the location away. I've done this many times, so I know exactly where I need to turn. Look ahead. You see that the road branches to the right. We go down there for about 100 meters."

Juan turned and continued on for a short distance. When the truck pulled to a stop, Samir opened the door and stepped out. He looked forward and could make out a stand of trees a few meters ahead. Juan soon joined him by the side of the truck. Samir glanced around and found it difficult to get his bearings. "Where's the border?"

Juan pointed toward the trees. "It is about 4 km past the trees over there. We park here so that people on the other side of the border have difficulty seeing us. You should gather your men here so that I can talk to them."

Samir turned and looked back toward the other vehicles. The men had climbed out of the trucks and were waiting for his orders. The leader walked back to Ahmed. "Have the men get their equipment ready and join me in front of my truck." Ahmed nodded and began giving instructions. A few minutes later, all of the men were standing around Samir and Juan.

Samir looked at Kamil. "Does everyone have what they need?"

"Yes, I explained to each of them what they were required to carry. Before we boarded the trucks, I personally checked each one to make sure that he had followed my instructions. They are all ready to go."

"Men, we're going to begin our journey to cross the border in just a few minutes. Juan is going to give you some final instructions. I want you to listen to him very carefully and do what he says. Does anyone have any questions?" Samir looked at each one of his men, but no one raised his hand. He then nodded to Juan to begin.

"It is very important that you follow my instructions. Failing to do so could result in our being unsuccessful in our attempt to cross the border. We are relatively safe on this side of the border. However, when we cross, there is always the possibility that we could run into border guards. If you fail to do what I say, it may result in your death or the death of your friends here.

"As you can see, it is very dark out here. It is very important that you pay attention to the man in front of you. If your mind wanders off, you may find yourself lost and those behind you will also be lost. Even in the dark, I know where I'm going. I have done this many times, and you are going to have to trust me. There is to be no talking of any kind. Even small sounds travel a great distance in this area. You should only speak in the event of a grave emergency and then, obviously, very softly.

"I will stop and let each of you know when we are about to cross the border. We may stop at various points to make sure we are not being observed. I may, at certain times, walk ahead and you will stay back. It is my way of making sure that our path is clear. It is about 4 km to the border and we will travel several kilometers beyond that, where you will meet our contact in the U.S. Does anyone have any final questions?"

When no one spoke up, Juan spoke to Samir. "Get them lined up in single file. I'm going to go tell the three other drivers of the trucks to go back." With that, Juan walked away.

Samir spoke to Ahmed and Kamil. "Get them lined up in single file and, once again, reinforce the instructions they just heard from Juan." Samir watched Ahmed and Kamil disappeared into the darkness to get the men ready to leave.

Juan walked back up to Samir and turned to watch the three trucks leave. "We will wait here for a few minutes to give them time to depart. Are you excited to begin your journey?"

"Not really. But I will be when we are safely across the border."

"I understand," Juan replied, "but you should stop and enjoy this moment. We're about to fool the Americans once again. I always enjoy defeating their attempts to control what we do. They think they're so smart with their technology and all, yet we always seem to find ways to defeat their attempts to stop us. You know their last president, the one who built part of the wall. He has helped our economy immensely."

"I don't understand," replied Samir.

"You have no idea how many jobs he's created for the men who now dig the tunnels under the wall. Shall we begin?" Samir nodded his agreement. Juan turned and began walking slowly toward the border.

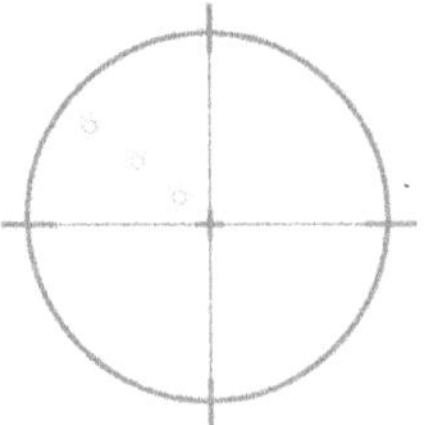

Chapter 19

Bill Jackson pulled his SUV off the dirt road, turned off the lights and shut off the engine. As his eyes adjusted to the darkness, he was once again surprised at how truly dark it got in the desert. To the east, he could make out the lights of El Paso.

He pulled out a beer from the cooler sitting next to him. Bill almost never drank on the job, but he was very nervous and needed some liquid courage to calm himself down. Taking a long swig, he wiped the few drops of liquid from his mouth with the back of his hand. Jackson took a deep breath and that seemed to help. Still, he was very concerned about what the night would bring. This was the third crossing where he would earn his money by looking the other way. He looked forward to the $2,500 he would receive for his work tonight.

However, this evening was going to be different. On the previous instances when he looked the other way, he just made sure he was not in the area where the crossing and hook up would occur. For some reason, Pedro had requested that Bill accompany him to the point where he would meet the people coming across the border. When he asked Pedro why, Pedro only replied that he had received those instructions from the people he worked with on the other side. Pedro had speculated that Bill was going to receive a nice bonus, which was being brought across the border tonight.

This side job was turning out to be very lucrative. Bill was flush with cash, but he made sure not to flash around his newfound riches. In fact, he had set up a separate account at a different bank and deposited all the money he received there. So far, he had not spent a single dime. He knew he had to be very careful if he wanted to avoid being caught.

Still, tonight's change in plans made him a little leery. It would be the first time that someone other than Pedro would be watching as he helped the people cross illegally. To protect himself, he had changed his appearance slightly. Tonight, he sported a fake mustache and wore a girdle that made him appear much thinner than he truly was. He had no intention of being caught because someone might observe him and later identify him.

Bill looked in his rearview mirror and saw headlights approaching. A few moments later, a rental truck pulled up and stopped beside him. He heard the door open and watched Pedro walk around the front of the U-Haul toward him. Bill rolled down his window and was greeted by the still-warm air. Pedro rested his hands on the door and looked at him.

"Well, Bill, are you ready to make some easy cash once again?" An easy smile lit up Pedro's face.

"The cash, as always, sounds great, but I am worried about having to meet those coming across with you. It really doesn't make a lot of sense to me."

Pedro started chuckling at his newfound friend. "Bill, you are just being a Nervous Nelly. Everything will be fine. Remember, I meet these people all the time. Nothing bad has ever occurred."

"Yeah, but you're not a member of the border patrol. I don't want to meet someone who can identify me."

"Don't worry. The only person you'll see is the guy bringing them across the border. He'll be the one carrying the extra cash for you. You are too valuable to them to allow anything to happen to you. I mean, man, you are sitting in the catbird seat. I should charge you a percentage as a finder's fee to set you up in this sweet deal, don't you think?"

Bill hoped that Pedro was correct, but he still had an uneasy feeling in his gut. "Right, but I'm the one taking all the risks. If you get caught, they will just deport you back to Mexico. If I get caught, I'll be doing some hard time in a place I don't want to be. Why don't you come around and sit in the car?" Pedro nodded and walked in front of Bill's SUV, opened the door and got in.

Bill asked, "So when and where do we meet them?"

Pedro took out a cigarette and lit up. After he took a drag and blew the smoke out of his lungs, he replied. "It's about two or three miles straight down this road and off to the side a bit. We're supposed to be there in about an hour. We should leave here in about 40 minutes. You know, because they're crossing in the dark, sometimes they're early and sometimes they're late. Normally, they are within 5 to 10 minutes of either side of the appointed time. You will follow me and I will lead you there. I will turn my truck around and face you so they can hop into back of the truck without seeing you. I'll wait in front of my truck and you can just remain in yours. If the guy bringing these people across wants to talk to you, he'll walk back to your car. That way, whoever is coming across won't see you. How does that sound?"

"That works for me." At that point, Bill's phone rang. He pulled it from his pocket and looked at the face. It was his ex-wife's number. He hit the answer button and said, "Hello."

Pedro watched Bill, quietly listening.

After a few moments, Bill spoke again. "Yes, I can do that. How about I pick them up at 10 on Saturday morning. I'll bring them back after dinner on Sunday. Is that okay?"

Once again, Bill listened quietly. "Okay, I'll see you then." Bill clicked the phone off and said nothing.

Finally, Pedro broke the silence. "Are you okay, man?"

"Yeah, I'm fine. That was my ex. She wanted to make arrangements for this weekend when I have my kids. You know, it still is hard to see her. I hate to admit it, but I'm still in love with her. When I pick up the kids for my weekend, I try to stretch out the time that I am at her place just to be with her. I know that probably just makes it worse for me, but I just can't help it."

"That sucks, man."

"Yeah, it really does suck, more than you can imagine."

After that exchange, both men remained silent, lost in their own thoughts. Pedro was glad he had never gotten married and this conversation reinforced his feelings. Bill, on the other hand, sat there watching his wife in his mind's eye. He could only hope that something might change between them.

Pedro saw the time on the SUVs dashboard. "It's about time we get moving. Just follow me and we will be there in a few minutes. Remember, stay parked in front of me, and if necessary, I'll bring our contact back to see you. Okay?"

"Sure, let's get this done." Bill pulled himself out of his reverie and once again became vigilant.

Pedro opened the door and climbed out. Soon Pedro was firing up his truck and driving off. Bill followed right behind him. His thoughts drifted back to his wife.

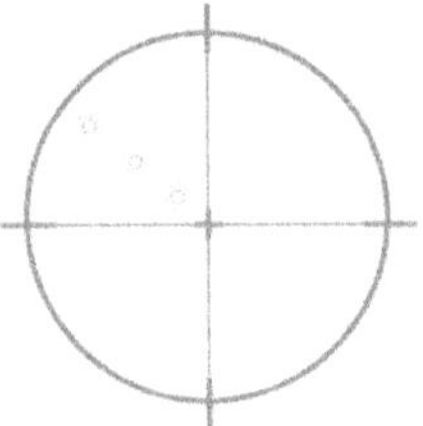

Chapter 20

Bill's ex-wife, Jean, hung up the phone. A deep sadness took hold of her. She could feel it clutch at her heart. She had really loved Bill for most of their marriage. It wasn't until shortly before the end that her love seemed to dissipate, and she knew that she could not go on. Bill was a good man, she knew that. However, somewhere during the course of their marriage, the spark of love had left them and both were sad and nearly despondent. The decision to end their marriage had not been an easy one. Jean was deeply concerned about the effect it would have on their children. But she knew in her heart of hearts that she could not go on with her husband.

Her conversation with Bill this evening was like every other conversation they had had since the divorce. He really never said much but listened to her closely. He routinely gave her whatever she asked for. Tonight, however, was a little different. Jean heard something in his voice that concerned her. It wasn't the sadness that normally came across when they talked. It was more of a concern. About what, she did not know.

Jean climbed the stairs to her children's bedroom. She opened the door and saw that both of her daughters were asleep. Hannah, her oldest, had bright red hair that was cut short. She was sleeping on her side with a very peaceful look on her face. She was probably dreaming of princesses. Hannah was at that age where everything was magical. That morning, she had told her mother that she would be a princess who would reign over her people with love. Hannah had said it with such tenderness her mother nearly cried. She walked over to Hannah and brushed some unruly hair out of her eyes.

Across from Hannah lay her sister Sarah. She was quite the beauty even at her young age. Her hair was a dark brown that reached her shoulders. Jean had never known a youngster as curious as Sarah. It seemed that everything she saw or touched raised questions in her mind. She brought those questions to her mother with the expectation that Mom would know every answer. Jean reached down and touched the back of her daughter and could feel it rise and fall with each breath she took. During these quiet times, she was overwhelmed with the love that filled her heart for these two young girls. Jean watched them for a few more minutes then turned and closed the door.

She returned to the kitchen, poured herself a glass of water, and proceeded to turn all the lights off before once again heading upstairs. Jean changed into her nightgown, removed the remaining makeup from her face, and looked in the bathroom mirror. She wasn't as young or beautiful as she remembered. The strain of the divorce, being a single mother to her two children and the simple toll of life could be seen in her face. Jean reached up and touched the crows' feet that were beginning to walk away from her eyes. It wasn't too long ago that those did not exist. Her smooth skin was a thing of the past.

Jean turned out the lights in the bathroom and got into bed. She lay down and closed her eyes but could not sleep. The conversation with Bill had left her unsettled, not because of what he said but rather because of what she felt. She knew he ached to return to his family. She also knew she would not allow that to happen. Every time Bill came to pick up his daughters, Jean could see in his eyes his desire for her. When he returned at the end of the weekend to bring his daughters home, she could feel his pain from not being with them during the week. Jean felt badly for him every time this occurred.

As these thoughts rolled through her mind, she could feel her stomach clutch with uncertainty. Before she drifted off to sleep, Jean decided to discuss her concerns with Bill when he came to pick up Hannah and Sarah on Saturday morning.

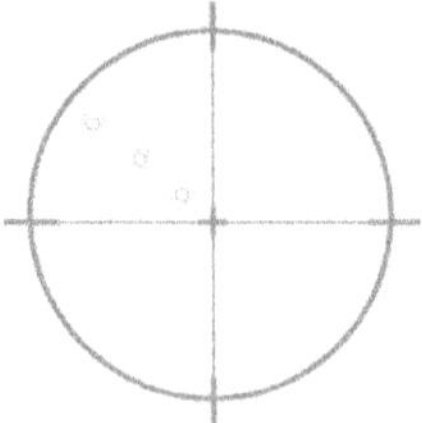

Chapter 21

They had been walking now for about an hour. The route they took was at times rocky and at other times hard-packed dirt. As Samir followed Juan, he was glad that this route was relatively flat. Because of the darkness, he was concerned that some of his men would twist an ankle or fall and break a leg. However, that had not occurred, and he realized how professional Juan was. The guide had not spoken to him since they had begun their trek, but suddenly Juan stopped. He whispered to Samir that everyone should lie flat on the ground. Samir turned to the man behind him and repeated the instruction. In short order, the entire line of men was lying down.

Juan who was next to Samir whispered, "I think someone is coming from our right and will probably cross in front of us."

Samir responded, "Who?"

"I don't know. We will just watch for a while." As he lay there, Samir also thought he could hear movement ahead of them. Soon, he believed he could see the outlines of six individuals walking from his right to his left. Samir could hear them talking in low tones but could not make out what they were saying. Juan leaned in toward him and said, "It appears there is another group also trying to cross the border. From what I could make out, they're going to use a trail about a mile to our left. They should not be of concern to us. We will begin moving again shortly."

Ten minutes later, Juan rose and passed the word. "We are very close to the border," he whispered to Samir. "I will be back in a minute. I am going to walk back and let your men know the situation." Samir watched the short, muscular Mexican as he made his way past the men in line. Within five minutes, Juan reappeared. "I think we can cross now. All of your men have been informed of the situation. Let's go." Juan turned and began to move away. Samir followed and the line of men behind him moved like a snake weaving its way home.

To Samir, the time seemed to pass very slowly. The pace set by Juan was slow and deliberate. As seconds stretched into minutes, and minutes into hours, Samir came to appreciate Juan's skill even more. Occasionally, he would stop and listen for something no one else heard. Twice, he halted the line and moved forward to investigate on his own. Each time he came back satisfied that the way forward was clear. Samir kept looking at his watch, afraid that daylight would soon arrive. However, whenever he checked his watch, only a few minutes had passed. The pack he was carrying seemed to get heavier with each step. He was looking forward to removing his burden and riding in the truck that waited for them.

Samir was just getting ready to suggest to Juan that they take a break when the Mexican brought the line of men to a halt. He whispered to Samir, "We've arrived. Our people should be about 50 meters ahead. I'll go forward and make sure that everything is as it should be." Juan walked slowly away. Again, it seemed like hours passed before he returned. "Our men are waiting for us, let's go." Once again, Samir and his men followed Juan into the night.

As they walked forward, Samir saw the outline of the large truck ahead. Pedro approached Samir and shook Samir's hand with a firm grip. "Hello, I'm Pedro and I'm going to guide you from here."

"Are you alone, Pedro?" Samir asked, looking the tall stranger up and down.

"No, as requested, the border patrol agent who is in our pay is in the SUV in front of the truck. Do you wish to talk to him?"

"Not just quite yet. I have some things to discuss with you and Juan first." He turned to Juan. "When are you expected back?"

"Not for several hours. In fact, I will probably go get some sleep before I begin my trip back to Mexico City. Do you need further assistance?"

"No, I was just wondering. Will you help the men get everything loaded in the truck and ready to move?"

"I will." Juan turned toward Ahmed and stated, "Will you have your men follow me please?" Juan did not see Samir's slight nod to Ahmed when their eyes met.

Samir turned toward Pedro and said, "Let's go meet your border patrol agent."

Pedro did not sense Kamil quietly follow them to the SUV.

Bill saw the three men approaching and stepped out of his vehicle. He did not like the fact that an additional person was approaching. He reached down and unbuttoned the flap on his holster. The first thing Bill noticed from the light of his open door was that neither of the other men were Hispanic.

"What's going on, Pedro? These men aren't Mexicans. What are you trying to pull?"

"What the hell, Bill, their money is good is anyone's. What's your problem?" Pedro retorted dismissively.

"I don't have a problem turning my back on a few Mexicans trying to make a better life for themselves. But these guys, I doubt if they're coming here to work under the table for some American business." Bill reached for his gun and started to pull it out of his holster when he found himself staring down the barrel of an automatic pistol with a silencer. Samir held it loosely, ready to fire. "Wait a minute, what's going on here?"

Samir smiled. "Funny that you should ask. Turn around." Bill did as he was instructed and Samir removed Bill's weapon from the holster. Samir shoved his pistol into Bill's back and said, "Walk away from the SUV."

Pedro blurted, "What the hell's going..." He, too, felt the brutal nudge of a pistol, this one held by Kamil.

Kamil whispered into Pedro ear, "If you know what's good for you, you will sit on the ground and shut the hell up." Pedro quickly obeyed. He looked at Kamil but only saw the barrel of his gun pointed directly at his head. Pedro's belly tightened and he felt fear like he had never known before and knew that his life might end very shortly. He couldn't move even if he had wanted to. He was simply frozen, unable to speak.

Juan heard the commotion going on outside the truck and walked to the back to investigate. He did not hear Ahmed walk up behind him in the truck, nor did he see the silenced gun in the Ahmed's hand. Juan saw the ground rushing toward him and did not feel his body when it hit the hard-packed soil. No words entered his mind. The bullet that had entered the back of his head and exited through his forehead made that impossible.

Samir followed Bill as he walked away from the SUV. When they were 50 meters away, Samir said, "Stop and turn around." Bill did as he was instructed, and Samir could see that he was terrified.

"Why are you doing this? I don't want to die," Bill pleaded. "Please don't do this."

Samir watched this American with disgust. "You've killed many of my friends and now it is your turn to die."

"I have not killed anyone and certainly not any of you."

With hatred in his eyes, Samir stated "Your country and countrymen have. That is sufficient for me." Samir raised his hand and pointed his weapon directly at Bill's head.

"Please don't. I have children," Bill begged. "Please don't kill me. I don't want to die." Those were his last words and thoughts as a bullet from Samir's gun entered his head and ended his life.

Samir smiled as he looked at the lifeless body sprawled before him. "You are the first of many Americans who will die by my hand." He turned and walked toward the truck. As Samir approached, he was met by Kamil. "Are we ready to go, Kamil?"

"Yes, we are ready."

Pedro, tears running down his cheeks, was made to sit in the truck driver's seat. Kamil turned and headed for the rear of the truck. With one smooth movement, Samir pulled opened the passenger door and pulled himself up and in. He looked at Pedro. "If you wish to live, you'll drive us to where we want to go. If you promise to say nothing, we will let you go. Do you understand?"

"Yes, and I promise."

"Did Kamil give you the address?"

"Yes, he did."

"Okay, drive us there. Do not speed or try to attract any attention. If you do anything out of the ordinary, I will shoot immediately. Do you understand?" Pedro nodded, tears still glistening on his cheeks. "Let's get going then."

The trip over the rough road to the warehouse they had rented previously took just over an hour. When they arrived, Kamil exited the truck, opened the large door to the warehouse, and Pedro drove in. Samir and Pedro got out of the vehicle, and Samir walked to the driver's door. While looking at Pedro, Samir stated, "I appreciate your following orders." Before Pedro could respond, Kamil shot him in the back. Pedro crumpled to the ground like a ragdoll without making a sound.

Samir opened the door to the back of the truck. He saw that his men had started to gather their packs. "Men, we've accomplished what some thought was impossible. We have entered America safely and with our weapons and explosives. Now is the time that our real work begins. We will leave tomorrow afternoon after we have had a chance to get some sleep and rest. Come on out of the truck."

As the men jumped down from the back of the truck, they saw three RVs waiting for them in the back of the warehouse.

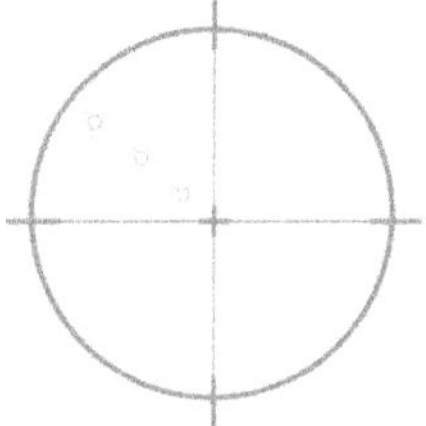

Chapter 22

Agent Rheingold was sitting in his office reviewing a report submitted by one of his agents regarding a bank robbery. As he quickly skimmed the report, he knew he wouldn't have to invest his time in this case. The agent assigned only had to meet with the two police officers who had arrested the subject. The soon-to-be defendant had given a full confession to the officers. The only question remaining was whether the case would be tried in the state or federal courts. As was the usual case, the local prosecutor had recommended that the feds take it over. The local officials would rather the feds invest their resources in obtaining a conviction rather than having the state do so. Rheingold approved his agent's recommendation that the case be forwarded to the U.S. attorney for filing of charges.

Rheingold placed the report in his outbox and reached for the next file requiring his attention. Being the special agent in charge of this field office required that he spend much of his day on administrative matters such as this. While his current position certainly gave him a higher salary and larger responsibilities, he missed the day-to-day operations and activities that kept most agents busy.

His thoughts were interrupted by a light tapping on the door. "Come in." The door swung open and the receptionist poked her head in his office. "What's up?"

"There are five agents from Washington here to talk to you. Do you want me to bring them into your office?"

"No, take them into the conference room. I'll be with them in a minute." Rheingold watched the receptionist close the door and heard her walk away. He assumed that the five agents were the ones Wyman sent to try to come up with leads on the terrorists. Rheingold quickly reviewed the files on his desk to see if any of them needed his immediate attention. Finding none, he rose from his chair and headed to the conference room.

When Rheingold entered the room, he saw the agents already seated at the conference table, three on one side, and two on the other. They had left the chair at the head of the table for him. Rheingold sat down and stated, "Hello. My name is Rheingold and I don't believe I've met any of you previously. Am I correct?" Each of the five agents nodded to him. "Would each of you introduce yourself and tell me how long you've been with the Bureau and in what capacity?"

The man to his left spoke first. He seemed to be the oldest of the five and appeared to be around 45 or so. He was about 6 foot 2 and just under 200 pounds. His black hair was cut short and parted on the side. His face was beginning to show the wrinkles that came with age and responsibility. "My name is Stu Williams and I'm the leader of this motley crew. I've been with the agency almost 15 years now and have cycled through a variety of assignments until my current one in the counterintelligence office." He looked to his left and nodded.

The agent to Williams' left spoke next. "My name is Jake Sanders. I've been with the Bureau for about seven years now. I specialized in bank robberies until I was transferred to counterintelligence. I've been there now approximately two years." Sanders was relatively short for an FBI agent, probably under 5 foot 10. His sandy blond hair was beginning to thin prematurely, but it was clear that he kept himself in outstanding shape. He carried himself as a man who knew how to take care of himself in any tough situation. Rheingold was sure he was much older than the mid-20s he appeared to be.

The agent sitting directly to Rheingold's right continued by introducing himself. "I'm Ethan Clark and I've been with the Bureau just under three years. After a year on the street, I was transferred to counterintelligence, I think, because I speak Arabic." Clark was a solidly built, stocky and of medium height. His brown hair was cut short in military fashion. His eyes, a light blue, added a sense of intensity to him. Clark had difficulty sitting quietly and gave off an air of raw physicality. He looked to his right and nodded to the woman sitting next to him.

"I'm Sherry Webster. I've been an agent for just over five years, doing a little bit of everything. Last month, I was transferred to counterintelligence. I assume I was transferred to this unit because our supervisor recognized my superior intelligence. These strong, burly men may not necessarily agree with my observation." Webster started laughing at the discomfort of her fellow agents. Rheingold guessed she was approximately 5 foot 8. The navy blue suit she wore showed her to be very trim and fit. Her straight blonde hair rested on her shoulders and her eyes seemed to twinkle. Obviously, she was able to hold her own with the other agents.

Rheingold had a big grin on his face when he looked at the last agent. "And young man, what do you have to say?"

"Well, I happen to agree with the comments Sherry just made. However, I was added last to this group of five because the smarts that Sherry possesses still did not raise the intelligence level of the group sufficiently for our supervisor." In response, Sherry elbowed the agent in his ribs while the other three agents laughed at her response. "My name is Jeff Turner. I've been with the Bureau just under a year. I think my supervisor assigned me to this group because of their advanced age." The other four agents groaned once again. Rheingold could see that Turner carried himself with an air of confidence that exceeded his youth. He appeared to be 23 or younger with longer, almost shaggy, brown hair.

Looking at Rheingold, Agent Williams continued. "As you can see, we actually have a lot of fun together. We've been working as a group now for about six months. Do you have any questions for us?"

Agent Rheingold shook his head. "No, Sam Wyman filled me in on each of you. What has Sam told you about this assignment?"

Williams answered for the group. "He filled us in on his conversation with you and your concerns about a potential terrorist attack on three professors in this area. He also told us that we were to report to you and you would report to him regarding any findings or concerns we may have. As I understand it, we are to maintain a loose surveillance on the three professors and hope to identify at least one of the terrorists by doing so. If we find such a person, we will apply for an arrest warrant to take him into custody for debriefing. Obviously, those actions will need to be cleared with you. We will keep you informed about everything so that if we need additional agents, you can make the appropriate request to Sam."

"What is your plan to carry out the surveillance?" Rheingold asked.

"We have rented three apartments in the same complex. Sandy and Ethan will be in one apartment posing as a married couple. Jake and Jeff will be in another apartment posing as students at the university. I'll be alone in the third apartment. We won't be watching them all the time because they would pick up on us sooner or later. Initially, Jake and Jeff will spend some time on campus to see if they can ingratiate themselves in some way with the Saudi students. Our hope is that we can make some positive contacts. But generally, we'll keep an eye on the professors and watch for anyone who may have undue interest in them. Do you have any suggestions for us?"

"Just make sure that your surveillance of the three men is sufficiently loose that they do not become suspicious. It will be very difficult for us to actually pick up on someone watching them, but with some effort and a little luck, we may be fortunate enough to find a terrorist before the actual attack starts." Looking at each of the five agents, Rheingold ended the conversation by stating, "Good luck. Now go find the bastards!"

Rheingold stood and shook hands with each of the five agents. He watched each of them leave and then returned to his office. He sat in his chair, pondering their mission. They seemed competent enough, but would need a good dose of luck if they were going to succeed.

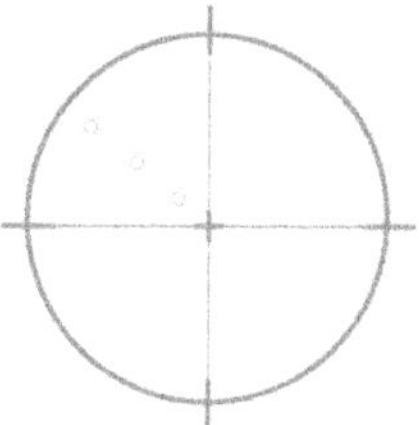

Chapter 23

Samir watched the men stretch their legs after getting out of the truck. Most of them headed toward the RVs to look them over. When he was ready, Samir called the men to come to where he was standing. "Sit down."

Obediently, the men lowered themselves to the concrete floor and sat cross-legged, attentive and focused on Samir.

"I'm going to give you some general information now and will discuss each team's mission later. To maintain our operational security, individual teams will not be told of the other teams' missions. We want to be sure that if you are captured you have no information to give to the authorities. So, I warn you now not to discuss anything with anybody other than the members of your team.

"I'm sure you would like to know about the RVs here in the warehouse. These will be the method you use to travel to your target location. Each RV will carry a single team. If you're concerned about driving one of these vehicles, don't worry. Each RV was rented by a couple living here in the United States who are dedicated followers of our organization. They will be responsible for getting you to your target and then safely away. You are to follow their instructions as it relates to your travel in their vehicle.

"Each of you will assume a new identity and will be issued a new passport that identifies you as being Egyptian. Your story is that you are related to the couple in charge of your RV. I do not believe that Americans can tell the difference between an Egyptian and a Saudi in looks or in names. You should remember that you're simply on a vacation in the United States. Your story will be that you are traveling by RV to meet relatives located in your target city. However, I do not expect that you will need to converse with any Americans. Any communication on your behalf will be accomplished by the couples you will meet shortly. The leader of each individual group will brief you on your target and your responsibilities in the attack. I can assure you that each of you has been trained thoroughly to accomplish your part of the mission. At this time, do you have any questions?" Samir saw a thin brown hand shoot up.

Samir nodded to a young man seated to his left. "Are we all going to be leaving for our targets at the same time?"

"No. Because each team will be going to a different city, you will leave in a staggered timeframe so that all of you will reach your target destinations at about the same time."

Another man raised his hand and Samir pointed at him. The man stated, "What about the resources we will need to carry out our attacks? Will they be in the RVs?"

"That's a good question, I'm glad you raised it. Each of you has brought across the border your personal weapons and some explosives. We have, however, had various explosives and tools shipped to warehouses near the targets. I have been informed that the shipments have arrived as planned. The leader of each group will brief you on this information when needed."

Samir once again looked at the group of men seated before him. "Does anyone have any more questions?" The men looked at each other, but no one raised his hand. "My guess is that more questions will come to you. If and when they do, address them to your team leader.

"I myself will lead team number one. Kamil will lead team number two, and Mohammed will lead team number three. Kamil, bring your team and your American drivers into the office so we can talk." Kamil, who had been standing with Samir, walked to the nearest RV and knocked on the door. Shortly, a woman appeared in the doorway and had a brief conversation with Kamil. The woman and a man followed

Kamil, who motioned to his men to follow him as well, and they entered the warehouse office. "The rest of you need to just wait patiently and I will call you into the office shortly."

In the office, Samir found the members of Kamil's team seated in straight-backed chairs facing an old desk or sitting on the ground. He strode behind the desk and sat down facing these men. He began his conversation by stating, "I want to introduce you first to the American couple who will drive your RV. Their names have been changed to avoid drawing any undue interest to themselves." Pointing to the stout man standing nearby, Samir stated, "This is George Smithson. Though he is clearly not American, the Smithson's story is that they Americanized their names when they became U.S. citizens, and he works as a janitor in Dallas. The story is simply that he is on vacation with his wife and each of you."

George had been born in Egypt and had moved to America with his parents when he was 10. Though educated in America, he had remained strong in his faith. Like many Americans, he was overweight for his 5-foot-6 frame. When he had been introduced, he had nervously ran his hand over his bald pate. Though he was in his late 40s, his face, chubby and wrinkled, seem to say he was older.

Samir next pointed to the woman standing beside George. "This is Molly Smithson and she works as a secretary in Dallas. You must understand that if you run into any situation when people are asking you questions, you should simply take them to George or Molly. They will resolve the issue.

Molly appeared to be older than George, perhaps having passed her 50th birthday. Molly had a sweetness about her that hid the true strength of her character. She dressed like a typical homemaker, and her hair was unremarkable in style and light brown in color. Molly, while not heavy, was stockier in build. Her face had a soft nature to it which again did not give any hint to her actual toughness.

"I am not going to divulge your target at this time. I want to avoid any inadvertent disclosure of that information to someone on another team. However, because your team has the longest distance to travel to reach your target location, you'll be leaving tomorrow morning. During your travel to the target, Kamil will explain the nature of your target and your responsibility in the attack. Don't worry about any of that now. You have time to relax and prepare for your departure tomorrow. Any questions?" Once again, none of the men raised his hand.

"George and Molly will now take you to their RV to familiarize you with it." Samir nodded to Kamil. "One more thing. Because of the number of men required for your mission, it will be tight quarters in your RV. You will need to take turns sleeping on the floor."

Kamil stood and motioned for his team to follow him. Samir also rose and followed the group out the door. He watched as the nine men followed George and Molly to their RV. Samir pointed to Mohammed and indicated that he and his team should come into the office.

George opened the door to the RV and motioned for everyone to enter. "Please take a seat if you can. I want to explain the basics of this vehicle to you. First, this RV is a 29-foot Thor. If you look to the rear, you can see a bedroom. That is for Molly and me. This table is where we will eat our meals. It also makes into a bed." George then placed his hand on the bed over the cab. "This bed sleeps two." Pointing to the sofa, George stated, "This will sleep two also."

George walked back to the small kitchen. "As you can see, this kitchen area is where we will prepare meals. There is no need for you to do so as Molly will take care of it." George then opened the door and indicated, "Here is the bathroom. There's also a shower for bathing. There's really nothing further you need to know about the operation of this RV. You will store all of your clothes and packs in the underneath storage units outside, but you should keep your weapons inside so they're not discovered by anyone. Let's go outside and get your packs put away."

Samir proceeded to give the same instructions to Mohammed's team and their American couple, Will and Brianne Jacobson, and then to his own team with Chuck and Samantha James.

Mohammad was a man in love with his mission. He had waited for this opportunity most of his adult life. Mohammad did not have the physical attributes of a strong or impressive man, but his dedication to their cause made up for any physical deficiencies he may have had. His dark eyes showed both passion and patience which made him an effective leader.

Will and Brianne had married at a young age. He had been 21 and Brianne was 19. Now, ten years later, they were the youngest of the set of drivers of the RVs. Brianne, now 29, was not what one would think of when considering a devout Muslim. While she paid lip service to her religion, she did have a deep hatred of the United States which was her driving force in helping Samir. Her twin sister had been killed in a missile attack on a refugee camp by the State of Israel, or in her mind, America's puppet state. Her dark hair rested upon her shoulders, and her black smoldering eyes could be appealing or dangerous depending on her mood. Brianne fulfilled her desires by manipulating Will by the simple force of her strong personality and overt sexuality.

Will, on the other hand, enjoyed being laid back and non-confrontational. He initially had not wanted to become involved with Samir and his mission. It had not taken Brianne long to bring him to her side of wanting revenge. Will was born in the U.S. to immigrant parents originally from Lebanon. He was certainly more American than Lebanese and enjoyed the finer things in life. He dressed typically American with blue jeans and polo shirts. At 6 foot, Will had the rugged look of an outdoorsman, an image he fostered with his friends. The chiseled features of his face hid the doubt in his eyes and the lack of strength of his own convictions. He was sure, however, that his internal weaknesses would not be noticeable during this mission.

Samir followed his men to the door and watched them walk toward the RV they would be traveling in. He saw Chuck and Samantha standing near the door.

Samantha was an attractive woman in her late thirties. Her hair was a soft brown that was usually done in a bun on the top of her head, and was a full-figured woman that still turned heads. Samantha and Chuck had met in high school and had been together ever since. She was not an outgoing type, but rather a quiet woman who kept her thoughts to herself.

Chuck was a confident extrovert who had no self-doubt. As he said often, "I am not always right, but I am never wrong." Chuck had a closely cropped beard, brown in color as was his longish hair. He stood a hair over 6 feet and had dark eyes which matched his soul and the secrets that resided there. He had met Samir in Paris and they had become close friends.

Samir returned to his seat, placed his feet on the desk, leaned back and reflected on the day's activities and the successful crossing of the border into the United States. They had been fortunate to get this far without being detected. Soon, he knew, the direction and leadership of the two other teams would shift to Kamil and Mohammed. He knew he had to trust their judgment and leadership abilities even though that was difficult for him. Samir liked having control, but these two teams would be on their own. If all things went well, the three groups would then join up for the attack on the professors.

Briefly, Samir wondered how Ahmed was doing as he scouted the professors' hometown. He smiled at the thought of their deaths. But Samir also had another plan in mind.

Exiting the office, Samir found Zuni sitting on a bench with a laptop. He walked up to the young man and squatted next to him. Zuni was Samir's resident computer nerd. Zuni was 17 but looked more like 15. He was 5 foot 4 inches tall, weighed under 130 pounds and his thin face had been ravaged by acne. Dark, horn-rimmed glasses rested on his short nose. Samir had found the young man at an Internet café in Paris where Zuni spent much of his time if he was not living on the streets. It did not take Samir long to discover the brilliance of the young boy with anything involving computers. Samir offered Zuni a new life in his organization where he would have available to him the best computers money could buy.

Zuni looked up at Samir and smiled. "Hi, Boss. Do you need me now?"

"Yes, now is the time for you to do what only you can do." Zuni beamed at the compliment Samir had bestowed upon him. "Have you been able to get hooked up to the Internet in a way that no one can find you?"

"I have been hooked up for some time. No one can trace me here for at least a week and they would have to be very good to do that. What would you like me to do?"

Samir gave the boy the names of the professors and the city where they lived. "I want you to hack into their computers and find out everything you can about them, their families, their lives and schedules. I need to know when I can grab one of them as a hostage by tomorrow morning. Do you think you can accomplish that?"

"Yes, that should not be a problem. I will have it for you when you wake up tomorrow, Boss."

Samir responded, "Good, I'm counting on you." Samir stood and left Zuni with his computer. He looked back as he walked away and saw the young man's fingers dancing across the keyboard.

He had not shared with Ahmed or Kamil this portion of his plan for the professors. In fact, what he was planning to do was not necessary in taking out his revenge on the professors. But it would give him great joy to do so.

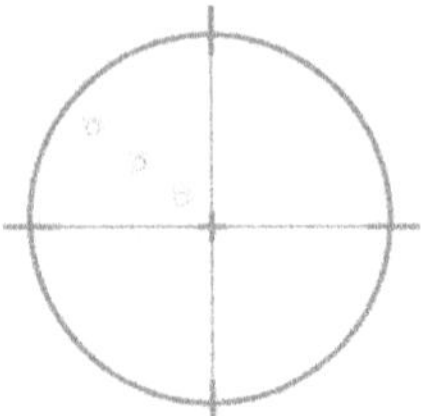

Chapter 24

Kamil awoke from his sleep refreshed and ready to go. He glanced at his watch and saw that it was just before 4 AM. This was the normal time he started his day as he needed only four or five hours of sleep per night. He was ready to begin his planned journey.

Kamil had been sleeping alone on the couch in the RV. He raised himself on his elbow, looked around, and saw that everyone else was still sound asleep. The Saudi listened to the sound of snoring coming from the bed above the cab of this class C RV. Kamil rose from the couch, stepped over someone sleeping on the floor and stretched his muscles before opening the screen door and stepping down the two metal steps. It appeared that no one else was up.

Walking to the middle of the warehouse, he saw the light was on in the office. Zuni was still seated in the corner of the warehouse working on his computer. Samir was sitting behind the desk. Kamil knocked lightly on the door. Samir looked up and motioned for him to come in.

Kamil sat down on one of the chairs in front of the desk. "You're awake early, my brother. Are you worried about the coming days?"

"No," Samir replied, "I am excited about our opportunities to strike. We have trained for this day for a long time. I'm confident that each of us knows our responsibilities and has the ability to perform the actions required. If it is Allah's will, we will be successful. Do you feel ready?"

"Absolutely. I have complete confidence in my team's ability and I'm excited to get on the road to begin this venture. What time do you think we should leave this morning?"

"I would direct that question to George and Molly. They have planned out your route and know the time required to reach your objective. It is important that you not draw attention to yourself. So, rely on their judgment on how fast they drive and the directions they take. For you, I think it will be necessary to stop at least once for the night at a RV park they select. Just make sure that your team acts appropriately at that location."

Kamil shifted in his chair. "I think it will be difficult for the members of our team to act like they are on vacation when they have such important work before them. I will warn them, once again, that impatience could bring problems to us. But they're good men and will do what is required. Do you wish to talk to them as a group before we leave?"

"Yes, I can, if you think that it is a good idea.

"I think it will be helpful for them to hear from you. Their loyalty to you is absolute, and I think speaking to them will be good for their souls. You can also set, once again, the expectations you have for them."

"I will do so then."

"I saw Zuni working on his computer. I think he has been up all night. Do you know what he's doing?"

Samir replied, "He's getting some additional information for me on my target."

Kamil and Samir talked for another hour before the others began to stir. Soon, many Saudis were walking around the warehouse. Each RV couple prepared breakfast for the members of their teams. A sense of excitement permeated the warehouse, in the tone of their voices and the determination in their eyes.

George walked up to Kamil and stated, "I think it is best that we leave at 9 AM. That is a time when many people start off on their vacations. Is that acceptable to you?"

"If that is your recommendation, it is certainly acceptable to me." Kamil glanced at his watch; they had about 30 minutes before they needed to depart.

"George, please get the members of our team and bring them to the office," Kamil said softly. "Samir has some final thoughts he would like to share with them." George nodded and left to round up the members of the team.

Kamil walked back into the office where Samir still sat. "My team will be here in a few moments. George has recommended that we leave in half an hour. Do you have anything you need to say to me before we leave?"

"No, as you know, I have complete confidence in you. In just a few days, the sun will shine on us for the glory of Allah." Samir glanced out the window and saw Kamil's team approaching. The men walked into his office and each took a seat. He looked at each one of them without speaking.

When it was obvious he had their attention, Samir began. "My friends, you're about to leave and head for your target city. I want you to know that I have the utmost trust in each and every one of you. The role you play is critically important as we attack the Great Satan in his own country. As you begin to carry out your responsibilities, remember that Allah will be watching you. Your actions will make him proud, your name will be spoken of with reverence and be remembered for many generations. Good luck and praise be to Allah." With that, Samir rose and shook the hand of each of the team members as they left his office.

Just before 9 AM, Kamil announced to everyone in the warehouse that his team was about to depart. The remaining members of the group came forward to bid farewell to their friends. Shortly after 9 AM, George and Molly got the RV ready to leave. Kamil ushered his team members into the tan RV, turned, shook Samir's hand one final time, then gave his leader a sincere hug. "If it is Allah's will, I will see you shortly after our attack and we will bring death to the professors."

Samir smiled and watched Kamil enter the vehicle. The door to the warehouse was raised and George drove the RV out into the street. After they had left, there was a brief silence in the warehouse as the remaining men pondered the beginning of their attacks.

* * *

Once they were on the freeway, Kamil addressed his men. "George and Molly have prepared a map for us, indicating the route we will be taking. Please familiarize yourself with it so you understand where we are. We will stop before the day is out and sleep at an RV park. Hopefully, we should arrive at our target city tomorrow or the day after. I'm also going to pass out to you photographs of our targets. I will speak with each one of you, outlining your responsibilities during our attacks. You should not be concerned with the actions you will take because you've been specifically trained to carry out your responsibilities.

"One final note. Remember, you cannot talk with anyone outside of our group about where you're going or what you're going to do. You are going on vacation with family members and will be visiting other family members. I'm going to hand out your Egyptian passports at this time. If Allah is willing, we will strike a great blow here in America, which will cause all Americans great fear."

The men nodded and indicated their readiness.

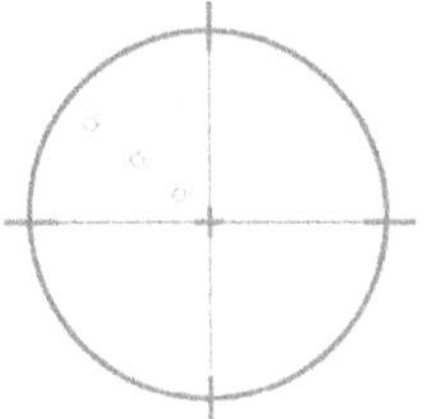

Chapter 25

My watch read 6:15 PM when I pulled into the restaurant parking lot. I saw that Mac and Ann had already arrived and had arranged for a table that held six. Sandy and I walked over, exchanged hugs and sat down. Mac and Ann had been sipping on beers. When the waitress came by, I ordered some water and Sandy asked for iced tea.

"Have you seen Leanne and Ty yet?" I asked.

Mac chuckled before answering, "Naw, you know he's always late."

Ann looked at Mac and stated, "You know that's not fair. We're always early and it's not even 6:30 yet. Just because you want to be the first one to order a drink, does not mean that everybody else is late."

I said nothing but smiled at Mac, waiting to see how he would reply. "Now, honey, you take things too seriously. I was just trying to see if I could get a rise out of DJ." Just then, Leanne and Ty approached and sat down.

Ty looked at me and asked, "What did he do this time? I saw her giving him the business again. You'd think he would learn. However, that may be too much to ask of him."

Mac looked at each one of us before stating, "Why are all of you picking on me again?"

We all responded at the same time, "Because you deserve it!"

Mac's shoulders slumped forward, a crestfallen look on his face. "You've really hurt my feelings."

We all responded once again, "Bullshit!"

Mac smiled as he looked at us. "Well, I had to try."

I looked at Ann. "And you have to put up with this all the time?"

Ann patted Mac on the hand and smiled at him sweetly. "Well, he does have some redeeming qualities."

"Let's not go there, please. You don't want to ruin our vision of him," I replied. "When we decided to have dinner, we all wanted to discuss where we should go from here. Any suggestions from anyone?"

Mac spoke up first, "Why are we always meeting during mealtimes?"

Ty responded. "Because we need to eat and that's the only time we can be sure you will be where we want you. On to more serious things, there's something I want to run by you guys. I believe that, however this comes down, we're going to be outnumbered. What do you think about reaching out to Derek and seeing if he would be willing to help out? As you know, he was in the service and can handle weapons. He clearly was the one we could rely on in Paris. But since he graduated, I don't know whether he has a full-time job. Has anybody heard what he is up to?"

Mac answered the question. "I talked with him about a month ago. He was interviewing for jobs at various police departments in Southern California. He was living with his parents and trying not to spend too much money. There's no question he'd be a great addition to our group."

"Why would we want to put him in danger, too? Hell, he's a great kid and just starting his career. I don't feel good about this." Sandy looked at the other two women and asked, "What do you think?"

Before Ann had a chance to respond, Leanne said, "I agree. I would feel terrible if something happened to him because he was trying to help us."

"I disagree with both of you," Ann responded. "First of all, he's a full-grown man and can appreciate the dangers he could face. Having heard what Mac said about his actions in Paris, I think that having him working with us would be a great advantage. If he doesn't want to come and help for any reason, I can understand that, and we would wish him well." Ann looked at each of us closely. "This is our lives we are talking about. We need whatever help we can get. Derek will help us kick ass and take names. I think it's a great idea."

I looked at Mac, "What do you think, Mac?"

"It's an interesting question and suggestion. I understand the concern that Leanne and Sandy have, but what Ty and Ann are saying makes sense also. The bottom line is that it is Derek's decision to make. If we don't ask, he doesn't have to make a decision. But I can tell you this, if and when those bastards come for us, I would like him on my side." Mac looked to Sandy and Leanne. "Do you guys feel really strongly about this? I think it would be difficult to ask him if you weren't on board. It's the kind of question, I think, we all have to agree on."

Sandy turned toward me. "DJ, what do you think? Should we ask him or not?"

I responded, "I understand your objections. However, Derek is a big boy. He can think for himself and make decisions that affect his life. We for damned sure could use his help when they come for us."

I could see that Sandy was torn. It was clear that she wanted no harm to come to Derek, but she also understood the advantages of asking him. A look came over her face that told me she had made a final decision. "I agree that this decision should be unanimous. I mean, we all should agree if we're going to put someone's life in danger. With that said, I'm in for asking him to join us."

Everyone looked at Leanne to see what her reaction was. She smiled and said, "I'm in, too. Let's ask him."

"I feel better already," said Ty with a smile on his face.

Leanne leaned over and gave him a kiss on the cheek. "Well you should, Big Boy. That's my hand on your thigh."

Ty kissed her back and said, "You are such a tease." Then he looked at Mac and me. "You know, I'm not really hungry now. I think we'll leave and go home."

Mac stood up and leaned over the table and stared at Ty. "Don't you even think about it. We've got business to discuss here, and I want another beer."

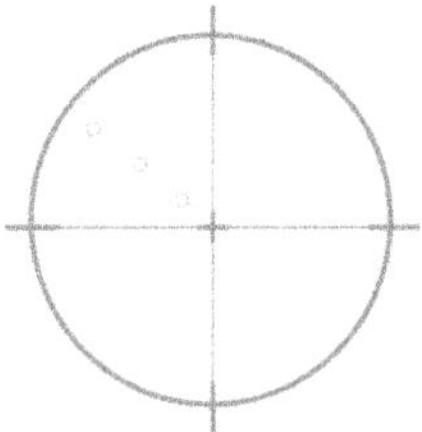

Chapter 26

Shortly after Kamil departed the warehouse, Samir called to Zuni and asked him to come the office. The slender young man hurried over with his computer and stood before him. Samir smiled at him, "Have you been able to get the information I need?"

"Yes, I have. I believe I have everything. Would you like me to explain how I was able to get this information?"

"Yes, please, but in layman's terms. Otherwise I won't understand what you're saying." Samir was not fond of admitting his lack of technical skills, but he trusted Zuni.

"Okay, but if I get too technical, please let me know. I had no difficulty finding or hacking into each of the professor's computers. From there, I was able to find their adult children's emails, which allowed me to hack into their computers. For DJ Anderson, I found that he has one adult daughter who has two children, twins aged 14. I also learned that his daughter's family currently is in Hawaii on vacation. They will not return to their home in Las Vegas until mid-January.

"For Mac MacDonald, I discovered that he also has one child, a daughter who also has a daughter. His granddaughter is five and is currently visiting her other grandparents in Seattle. I was not able to discover when she would return.

"As for Ty Smith, I found some interesting information. His son lives in Mesquite, Nevada, with his wife and their young daughter, who is four."

Samir asked, "Why is that information interesting?"

"I learned that the wife, Julie, would be taking their daughter, Kelsey, to a local theater the day after tomorrow to see *The Nutcracker*, a ballet that is evidently often performed during the Christmas season. I looked at the theater and the area surrounding it. There appears to be a parking lot on the side of the building. They have two vehicles, a truck and a sedan. I believe the father drives the truck and the mother the car. I also have the make, model, and license number for both vehicles.

"I discovered that the family also has a Facebook page. I was able to access that and have found photos of the mother and the child. It is my opinion that this is the best option available to you. I can provide you with all the information you need such as the address of the theater and the time of the show. Do you need anything else?"

Samir smiled at Zuni. "You've done a very thorough job, Zuni. I'm proud of your work. Can you get that information printed out for me? If so, I'll take it from here."

"I have that right here for you. I assumed you would want a hard copy."

"Thank you, Zuni. I will let you know if I need anything else." Samir watched the young man leave his office. Samir closed his eyes and saw the vision of Salah before him. You will be avenged, my friend, in more ways than one.

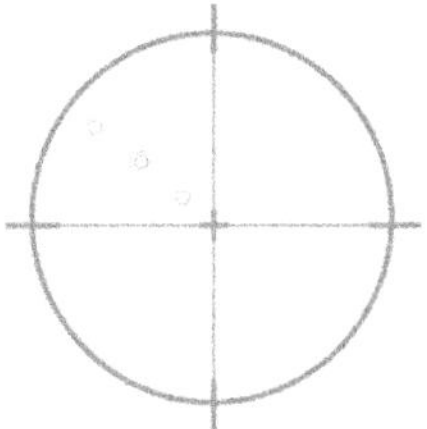

Chapter 27

Mohammed was itching to get on the road. Waiting around did nothing but raise his anxiety. He understood why he was scheduled to leave in the late afternoon rather than at the same time Kamil left, but he was ready to go now. Mohammed looked at his watch and saw they were still over an hour from their departure time of 4 PM. He turned to head for the RV to make sure he and his men were ready to leave.

As Mohammed walked toward his vehicle, he heard Samir's voice call to him. He turned and saw Samir standing just outside of his office and motioned for him to enter and sit down.

Samir began the conversation by asking him, "Are you ready to leave?"

Mohammed nodded vigorously and said, "Yes, I do not like this waiting and wish we could begin right away."

"I understand your desire to begin immediately. However, as you know, our attacks have been planned very carefully. We do not want the three RVs leaving at the same time as it may raise some suspicion. By leaving as we are scheduled to, we all should reach our destinations about the same time. Sometimes patience is more important than being aggressive."

"I understand what you're saying. While I am and can be patient, I have an overwhelming desire to strike at America. Waiting just makes it difficult."

Samir smiled at the man before him. "I know what you're feeling. I, too, am excited at the prospect of striking the Great Satan. I, too, must resist my own desires for this mission to be a success. In any event, your team will be leaving within the hour. I'm going to ask you, as I did Kamil, whether you think it would be helpful for me to speak to your team before you leave?"

"I believe, without question, your words to my men would be a helpful motivating factor in their success. Do not misunderstand me; my men are ready to do battle. They are as dedicated as any group I have known, but you are their inspiration in our cause. Should things become difficult, your words will ring in their ears and will give them strength to continue on."

Samir was pleased to hear Mohammed's comments and felt gratified that his men would hold him in such high esteem. "Go out and bring them back here." Mohammed rose from his chair and strode out.

Within a few short minutes, Mohammed had returned with his men in tow. Samir gestured for them to take their seats. "Well, men, your time to leave is drawing close. I wanted to talk to you for a moment. If you're like me, this waiting is very difficult. I know that my team and I ache to begin this mission. As you know, we will not leave until tomorrow morning. Each team leaves at a different time for two reasons. First, we don't want to raise suspicion among the Americans because three RVs were traveling together. Second, we want each team to arrive at its target location about the same time as everyone else. Leaving when you do meets both those concerns.

"You know you have been chosen personally by me to be members of this operation. I am confident that each of you will perform your responsibilities completely. I want you to understand that if you are successful, you will help bring the Great Satan to its knees. Your name will be raised up by others and you will be remembered for many years as a faithful soldier for Allah. There is no greater tribute that can be given to anyone than having your name praised by Allah. After you have completed your mission, we will meet once again to carry out further actions against the Americans. Your journey today is just the beginning in bringing America down.

"I want you to go forward understanding the importance of your mission, the importance of your place in that mission, and the rewards that await all of us. Do any of you have any questions?" Seeing no response, Samir finished," May Allah shine his face upon you. Good luck and we will see you again after your attack."

Mohammed stood and led his men out of the office. Samir watched them walk toward their RV before walking over to his pack, which was sitting in the corner of his office. He reached in and pulled out a burner cell phone. He dialed the number he had memorized, and after three rings, it was answered by a man who simply said, "Hello?"

Samir responded, "I am ready for your services. As soon as we hang up. I will be sending you the information you will need. You know what I want done, correct?"

"I do."

"Good. When I hang up, I will deposit in your account one half of the amount we agreed upon. Call me when you are ready to perform the second part of our agreement. Any questions?"

"None. I will call you when we are ready to proceed."

Samir disconnected the call and immediately removed the Sim card and battery from the phone. He smashed the phone, cut up the Sim card, then picked up the remains of the phone and Sim card, walked to the bathroom and flushed the items down the toilet. Samir returned to his office with a big grin on his face. Things are coming together quite nicely, he thought.

Mohammed stopped his men and announced to the remainder of the men that his team would be leaving shortly. As with Kamil's team, the remaining men came forward to speak briefly with the members of Mohammed's team. There were solemn handshakes and wishes of good luck. Once that had been completed, Mohammed led his men into the RV for the beginning of their journey. Will started the vehicle and drove slowly through the open door of the warehouse and onto the street outside.

Like Kamil before him, and following the instructions he had been given, Mohammed spoke to his men only when they were on the freeway. He, too, handed out photographs of their target destination. Mohammed told them that they would drive for about five hours today and then camp overnight at a location picked by Will. He further informed them that they should reach their target city the following day.

Brianne, Will's partner, left her captain's seat in the front, came back, and stood before the men. She smiled a toothy, red-lipsticked grin at them. "The drive to where we will spend the night will not take too long. I will fix our evening meal when we arrive at that location. If you're hungry before then, there are some snacks in this cabinet," she said, pointing over her head. "The trip tomorrow will take most of the day. It is important that you relax so you will be ready when we reach our target city." She then returned to her seat.

Each man had found a seat and began to think about the days ahead. Some were arrogant as they thought of their own abilities. Some prayed to Allah for the strength to carry out their responsibilities in such a way that would bring them glory. Some, though they would never admit it, felt fear rise in their stomach—fear that they would fail to carry out their assigned duties, fear that they would be stopped by the Americans, and fear that they would die without having pleased Allah. As these thoughts passed through their minds, the vehicle that carried them to their destiny rolled on, across a flat, barren landscape.

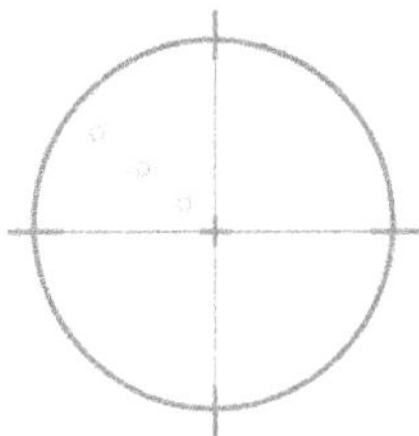

Chapter 28

Ben McCall was sitting in his office staring at the phone. He had just replaced the receiver in its cradle. McCall was the supervising agent of the border patrol office in El Paso and had been in that position for 12 years. Prior to that he was assigned to the Washington, D.C. office. Today he was worried.

Standing 6 foot 2, he was a well-built man who exercised regularly, and his physical appearance drew respect from those around him. Even though it was beginning to show streaks of gray, his hair was mostly black and touched his collar. McCall's face was just beginning to show the lines of age and responsibility. His brown eyes were a natural draw for women until they saw the coldness that appeared during times of stress.

The cause of his concern this morning involved one of his agents, Bill Jackson. Jackson had been on duty the previous night and had not reported in after his shift. Occasionally, agents would forget to call in and just return to their home. McCall had called Jackson's home phone and cell phone, but after a few rings, both went to voicemail. McCall couldn't fight the nagging feeling in his gut that something had happened to Jackson. He had noticed that Jackson had begun to drink more than he should, so it certainly was possible that he was drunk somewhere. McCall needed to get to the bottom of this, if for no other reason, than to relieve his own anxiety.

He had called a meeting with three of his agents to begin at 9 AM to share his concerns. McCall looked at his watch and saw that it was time for him to go to the conference room. The three agents were waiting for him. McCall sat down at the head of the polished table and glanced around. To his left was Jeanette Hauser. Her short brown hair framed her round face and highlighted her light brown eyes. She was 25 and new to the border patrol, standing 5 foot 7, weighing approximately 150 pounds. Jeanette's work performance had been steady but unspectacular. On the positive side, she had scored highly in the firearms training.

The second agent, a forty-something named Jared Isom, was more experienced than Hauser. He had come to the border patrol some five years ago and had developed into a very competent agent. Isom was of average height; his most outstanding characteristics were his curly red hair, cut short, and the wealth of freckles covering his friendly face. He had a quick smile, but like many redheads, was also quick to anger.

The third agent in the room, Jason Crow, was a recent hire. He stood 5 foot 10, with sandy blond hair and blue eyes. Jason, like his peers, had been driving the border since he finished his training. He had not been an agent long enough for McCall to develop a good feel for him.

McCall opened the meeting. "Good morning, thanks for coming. I know this meeting was called at the last minute. However, a situation has come up that we need to deal with. Do each of you know Bill Jackson?" The three agents nodded their heads in the affirmative. "He was on duty last night but failed to check in at the end of his shift. I've called both his cell phone and his home phone and received no answer. Now this may be nothing and there's probably a good reason for him not checking in and for not answering his phone, but I want you three to check where he went last night and see if you can find anything. You can go down to dispatch and see where he told them he would be working. Then figure out how you want to split up the area to see if you can find him. I'm also going to send someone to his house to check on him just in case he has his phones turned off. Any questions?"

Jared looked at the other two agents. "We'll get on this right away, sir, and hopefully get an answer to you before noon."

"Good, call me when you learn anything." The three agents got up and strode quickly out of the conference room. He slowly rose and headed for his office. If they were lucky, they would find Jackson sleeping off a hangover at his home.

Within 20 minutes and after several phone calls, the three agents had determined the direction Jackson had been heading. In short order, they had divided the area to be searched into three sections using their GPS. Each of them got in a vehicle and headed toward his or her respective area of responsibility.

As Hauser drove toward the area she was going to search, she realized it was a place where immigrants tried to slip over the border. It took her about an hour to reach her assigned section, which she had been to many times previously. After nearly 30 minutes of traveling down various dirt roads without finding any trace of Jackson, she saw a vehicle in the distance. As she drew closer, she saw the border patrol crest on its side. She pulled up beside it and got out of her vehicle. Unsnapping her sidearm, she walked to the driver's side, looked in the window, and found it empty. She did see, however, that the keys were still in the ignition and there appeared to be relatively new tire prints in the dirt road. Her attention was drawn to the side of the road. Hidden behind some bushes, she found the body of a young man. She reached down and checked for a pulse and found none.

Hauser pulled out her cell phone and dialed McCall's number. She heard him say, "Ben McCall."

"This is Hauser. I found Jackson's car, but it's empty. Not too far away, I found the body of a young Hispanic male. Since it appears that he was shot, I suggest that you send some people here to investigate this."

"Text me your GPS coordinates. I will get someone there right away. Call Isom and Crow and have them join you. Search the area around the car's location to make sure Jackson isn't there. Let me know what you find."

Hauser immediately called the other two agents and asked them to join her as soon as possible. Hauser then searched the area around the car, but found nothing else. She expanded her inspection by walking in an ever-widening circle around the vehicle, careful not to step on any possible clues. Hauser decided to increase the distance by 25 yards for each circle. As she was walking on her second circle at 50 yards, she observed a pile of brush with a boot sticking out.

When Hauser pushed aside the weeds and other brush, she jerked back when she saw the body that lay there. It was Bill Jackson. He was lying on his back and it was obvious he had taken a round to his head. Even so, she knelt down to check for a pulse but found none. There appeared to be a look of fear on his face, and she wondered what he had seen in those last seconds of his life. Hauser stood, took out her cell phone and called McCall once again.

"I've found Jackson. He's been shot in the head."

"Stay with his body. I'm on my way. Are Isom and Crow there yet?"

"No, they haven't arrived, but I expect them shortly."

"When they arrive, make sure they seal off the crime scene. I will get a forensic unit out there to see what they can find. How are you doing?"

She responded, "I'm fine. You don't need to worry about me."

"Okay, keep me updated, and I'll see you soon." As he put the phone down, McCall knew that later he would have the difficult job of notifying Jackson's ex-wife of the border patrol man's death. He also knew how heart-wrenching it would be for Jackson's wife to inform their children that they would no longer see their father.

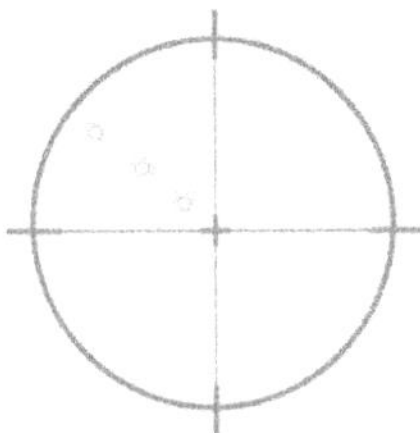

Chapter 29

Prior to leaving the warehouse, Kamil had talked to George at some length about the route they would travel to Seattle. George brought up Google maps on his computer so that they could have an idea of how far they should go each day. Kamil wanted to reach Seattle in the early afternoon so the men would have time to get a feel for the area. After some discussion, George and Kamil decided that it would probably be best to stop twice on their journey. They would travel to Moab, Utah, the first day. The next day would take them to Baker City, Oregon. On the third day, they would complete their trip to Seattle.

Kamil looked at his men. The excitement of beginning their mission had worn off and quickly had given way to the boredom of traveling great distances on American freeways. George and Molly took turns driving, usually exchanging seats when they stopped to get gas. Soon the men developed an unspoken routine of half of them napping and the other half reading or looking at magazines they had brought with them. They did not stop for lunch, but Molly fixed sandwiches for them around 2 PM. George did some calculations and informed Kamil that they should arrive at the Moore Valley RV resort in Moab between 7 PM and 8 PM that evening. Molly had called the campground and reserved a site for them.

Kamil's men complained of the boredom that this traveling involved. He kept them up to date as to their progress and at what time they expected to arrive. Kamil sat down on the couch, and the man next to him stated, "How big is this damn country? It seems like we travel for hours and hours and get nowhere. How far is it from El Paso to Seattle?"

Kamil responded, "It is about 1,700 miles."

"That means nothing to me. What is it in kilometers?"

Kamil took out his phone and googled a miles/kilometer conversion app. He looked up from the phone and told the man, "About 2,735 kilometers."

The man rolled his eyes and stated, "I will be dead long before then. Boredom takes no prisoners. Perhaps, I should just kill myself now and end this misery and the misery to come." He saw the look of concern came over Kamil's face. "Don't worry, I'm only joking. But next time, I suggest we pick a small country like Monaco." Both men chuckled.

Kamil stood up and looked down at the man. "Next time, I think we should land in Moscow and attack Vladivostok."

The man pantomimed putting a rope around his neck and hanging himself. "You're killing me, Kamil." The man then slumped on the sofa as if he had died.

Just after 7:30 PM, the RV with its towed car pulled into the RV park. George walked into the office and returned shortly thereafter. He held some papers in his hand which he said was their rental contract and map of the park. A few moments later, George pulled into their assigned site, and he and Molly left the motor coach to complete the appropriate hookups. Molly returned shortly thereafter and began preparing spaghetti for their dinner.

The men were hungry and ate quickly. Kamil concluded the meal by stating, "In a few minutes, we're going to begin taking showers. Only two men will go to the shower building at any one time. Do not waste time in the shower. We're going to leave early in the morning. Our next stop will be in Baker City, Oregon, which is about a 10-hour drive." That information produced a groan from most of the men. Kamil continued, "To make you feel better, our travel time for the following day will be half of that." Kamil's statement caused two men to perk up, but the remainder continued to grouse.

By 10 PM that evening, most of the men were settling in for the night. Kamil and George had been keeping watch on the RV park to see if there had been any reaction to their men showering. Kamil said, "I have not seen anything suspicious, have you?"

George answered, "I've not seen anything either. It's cold outside and that keeps people in their RVs and out of other people's business. I think we're fine."

George and Molly were up at 5 AM to begin their day. Molly put together a breakfast of fruit and yogurt again while George stepped outside the RV and prepared it for the day's travel in the dim dawn light. As they moved about, Kamil and his men began to wake up. Once they finished their breakfast, George climbed into the driver's seat and pulled out of their site. Several of the men lay back down to get some extra sleep while the others quickly got bored again. The second day of travel was a repeat of the first—almost.

Just after 6 PM, George pulled the RV into the Oregon Trails West RV park. Like the previous night, he walked into the office and obtained information about his assigned site. Within five minutes, the RV pulled into that spot, and like the previous evening, George stumbled about in the dark and got the RV hooked up, while Molly walked into the small store and bought several cans of beef stew. She returned to the RV and in a few minutes, the men began to smell the results of her efforts.

The routine that evening copied the night before. By 9:30 PM, Kamil began to hear snoring permeate the air.

The quiet in the RV was suddenly interrupted by someone pounding on the door. "Hey friend, open up!"

Kamil motion to his men, who were now awake, to move into the back bedroom. He then whispered to George, "Get rid of whoever that is."

George walked to the door and opened it. Standing before him was a man who appeared to be in his late 60s, dressed in jeans and a plaid flannel shirt. George smiled at the man and said, "Can I help you?"

"You certainly can," the man replied and pointed to the coach parked next to George's RV. George noticed the slur in the man's speech. It was obvious he had too much to drink. "My wife and I would like you to come over and have a drink with us."

"I'm sorry, I don't think we can do that since were pretty beat and want to go to bed."

"Oh, come on, man, you have time for a little snort." This conversation continued for a short while as the man would not take no for an answer. Suddenly, his voice started to rise in volume as he insisted that George join him. George looked at Kamil, who nodded at him.

Kamil walked up behind George and looked at the man, who said, "Who's he?"

"I'm George's brother," replied Kamil. "A snort sounds good to me."

Pointing at Kamil, the man responded, "Now, I like him. Come on over and meet the wife." George and Kamil followed the man to his RV. "Margie, I want you to meet our neighbors." He turned to Kamil and George, "I don't think I got your names."

George answered, "I'm George and he's Ralph."

Margie reached over and shook each of the men's hands. She pointed at the couch and asked them to sit down. "I'm sorry if Les here has been little pushy. He just likes to meet new people."

The grizzled, gray-haired man smiled at each of them as he began to pour them a drink. "I'm Les, Les Stevenson. I make a strong drink. Hope you like it." He gave everyone their drinks and peered at the two men as if he had not seen them before. He looked at Kamil and stated, "You said the two of you were brothers?"

"That's correct."

"Now that you're in the light, you don't look like no brothers to me. In fact, you don't look nothing alike." Les steadied himself on the dinette.

Margie interrupted him. "Now, Les darling, don't go getting angry just because you're drunk. These men are guests in our home."

After finishing his drink, Kamil stood up and smiled at Margie. "I think its best that we go back to our place. We are leaving early tomorrow." Kamil reached out and shook Margie and Les' hands. "Thank you for the drink. Les. You're right, you make quite a drink. It will help me sleep tonight."

Margie shut the door behind the two men as they left and stated, "They were very nice gentleman, Les."

"Something is very fishy about them and I want to find out what it is," Les replied.

Margie looked at him with sadness in her eyes. "You're just an old fool. Let's go to bed.

***

As soon as George and Kamil returned to the RV, the men asked what happened. Kamil quickly explained what had occurred. Soon, though, everyone had fallen asleep once again. The incident with Les had left him unsettled. However, he too, was tired and soon his deep snores joined those of his men.

Kamil and George had decided to leave the park at about 8 AM. As they pulled out onto the freeway, they were greeted by blue sky and sunshine. This is a good omen, thought Kamil, to begin their final day of travel, knowing that they would soon reach Seattle. As the hours passed, Kamil noticed that his men's attitude had changed back from boredom to excitement. Each of them knew that by the end of the day, they would begin the preparations for their attack. That sense of anticipation seemed to make the hours pass quickly.

Soon the RV was on I-90, which ended in Seattle. The men looked eagerly out the windows as they entered the suburbs of Seattle. They crossed a short bridge and soon found themselves on Mercer Island.

One of the men exclaimed, "The road ahead appears to be floating on the water. How can that possibly be?"

George answered the man, "This lake is too deep to allow bridge pilings to reach the bottom. Therefore, the Americans developed these floating bridges to move traffic from Seattle across this lake. It really is a marvel of engineering."

The men continued to stare at the bridge they were traveling on and were amazed by its ability to float on water. The RV continued on and soon came to Interstate 5, which gave the men a view of Seattle proper. George took the exit for Seattle North through the city. The men were amazed at the height of the buildings and the beauty of Puget Sound. George continued on I-5 N and then took the exit for 520 E. Soon the men were on the Evergreen Point Bridge and, once again, were stunned at how this concrete structure floated on water.

After crossing the lake, the RV turned south on Interstate 405 in the direction of the Trailer Inns RV park in Bellevue. It did not take long for George to check in and drive to the site they had been assigned.

Kamil stood before his men once again and stated, "Molly will be preparing a late lunch momentarily. After that, we will begin the preparation for our attack."

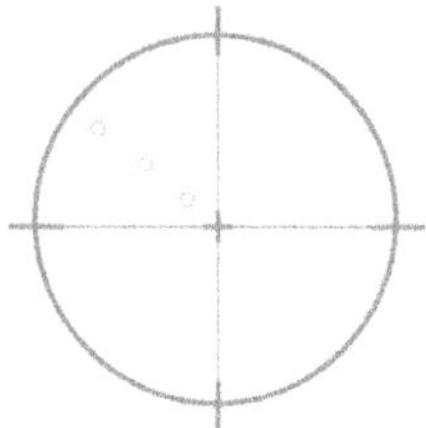

Chapter 30

The sun was just peeking over the horizon when Samir awoke on the cot he had placed in the office. Even though his portion of the mission would start today, he had slept peacefully without interruption. He was confident in the plan they had devised and in the people who would carry it out.

He walked out of the office and glanced toward the vehicle that would transport them to the target. Samir saw some movement through the windows and realized that others were up also. He walked toward the RV and opened its door. The men were sitting on the couch and at the dinette. As Samir entered, he could smell freshly brewed tea. Samantha, standing by the stove, smiled as he entered and handed him a full cup. Samir looked toward the back and saw that Chuck was occupied in the back bedroom.

Samir looked at his men and stated, "We will be having breakfast shortly. I want to be on the road by 9 AM." As he finished talking, Samantha brought over some yogurt and fruit. The men ate slowly as they discussed the coming mission. Samir listened to the conversation but did not inject himself into it. He was satisfied to just listen and check the mood of his men. They appeared to be in high spirits and were confident they could carry out their mission successfully. Samir helped himself to some fruit and yogurt.

It was about 7:30 AM when the men had finished their tea and breakfast. They looked at him expectantly and he knew they wanted to get started. Samir could feel the excitement in his own stomach and shared their desire to be on the road. However, he knew that this mission had been planned carefully and there was no reason to deviate from it by leaving early. Samir looked at his men and said, "I want you to get your packs out and double-check that you have everything you need. Let's make sure we don't leave anything here that either we need or could be used against us in the future. Following that, let's get this warehouse cleaned up so that there is nothing that would make the owners suspicious."

One of his men spoke up, "When are you going to tell us our objective and what the plan is?"

Samir smiled to himself and knew that if he was one of his men, he would have the same question. Samir looked not only at the man who spoke, but at all of his men. "You will learn all the details once we are on our way. Have just a little more patience. Let's get ready so we can leave."

Samir sat once again at the desk in his office and looked out the window to see the men scurrying about. He had finished cleaning out his office, so he too would be ready to leave. Samir glanced at his watch and saw that it was almost 9 AM. He then headed toward the RV. The men had completed their work and were gathered near the RV's door. Samantha stood next to the door of the warehouse. Samir motioned to his men to get aboard and nodded to Chuck. Once everyone was seated, Chuck started the vehicle and drove toward and through the door. Samantha closed the warehouse door and rejoined them. She took the front passenger seat and buckled herself in. Chuck then headed for the highway.

Samir stood and faced his men. "Now is the time for you to learn of the target's location." He handed out a series of maps, as had been done with the previous two teams. "We are headed for Las Vegas. It is a place to go if one wants to gamble or to pursue other immoral activities. This is the town where gambling is king. There are many places to go to listen to obscene music or to watch women dance without wearing any clothes. It is a place of such decadence, that it is, in and of itself, a smear on the face of Allah. We will attack it in such a way as to send a message to all Americans that this activity will no longer be tolerated." Samir watched the men break into smiles. It was easy for them to understand why this city had been chosen as their target. Samir also gave them photos of Las Vegas. "Study these so you have a sense of what we will be facing. This afternoon, I will tell you the plans for our attack."

Samir watched his men look through the photographs. They were almost like children in their excitement. He would let them enjoy this moment for he knew that their road ahead would be very difficult. Samir had kept the hardest and most complicated mission for himself. He believed that he had the right men with the appropriate training to strike a devastating blow against the Great Satan. When this attack had been completed, Samir would then be free to turn his attention toward the three American professors.

In his heart of hearts, he questioned whether his focus on the three Americans was ill advised. However, he had convinced himself that killing them would send a message to not only America but to all who opposed them that he was a man not to be taken lightly. These Americans would understand that he could strike with impunity by killing their people and disrupting their economy. Every government would know that his group could strike at the very heart of their country and to the heroes they looked up to. His attacks would strike fear in the soul of every American. They would begin to doubt the ability of their government to protect them even in their own country.

Samir looked out the window and watched as they passed through the dull, dusty landscape.

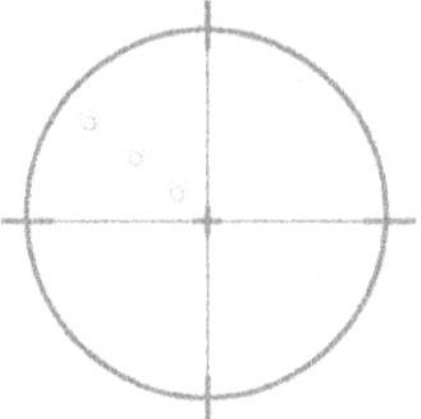

Chapter 31

I pulled into the university parking lot that served the president's office. While I was on time, I saw that both Mac and Ty had already arrived and were waiting for me on the sidewalk. As I walked up to them, I said, "Mac, I thought they had banned you from the university some time ago."

"You haven't been here five seconds and you are already on my butt. I know that sometimes I give you a bad time, but I also give you at least 10 seconds to get acclimated."

"Ty, I think I might've hurt his feelings. No, that can't be right. He has no feelings. Ty, you know, I thought you were getting better, but seeing you here with him made me realize I was wrong. However, I still have hope for you, but you really need to watch who you hang around with."

Before Ty could say a word, Mac continued, "Ty, I warned you about him. When I am long gone, you'll be his main target. You should thank me now for shielding you as long as I have."

Ty looked from one to the other. "The only thing you two have in common is the incredible amount of bullshit that you are able to generate."

"You know, you're right. It's kind of cool, isn't it?" Mac turned to me, stuck out his hand and said, "How you doing, buddy? Ty is always so serious, don't you think?"

I responded quickly, "No kidding. I guess we are just going to have to keep working on him. Well, are you guys ready to go see the man?"

"Do you have any idea why the president wants to see us? I don't know about you, but I haven't heard a word from him since our last meeting," Ty said.

I responded, "Your guess is as good as mine. The only thing I can think of is that he finished discussions with both the regents and the trustees. Well, there's no time like the present to find out. Let's go talk to him."

The three of us walked to the building and made our way to the president's office. As we walked in, the dark-haired receptionist greeted us. "Hey, guys, what's going on?"

Mac walked over and sat on her desk. "I don't know about these two morons, but I've come to talk with you."

She smiled at him sweetly and responded, "You are so full of BS. The president was right when he told me about you. He's waiting for you if you can manage to make your way into his office."

As we opened the door to his office and entered, Jack pointed to the conference table and we sat down. Mac spoke first. "You asked for our presence, Your Eminence. We are here at your disposal."

The president rolled his eyes at Mac and then looked at the two of us. "Perhaps it would be best if we had him taken away. I know of a padded room they could try to hold him in. However, before he gets going trying to justify his existence, I have some news for you. I've met with the Board of Trustees and the Board of Regents and discussed our little problem. Needless to say, they were not happy to hear what was going on. As I suspected, they absolutely do not want any potential danger threatening our students. So, you won't be allowed on campus until further notice.

"They are, however, understanding of your plight. They also know that it would not only be wrong, but a terrible public relations move to terminate you. Therefore, they confirmed your leave of absence to see if this matter resolves itself. Your classes will be taught by adjuncts for spring semester. Has anything new come up that I don't know about?"

I shook my head. "No, other than we are preparing ourselves for what might come. We've heard nothing from the FBI or anyone else in the government. Frankly, we are at a loss on what to do from here." I looked at Mac and Ty and invited them to share any thoughts that they might have.

Mac looked at the president and said, “That really is about it. We will keep getting ready for an attack, should it come, and if we learn anything that affects the university in one way or another, we will let you know. By the way, am I going to get paid for not working, too?”

“Mac, I don’t know if you remember,” the president replied, “but you don’t work here anymore. Just why do you think you would get paid?”

“Well, sir, these two jokers,” he said, pointing toward Ty and me, “aren’t worth what you’re paying them now. At least with me, you’ll be getting a man of substance on the payroll. You know, just saying. It feels like another liberal conspiracy against me.”

“You know, Jack,” Ty interjected, “it would make sense if we could just leave him here with you. He can be a paid protector.”

“Ty, I think you should take him and get your collective butts out of here before I review my decision to make it a paid—as opposed to an unpaid—leave. They don’t make a padded room big enough to hold me in if he were my protector. Now get the hell out of here and take him with you.” He was smiling.

As we walked out, Mac stated, “You know, he really likes me. I can tell. Don’t you agree?”

We approached the receptionist. “Would you mind if we left Mac here with you? He seems to be quite fond of you.”

She stood and pointed toward the door leading out of the office. “Out, take him out. If he says one more word to me, I’m going to call his wife.”

I turned to talk with Mac and saw that he was already out the door and heading down the stairs. Ty and I caught up with him at the cars. He looked at each one of us. “You know, I can take almost any kind of threats, but the last one was over the line. I just don’t understand why a guy can’t have a little fun around here. By the way, you guys want to grab a beer before you head home?”

Ty gave Mac a fist bump and answered, “Lead on, my man, I will follow you anywhere.”

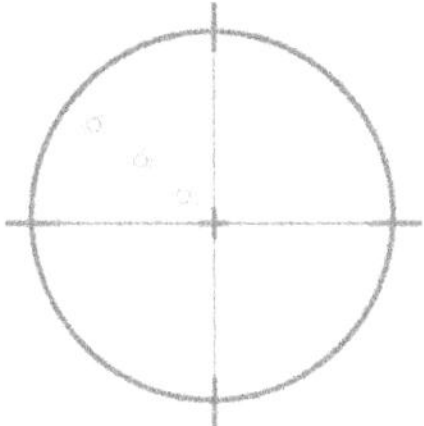

Chapter 32

Ahmed had rented a car in El Paso and had driven across the country on his own. When he entered the small town, he drove around until he found a hotel that would rent a room by the week. He walked into the office and saw a youngish, chubby man standing at the receptionist counter. The man looked up and smiled at him. "How can I help you?"

"I need to rent a room. Probably for more than a week or so. Do you have anything available?"

"Yes, we have several," the clerk responded.

"Your sign outside said they have partial kitchens. Is that correct?" Ahmed asked.

The clerk nodded his head. "Yes, that's correct. Each room has a small refrigerator and a microwave. If you wish to eat in your room, there is a grocery store two blocks down the street that can fill all your needs. The room also has free Wi-Fi, a 42-inch, flat-screen TV and the most comfortable bed you'll find in town. All of this for $49 a night or $300 a week. How does that sound to you?" The clerk smiled a buck-toothed grin.

"That will do," Ahmed responded, "I'm sure I'll be here for at least a week."

"Are you visiting your son?"

Ahmed looked at the man very closely. "I'm not sure what you mean?"

"You look like you're from Saudi Arabia. There are a lot of Saudi students at the university and I just assumed one of them might be your son. There are no Saudi women on campus, so I understand, so it must be your son or perhaps your brother. Am I that far off base?"

"No, no, you're right on target. I didn't realize there were that many Saudi students studying at the university here."

The clerk responded, "I've heard they're up to 100 Saudi students at the university now. I don't know for certain, but that's what I've heard." The clerk continued with the registration process for Ahmed and, when that was completed, handed him his room key with directions to his room. "If you need anything, just let me or whoever may be working at the desk know."

The clerk watched as Ahmed left the reception desk and walked toward his room. It's interesting, he thought. No family member has ever visited a Saudi student before. The clerk would know; the city was small enough that that news would've made the rounds. He wondered if he should alert the university.

* * *

After he got settled in his room, Ahmed left to drive around the city. He needed to familiarize himself with the layout of the town and where the professors worked and lived. Still sitting in his car, he pulled out his cell phone and dialed the number. After a few seconds, a voice answered. Ahmed spoke quietly in English, "Hadi, this is Ahmed. I'm a friend of your father's." This was the code he used to identify himself to Hadi. He would never speak in Arabic because of the NSA capturing and reviewing phone conversations. Arabic would be a sure way to draw their attention.

Hadi responded appropriately, "I've not seen my father for a long time." There was a short pause and Hadi continued, "I assume you need my assistance. I did not expect anyone to contact me so soon."

"I understand. It was not originally planned this way. Where can we meet?"

"Where are you now?"

"I am in the parking lot of my hotel." Ahmed told him the name of the hotel. Hadi suggested a park two blocks from Ahmed's hotel. "I'll see you there in half an hour." After disconnecting the call, Ahmed spent the next 30 minutes driving around town. He ended up at the park suggested by Hadi. Ahmed walked into the park and found a picnic table that was unoccupied.

Soon, he observed a man he believed to be Hadi approaching him. Ahmed rose, shook his hand, and invited him to sit. He did not explain to Hadi why he was there. "I'm going to be here for about a week and will need your help on a couple of matters. I need to rent a small warehouse. It would be best if there are no other buildings nearby. So, however you do that here, I need you to find it for me. Once that is lined up, I will need you to buy things for the warehouse, like sleeping bags and other necessities. I need this warehouse as soon as possible. After you've completed that, I want you to find me the addresses of professors Anderson, MacDonald, and Smith. Can you do that for me?"

Hadi responded quickly, "I should have that for you by tomorrow. I've made friends with someone who works in a property management firm. I'm sure they can find a warehouse for me. My guess is that the professors are listed in the phone book so that's not going to be a problem either."

"That will work fine for me. Call me immediately when you have made arrangements for the warehouse."

"I assume you are planning something here or nearby. Am I going to be able to help you with that?"

Ahmed eyed the young man closely. "Prior to coming to the United States, did you receive any training in firearms or explosives?"

"No, nothing like that," Hadi responded, "It's my dream to be able to assist you in a strike against this country. I don't know how long you've been here, but it doesn't take long to see why it is called the Great Satan. They have absolutely no respect for Allah or even their own God. The women dress in the briefest of outfits and have no regard for themselves. I've not been here that long, but it seems the most important thing in their lives is money and what they can spend it on. I see many students here who spend as much money on gaming as they do on their education. It is absolutely appalling. So, I want you to know that I am prepared to do anything you ask that will serve Allah."

Ahmed's eyes had not left the young man and he replied, "I will keep that in mind and see if I can find a way for you to serve our cause. However, at this point, you should exercise extreme caution in keeping my presence here secret. You should mention it to no one, Saudi or not. Is that clear? I cannot tell you how important it is that you follow my instructions."

"I understand what you're telling me, and I will follow your instructions to the letter."

"Good, it is important that I know I can trust you. We will separate now, and when you have the information about the warehouse, I want you to call me immediately." With that, Ahmed stood and walked toward his rental car.

Book Three
The Next Move

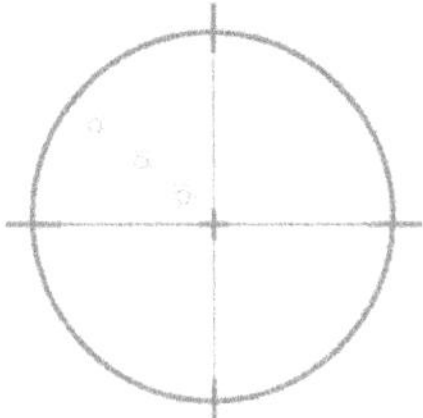

Chapter 33

A dark red Ford sedan pulled up directly across the street from the theater and parked. Tommy, who was driving, stated, "This is probably as good of view as we will get." His watch read 6:15 PM. He remarked, "I'm glad we got here early. Since the show starts at 8 PM, I would expect people to start arriving about 7:30 PM. Want to get something to eat? We've got some time to kill."

"No, let's not take the chance that they could be here early. We'll just wait," Phil replied. Phil was a big man who used to lift weights competitively. While he no longer did that, he still had the muscles of his previous life. Tonight, he wore jeans, a sweater, and a Raiders hat that covered his bald head. Phil had a smile that seemed to light up his eyes, which drew people to him. Unfortunately, he rarely allowed that smile to come out unless there was something specific he wanted from someone. "Are you good with that, Tommy?"

Tommy simply nodded, tilted his seat back and closed his eyes. Tommy was a high-school dropout who simply drifted from one crime to another. His long brown hair fell below his shoulders. Tonight, he had it tied up into a ponytail. He, too, was dressed warmly and was beginning to feel that they had arrived too early. He was concerned that staying in his car for an hour might draw attention to both of them.

Just after 7:15 PM, cars begin to arrive and park in the lot next to the theater. Phil and Tommy each had a copy of the photographs that Samir had emailed. Phil used his binoculars to look at the cars and their license plates. Just before 7:40 PM, Phil stated, "There's it is. It's just turning into the parking lot."

"I've got it," responded Tommy.

The two men watched the vehicle park and saw the lights turn off. A woman got out of the driver's seat and opened the rear passenger door to help a child out of a car seat. She walked through the parking lot holding the child's hand and entered the theater.

"That's her," stated Phil. "She looks just like she does in the picture."

Tommy nodded his agreement and said in a surprisingly loud voice, "That's the kid, too."

The two men stayed in their car while other theatergoers came, parked, and entered the theater. They waited until the play had been going for almost 30 minutes before moving their car into the parking lot. Tommy approached the woman's car and saw no blinking lights that might have indicated an alarm system. It was very easy for him to pop the lock and open the door. He reached in and pulled the lever, opening the hood. Phil pulled the hood up. In short order, he had disabled the engine so it would not start. The two men returned to their car to wait.

When the play ended, people started streaming out of the theater and heading for the parking lot. Phil and Tommy were standing just outside the theater and joined those walking toward the parking lot. They stayed several feet away from Julie and Kelsey.

Julie opened the rear door and helped Kelsey into her seat. Kelsey's eyes were alive with the excitement of the play she had just seen. She could not stop talking to her mother about it. Julie got in the driver seat and attempted to start the car. She quickly realized that something was wrong because all her efforts at starting the vehicle had failed. By that time, the parking lot was nearly empty. Julie decided she would have to call her husband to come and get them. As she pulled out her phone, she saw Phil and Tommy approaching.

Phil smiled at her and stated, "Having some car problems, ma'am?"

"Yes, the stupid thing won't start. I was just going to call my husband."

"Before you do that, why don't you open the hood and I'll take a look. I'm a mechanic and it may be something very simple." He walked to the front of her car and stated, "Okay, open it now."

As she reached down and pulled the lever that opened the hood, she felt a sting on her neck. She turned to the left and saw Tommy standing next to her with a smile on his face. Julie started to say something and then fell forward against the steering wheel.

Tommy opened the back door and smiled at Kelsey. She looked at him in alarm and said in a high, quavering voice, "What are you doing? Mama, what's going on? What's wrong with my mama?" She began to cry quietly.

"I brought this present for you from the theater." Tommy handed her a stuffed animal and as she reached for it, he brought the vial with the needle attached and injected the contents into her arm.

Kelsey yelled, "Ouch, that hurt," before she too drifted into unconsciousness.

"Let's get this done, Phil, before anyone takes notice." Tommy removed Kelsey from the car seat as Phil gently closed the hood of the car. Phil closed the car doors and led Tommy, who was carrying Kelsey, to their car. Once Kelsey was in the rear seat and buckled in, the two men got into the car and drove off.

Phil looked at Tommy. "How much propofol did you give them?"

"They both will sleep for 2 to 3 hours at least. We'll be in Vegas before either one of them wakes up." Phil took out his phone and dialed the number.

One of Samir's phones began to ring. Because only one person had the number to this phone, he knew who was calling. "Yes?"

"We have her. I will send you a photo in a moment. We will be ready to make the call at 1 AM. I will call you then." Samir heard the phone disconnect and 30 seconds later, Samir's phone beeped. Soon he was looking at a picture of the sleeping girl, her blond curls a mess.

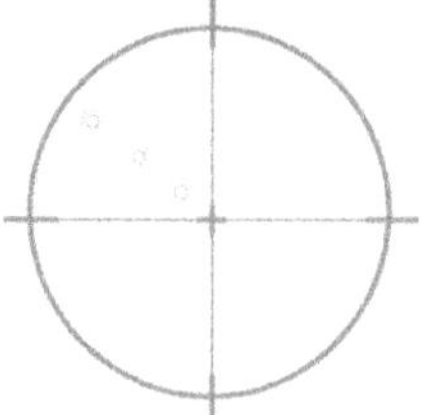

Chapter 34

Clint, Julie's husband, was getting worried. He had expected her to return from the play 30 minutes ago. For the third time, he hit the number for her phone. It rang four times and then went directly to voicemail. Thoughts ran through his mind of both his wife and child being in a serious auto accident. He decided that he could not wait any longer. Clint walked into the garage and climbed into his truck, and soon was on his way toward the theater. Ten minutes later, he saw Julie's car standing alone in the theater's parking lot.

He pulled up next to it, climbed down, and approached the driver's side. His wife was slumped over the steering wheel. Quickly, he opened the door and took her into his arms. He shook her gently. "Julie, wake up, wake up." He turned to look into the back seat and found it empty.

"Oh, my God, what has happened?" He felt and found a pulse on Julie and could see that she was breathing. Still, he was unable to wake her.

He took out his cell phone and dialed 911. He quickly described the situation to the dispatcher, who told him that she the police and an ambulance were on their way. He could hear the sirens as they approached.

* * *

The phone rang, jolting me out of a sound sleep. My alarm clock read 12:45 AM. I picked up the handset and said, "Hello."

Samir answered, "Good morning, Professor, I assume you know who this is. I need to talk with you and the other two professors right now. I will give you two minutes to conference them in."

When I started to speak, Samir interrupted me and stated, "The two minutes begins now. I suggest you not waste your time."

Surprised, I cleared my head and quickly conferenced both Ty and Mac into the conversation and said, "We're listening."

Wasting no time, Samir continued, "I'm only going to say this once. My men have taken someone close to you. I know you probably don't believe this, but I'm going to call you back in a half an hour. That will give you time to make some calls, and I will confirm it to you when I call again." Samir disconnected the call.

Both Ty and Mac immediately started to talk. I stated, "Be quiet for a minute! He must be talking about our family members, probably our kids. Let's call them and see if anything is amiss. When he calls back, I'll conference you in. If you find out anything, call me immediately and we can talk about it before he calls back."

I heard both Mac and Ty hang up. Sandy had heard my part of the conversation and asked, "What the hell's going on?"

I quickly explained the situation to her and told her I was going to call our daughter, Jill, to see if her family was okay. Dialing the number, I waited for Jill to pick up.

Since she was currently in Hawaii, I did not wake her up given the time change. She stated, "Why are you guys up so late? You should be getting your beauty rest."

"Jill, what I have to say to you is very important and I don't have time right now to explain. You know our old friend Samir, he just called and said that his men had taken someone close to Mac, Ty, or me. He gave us time to confirm whether someone was missing. Will you make sure the girls are safe, right now? I'll hold on."

"Yes, just a minute and I'll check." I heard her stand up and heard her husband ask what the hell was going on. A few seconds later, Jill came back on the phone. "Both kids are sound asleep, so it's not us. Can you tell me more?"

"No, I can't, but I'll have your mother call you on her phone." I hung up and waited to hear from Mac or Ty.

Mac called a moment later, "I just got a hold of my daughter and everything is good with her."

"Okay, let's hang up until we hear from Ty." Ten minutes passed before Ty called back in a state of shock.

"My God, DJ, I think they've taken my granddaughter Kelsey! I called my son, who is at the police station. Julie and Kelsey had gone to see *The Nutcracker*. Clint was at home waiting for them and then began to worry. He drove to the theater and saw Julie's parked car. He went up to the car and found her sleep and slumped over the steering wheel. Evidently, Julie had been drugged and is still not awake. Kelsey is nowhere to be found. My God, what are we going to do?"

"We need to hang up now and wait for Samir to call. After we talk with him, we'll figure out what we need to do. Don't worry, Ty, we will take care of this."

"I can't believe this is happening." I heard Ty hang up.

It seemed like hours before my phone rang again. "Yes?"

I recognized Samir's voice. "Please conference in the other two before we continue." Soon I had both Mac and Ty on the phone. Samir continued, "I assume you have confirmed what I've told you."

Ty responded, "Listen, you bastard, if you hurt my granddaughter in any way, there is no place on this earth you can hide. Because I will find you, and you will die a slow and painful death!"

Samir begin to laugh and then stated, "And just what are you going to do? Your threats don't concern me. I'm going to send each of you a photo of the young girl so there is no doubt in your mind that I have control of her. I'm also going to send you a video you might enjoy. You can think about it for a while and I'll call you tomorrow to tell you what I want." The phone went dead.

A second later, my phone beeped and I saw an attachment on a text. I clicked on it and saw a photo of a young girl. I asked Ty, who along with Mac, was still on the phone, "Is that Kelsey?"

"Yes, that's her." I heard Ty stifling a sob.

The phone beeped again and I open another attachment. It was a video of Kelsey sitting on the hood of the vehicle. I heard someone in the background say, "What would you like to tell your grandfather, Kelsey?"

Kelsey looked at the camera and said simply, "Grandpa, help me. I'm afraid!" The video stopped.

I heard a cry of anguish coming from Ty. "Oh, my God, what are we going to do?"

Mac answered first, "We're heading for Vegas!"

Irritated, I asked "What are you talking about, Mac?"

"Play the video again," he said. "Look at the reflection in the window. You can see the Stratosphere in the background."

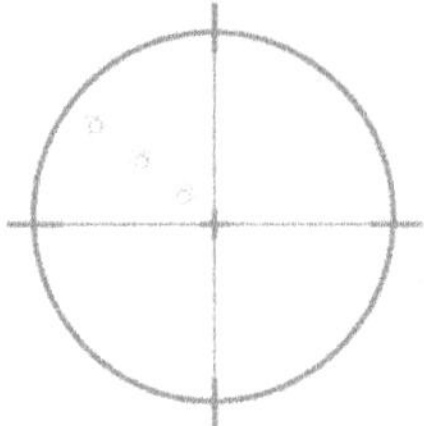

Chapter 35

In Samir's RV, the mood had changed dramatically. As their journey began, the men were excited to be moving. However, boredom seemed to take over as the endless miles passed by. Like children, the men continually asked how much further until they reached their destination. Each time that occurred, Samir would discuss the issue with Samantha and Chuck. Many times, they would refer to MapQuest to obtain an answer, which was then passed on to the men. To save time, they did not stop for lunch. When the time came to eat, Samantha prepared turkey sandwiches and chips for the men.

As one man received his plate, he complained that the food was not to his liking. Samir addressed that issue immediately. "I understand why you may not like this food, and perhaps I should have talked about this before. We will not be eating the food we are accustomed to. We will be eating like everyday Americans. We could stock our refrigerator with more familiar foods, but if we were stopped, it would make it more difficult to explain our cover stories. So suffer through the Great Satan's food. We will have plenty of time later to celebrate according to our own customs. Does anyone have any questions?"

No one raised his hand, but unhappy expressions marred some of the men's faces.

"Good, I'm glad that you understand. Now is anyone as bored as I am with this trip?"

Immediately the men began complaining and laughing at themselves. Just as Samir had hoped, this gave his men something else to focus on.

After about eight hours on the road, Samir walked to the front of the RV and spoke to both Samantha and Chuck. "At the rate we are going, when do you think we will arrive in Las Vegas?"

Chuck responded, "Samantha and I were just discussing that. If we continue on as expected and have no unnecessary delays like road work, we will arrive in Las Vegas quite late. My best guess is that it would be after 10 PM."

"Will that cause any difficulty at the RV park that you have chosen for us?"

"I'm sure we can get in the park and to our assigned site. However, I know the men will want to get out and stretch their legs and generally shake off being cooped up all day. Many of the other campers will have gone to bed by then and the men's activity could draw attention to us. There is another option we have available to us, which is to stop earlier than we planned. For example, we could stop in Kingman, Arizona, for the night. That would put us there in time to have dinner and get some exercise before going to sleep. Samantha has checked out an RV park that would suit our needs. What do you think?"

Samir knew that an earlier stop would be best for the men. "If we stayed in Kingman, how long would it take us to get to Las Vegas tomorrow?"

Chuck responded immediately, "Less than two hours, I expect."

Samir pondered this potential change in plans. "Okay, let's stop in Kingman. If we plan to be on the road at 9 AM, that will give us plenty of time tomorrow to do what needs to be done."

"Kingman it is then." Chuck looked at Samantha. "Why don't you call the park and get us reservations? Let them know we should be there in a couple of hours."

When she completed her call, Samantha looked at Samir and nodded that all was in order."

"Good." Samir then went back to where his men were seated. "I have some good news for you. We're going to stop earlier and spend the night in Kingman, Arizona. We should get there in about two hours. In the morning, we will leave at 9 AM and should be in Las Vegas within a couple of hours." Smiles lit up the men's faces as they welcomed his news.

Just after 7 PM, the RV pulled into the Diamond Village RV park. Chuck got out of the RV and walked into the office. A few minutes later, Chuck reappeared holding papers in his hand. He turned and looked at Samir. "Everything is good and I have our assigned spot."

"Did the clerk appear to be suspicious of anything?" Samir had been watching Chuck through the window and saw nothing unusual but wanted to make sure.

"No, it was clearly routine. I see no problem whatsoever." With that, Chuck put the vehicle in gear and drove forward. A few moments later, the RV pulled into their assigned site, and Chuck and Samantha got out and prepared the RV for the night. Samir allowed his men to get out and walk around the camp site, but with the stipulation that only three men could leave the vehicle at any one time. Samir did not want to draw attention to the number of people who were in the RV.

A short time later, Samantha began preparing dinner. The men watched her prepare and then serve pasta and a salad. It had been quite some time since their earlier meal and the men were quite hungry. She made enough so that each man could have two servings.

Samir could see that the day had taken a toll on the men's energy. After a while, he stated, "It's been a long day men. I suggest that we get some sleep now. Our real work begins tomorrow." The men began to take the places where they would sleep for the night. Soon most of the men were sleeping, some snoring. Samir drifted off to sleep, also.

Samir awoke with a start after hearing something outside. He opened his eyes and saw that it was daylight. Looking out the window of the RV, he saw quite a few campers up and moving about. Samir watched for a few moments to make sure that nothing was unusual. Even though it was early in the morning, he saw some RVs leaving the park. He walked to the back of the RV and saw that Samantha and Chuck were already dressed. "I think we should get breakfast ready now. Should we have the men shower in the building over there?" He pointed to the gray cinder-block building not far from their location.

Chuck answered, "That should not be a problem. However, I suggest that only three shower there and everyone else showers here in the RV. That would allow us to get on the road even earlier."

Samir quietly woke each of his men and explained the plan. In short order, Samantha had prepared eggs and toast for the men. Like the night before, they were ravenous and finished their meals quickly. Samir chose two other men to go with him to shower in the building. He told the remaining men to shower quickly in the RV.

As he and the two men walked to the shower building, many people in the park greeted them. As he passed one RV, he saw a man standing in the door of the RV, watching him and his two men very intently. As he passed, he smiled at the man and nodded. The man did not respond but continued watching them as they walked toward the building.

Each of his men showered quickly, brushed his teeth, and combed his hair. Samir enjoyed the simple pleasure of a shower. It refreshed him and was a pleasant way to start the day. As he left the shower building with his men, he noticed the man in the RV had not moved from the doorway. Once again, the man looked at them in a most suspicious manner. Samir looked at his two men and said, "Keep going to the RV. I'll be there shortly." As they were walking, Samir veered toward the man who had been observing them. "Good morning. How are you today?"

"I'm fine, thank you," the man responded. "What are you up to?"

Samir smiled and responded, "We arrived here last night and will be taking off shortly for Vegas to spend one day with my brother who lives there and then on to LA. But first, we're going to try to not lose too much money at the casinos. We'll see how it goes. How about you?"

"We're here for a few days. My wife has some family here in Kingman. Where are you from?"

Samir did not like where this conversation was going. The man was too inquisitive. "We live in Charlotte, North Carolina. We all work in the tech industry there. I like that area better than Boston where we worked previously. Sure is nice to have some time off though. Well, I'd better get going. The tables in Vegas are waiting for us. Nice talking to you." Samir didn't wait for response and headed toward his RV. When he entered, all of his men were watching him.

Chuck asked, "What was that all about?"

"That guy seem to be very suspicious of us. I walked over to have a conversation with him to see if I could help resolve any concerns he may have about us."

"So how did it go?"

"I couldn't tell. He was very hard to read. There's nothing we can do now so let's head for Vegas and concentrate on the work we have there. I want everybody to stay hidden except the two guys who went with me to the shower building and, of course, Chuck and Samantha."

The couple got the RV ready to hit the road. Once they completed those chores, Chuck fired up the vehicle and drove toward the park exit. Samir had decided to sit in the front passenger seat and made sure his window was down as they started out. As they passed the man he had talked with, Samir leaned out the window, waved, and stated, "Have a great day." The man did not respond to Samir in any way. As they turned out of the RV park, Samir looked at Chuck. "There's nothing we can do about him. Let's just stick to our plan."

Neither Samir nor Chuck saw the man pull his cell phone out of his pocket, dial a number, and begin talking. He did not complete his conversation until the RV was far away from the RV park.

The next two hours passed quickly as they covered the miles to Las Vegas. Soon he could see the Las Vegas skyline. Samir called his men to the front and pointed out the window. "There's our target and guiding us to it is the Stratosphere." They continue to drive straight toward Las Vegas. They followed the signs to 215 W. and when they reached I-15, they headed south toward Los Angeles.

Samir looked at Chuck and asked, "Why are we going south?"

"Our RV park is just south of here." A few minutes later, Chuck exited the freeway. Soon they entered the Oasis Las Vegas resort. It was from this location that their attack would be coordinated.

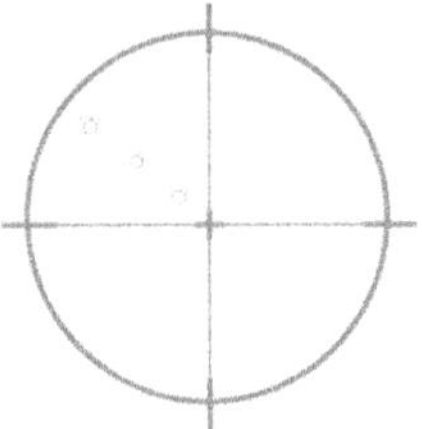

Chapter 36

Will was driving his RV on the freeway at a steady 65 mph. Brianne, who was sitting in the passenger seat, and Will appeared to be the typical American couple enjoying the warmer weather of the American Southwest. Mohammed and his men were resting as much as they could, given their excitement about starting their mission. Like Kamil ahead of him, Mohammed had talked to his men about their mission in San Francisco. They recognized the difficulties inherent in their task but were determined to successfully complete their assignment.

Will had planned to stay at an RV park in Tucson, which was just under a five-hour drive from El Paso. About halfway to Tucson, Will sat up straight in his seat and stated to Brianne, "Look what's behind us."

Brianne leaned forward and looked back through the side mirror. "What are we going to do?"

Will looked over his right shoulder and shouted at Mohammed. "Mohammed, you need to get up here immediately." As Mohammed approached, Will continued, "We have a state trooper behind us and he just turned on his lights, which requires me to pull over. You should get everyone hidden immediately, and don't do anything unless things turn bad. It's probably nothing more than a normal traffic stop." As Mohammed left, Will began to slow and signaled his turn to the side of the freeway.

As Mohammed approached his men, he barked, "We have a police officer behind us who is pulling us over. We will do as we initially planned. Two of us in the shower, two in the bathroom, and two in the bedroom. Make sure you have your handguns with you but do nothing unless I order it. Now, move quickly to your positions." Mohammed watched as the men went to their assigned locations before stepping into the shower with Abdul.

As Will brought the RV to a stop, he observed the state patrolman pull in behind him and park at an angle to provide him some protection from vehicles on the freeway. The officer walked slowly to the passenger side of the RV. Brianne, who had rolled down the window, smiled as the officer approached. The officer began, "Good afternoon, ma'am."

Brianne responded immediately, "Hi, officer. Do you want to talk to me or that terrible driver I sometimes call my husband, who happens to be driving today?"

"Now, dear, I'm sure the officer does not want to hear your opinion about my driving. What's up, officer?"

"Do you know why I pulled you over?"

Will shook his head back and forth and said, "No, I really don't. What was I doing wrong?"

"I've been following you for about five miles and you've been consistently going seven miles per hour over the speed limit. That puts you at 77 mph. Did you think we would not stop you for going that fast?"

Will answered immediately. "Not at all, officer. I set my cruise control at 65 mph. Either your speedometer is off or mine is. I expect you have yours tested all the time so, I guess, it's this old beater of an RV that is out of whack. I assure you it wasn't intentional. I know, however, that is no excuse and I am responsible for how fast I go."

Since the shower was on the right side of the RV, Mohammed could hear their conversation.

After asking for and receiving Will's license, registration, and proof of insurance, the officer asked, "Do you have any weapons in the vehicle?"

Will sounded surprised when he answered, "No, I don't have any weapons at all. Is this an area where I need to have protection?"

"No, I was just wondering. Do you mind if I have a look around inside?"

"No problem, officer." Will got out of the seat and headed toward the door. In a voice loud enough for Mohammed and the others to hear, he said as he opened the door, "You're certainly welcome to come into our humble abode."

Mohammed brought his gun up in front of him. It had a silencer attached to it. He intended to eliminate the officer quietly. If he did so, they would drive off and would have to ditch the RV and the officer's body some place and then figure out how to continue their mission. Mohammed was sure that the trooper had radioed the license number and type of RV he was stopping to his dispatcher. He continued to listen to the conversation between Will and the officer.

The officer smiled at Will and said, "I don't think you are doing anything illegal, but since you are stopped, I would like to see the inside of your RV. My wife and I've been thinking about buying one for some time." The officer looked around the interior. He did not open any doors or try to examine the bathroom, shower, or bedroom. "What kind of mileage do you get with this rig?"

"Oh, probably 7 to 8 miles per gallon on a good day. I've got to tell you a story though. When I first got this rig, we were on a trip and I was averaging 13 to 14 miles per gallon."

"You're telling me..."

Will held up his hand and interrupted the officer. "What was occurring, was every time I filled up, the pump stopped at $100. Based on that, I calculated my mileage. What I didn't realize is that the tank was not full, but rather the pump shut off at $100. I was stupid enough to think that I filled the tank and thus I was happy to be getting 13 to 14 miles to the gallon." Will started laughing and he was quickly joined by the officer. "Unfortunately, I understood that stupid is as stupid does. I have obviously lost too many brain cells as I have gotten older."

The officer was still laughing as he turned to the door of the RV and stepped out. Will followed him down the steps and the officer turned to face him. "I'm not going to give you a ticket today because I've really enjoyed talking with you. But please readjust your cruise control so someone else down the way doesn't stop you."

Before Will could answer, Brianne yelled out the window, "Well, dear, what's this going to cost us?"

The officer was laughing as he reached out to shake Will's hand. "I think you're going to get enough punishment from your wife. Good luck and enjoy your trip." The officer handed Will his documents, turned and walked back to his car.

Will stepped back into the RV and closed the door. He walked forward and sat in the seat, smiling at Brianne. "You played that role very well." Will put the RV in gear, signaled, and pulled out onto the freeway. Within a minute, the officer passed them and headed on his way. Brianne turned and looked backward and stated, "Everything is okay."

Mohammed and his men left their hiding spaces and sat down. Mohammed knelt behind Will. "That was close. If he had opened the door to the shower, I would've had to kill him, and that would have put our whole mission in jeopardy. Allah will smile upon you for how you protected us today."

The trooper was several miles ahead of the RV when he reported his contact to the dispatcher. "I stopped an RV for speeding. Nothing out of the ordinary."

"If you haven't made your quota for tickets, I suggest you make it a priority. The lieutenant is on the warpath again."

"Roger, will do." He had no idea how close to death he had come.

After a couple more hours of uneventful travel, Will pulled into the Prince of Tucson RV Park. In short order, like those before him, he pulled into his assigned site. Unlike Samir and Kamil, Mohammed had his men remain in the RV. He did not want to take any chances that his men might raise concerns among those at the park after their close call with the trooper.

Mohammed's men showered in the RV rather than using the public showers. After dinner, the men soon went to their assigned spots and curled up to sleep. Mohammed kept looking out the windows of the RV for some time to see if anyone was exhibiting any undue interest in them. Seeing none, he, too, fell asleep.

The next day, the men awoke early and found Brianne making breakfast for them. Within the hour, they were on the freeway again. The second day's travel was much like the first and ended in a quiet RV park. On the third day, they arrived in the San Francisco area. Mohammed decided not to stay in an RV park in the Bay Area. Instead, he had called his contact and inquired about the warehouse that was filled with the armaments he would need. The man gave him the address and then met the RV at the warehouse.

As the man left, Will carefully drove into the warehouse and parked the RV. He, Brianne, and the men were happy to get out of the rig and stretch their legs. Mohammed informed them that they would inventory materials in the warehouse that afternoon and evening, and that tomorrow, they would begin the preparations for their attack.

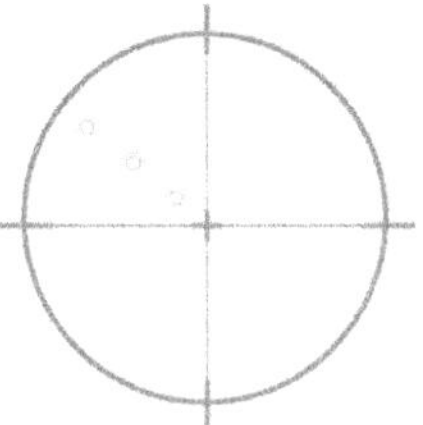

Chapter 37

It was 2 AM when I pulled up to Ty's house in my blue F150 Supercab. Ty was sitting on the porch waiting for our arrival and within minutes, Mac pulled up behind me in his truck. We had decided to leave immediately for Vegas and see what kind of plan we could develop on the way. Mac and Ty got into my truck while our wives got into Mac's vehicle.

Once we were on the freeway headed for Vegas, Ty spoke up. "I have an idea on what we should do. Just hear me out. I have a friend on Metro who works undercover. I want to give him a call, explain what's going on, and see if any of his informants might have heard something on the street that might help us."

"Good idea," Mac responded, "I know someone I can call also. If we're lucky, maybe we'll get a lead and can develop a plan from there."

I looked at both of them. "Not a bad idea. Certainly better than anything I can come up with." I drove while both Mac and Ty worked their phones. I glanced in the rearview mirror and could see our wives not far behind.

The miles seemed to crawl by as we waited for call-backs. Both their contacts had agreed to start making calls and see what they could find out.

Ty was clearly and understandably agitated. "I'm going to kill Samir regardless of what happens with Kelsey. And when we find where she is, I'm going to go in and kill anybody over the age of 10." He continued making threats about anybody and everybody who might be involved in this case.

Mac turned around and looked at Ty. "If we find out where she is, Ty, you can stay in the car and DJ and I will take care of it."

Ty exploded, "What the hell are you talking about? You and no one else will stop me from going in to save my granddaughter. You understand me?"

"Listen to yourself, asshole," Mac responded. "You are so hyped up and out of control that you would probably kill Kelsey by mistake. If you want to go after her, then you need to get a grip. If you can't, I'm going back home right now."

I looked in the rearview mirror and saw Ty's face filled with anger. For a moment, I was worried he might shoot Mac.

Mac continued to look at Ty and there was a fierceness in his voice that I had not heard since Paris, when he said, "Well?" There was a short pause before Mac continued, "Ty, I will go to hell and back to get your granddaughter. But you need to understand, I will not be part of a killing spree because you don't have your shit together."

"I understand, Mac." He started to speak again, but his voice cracked and he could not go on. "I trust you, Mac, you know that. If and when we move, I promise I'll be under control. Furthermore, you make all the calls on how this comes down. Are you good with that?"

"Yes, I'm good with that."

I spoke next, "You both scared the shit out of me. I thought there might be a gun battle right here in the truck."

What I didn't know was that both Mac and Ty agreed with what I had said.

The tension that still existed in the truck was broken when Ty's phone rang. He answered and listen for several minutes. When he hung up, he smiled at both of us. "I think I know where she is. My friend's informant said he had heard rumors that an abduction was going to take place. A guy named Tommy was supposed to be involved. He's going to text me the guy's address."

As we came over the hill, Vegas came into view. Ty had received the address, typed in the GPS, and we headed there immediately to check it out. It was located in an area of town not known for its law-abiding citizens. Tommy's address turned out to be a three-story apartment building; Tommy's apartment was on the first floor. We pulled over to the curb across the street from the building. No lights in the building indicated that no one was awake in the apartments. In fact, the entire area seemed quiet.

After some discussion, it was decided that Mac and Ty would enter through the front door. Since Mac had experience in picking locks, he didn't think this would be a problem. Our wives had pulled up behind us and Mac said he wanted Ann and me to cover the back door. He got out of the truck and walked back to tell Ann what her role would be. He returned to our car and looked at me. "You and Ann should head to the back door now, and in five minutes, Ty and I will go in. Don't let anybody escape."

I nodded at him, got out of the car, and met Ann, now standing outside of her truck. She smiled at me and said, "Okay, Big Boy, let's go."

I gave Sandy a thumbs up and followed after Ann. It took us three minutes to reach the rear of Tommy's apartment. We each stood on different sides of the door. I was not concerned about being seen given how dark it was. Now, all we had to do was wait for Ty and Mac to do their job.

Mac and Ty walked slowly to the front door. Mac knelt down and worked the lock. In 30 seconds, Mac had done his work and slowly opened the door. The men then entered the apartment with their guns raised, ready to meet any threat. They each had a small flashlight, which they used to search the apartment.

Ann and I were waiting for gunfire to erupt when suddenly the back door opened. Both of us had our guns raised and were ready to fire. Mac poked his head out the door and exclaimed, "Holy shit, don't shoot, it's me. Come on in." Ann and I followed him into the apartment. Mac continued, "No one's here and we haven't found anything that would lead us somewhere else."

Ty walked up and whispered, "We found nothing. I suggest we get out of here."

I glanced at Mac and said, "Damn, Mac, you scared the shit out of me when you opened the door. I may have to change my pants."

At that moment, Mac's phone rang. He answered, listened and said nothing. He hung up, looked at us and smiled. "Damn, I must live right; we have a new lead. Let's go. Ann, you follow us."

We climbed back into our respective vehicles, I started the engine, and asked, "Where do we go?"

"Well, guys, my buddy says he has an informant who wants to talk to us. I think we're going to enjoy this, too." I drove for about 20 minutes, following Mac's instructions, and soon pulled into the parking lot of a seedy strip joint. The three of us got out and walked back to where Ann had parked.

As we approached, she rolled down her window and said, "What the hell is this?"

Mac answered, "Our informant is a dancer inside. She wanted us to come down and talk with her."

"I'm going in with you guys."

Mac responded, "No, you're not, Ann. It's not a place where nice girls go. Besides, she won't talk if you're there."

"Listen, Asshole, if you're not back here in 15 minutes, I'm coming in with my gun drawn. I don't need to be no damned nice girl."

The three of us walked up to the heavy door, pushed it open, and walked in. The lights were on low, but not too low to avoid the show, and the music was blaring. I was surprised to see that even at this late hour, the strip joint was almost full. Mac had us sit at a table while he went up to the bartender. Soon, he returned and sat down with us. Not two minutes later, one of the dancers walked up wearing something that left little to the imagination.

"I'm Renee. The bartender said you wanted to see me." Mac quickly explained why we were there and Renee said, "Come with me. I have a place where we can talk in private." She led us to a small private room in the back where she had us sit on a sofa. She started a slow gyrating dance. She saw the surprised look on our faces." I need to make it look like I'm working."

Mac leaned over to me and whispered, "We are in deep shit if Ann comes in and sees this."

Looking at Mac, Renee continued, "Your friend contacted me and asked if I might be able to help. The truth is, I'm not sure, but here's what I have." Her hip rolls and gyrations continued causing Mac to wet his lips. "One of my regulars was in here a few days ago. We were in one of the back rooms having a good time. He was about ready to leave, so I asked him when I would see him next. Phil told me it would be a few days because he had a job to do. He said he was going to become a daddy for a short time.

Mac asked her to clarify a few things, which she did. He stated, "Who is this guy and do you know where he lives?"

"I only know him by his first name, Phil. I've been to his place a couple times, so I can give you his address."

I asked her, "Is this going to put you in a bad situation giving us this information?"

She looked at me and smiled. "It doesn't matter. No one should be messing with kids."

Mac smiled at her and said, "Thanks, and great dancing by the way."

She returned his smile and said with a wink, "Come see me anytime and I'll give you a special discount."

After thanking her and slipping her a couple of bills, we headed for the door. Mac pushed it open and almost knocked down Ann, who was being followed closely by Sandy and Leanne. He smiled at the three of them and said, "Are you ladies looking to apply for a job?"

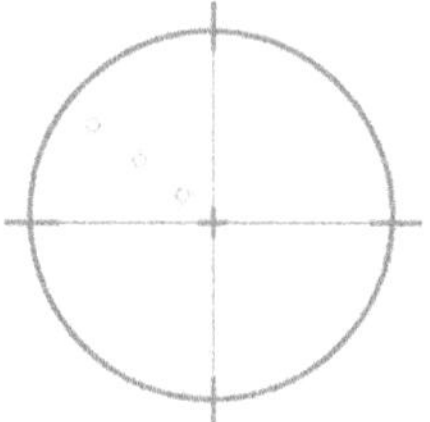

Chapter 39

As we headed for Phil's apartment, I asked, "It's almost daylight. How are we going to do this?" There was an eerie silence as each of us contemplated this question. I continued, "Well, why don't we wait until we can see the location?"

"I think that's our only option at this point," said Mac. No one said another word until we pulled up in front of Phil's house. It was a small home that had seen better days. The front yard was overgrown with weeds. The house itself was in need of a good painting, which was not different from the other houses on the street.

Ty spoke first, "Hey, Mac, why don't we use the 'drunk at the wrong house' routine? I can't think of anything else that would work, how about you?"

"That just might work, Ty. I'd better be the drunk though. We don't want your granddaughter to see you and give it all away. DJ, you and Ann go cover the back door again."

"I'm on my way," I responded. "See you inside." I got out of the truck and headed for Ann. When she saw me coming, she opened the door and stepped out.

"We're in the back again?" I nodded at Sandy and we headed for the side of the house.

A few minutes later, Mac and Ty walked up to the front door of the house. Mac looked in the front window and saw a small man sleeping on the couch in the living room. He looked at Ty and pointed toward where the man was sprawled. Ty took his place to the left side of the door and Mac stood slightly to the right. Mac knocked on the door and started weaving back and forth. When no one answered, Mac started knocking louder and began asking for Jim.

Soon, the skinny guy heard the knocking and struggled to his feet to answer the door. He opened the door, saw Mac standing there, and asked, "What the hell do you want?"

Mac started to weave back and forth more than before and reached for the wall to hold himself up. "Where's Jim? He told me to meet him here. Who the hell are you?"

"Well, I'm sure as hell not Jim, so get your ass out of here."

Mac continued the charade. "You don't understand. Jim told me to come here."

Tommy pushed Mac out of the door and showed him his gun. "No, it's you that don't understand. If you don't leave, and soon, I'm going to shoot you right between the eyes. Now, do you understand?"

Tommy, who now had his back to Ty, was clearly done with Mac. Ty reached up and grabbed Tommy's long, shaggy hair, pulling it back, and placed the barrel of his revolver against the man's head. At the same time, Mac grabbed his gun. Ty whispered, "If you don't do exactly what I say, I'm going to kill you deader than shit. You never should have grabbed my granddaughter. Just give me one excuse so I can kill you. Now, where's Kelsey?" Ty looked at Mac and saw him shake his head and Ty just smiled. Ty pushed Tommy into the living room, threw him to the floor, and Mac slammed his boot into Tommy's back, holding him down.

When Ty saw that Mac had Tommy under control, he turned to head to the back of the house to find Phil.

Mac, with some urgency in his voice, whispered, "Ty, I'll take care of Phil while you watch over Tommy."

Tommy seemed startled that Mac used his name.

Ty grinned at Mac and stated, "Don't worry, Mac. I've got this. She's my granddaughter, not yours."

"Don't screw this up, Ty, or we will be in a world of shit."

Ty quietly crept down the hall, peered into the first room, and saw Kelsey sleeping on a twin bed. He almost cried, but knew, however, that he had to take care of Phil before going to his granddaughter. He moved to the next room, looked in, and saw no one. Suddenly, the bathroom door opened, Phil walked out to see Ty's gun pointed at his head. Ty said with an edge to his voice, "Give me a reason to kill you. Just one."

Ty looked down and saw Phil's gray underwear turn dark. He smiled at Phil and said, "I guess I'm enough to scare the piss right out of you." Ty ordered him into the living room.

As Phil passed Ty, he pushed Ty's gun down and took a wild swing, aiming for Ty's head. Ty ducked under the swing and viciously brought his knee into Phil's crotch. Phil groaned and fell to his knees. With no remorse, Ty, with all his strength, kicked him in the face. Phil fell unconscious on the floor. Ty grabbed the big man by the collar and dragged him into the living room.

Ty looked at Mac and stated, "The sonofabitch had to make it hard. Watch them, but don't kill them, while I let Ann and DJ in." As he was doing so, Sandy and Leanne came through the front door.

Ty nudged Leanne and said, "She's in the first bedroom on the right."

Soon Leanne, with tears in her eyes, reappeared, holding Kelsey tightly in her arms. Kelsey jumped down, ran over to Ty, and gave him a big kiss. "Grandpa, you did come to help me." Her little arms wrapped tightly around his neck.

He pulled her back to look at her and whispered, "Did they hurt you? Are you okay?"

"No, they didn't hurt me. I'm good now that you're here."

Mac spoke next. "Ann, go get me the rope in the back of the truck." She returned a few minutes later and handed the rope to Mac. In short order, he had both men trussed up. He squatted down before each of them and stated, "Just in case you don't understand what I just did, let me explain. I have tied your hands and feet together behind your back and then wrapped it around your neck, which as you can tell is pulled tight. If you try to escape, you'll merely choke yourselves to death. From my perspective, I hope you do try to escape because it will save all of us a lot of trouble."

As we turned to leave, I asked Mac, "Are you just going to leave them there?"

He gave me his infectious grin and stated, "No, I'll call my buddy to come and get them. It shouldn't take him more than an hour so." He grinned at me again.

Leanne pointed at the two men and asked, "Are these the guys who are responsible for kidnapping Kelsey?"

Mac answered, "Yes, these are the men."

Leanne, screaming, launched herself at the two men. With tears streaming down her eyes, Leanne kicked both men. Sandy and Ann pulled her off of them as she vented her rage in the only way she knew how. "You dirty bastards. Ty, kill them. Please kill them now."

Ty walked over and knelt next to Phil and whispered into his ear, before quickly jumping back to his feet. "Oh, damn!"

Ty walked toward me and I asked, "What was that all about?"

"I threatened to kill him then and there just to scare him a bit. I'll be damned if he didn't shit his pants."

An hour later, we were knocking on Clint and Julie's door. They opened the door together and saw Kelsey in Ty's arms. He handed the girl to Julie, who could not stop crying. Ty quickly explained what happened and stated, "You can't stay here for a while; I'm sure they know where you live. I've got a room reserved for you at the Bellagio. I want you to stay there, safely away from here!"

"I understand," said Clint.

Book Four
Attack on the Cities

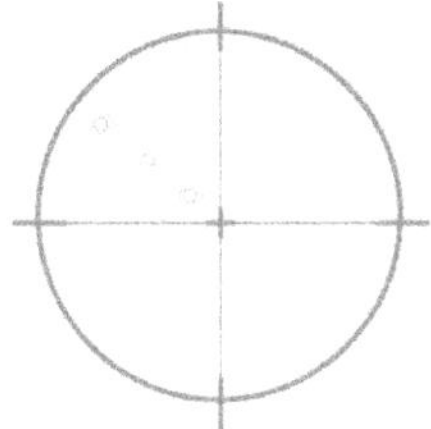

Chapter 40

My phone rang early the next morning as I sat in front of my fireplace enjoying a cup of hot coffee. The fire was roaring as much as a gas fireplace could roar. I was feeling very good about what we'd accomplished the day before. I laid the paper I was reading on my lap and reached for the cell, punching the answer button. I mean who uses a landline anymore? "Hello?"

"Professor Anderson?"

"Yes, that's me"

"Hi, Professor, this is Riaz. I hope I didn't call you too early."

"Not at all," I responded, "I'm just sitting here reading the newspaper and enjoying some coffee. What's up with you?"

"Is it possible that we could meet this morning? I have something I'd like to talk to you about."

"Of course, we can meet." I looked at my watch and saw that it was just after 8:30 AM. "Why don't we meet at Starbucks, at say, 10?"

"That works for me," Riaz answered. "I'll see you at 10."

Riaz was the Saudi student who told me he would keep me informed of any changes in their community. Maybe we're getting lucky, I thought. Perhaps he had something significant that could put us a step ahead of Samir. I felt like we were always running behind him and simply unable to catch up. I picked up my phone once again and called Mac. The phone rang three times before he picked up.

"Why are you up so early?" he asked. "I thought it was a rare day that you woke up before noon."

I could hear him chuckling over the phone. "Listen, Mac, I have some information for you. It may be important, but I'm not sure. My Saudi student just called me and wants to meet. We're having coffee at Starbucks at 10."

"You want me to go with you?"

"No, he doesn't know you and I want him to feel as comfortable as possible. I just wanted to give you a heads up about what was going on."

"Are you trying to tell me that I make people uncomfortable?"

"That is not what I was trying to say, regardless of how true it might be. I think he might be a little concerned if he was found talking with two of the professors who were involved in the Paris attack."

There was a pause before Mac responded. "I can understand that but let me tell you something. I haven't had a beer yet this morning, so no one will be uncomfortable around me. However, after talking to you, I may have to start drinking something stronger than coffee. Do you realize that you do that to people?"

"Only to you my friend, only to you. I'll call you after the meeting. Will you give Ty a call and pass on that information?"

"Consider it done," Mac said.

With that, I ended the phone call, got out of my chair and headed for the bathroom to shower before leaving. The clock showed 9:45 AM when I walked into the garage and got into my truck. Sandy was out shopping so I couldn't tell her what was going on. I drove to the only Starbucks in town, parked the car, and walked in.

No one was in line and I ordered my standard venti latte. My drink was produced soon enough; I took it and sat in the corner. A couple of minutes after that, Riaz walked in. I motioned for him to come over and take a seat. "What would you like to drink?"

"How about a grande black tea with cream?"

"Would you like something to eat also?" Riaz shook his head back and forth. I smiled at him and said, "I'll be right back with your drink." Since there was still no line, I was able to get his drink, pay for it, and return to the table within a few short minutes.

"Here you go." I placed the drink in front of him. He was very slim and his clothes seemed to hang from his body. The most remarkable thing about him were his hands with their long fingers. He looked as if he were made to play the piano. His black hair came down over his ears and yet one could almost detect some gray in it even though he was only in his early 20s. I knew that Riaz was much tougher than he appeared. His goal was to complete his degree in criminal justice and go to law school. He had told me that he wanted to prepare himself so that he could reinvent the criminal justice system in his homeland. Given its adherence to Sharia law, that was quite a lofty goal.

"How have you been, Riaz?"

"You know how it goes at this time of year. I have finished my finals. But I did not want to meet you here to talk about me."

As I looked at him, I could tell Riaz was troubled. "What do you want to talk to me about then, Riaz?"

He looked at me with some uncertainty. "I'm not sure how important this is, but I thought I should tell you. There have been some rumblings in the Saudi community about a newcomer who might be here. It is really nothing concrete, but I've heard it from more than one individual. When I asked them about it, they said they had heard it from someone else who wasn't totally clear about it either. Supposedly, this new person does not want to be involved with us. That in and of itself is very unusual, since we have such a strong support network within our community. I would take it that whoever is here does not want that information known. Yet again, it is certainly possible that this is simply a rumor. You know how those things fly around."

"Has anyone seen this person around the city?" I asked.

"No, if someone had actually had seen him, it would not be a rumor. I personally believe that there is no one we need to be concerned about, but I did not want to make that decision, so I called you."

I thought about that for a while before stating, "You did the right thing, Riaz. I appreciate your acting as you did. I have to ask you; you seemed a little concerned when you phoned me this morning. Also, you look a little troubled now. Is there something I should know?"

He brought his eyes to meet mine. "I am concerned and so should you. In fact, I'm scared. You do not know these people like I do. If the terrorists had any inclination that I was talking to you, I would die a terrible death. The problem, you see, is I don't know who I can trust in the Saudi community. They all profess to be against terrorism of any kind, but I know that's not true. I know that some of them would like to see changes not only in the world, but especially in Saudi Arabia. What I don't know is how far they would go to accomplish that. The mere fact that they exist places me in danger. From now on, I will not meet with you further, but if I have information for you, I will call you on the phone. I just wanted to tell you this in person."

"I understand what you're saying, Riaz, and I want you to know how much I appreciate your willingness to talk with me. I would not do anything knowingly that would put you in danger. If you feel for any reason that you are threatened, please call me and I can get protection for you."

"Thank you, Professor, but if I need protection, I am already dead."

I watched him walk out the door and get into his car. He drove off without looking back. I immediately called Mac and informed him what I had been told. "Would you call Ty and let him know? I'm going to call the chief and fill him in also."

When I hung up, I changed my mind. Instead of calling the chief, I decided to go to the police station and talk with him in person. When I arrived, his secretary showed me right into his office. I laid out for him what Riaz had told me. "Chief, I don't know whether it's a rumor or not, but I think it's worth looking into."

The chief responded, "I agree. I will let my officers know to be on the lookout for a Saudi they are not familiar with. I'm also going to have one of our investigators check with the hotels and B&Bs to see if they have anyone staying in their facility who might fit the bill. I think it's getting down to crunch time. Maybe we'll get lucky with one of the hotels and find the guy in time."

After thanking the chief for his help, I drove home. Sandy was there when I arrived and I shared everything I had learned. To say that she was concerned would be an understatement. She, like me, knew that we had to be very alert from this point on.

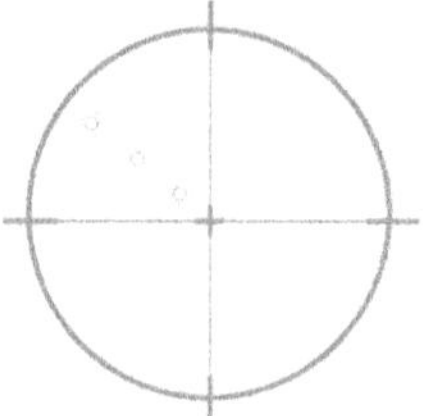

Chapter 41

It was about noon when Mael walked out of his office and down the stairs to the street below. He had never taken an elevator because he knew his outstanding physical condition would suffer if he did not keep going up and down the stairs. Maintaining his physical condition was extremely high up on his list of mandatory activities. Having worked on the streets for as long as he had, his ability to stay alive depended on the shape he was in. There were many men who had tried to take advantage of him but wound up being surprised by his ability to take care of himself, to their detriment.

Mael was headed for a meeting with Pierre at a small restaurant not too far away. Because of their busy schedules, it was often easier to meet at a restaurant than at their offices. This restaurant catered to a higher-end clientele and its employees were known for their discretion and ability to keep secrets.

As soon as he entered, Mael was greeted by the maître d'. "It is good to see you again, sir. If you will follow me, I will take you to your table."

They wound their way through a maze of tables. Soon he was at a booth in the back of the restaurant where his boss awaited him. Pierre stood and shook hands with Mael. After Mael sat down, he asked, "Have you ordered yet?"

Pierre responded, "Yes, I have. What would you like today?"

"I am having a salad, that's all. I gave my order to the maître d' as we walked back here. I have something for you which might be of interest." Mael reached into his coat jacket and pulled out four pieces of paper. On each was a drawing of a man. "My people worked with the farmer, who we believe was the only person who saw four of the terrorists involved in the attack on Paris. My men were at his farm yesterday and he agreed to work with the sketch artist to see if they could develop a drawing of the four men." Mael spread the four pages out before Pierre.

Pierre looked at each of the drawings for several minutes. "These drawings do not appear to be anyone I have seen previously. Do we have any idea whether these drawings are accurate in any way? As I recall, we have no real proof the men the farmer saw were even involved in the terrorist attack. Isn't that correct?"

"Not anymore," Mael responded. He pulled out another sheet of paper with a photo on it and placed it next to one of the drawings. "What do you think of this?"

Pierre studied the two pages carefully. "It appears to be the same man."

"The photo is one of the terrorists killed at the professor's hotel. In fact, this man was identified by one of the professors as the individual leading the attack. His name was Salah. If the photo and the drawing are the same person, I believe that gives us clear evidence that these other three drawings may show the men who were involved in our attack. In fact, I would expect that one of these men in the remaining three drawings is Samir, the leader of the entire attack on Paris. You remember, I'm sure, that the information we received from the professors was that Samir clearly knew the man in the photograph whom he called Salah."

"I see where you're going with this, Mael. I suggest that we get this information to the appropriate officials in France so that it can be distributed throughout the country. Would you agree?"

"Absolutely. I also think we should a send this information to our friends in the U.S. If they are lucky, these drawings may help them stop an attack before it begins."

At that point, their waiter appeared with their meals. Mael began eating the salad while Pierre enjoyed his crêpe. The men sat silently lost in their own thoughts for a few moments.

"Mael, do you really believe that these drawings are of the terrorists we're seeking?"

"I do. I only wish we would've had them available to us prior to the attack on Paris. The outcome might have been very different. I think that's why it is extremely important that we share this information with the U.S. Do you agree?"

"Yes, in fact, I do. If for no other reason than to avoid a missed opportunity. You can explain to the Americans why we believe these drawings may be accurate and let them decide how they wish to proceed with that information. So, you certainly have my permission to give them this information and any explanation you believe would be helpful."

"Thank you, I will do so."

"Anything else?"

"No, but when something presents itself, I'll get that information to you." Mael shook hands with Pierre and left the restaurant. Even though he had not told Pierre how he felt, he was quite excited about the drawings. He was certain that the men depicted on those sheets of paper had indeed been deeply involved in the attack on Paris, and might also be preparing an attack on the U.S. Because of that, he wanted to get these drawings to the Americans as soon as he could.

After he had returned to his office, Mael called his secretary in to speak with her. He handed her the drawings and explained their significance. Mael told her it was of vital importance that this information get to the officials in the United States. He gave her the names and phone numbers of the U.S. individuals he wanted to receive copies of the drawings. Mael then indicated which French officials should also receive them. He asked her to make sure those men received the information as soon as possible. She nodded and left his office to carry out his instructions.

Mael leaned back in his chair and paused to think for a moment. This is our first break in the case, he thought. We need to find these men and determine whether they were responsible for the attack on Paris. The people of France deserve that.

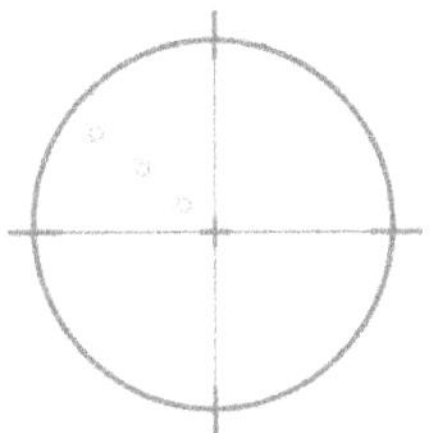

Chapter 42

In the FBI building in Washington D.C., Sam Wyman was seated behind his desk, working on his computer. He heard his phone beep, indicating he had received a new message and Sam brought up his email on his computer to see what had come in. It was from Mael Cousеau within the French counterterrorism office. He had met Mael after the attack in Paris when he had traveled there to offer any assistance the FBI could give. Sam had only been in Paris a few days but had come to respect Mael. Mael was clearly a cut above most French intelligence officers. They had dinner one night and talked long into the evening about the attack and Sam's concern for something similar occurring on U.S. soil.

Sam clicked on the email, read through it quickly and then opened the five attachments it contained. The attachments appeared to be four hand-drawn sketches, and the fifth, a photo. The email indicated that these individuals could be the leaders of the Paris attack. Without hesitation, Sam picked up the phone and dialed Mael's office. He had to wait just a moment for Mael's secretary to connect him. Sam heard Mael come on the line. "Hi, Sam, you must've received my drawings. What do you think?"

"Can you tell me how you came up with these?"

"Of course. After the attack here, our office was contacted by a farmer who lived not too far outside of Paris. He told us that a house a short distance from his had been rented by four Middle Eastern men. The man explained that he had gone to their house to check what was going on since it was normally empty. The farmer was invited in to share a beer with them. He really didn't think anything about it until after the attack. We had one of our sketch artists work with him. These drawings are the result of that work. You will also notice that one of the drawings matches a photo I just sent you. That photo is of one of the terrorists killed in the attack on the three American professors and their students. In fact, one of the professors told me that the man in the photo was the apparent leader of that attack. His name was Salah, and evidently, he was a friend of Samir, the man who has threatened your professors."

Sam had told Mael of the threats in a previous call. "So you think that these men may be the ones who are after the professors and that the other three could be here now?"

"That's exactly what I'm thinking, Sam. Whether it is or not, I thought it was best for your country to be informed of this new information and act on it as you see fit. Frankly, it may be the best lead we have for the attack here in France. At least, that's how I look at it."

In response, Sam stated, "I think you may very well be right. I'm going to get copies of these drawings out to everybody in our government. You know, maybe we'll get lucky and someone will recognize them. My guess is the Bureau will want that information given out to the public. Mael, I want you to know how much I appreciate your help in this matter. It's important that we all work together to beat these bastards."

"I agree with you, Sam. Good luck and if you need anything from us, just give me a call."

"I will. Thanks again." Sam hung the phone up. He called his secretary in and gave her orders to distribute the drawings to all FBI offices and police agencies, and also to have them placed on the bureau's Facebook page. When Sam hung up, he called the director to update him. He was told to get the information to the public information officer so it could be released to the press.

Sam then called Agent Rheingold. Within two rings, Rheingold answered the phone, "Hey Sam, how are you doing?"

"Good, Art. I have some important information for you. I'm going to forward an email to you that I received from the French Counterterrorism office. Attached to it are four drawings and a photo. The drawings are the result of a sketch artist working with a farmer who may have seen four of the Paris terrorists. The photo and one of the drawings look like the same person. That person was killed in the attack on your professors. Our best guess is that the other three drawings show other leaders in that attack, including Samir. I suggest you may want to get copies to the local police agencies and to the professors. I can't tell you for certain that these are the terrorists coming to this country, but it's the best lead we have."

Art responded, "I don't know if the drawings are accurate or not, but it is certainly a better lead than anything we have now. I'll get copies out immediately. You have any other good news for me?"

"Nothing at this point. Let me know if you come up with anything as a result of releasing these drawings." Sam hung up the phone.

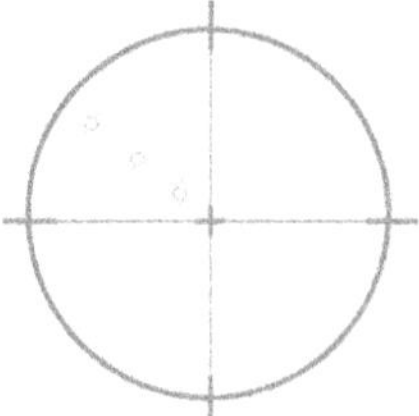

Chapter 43

Samir joined Samantha at the dinette table. He smiled at her. "Did you make the arrangements I spoke to you about?"

She returned his smile. "Yes, I've completed each of those tasks. I've made three room reservations at each hotel, the Wynn, the Bellagio, and the Venetian. Each room is on a separate floor. At each hotel, the reservations are for Omar Abbas, Saad Darosa, and Nasser Maj. Those were the names you gave me, correct?"

"Yes, that's right." Samir turned and motioned for Chuck to join them. "I want you to unhook the car and take Omar, Saad, and Nasser to the Wynn, Bellagio, and the Venetian respectively to check in. Prior to that, take them to a thrift store and have them buy three suitcases each and some cheap clothes to fill them. Also, have them buy three or four newspapers that they can leave in their rooms. When you have completed those tasks, bring the men back here." Samir watched Chuck get the three men and drive off in the direction of the Strip.

When Chuck and the three men reached the first hotel, the Wynn, they pulled into valet parking. Chuck informed the uniformed man who came to his car that they would be there less than an hour. He followed the three men to the reception desk. Omar was in the line to the far right.

The young clerk, a pretty girl, stood about 5 foot 4 and had light brown hair done up in a bun. She pulled up Omar's reservation on the computer and stated, "I see you're here for five days, is that correct?"

"Yes, that is correct."

She took his credit card, ran it through the charge machine, and handed it back to him along with his room key. "Is there anything else I can help you with, like restaurant reservations or shows?"

"No, that will not be necessary," Omar answered. "Thank you for your help." Omar turned and walked away from the reservation desk. When he was a few feet away, he turned and looked at her again. She smiled at him. Then Omar walked to the elevators.

Michaela turned to her friend, Jamie, who was standing next to her. "There's something very weird about that guy."

"Which guy?" asked Jamie.

"The guy whose reservation I just took care of. I'm not sure why but he gave me the creeps. If I could explain why, I would bring it to the attention of our supervisor. Weird, just another day in Las Vegas, I guess."

***

Meanwhile, back at the RV, Samir told Samantha, "I want you to call and see if you can reserve two helicopters that seat three plus the pilot. I want them reserved for New Year's Eve at 11 PM. If they ask why you want to reserve them for that time, explain that you want to watch the fireworks from high in the sky. You can tell them you are willing to pay a premium for their service. If they question you too much, just ease out of the conversation. Do you understand what I'm trying to accomplish?"

"Yes, and I don't think there will be a problem. I will do that right away."

"You told me previously that our contact here has rented us a warehouse. Am I right?"

"That is correct," Samantha responded. "He is waiting for a call. Would you like me to phone him and arrange a time to meet him at the warehouse?"

"No, have him meet us here at 4 PM. He can then take us to the warehouse. Let me know when you have made all of these arrangements." Samir left Samantha at the table with her computer.

He spent the next several hours reviewing the list of materials they would need to purchase. He also telephoned his local contact in Las Vegas, who had found the man he would need. Samir arranged to meet the man at a local park at 7 PM.

Three hours after they left, Chuck and the three men returned to the RV. As the four men entered the RV, Samir asked, "Is everything satisfactory?"

Chuck responded first, "Yes, we had no trouble finding the luggage and the clothes they needed. Each man has successfully checked into his respective hotel."

Samir gave a thumbs up to each of the men. "Chuck, you'll need to take the men back every evening and make sure the rooms appear to have been lived in. You know, make the bed look like someone slept there and have some partially eaten snacks around. We don't want housekeeping to raise any questions. Understood?" Chuck nodded.

Just before 4 PM, the man taking them to the warehouse arrived. He introduced himself as Gary Bell. After shaking hands, Samir asked, "Are you ready to take us to the warehouse?"

Gary responded, "You bet, let's go. My car is parked over here."

Samir nodded toward Chuck and responded. "Can you let him drive your car? He needs to know how to get us there. Samantha can follow us in our car."

"Not a problem. Chuck will drive my car and I'll just give him directions. If he's like me, he needs to actually drive it to remember it."

Chuck spoke up, "I'm with you on that."

The three men got into Gary's car and drove off with Gary providing the appropriate instructions. When they arrived at the warehouse, Gary got out of the vehicle and walked to the door. He took out a set of keys and opened the door to the office. Samir, Samantha, and Chuck followed him in. Gary proceeded to give the two men a tour of the warehouse and its features. He also pointed out to them the boxes that had been delivered previously. Samantha looked at Gary and asked him to open the roll-up door. He did so and she drove his car into the warehouse. Chuck then closed the door.

Gary seemed a bit confused when he asked, "Why are you bringing my car in here?"

Chuck walked up behind him and whispered in his ear, "So we can put your body in the trunk without anybody seeing it." Gary turned around looking at the man sharply. His expression turned to one of stunned surprise when he looked down and saw the knife Chuck had shoved into his stomach. Chuck only smiled, twisted the knife, and pushed it up under Gary's rib cage.

Chuck lowered the knife and let the body slide down to the floor. Samantha quickly opened the trunk; Chuck and Samir lifted the body and placed it inside.

Chuck looked at his wife. "I want you to follow us. I'm going to lead you to a casino parking lot where you can park his car and then we will head back to the RV park." Samantha got into Gary's car and exited the warehouse. Chuck pulled the door down and he and Samir walked out of the office, locking the door behind them. As they drove off, Samir looked back and saw Samantha following them. A few minutes later, they pulled into Caesars' parking lot.

Samantha parked Gary's car far away from the elevator and wiped it down. She locked the door to the vehicle and got in the back seat of Chuck's car. They were minutes away from the RV park. Samir looked at his watch and saw that it was just after 5 PM. Everything was going according to schedule.

Samantha proceeded to fix dinner for the men. This time they had pan-fried chicken and small baked potatoes. During dinner, Samir told the men what would occur the next day. "In the morning, we'll leave this location and head to the warehouse. We will go over the material we've had delivered and determine if anything else will be needed." Samir looked at his watch and continued, "Chuck and I have some business to attend to now. You men can relax and get ready for tomorrow."

Samir and Chuck walked to Chuck's vehicle. It was a short 10-minute ride to the park where they were to meet the man whose help they would need to carry out the attacks. Chuck pulled into a parking space, and the two men walked into the park. They saw a man sitting on a park bench by himself. Samir walked up to the man and said, "I'm Michael Jackson. Who are you?"

The man chuckled and finished the code by stating, "I must be Janet Jackson then." He stood and shook hands with both Chuck and Samir. "I'm glad to see that you made it. Are you ready to conclude our arrangement?"

Samir smiled. "I'm more than ready. Do you think you can do what we've asked?"

"I wouldn't be here if I wasn't sure. But what's important to me is the money. Have you got it?"

Samir responded, "Before I give you any money, I want you to tell me what you will do."

"Fair enough. Beginning at 9 PM on New Year's Eve and concluding before midnight, I'm going to go to the Wynn, the Bellagio, and the Venetian." The man continued to explain exactly what he was going to do. "I assume that's correct?"

"Yes, that's exactly right," responded Samir. "Now for the money." Samir reached into his coat pocket and pulled out a package, which he handed to the man. "Please open and count it. You should find $50,000 there."

The man spent several minutes counting the money. "It's all here. When do I get the remaining $50,000?"

"I will meet you here at 1 AM on New Year's Day. That should give you sufficient time to perform your work and get to this location. It will also give me enough time to know that you completed your work successfully. If so, I'll give you the remaining $50,000. Then I don't want to ever see you again."

"That works for me," the man responded. He stood up and shook hands with each of the men once again. "I'll see you at 1 AM."

By the way," Samir stated, "I suggest that you not skip out with our money. It would not be good for your health."

The man smiled and responded, "I thought that might be the case."

Chuck drove Samir back to the RV park. "I'll take the guys to the hotels to make sure their rooms look lived in. We should be back in a little over an hour."

Samir entered the trailer and told the three men to go with Chuck. He sat down and smiled at Samantha. "I must say, things are going very well. Very well indeed."

Samir walked into the back bedroom and sat on the bed. He had let the professors stew for some time now. Samir dialed the professor's number and waited for him to answer.

When I picked up, Samir said, "I think you know who I am. Conference the other two in right now."

"And why would I do that?" I responded with a smile on my face.

"I suggest that you not play games with me, Professor. I have no hesitation in killing that little girl. So get the other two men conferenced in now."

"Samir, I just sent you a text with an attachment. I suggest you open it."

Samir heard his phone beep, saw the attachment, and clicked on it. A picture appeared, showing the three professors, Kelsey, and a newspaper with the date clearly visible. Each of the professors was giving him the finger. When Samir realized what he was looking at, he stated, "You think this changes anything?"

"Actually, I think it changes a lot, asshole. We have Kelsey, and Phil and Tommy are spilling their guts to the police right now. You may want to keep a lookout over your shoulder." I ended the call with an even larger grin spreading across my face.

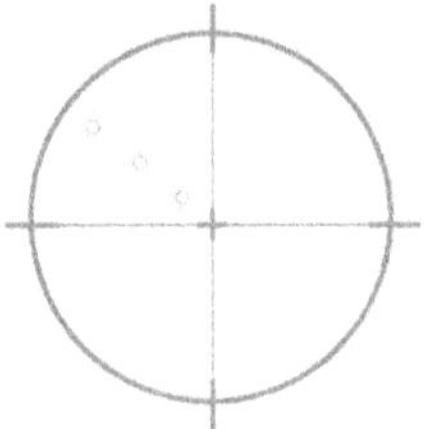

Chapter 44

Kamil called for Majid, Moiz, and Asad to join him at the dinette table. Once they had taken a seat and looked at him expectantly with their dark eyes, Kamil stated, "We are going to take a look at your target. You have looked at photos, have you not?"

Majid answered, "Yes, we have examined all the photos you gave us very closely. There were several of this target."

Holding one of the photos, Kamil pointed as spoke, "The older part will be attacked by a truck filled with explosives. Moiz, that will be your assignment." Kamil then looked at Majid and Asad. "The newer part will be your assignment. We had initially planned to use a truck bomb on that. However, the engineers we consulted could not assure us that an attack of that type would be successful, so we've designed a different form of attack for you. Both of you will drive a small boat and detonate the explosives at the appropriate time. If you have looked closely at the photos, you will understand what I have in mind."

Majid answered once again, "Yes, that makes sense to me."

"Okay, let's go check it out with George." The four men exited the RV and found that George had unhooked his car. They all climbed in and left the RV park. George had previously entered the route he wished to follow into his GPS system. He followed the singsong orders of the woman speaking to them from the little machine. They drove westbound. As they passed near the midpoint, Kamil stated, "It is about at this point that we should detonate the explosives."

"Do you have an idea on how we can do that?" Asad asked.

"Yes, we are going to have a red blinking light on the top of Moiz's truck. You will be in your boats a sufficient distance away so you can see his vehicle approach and stop. Once he has stopped, you'll move your boats forward to the same location. When the boats are properly positioned, Majid, you'll give the order to execute to Moiz and Asad."

"How will I do that?"

"Each of you will have cell phones. You will be joined in a conference call. When you're ready, Majid, you will say you are going to count down from five and when you hit zero, everyone detonates the explosives. Do you have any questions?" The men shook their heads in the negative. "Okay. Tomorrow we will obtain the truck and the boats and prepare them for New Year's Eve."

When he and the other men returned to the RV park, Kamil asked Ali and Jawad to join him at the dinette table. "We are now going to go to your target location. Did George give you the photos of the target?"

Ali responded, "Yes, he did, but I could not determine why we are attacking that target or how we are going to attack. Can you explain that?"

"Of course, I will. This target was chosen as a result of research we did many months ago. We actually found an article in the Seattle paper that described how to attack the target. This point of weakness is commonly known as the Ballard Locks." Pointing at the map before him, Kamil continued, "On the Lake Union side of the locks, the water level is 20 to 22 feet above that of Puget Sound. Boats traveling from Lake Union to Puget Sound enter the locks and then are lowered to the level of Puget Sound. Those boats traveling from Puget Sound to Lake Union enter the locks and are raised to the level of Lake Union. You are going to destroy each end of both locks."

"What effect will that have?" Jawad asked.

"The destruction of all four doors will allow the waters of Lake Washington and Lake Union to rush into Puget Sound. It will cause a major disruption."

Ali spoke up again, "Are we to martyr ourselves in this operation?"

Kamil smiled at the question. "No, that is not the plan. Tomorrow, George and the two of you will visit the locks and take the tour that is offered. That is the best way for you to familiarize yourself with the locks. At the designated time, your role is to place the explosives at each end of the locks and set them to detonate at midnight. Once you have set the explosives, you will return to the car to return here. It is unclear whether anyone will be on duty at the locks. If so, you will eliminate them.

"I also have a second mission for you which will take place earlier in the day. Part of the transportation system the city relies on is a series of water ferries." Kamil quickly outlined the attack before placing in front of each man a series of plans. "These are schematics showing each level of the ferries. You need to memorize these plans. After tomorrow's tour of the locks, George will take you on ferry rides on all four boats so that you know what you are dealing with. Much of the success of this mission rests on your being able to carry out your attacks. You have been selected because we're confident that you can and will succeed."

Kamil then asked Hossien, Mohammed, and Yaser to join him to discuss their operation. As soon as all three had been seated, Kamil began. "Each of you will be driving a truck bomb for your part of our mission." Referring to the picture on the table, Kamil began to explain how their attack would be carried out. He pointed at one photo. "One of you will be traveling eastbound and two of you will be traveling westbound and when you come parallel to each other, you'll bring your truck to a stop and detonate the explosives. It is quite simple. Are you prepared to do this in the name of Allah?"

Yaser asked, "How will we know when we are parallel to each other?"

"The truck traveling eastbound will have a red light on top of the cab. Are you ready?" responded Kamil.

Kamil looked at the three men. They smiled and answered in unison, "Yes, we are."

"I thought you would be. This is a time when you're in the right place to strike a mighty blow against America, which will bring you great favor with Allah. The bridges are packed with evening rush hour right now. Later this evening, George and I will take you on a ride so that you may see your route. We will let you know when it is time to go."

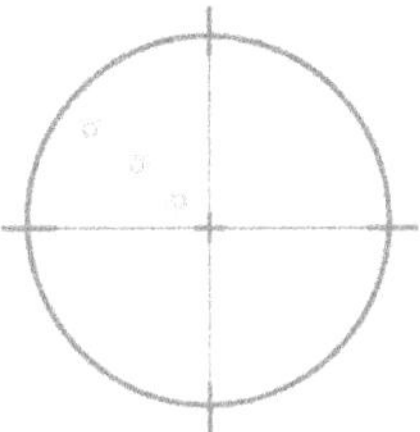

Chapter 45

I received a call from the Chief Martin, asking if Mac, Ty and I could come down to his office as soon as possible. I called my two friends and we agreed to meet at the police station in half an hour.

I was the first one there, but within five minutes, both Mac and Ty joined me. The three of us walked into the police department and were immediately ushered into the chief's office. We were surprised to see Agent Rheingold sitting there.

Mac immediately burst out, "We didn't do it, and if we did, you can't prove it."

Everyone chuckled at Mac's opening, even Agent Rheingold.

Mac continued, "Well, guys, if you're not going to arrest us, what's going on?"

Rheingold spoke up first. "I brought some new information to the chief this morning and we both agreed we should share it with you immediately."

Needless to say, he had our attention. Neither he nor the chief were smiling so I expected this was quite serious. "We're all ears. What's going on?"

Without skipping a beat, Rheingold continued, "My superior in D.C. contacted me this morning with some interesting, if not startling, information. One of his contacts in the French Counterterrorism Office sent him an email. To make a long story short, the email had five attachments, four drawings and a photograph. I've got copies here for each of you." Rheingold passed each of us a complete set of the attachments. "Does anyone look familiar to you?"

I shook my head, "I don't recognize anybody. Mac or Ty, how about you guys?"

Mac answered quickly, "I remember the guy in the photo. He was one of the terrorists at the hotel. In fact, DJ, he's the one you killed toward the end of the attack. I think his name was Salah. He was the one Samir was trying to contact. He doesn't look familiar to you?"

"No, not at all. But, as you might recall, I wasn't in very good shape at the time."

"I don't believe you were there when this guy came in, Ty. It looks like this drawing is of the guy in the photo. Is that correct?"

Rheingold answered, "That's what the French think as well. Do you recognize any of the other three men in the drawings?"

Mac picked up the drawings and studied them closely. "I don't think I saw these men when we were in Paris." Mac looked at both of us, "How about you guys?" Both of us shook our heads in the negative. Looking at Rheingold, Mac asked, "Do you know who these men are supposed to be?"

"No, and neither do the French. However, they are speculating that these three men were among the leaders of the attack on Paris, and one of them could be Samir. If that is the case, it may be a big break as we try to keep you guys safe. These copies are for you to use as you see fit. I would recommend, however, that you show them to your wives and your neighbors. The chief will get copies to the university officials. Chief, do you have anything else to add?"

"Listen, guys, this may go a long way in ending this problem. All of my officers will have these drawings in their squad cars. I have two investigators who will be contacting all the hotels in the city and showing them these drawings to see if we get a hit. The university police chief is going to have his officers talk with as many Saudi students as they can find. Hopefully, one of them will have seen one of the three men depicted here. If you have any suggestions on what additional steps we can take, I'm open to them."

Ty responded for us. "It seems to me that you've done everything that you can. If one of these guys is recognized around here, that certainly eliminates any question about if they're coming for us. Given the kidnapping of my granddaughter, which we told you about previously, any talk about whether they are coming for us is probably wishful thinking."

I had a question. "Are these drawings going to be given to the press? That would certainly help you find these guys if they're here."

The chief answered. "That raises an interesting issue for us. If we tell the public that potential terrorists might be in town, it could set off a panic. Furthermore, that could place our Saudi students in danger by some of the not-so-bright men in this town. So, the question is how do we do that?"

Mac stated, "That sounds like a lot of 'what ifs.' I'm more concerned about what happens to the three of us and our families. Since they have already shot Ty, stalked our extended family and kidnapped Ty's granddaughter, I am certainly a lot less concerned about the Saudis than I am my own family."

Rheingold addressed Mac's comments. "While I understand how you feel, Mac, that does not eliminate the potential danger to some innocent students. However, I think there is a way to accommodate both concerns. How about we tell the press that these guys are wanted for things they did overseas and that we have learned they may be passing through the area? If they press further, we just tell them this is the only information we received from France. What do you think about that?"

"I think I can sell that," the chief replied.

I looked at Mac. "That will work for me. Mac, how about you?" Mac nodded his assent. I looked at Ty.

"I can go with that also."

Rheingold chuckled. "You see what great minds can do together." The look he received from Mac could have bored through several levels of steel. It was clear that Mac wanted no part of any political correctness. The silence was quickly becoming awkward.

The chief brought us back to his concerns. "I have another question I think we need to address. What happens if one of us or our employees sees one of these guys on the street? What do we do then?"

Rheingold stood up. "I think the best course of action is that everyone in this room should be notified immediately. Following that, both the city's S.W.A.T. team and whatever manpower we have available from the Bureau should be directed here. Then we can formulate a plan to take these guys down. I think the chief and I could probably work out the details about the joint assault between ourselves. I assume the three of you will work out whatever plan you think appropriate for your safety."

Mac was still not very understanding when he stated, "You can bet your sweet ass on that!"

The discussion carried on for a few more minutes and then the meeting broke up. The three of us left the chief and Rheingold trying to work out their plans. As we reached our cars, Mac erupted, "This is just government bureaucracy. They'll spend more time making their plans that will never come to fruition. As far as I'm concerned, we should kill those guys as soon as we see them. We should shoot first and ask for forgiveness later. There is not a jury in this town that will convict us of anything if we're killing a bunch of terrorists."

I looked Mac straight in the eyes and stated, "I agree with what you're saying, but what if the person you kill is not a terrorist? Would you still be so confident that they would not convict us? Let's go home and explain what we know to our wives. We need to fine-tune our plans also, so let's meet up tonight." Both men nodded their agreement. We started for our respective homes, each wondering what we were going to do.

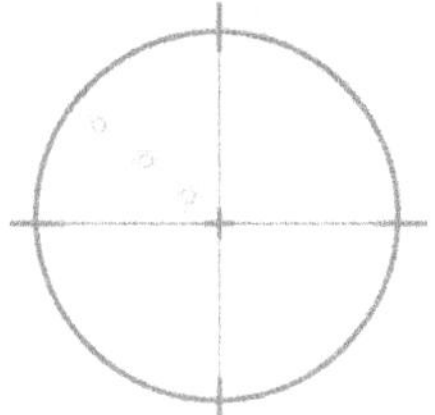

Chapter 46

Chuck woke up early the next morning and found Samir already awake. He walked up to him and asked, "What are you thinking about? You seem to be deep in thought."

"I'm concerned about the guy at the RV park the other night who seemed so suspicious of us. I think we should move the RV into the warehouse. We could be found fairly easily if we stay here, but it would be much more difficult to find us in the warehouse. What do you think?"

"Well, we don't really know whether or to what degree that guy was interested in us. It might be that he simply acts that way with everybody. However, if he was suspicious of us, it would seem that leaving this park would be a good idea. As a practical matter, it may hurt us to stay, but it doesn't hurt us to leave and head for the warehouse. I think your suggestion is a wise one."

Samir was silent for a few minutes as he continued to consider his options. "Okay, let's do it. After breakfast, we'll move to the warehouse. We should get everybody up and moving."

Chuck headed to the rear of the RV to wake Samantha and Samir did the same with his men. While Samantha prepared breakfast, Chuck went outside to empty the black and gray water tanks, then refilled his fresh water supply. He wasn't sure exactly how long they would be staying in the warehouse, but he knew he should be prepared to be there a while.

When his men were eating, Samir spoke to them. "We're going to leave this park now and head to the warehouse where we will stay until our attack has been completed. That will limit our contact with other individuals and allow us to walk about without attracting attention.

When you are finished eating, take turns going to the shower and get ready to leave. No more than two of you are to be in the shower building at any one time, and make your showers quick so that we can be on our way."

Chuck and Samir left the RV first to go to the shower building. They did not spend more than 10 minutes getting showered and shaved. When they returned, Samir saw that the men had already paired off for their trip to the showers. Within the hour, they were ready to leave.

As instructed, Chuck went to the park office to check out. He let it be known that they were now heading for Los Angeles. Upon his return, Chuck once again sat in the driver's seat, started up his rig, and pulled out of their spot. The RV, followed by Samantha in the car, exited the park and headed to the warehouse. The traffic was light as they drove through the back streets. When they arrived, Samir stepped out of the RV, went in the small door to the right of the roll-up door, and opened the door to the office. Shortly, the heavy metal warehouse door rolled up, and Chuck drove in and parked followed by Samantha. Samir closed the door as his men began exiting the RV.

Samir approached Chuck and stated, "I want you to take off now and pick up the items we previously discussed. We might as well finish that while we have time. Do you want to take anybody with you?"

"No, I can take care of that myself." A few moments later, he drove out of the warehouse and headed toward a hardware store he had discovered on Google the night before. It took about 20 minutes for him to reach the store. Chuck exited his vehicle and walked in. He saw that it was a typical hardware store, where anyone could get advice on home projects and pick up the material needed. Chuck walked up and down the aisles before he found what he was looking for. He took three cans from the shelf. Chuck also picked up three other items and headed to the checkout line. He was the second person in line and shortly stood before the clerk. Chuck placed the items on the counter and smiled at the clerk.

The clerk returned his smile and asked looking at the cans, "Do you really need three of these?"

Chuck gave her a big grin and chuckled. "No, I don't. But I have two kids who each need one. I know they'll never get one on their own. So rather than having them bug me by asking to borrow mine, I'm getting these for them. It costs me a little money but saves me a lot of time."

The clerk looked to be about 45 or so and nodded her agreement. "Isn't that the way it is? My kids are in their early 20s and still cost me a lot of money. I like the way you think. I may do the same thing." Chuck paid cash for for the items and headed for the door. Soon he was on his way back to the warehouse.

Less than an hour after Samir and his group had left the Oasis Las Vegas resort, a state trooper's vehicle pulled in and parked in front of the resort's office. Entering the reception area, the trooper was greeted by the woman behind the counter. "Hi, officer, what can I do for you?"

"I'm trying to find an RV that was headed to Las Vegas." He handed her a piece of paper with a license plate number on it. "Has this vehicle been here?"

She picked up the paper and looked at it. "Let me check," she stated. The woman sat down at her computer and entered the plate number. "Yes, here it is. Let's see, they arrived yesterday. Yes, now I remember this RV. They checked out and left about an hour ago."

"Did they say where they were going?"

The clerk thought for a moment. "As I recall, they mentioned they were going to Los Angeles."

"What else can you tell me about them?" the trooper asked. "Do you know how many people were in the RV, what they looked like, or anything they did while they were here?"

"No, not really. You know, I see so many people every day. They were like all of our other guests. Nothing unusual stands out to me. Here is the name they registered under." She slid a piece of paper across the counter that had a name written on it.

The trooper took out one of his cards and handed it to the clerk. "If you can think of anything else, please give me a call. It's important."

"I certainly will."

The trooper left the office and got in his vehicle. He picked up his cell phone, which was resting on the console, and called his supervisor. "I am at the Oasis Las Vegas resort. The RV we are looking for arrived here yesterday and left this morning. The clerk here had no information on them other than the name they registered under. She said they mentioned heading for Los Angeles." After answering a few brief questions, the trooper concluded his call.

The supervisor wondered what he should do with this new information. His agency had received a call from a concerned citizen two days ago. The man had described what he thought was a group of suspicious Mideastern looking people in the RV park where he was staying who said they were on the way to Las Vegas. As a way of checking up, the supervisor had sent his troopers to RV parks in the Las Vegas area. He decided he would pass this information on to the local FBI office. The supervisor picked up the phone and began to dial the number. He hesitated for a moment as he thought of what he would say. He realized the information he had was vague, incomplete, and perhaps of no importance at all. Hanging the phone up, he decided that he would send an email to the California Highway Patrol instead and let them handle it.

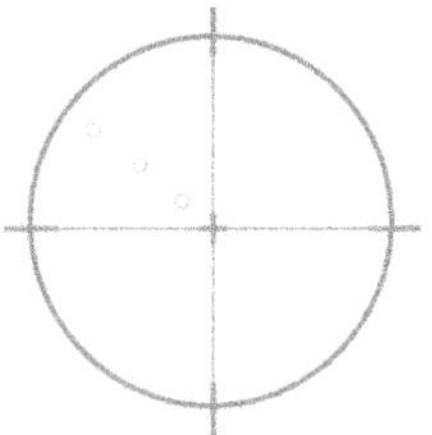

Chapter 47

It was a short drive from the FBI building to the White House. Sam had been there a couple of times before to brief the President on terrorism issues. The director thought this new information from France justified bringing the President into the loop about this potential attack. It did not take long for Wyman to be cleared through the guard station and to be taken into the White House. He was escorted to the President's secretary's office, just outside the Oval Office. She informed Wyman that the President was in a meeting that was lasting longer than expected. He smiled at her and sat down awaiting his turn.

Within ten minutes, the Secretary of Commerce came out of the Oval Office and told the secretary that the President was ready for his next appointment. She beckoned Sam to follow her as she walked to the door of the Oval Office. She knocked quietly before opening it. The President looked up, saw Sam, and told him to come in.

"Hi, Sam, why are you bothering me today?" he said with a smile. The President was a tall, slender man, with a graceful stature. Since taking office, he had added a little weight to his middle, but a good workout routine established by his doctor kept that under control. His dark brown hair was short. For a man of 50, he was lucky not to have some gray streaks in his hair, especially given the pressures of his job. Since he was from Colorado, his rugged facial features were expected. The President's reputation was one of stellar integrity, someone who knew the issues and how to wield the power of his office. He was a welcome relief from his predecessor, who didn't know a lie that wasn't worth telling.

"Well, Mister President, we have some new information that the director felt you should be made aware of. I'm sure you remember the attack on Paris a few months back."

The President nodded his head before he spoke. "It still astounds me that the terrorists were able to pull off that attack. From what the French have told me, they had no inkling of any kind that it was coming. My guess is their economy will not recover for at least five years. I'm sure it is going to cost us a lot of money trying to help them put everything back together."

"Mr. President, of course, you remember the three American professors and students who fought off the terrorists at the hotel in Paris?" The President nodded. "Well, a man named Samir, who is now believed to be the leader of the terrorist attack in Paris, recently contacted Professor Anderson. He said that he was coming to kill him and the other two professors who were with him in Paris. Shortly after the call, one of the professors was shot and wounded by an assassin. The professors actually caught up with the man and he was subsequently killed. Also, a granddaughter was kidnapped at the direction of Samir. Amazingly enough, the professors managed to recover her. The professors and their families are taking this extremely seriously, given what they endured in Paris and the most recent actions. The university is also taking protective measures. We've been working with local officials and the border patrol to see what we could do. Because the threat was so vague it has been difficult to respond to it in any meaningful way.

"Today, I received from my counterpart in France a photo and four drawings prepared by a sketch artist in their country. He believes it is of the leaders of the attack on Paris described by a farmer who saw them or at least the officials in France believe it's them. The photo is of one of the terrorists killed at the professor's hotel." Sam placed a photo and sketches before the President. "As you can see, the photo looks just like one of the sketches drawn based on the description given to the sketch artist. This seems to tie the people depicted in the sketches to the terrorist group. The French officials think one of the other men is Samir, the leader of the attack in Paris. Because of the connection between Samir, the professors, and Samir's capabilities, we believe there may be a real threat against them. If that's correct, that attack could come at any time. One of the professors also told my agent that he believes that Samir will come after them. However, he also believes that Samir was likely to plan additional attacks in the U.S. He didn't think that Samir would come just to kill them.

"Now, sir, as I told you previously, I'm here just to provide you with this information. We're not asking you to take any action at this time, but we didn't want you to be surprised if something happened."

The President spoke. "Let me see if I have this straight. The terrorists who attacked Paris may be in our country now or in the near future to kill three of our people and may stage additional attacks against this country. Is that about it?"

"Yes, sir, that's correct."

"And you're giving me this report only for information purposes and without any request for action on my part. Is that correct?"

"Yes, sir, it is."

The President looked at Sam and shook his head. "This is a hell of a job I have. Are you sure I can't do something for you? I am the most powerful man in the world, and yet, I feel so helpless in these types of situations."

"I understand what you're saying, Mr. President. To answer your question, there is nothing further we need at this point. If there were, you can be sure I would ask you for it. Also, the sketches will be released to the public tomorrow. I have a copy for you as well. The cover story we're putting out to avoid public panic is that these men are wanted overseas and we've been requested to watch for them."

"Okay, Sam, I want you to talk with my press secretary and let him know what the story is. I am sure as soon as these photos are released, the press are going to have a lot of questions they want answered."

The President stood and shook Sam's hand. He walked to the heavy wooden door, opened it, and asked his secretary to get Sam in to see the press secretary as soon as possible. Sam watched the President return to his office shaking his head and mumbling under his breath.

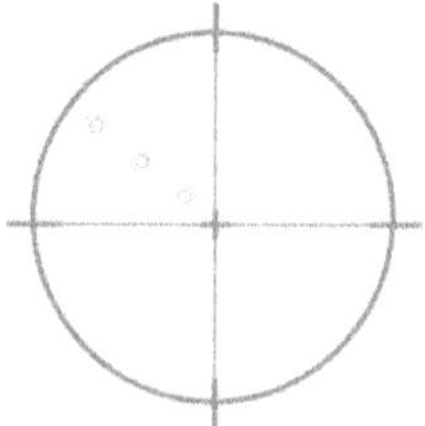

Chapter 48

Mac and I were sitting on his deck waiting for Ty and Leanne to arrive. After our discussion at the chief's office, we had realized that the sooner we finalized our defensive plans, the better situation we would be in. Sandy and Ann were in the family room talking. Even though it was quite chilly, Mac and I had decided to sit outside for a while. Mac got up and headed for the door. "Where you going, Mac?"

"I heard a car drive up. I'll be back in a couple of minutes."

I hadn't heard anything that would lead me to believe someone had arrived. Sometimes it surprised me how acute Mac's hearing was. As long as I had known Mac, he continued to surprise me with his heightened senses and police skills, which had not diminished since retiring from the department. He was a good one to have around when a problem like ours arose. While I was pondering those thoughts, the door suddenly opened, pulling me out of my thoughts, and Mac and Ty walked out. "Hey, Ty, how are you?"

"I'm good, but I would be much better if Mac got me a beer."

Mac looked at me. "Would you like one, too?"

"Sounds great, thanks," I answered. A few minutes later, Mac emerged and joined us. "Mac, are you still drinking this dishwater beer? I would've thought you would like the microbrews."

"Asshole, the truly great beers never change," Mac replied.

"Just saying, Mac."

"Just saying, DJ."

I changed the subject. "I think we need to make a plan today. Have you guys given any additional thought to what we may want to do since we met with the chief and Rheingold?"

Mac stood and looked at both of us. "If we're going to start talking business, we might as well go inside and have our wives join us. If we don't, we'll just have to go over everything we talk about twice." Ty and I got up and followed Mac into the house, where we joined Sandy, Ann and Leanne in the family room. All three of them were sitting on the couch and each had a glass of wine in their hand.

"Ladies, are you ready to continue our discussion on where we go from here?"

Ann answered for the three of them. "Of course, we are. I assume you were smart enough not to start outside without us present?"

"You know us so well, Ann," I replied. "You see, you can teach an old dog new tricks. And of course, then there is Ty and me. We do appreciate the work you've been doing with Mac, and we are hopeful that he will continue learning new things."

Mac pointed his finger at me. "You know, DJ, it's not polite to denigrate people in their own home."

"Damn, Mac, I didn't know you knew big words like denigrate. I'm impressed."

"Oh, shut the hell up. Let's get back to business." Just then, the doorbell rang. Mac got up from his seat and walked to the front door. A few seconds later, he walked back into the room and stated, "Look what the wind blew in."

Standing next to him was Derek. All of us got up to greet him, Ty and I shook his hand and he received hugs from all three women. Mac then addressed him. "It's about time you got here. What the hell took you so long?"

"What are you talking about? I got here as soon as I could. I was afraid if I took too much time that Mac, being the age he is, might pass on before I could get here."

"Geez, I don't remember Derek being so smart," I said.

Before Ty could enter into the conversation, Mac replied laughing, "That's because you are so old, DJ."

Pointing at Mac, I answered, "Who is this guy? Does anybody know what retirement home he came from?"

Sandy sat back down and looked at Derek. "I'm sorry you have to see these two old men deteriorate right in front of your eyes, but if we're lucky, they may be able to add something to our conversation, which we are just about to begin." She pointed to a chair and Derek sat down.

Derek had just graduated from the university and moved to LA to find a job as a police officer. At his age, he really looked more like a surfer dude than a law enforcement officer. Derek was tall, about 6 foot 2, with medium-length blonde hair. He appeared to be 225 pounds of pure muscle. Easy going with a great sense of humor, Derek attracted people to him. A smile was quick to come to his face but underneath that happy exterior was a former soldier who was ready to take aggressive action against those who might cause him or his friends' problems.

We chatted for a few minutes before Sandy brought us back to the task at hand. "DJ, why don't you bring Derek up to speed on what is going on?"

"Okay. I don't know how much Mac told you before, Derek, but Samir, the terrorist from Paris, called and told us he was going to come and kill the three of us. We've contacted the FBI and our police department. He sent an assassin who shot and hit Ty in the arm. Obviously, we plan to take whatever defensive measures we can. However, things got very interesting today." I gave Derek a brief rundown about the information and the drawings we received. I also filled him in with everything we had done since Samir's call. "You had to fight Samir and his men before, so you understand what we're up against. The question we have for you is that we could use your help and want to know if you might be interested?"

"Well, guys, I don't have anything else better to do, so why not?"

Sandy stated, "You understand, Derek, that this is going to be very dangerous. We expect it to be very violent, given what happened in

Paris. You are just starting your life and we don't want you to..." Sandy began to choke up.

Mac finished her thoughts. "Derek, we need to be clear about this. Simply put, you could be killed. As you know, these guys don't play games nor do they mess around. This is really our problem, not yours. We need you to consider whether you stay and become involved very seriously."

"I know exactly what these guys are capable of and wouldn't expect anything else. By coming here, they are threatening not only you but everyone in this country. I think the sooner we eliminate them, the better off we all will be. So, I'm definitely in and I don't want to hear about this again. Agreed?"

Sandy replied, "Agreed. Welcome aboard. We're really glad to have you with us."

Ty continued the conversation. "I want to bring up one of my many concerns. How can we truly protect ourselves when we are all at different houses? We don't know how many people these guys will bring at us, but if they can keep us apart, their job becomes much easier. It seems to me we have to figure out how we can all stay together. If they come after us, they should face all of us at one time."

Those comments started a lengthy discussion among everyone, but, in the end, common sense led us all to the same conclusion. Ann brought the discussion to a new focus. "It seems to me that the only option we have is that everybody should move in with us. We're surrounded by a hundred acres and you guys are lucky if you have a quarter acre each. The options we have available to us here are much greater than anywhere else." She looked at Mac and asked, "Honey, what do you think?"

He responded to her question. "Before I agree, I want an ironclad contract saying that DJ will pay for any damage to our property."

I looked at him with cold eyes. "Fine, I will draft it. You really are a crusty old bastard."

"You draft it? That's like having a fox guard the chicken coop," Mac answered.

"Listen, you old..."

Mac interrupted me, "I'm just joking, DJ. You've lost your sense of humor, as minimal as it was to begin with."

"Dammit, I'm mad," I yelled.

Sandy spoke up. "Both of you shut up and let's get back to work."

Mac started over. "Frankly, I think our place is the only option that gives us a chance to defend ourselves. As you know, there are paved roads on the north and south sides of our property. There are two entrances to the property, one from each road. However, someone could decide not to take those roads and come over the ranch land. If we're going to stay here, we have a lot of work to do. Ideas?"

Derek started first." You know, it would be easy enough to set up video equipment to cover the entrances and roads. We can do regular video for the day and infrared for night. All of this could be tied into a central command here in the house. I've done that before, so I could set it up for you. I'm sure the equipment is available in town."

"How do we cover the open spaces around the house and specifically the ranchland? I asked.

Derek responded, "I'm sure I can come up with some electronic equipment that will cover all that area and feed it into one location."

A discussion ensued where we talked about other methods of defense. The pros and cons of each were debated and decided upon. We then discussed and decided how we would institute each of these plans.

After everything seemed to be covered, Mac raised another subject. "I think we need to open our minds to other options on how we can cause these people problems." He had a sly grin on his face.

I stated, "You crazy old bastard. It sounds to me like you're considering an adult version of *Home Alone*."

His chuckle grew into more of a belly laugh. "There's no reason we can't have a little fun while we do this, is there?"

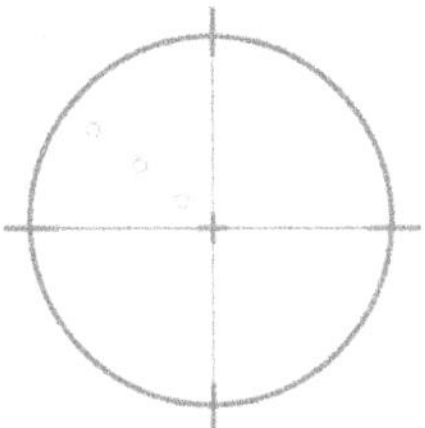

Chapter 49

Kamil had George looking for boats on Craigslist. George found two boats, each 18 feet long with open bows that met their needs. After a relatively brief discussion with each boat owner, George agreed to purchase the vessels subject to a test drive. George also found on Craigslist a Ford pickup truck, which he also agreed to buy subject to a test drive, which he and the owner scheduled for that evening.

Kamil contacted the man who had arranged for a warehouse in North Seattle. He confirmed that several recent deliveries had been made there. Kamil smiled as he thought how perfectly his plan was coming together for him.

The next morning, George and Kamil drove the truck to the boat launch in Kenmore. They arrived about 8:15 AM and watched an older man putting a boat into the water. The man was accompanied by his wife, who was driving the truck, and was just pulling the trailer out of the water. George approached the man and identified himself as the potential purchaser. After a 15-minute test drive, George indicated that the boat was just what he wanted. He paid the man in cash and completed the necessary paperwork. The man disconnected the trailer and helped George attach it to his truck; then they loaded the boat onto the trailer.

After a final handshake, the man and his wife drove off and Kamil and George headed back to the warehouse. Molly and the remaining men had already arrived with the RV and car. George drove into the warehouse and unhooked the trailer and boat. George and Kamil then headed back to the boat launch to check out the second boat.

When the two men pulled into the boat launch, they saw that it was empty of any boats or people. Within five minutes, the second boat they wanted to purchase entered the launch area. George and Kamil walked up, met the owner, and soon were testing the second boat. Again, after a short test ride, George indicated he was satisfied with the boat. They returned to the launch area and loaded the boat onto the trailer. George paid the man and once again completed the paperwork. They followed the man out of the launch area and set course for the warehouse. As before, George parked the second boat and trailer in the spacious building. Kamil informed Ali and Jawad that they were going to the locks with George to take the tour.

After the car left, Kamil motioned for Majid and Asad to join him where the boats were parked. "Each of you has been trained to operate small boats such as these so let's go over the controls and give you time to familiarize yourselves with your boat." He and Majid climbed into the first boat and Kamil explained how the boat operated. He left Majid looking over the boat and climbed out and down. Then Asad joined him in the second boat. Kamil briefed Asad as he had Majid.

When they were ready, he led Majid and Asad to where the crates had been delivered. The men opened all the crates before them and confirmed that each contained the explosives they needed. Kamil continued, "I want you to take the explosives for your boat and pack them into the bow. You will then need to run the wires for detonation to a position near the driver's seat. I know you have been trained in the use of explosives. Do you have any hesitancy in preparing these boats?"

Majid answered first. "No, I think it will be quite easy, actually."

Asad nodded. "I agree, it should not be a problem."

Kamil smiled at both of them. "When you are finished, let me know so that I can inspect your work and please be careful. We do not want the explosives to fire prematurely."

"I have one other question," Asad stated. "Are you sure the boats will operate properly? I don't want our attack to be delayed because of mechanical issues."

"I don't think that will be a problem," Kamil responded. "Once you're on the water, just stick together and take your time. You will have plenty of time to reach your target. The only concern I would have is that the boat won't start, but each boat started right away when we purchased them this morning, so that shouldn't happen. I also checked each of the boat's gas tanks this morning and saw that they were full. Therefore, there's nothing to worry about as far as that's concerned. When it is time to go, George or I will take each of you and your boat down to the launch area. Before we leave you, we'll make sure that the boat is running and in proper working condition. As long as you take your time, you should be fine."

Kamil then walked into the RV and found Molly on her cell phone. When she finished her conversation, Kamil asked, "What progress have you made in securing the trucks for us?"

"I have rented four U-Haul trucks from four different locations. Two are 12 feet long and the other two are 10 feet. We can actually go get them now if you want to."

"Yes, let's do that while we have the time. How far are they from here?"

"Each rental location is within 20 minutes of this warehouse. It's been my experience that it takes about a half hour to do all the paperwork. So, this process will take probably 3 to 4 hours."

Kamil responded, "Let's go get it done."

Just over three hours later, Kamil drove the pickup into the warehouse, followed by Molly driving the last U-Haul truck. Kamil called his men over to his location. Previously, he had given them orders to load the remaining explosives into each truck as it was brought in. "How's the loading process going?"

Asad answered. "The first truck is loaded and armed. The second truck is loaded and Majid is working on the detonator now. The third truck is about half loaded. It shouldn't take us more than another half hour to finish the third truck and then we can begin work on the truck you just brought in."

Kamil nodded his approval. "I will inspect the first truck now and then each one when it has been completed."

* * *

George and two of the men, Ali and Jawad, were on their second ferry trip of the afternoon. George was confident that both men were ready for their assignment. The men walked around the ship unhindered. While they did not go into the nonpublic areas where they would later need to go to complete their task, the men discovered how to enter those areas. Once Ali and Jawad were below the main decks, it would be critical to avoid ferry employees. The plan was to have the detonations occur at about 11:30 PM on New Year's Eve. It was hoped that this would divert attention from the second wave of attacks.

It seemed to George that with a little luck, they would be able to pull off this mission.

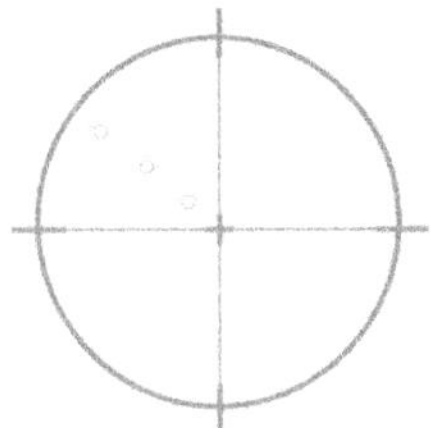

Chapter 50

Ahmed was sitting at a small table that had come with the warehouse they had rented. He was surprised when his phone rang. It was a burner phone and the only person who had the number was Samir. He answered, "Samir, my brother, how are things going where you are?"

"Very well indeed, I must say. Things are progressing as planned. I've talked with Kamil and Mohammed and for the most part, things are going well for them also. What progress have you made?"

"Right now, I'm sitting in the warehouse. It is pretty bare-bones but will meet our needs. I also have the addresses of the three professors and have driven by each of their houses. I was surprised to learn that two of the houses are currently for sale and it does not appear that anyone is living there. The other house is on a large ranch and very difficult to approach. The bottom line is we are prepared to go forward. I trust you will be bringing with you all of the armaments necessary to conclude our work here."

"Rest assured, we have everything to carry out our objective. I assume you'll have a plan developed for us when we arrive, Ahmed?"

"Yes, I believe so. I have an individual here who not only is willing to help us but would like to be a part of our plan. He is a true believer. I still have many things to accomplish and will explore the various alternatives to carry out our mission. I should have them ready for you to review and consider when you arrive. Do you have an idea when you will be here?"

"Hopefully, we will leave here shortly after midnight on New Year's Eve. I should be able to reach your location before sunrise. The other two will take one or two days more before they arrive. Have you had any difficulty traveling around the city given that you are a Middle Eastern man?" Samir asked.

"No, not at all. We're lucky, I think, because there are so many Saudi students going to school here. Because of that, I think the community has become used to seeing Middle Eastern men walking around. In fact, when I stayed at the hotel the first night I was here, the clerk asked if I was a father or brother of one of the students. I was a little insulted that he used the word father. I'm certainly not old enough to have children the age of the Saudi students here."

"Ahmed, I'm very concerned that we may not have an appropriate plan of attack against the professors. It would be best to get them together because if we attack them individually, the first one could give the others a warning of our presence. Therefore, figure out the best options we might have. I expect that the FBI and other agencies will be after us with a vengeance as well. I don't want to spend a lot of time there if we can avoid it. After we kill the professors, we need to follow through with our escape plan and leave this country far behind us."

"Samir, I truly believe Allah is with us. We will bring this operation to a successful conclusion. I look forward to seeing you when you arrive."

"I will see you soon, my friend. Make sure you dispose of the cell phone you're using. We will use phone number two for our next conversation." Samir terminated the call.

Ahmed immediately went to his car and drove away from the warehouse. He stopped in a residential area, placed the burner in a brown paper bag to hide its presence, and threw it into a garbage can. He didn't want that phone anywhere near him.

***

While it was against the law for the NSA to record domestic conversations, for the last year, they had been doing so anyway. The conversation between Ahmed and Samir was one of the calls that was captured. It was run through a software program designed to identify certain critical words in a conversation. When that occurred, the conversation was sent to an expert to analyze. Within an hour of Samir's disconnecting the call, an expert was reviewing this conversation and would, if necessary, bring it to the attention of those who could initiate action based on this conversation. In a matter of hours, the FBI knew about the conversation.

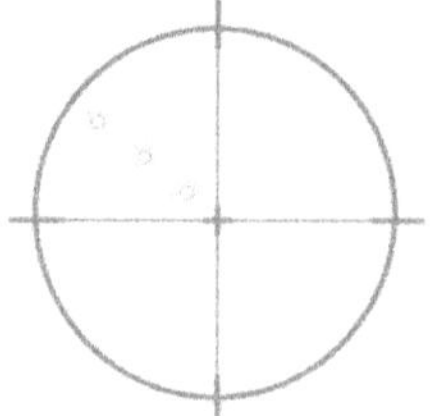

Chapter 51

Mac was sitting on the couch in the family room when he felt his phone vibrate. He reached into his jeans and pulled it out. "Hello?"

"Hi, Mac, how are you doing?"

Mac immediately recognized the Chief Martin's deep voice. "Good, and you?"

"I've been better, I can tell you that. I tried to call DJ, but he didn't answer his phone."

"I think he just got out of the shower. Do you need to talk with him?"

"I would like to talk to all of you at the same time. Can you make that happen?"

"Give me a minute or so. I'll call you back."

After rounding us all up, Mac dialed the chief's number and then spoke into the phone. "Okay, chief, you're on speaker and everyone, including our wives, are listening. What's up?"

"Well, I have some news for you. I told you I was sending investigators out to check with the various hotels and B&Bs here in the city to see if we might get a hit. Well, we did. One of my officers walked into one of the smaller hotels and showed the drawings to the manager. He recognized one of them. Do you have the drawings there?"

Mac responded, "Yeah, they're here on the table."

"Do you see the one where the man is smiling? That's the one he recognized. The officer asked him where the guy was and the manager said he left after only one day, even though the man had inquired about renting for a week. The man did not leave any forwarding information, but just took off early the following morning. There's not much else that we learned from the manager, but we now know that at least one of the men has arrived. It certainly is possible that he left after being here only one day. We just don't know.

"Every officer currently on duty has been provided with this information. I will make sure that each shift is also given that same information. The officers are very cognizant of the potential danger that exists and will be on the lookout for this guy."

Ty asked, "Was he driving a vehicle and, if so, do we know what kind or what the license plate is?"

"I forgot to mention that. We have the license plate number that was on the registration form at the hotel. The manager did not check to see if it was accurate, so we simply don't know if it is. When he was asked about the type of vehicle, the only thing he could say was that it was a dark sedan, nothing more specific than that. We do know that it was an out-of-state plate and my officers are actually running that now. I'll let you know what we find out. However, I can't imagine these guys giving anybody accurate information...Hold on a minute. One of my guys wants to speak to me."

When he spoke again, the chief said, "Just as I expected, the plate is not accurate. I don't know if I mentioned it to you, but it was a Florida plate. When my officer checked with the Florida DMV, they were told that it is a real plate registered to a white minivan."

Ty piped up, "A dead end. I can't say that I'm surprised. What's next, Chief?"

"I'm going to call Rheingold and pass on this information. Because it appears that the men or at least one man is here, I am going to ask him to see if he can bring in any reinforcements for us. I'll also inform the sheriff's department and the Highway Patrol and see what they can do for us, too. Other than that, I think we have to wait for their next move. Do you guys have any suggestions?"

"I don't have a suggestion, but I do have a question," stated Mac. "What are your instructions to your officers if they should see the guy?"

"They have been instructed not to stop him, but to call for backup immediately. I want them to keep the guy under surveillance if they can, and not do anything stupid. You know, some of these officers are young and gung ho. If they don't follow my instructions, they could end up on a slab at the coroner's office. I tried to make it very clear to them that these are not the usual drunks or shoplifters they deal with. I'm afraid this could be a tragedy waiting to happen."

"You're absolutely right, chief. If your officers follow your directions, they have a much better chance of staying alive."

"Amen to that," I stated. I could almost feel the wounds I received in Paris all over again. "Thanks, Chief, for keeping us informed. Please let us know if you find anything new."

"I definitely will," he replied. "Good luck, guys."

We heard the phone click off.

Sandy spoke up, "I don't mind telling you I'm afraid. Do you think what we have planned is sufficient to keep us safe?"

Ann answered, "If those terrorists show their faces around here, I'm going shoot their balls off and then kill them."

Mac had a big smile on his face. "I just love that woman. Don't you just to love her?"

Ann patted him on the knee. "There he goes trying to get lucky again."

That broke the tension and we all started talking at once. The general tenor was concern and determination. We knew we were in a difficult situation and the only responsible thing to do was to prepare ourselves as well as we could. There was still plenty of work to do outside of Mac's house. One person would always stand guard, watching both entrances. All of us would be armed at all times and keep our rifles nearby.

I turned toward Mac and asked, "Do you have any comments you want to add?"

He looked me right in the eye and said, "This is Paris all over again. The bastards are really here."

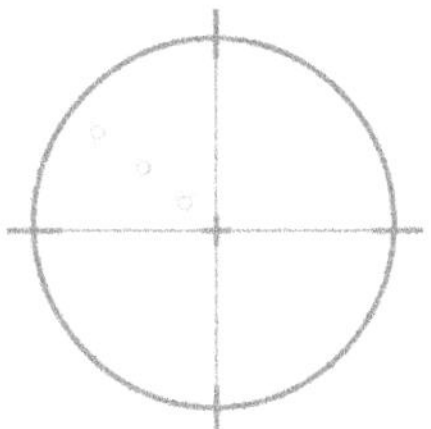

Chapter 52

Mohammed slept fitfully during the night and woke up at 6 AM. He saw no need to disturb his fellow freedom fighters, so he quietly exited the RV with his prayer rug and walked to the windows to either side of the warehouse's roll-up door. As requested, his contact had covered the windows with black cloth before they arrived. Mohammed pulled back the cloth to look outside. The warehouse was one of several located in an industrial area. He watched for a while but saw no movement into or out of any of the other buildings. This was not unusual given the time of the morning. He decided to have one of his men keep a lookout during the day and determine what times traffic in and out of the area was the highest. He spread out his rug out on the floor, knelt and began his morning ritual.

This warehouse, like the others that had been rented in Las Vegas and Seattle, had a small office. The office had two doors, one that opened to the outside and one to the inside, which was the preferable way to enter the warehouse. Mohammed went into the office, sat down in the creaky desk chair, and began to go through the day's activities. His thoughts were interrupted by Will, who walked into the office and sat in one of the empty chairs lining the walls. "Well, Mohammed, what's planned for today?"

"I was just thinking about that. I want Abdul, Bakir, and Jalal, who will be in the boats, to go with us when we investigate the target. The other men I will leave here to do an inventory of the armaments stored here in the warehouse. We also need to rent the trucks and arrange for the purchase of two boats that are required. Tomorrow, you will show the two men who will be driving the trucks to their point of attack."

"I'll get Brianne to work on the truck rentals and I can check Craigslist to see what boats I can come up with."

"That works. Will you also unhitch the car from the RV so we can take off after breakfast?"

"Okay, I'll get Brianne up and moving on breakfast, too." Within a few minutes, Brianne was busy in the RV's galley. Once the men had eaten, Mohammed called Abdul, Bakir, and Jalal into the office. "Today, Will is going to drive us around so we can look at the target up close. We will leave here in about half an hour, so be ready to go."

The three men left Mohammed's office. He then asked the two remaining men, Fahd and Talib, to join him. "The other men and I will be leaving shortly to do a reconnaissance of their target. While we are gone, I want you to unload all the materials stored here and take a complete inventory of everything we have. We will be back here in three or four hours. After that, our driver will take you on a reconnaissance of your target also. Do you have any questions?"

The two men facing Mohammed did not respond, which he took as evidence that they had no questions.

Five hours later, Mohammed and the other men returned from their reconnaissance trip. Because of heavy traffic, the trip had taken longer than expected as they searched for the locations to view the towers without creating any suspicion.

"It seems pretty clear to me that we have our work cut out for us. First, we have to make sure each of us can make it to our assigned target in a timely manner. Second, we need to prepare the explosives so that we can attach them as quickly as possible. We're not going to be martyred during this attack because it is important that we meet up with Samir for the final attack. So, for the remainder of the day, I want you to work on the explosives. Do you have any questions?" Mohammed asked.

One of the men raised his hand. "How many of the explosives can we use?"

"Remember, we still have two trucks that will need to be filled with explosives also. You need to use enough explosives to bring the towers down, but leave sufficient explosives to be loaded into the trucks. I want you to go out and discuss this among yourselves. Use each other's expertise to determine how much is needed and how they are to be placed. Now, get to work."

The three men walked out of the office engaged in an animated conversation. Mohammed knew that each of these men had received extensive training in the use of demolitions. He was confident they would come up with the appropriate answers.

Then Mohammed asked Fahd and Talib to join him in the office. They would be driving the trucks. Together, the three men headed for Will's car, a non-descript silver sedan, where Will was waiting.

"Now we're going to show you the route you will take to accomplish your mission. When you leave the warehouse on New Year's Eve, you will have a GPS unit to guide you to your target. So today, I don't want you to memorize this route, just become familiar and comfortable with where you will be going."

The men nodded eagerly and gave their full attention as Will drove toward their target.

When they returned to the warehouse sometime later, Mohammed found Brianne working in the office. "Have you been able to rent the trucks?"

She nodded and said, "Yes, I have reserved two 10-foot U-Hauls. We can go pick them up anytime." Will walked into the office.

"Will, Brianne and I are going to pick up the trucks. Why don't you start finding the boats and pickup truck on craigslist for us?"

"Okay, when would you like to pick them up?"

"Tomorrow morning," Mohammed answered. "Let's go get those trucks, Brianne." Leaving Will in the office, the two headed for the car. A few moments later, they drove out of the warehouse heading to the first of the U-Haul dealers.

Two hours later, Mohammed drove the car back into the warehouse. He was followed by Brianne, driving the second rental truck. One hour previously, they dropped off the first truck, which was in the process of being loaded with explosives. It would not be long before the men could begin work on the second truck.

Mohammed walked into the office just as Will hung up the phone. "Any luck with the boats?"

Will grinned at Mohammed and stated, "I just finished the arrangements for both boats and a pickup to pull them. I think we're good to go."

"Good work, Will. This is all coming together just as we hoped."

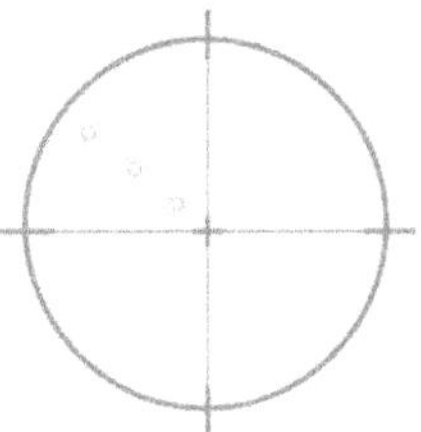

Chapter 53

Mac, Ty, Derek, and I were on our way to the police station once again. I'd received a phone call from Rheingold requesting that we come to the chief's office immediately. When we arrived, we saw what appeared to be the city's S.W.A.T. team forming up outside the station. We walked past the officers and went directly to the chief's office.

Rheingold ordered us to sit down and pay attention. Mac was about to object to being ordered around when I grabbed his arm and said, "Something's going on. Let this thing play out." Mac looked at me, nodded, and sat down.

Rheingold dove right in. "There's been some new information I think you need to know about. The National Security Agency picked up a phone call from this area which we believe is from one of the terrorists. They were able to track the phone to a house not too far from here. We obtained a federal warrant to enter and search the house, and will be executing the warrant shortly. If we catch the guy, I want you there to see if you can identify him."

At that moment, four men and a woman entered the office. Each was dressed in bulletproof vests with letters FBI on them.

Stu said, "Let's dispense with formalities. Hi, professors. I'm Stu Williams, FBI." He turned to Rheingold. "We're ready to proceed. The five of us will do the actual entry into the house. We coordinated with the city's TAC squad, who will provide perimeter security and backup."

"What approach to the house are you going to use?" asked Rheingold.

Stu continued, "Since it is still daylight and the house is in the middle of the block, we will park our vehicles out of sight at both ends of the block. We will then approach as quickly as possible and enter the front door. I think we will be able to reach the door without being seen and should have the element of surprise with us."

"Okay, let's go." We followed Rheingold, the FBI, and the S.W.A.T. team out of the building. Each of us had been supplied with radios and earbuds to follow the radio communications during this operation.

I heard Rheingold give the order to go. Immediately, the FBI and S.W.A.T. team officers began moving toward the house in question. We had been warned to stay away during the actual entrance to the house. When the officers had reached the houses on either side of the house in question, they paused for just a moment. I then heard Williams shout, "Go, go, go!"

We could hear the sound of the door being broken down and shouts of "FBI, get down." Following that, the sound of guns firing filled the air. As quickly as it started, the firing stopped and a deafening silence took its place.

Suddenly the radio cracked, "Rheingold, this is Williams. Three bad guys down and one of us. We need ambulances immediately."

At a run, Mac, Ty, and I followed Rheingold to the house. As were about to go up the stairs to the entrance, Williams walked out. "There are no terrorists here, but it looks like we have a drug house. There appears to be heroin and meth being packaged for sale. When we entered, the three guys in the house drew their weapons and began firing. They were taken out almost immediately, but hit Turner in the throat. It must've hit his artery; he died within minutes. The house and the surrounding area are being searched as we speak."

Fifteen minutes later, Williams walked out of the house carrying a cell phone. "This was found in the garbage out back. My guess is that it was ditched there by one of the terrorists."

I looked at Mac. "Damn, Mac, it's started for sure now."

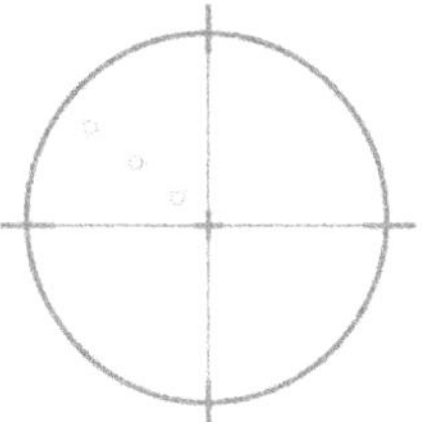

Chapter 54

Hadi walked out of his apartment and slowly ambled down the street. His destination was the small commercial building that acted as a mosque for the small number of Muslims in the city. Since his meeting with Ahmed, jumbled thoughts continued to float through his mind. He knew where his heart stood. Hadi wanted to do what he could to make his family proud and bring glory to Allah. While he knew where his heart stood, his mind, however, twisted his stomach in knots.

While still living in Saudi Arabia, he had been approached by the imam of his mosque. It was not necessarily unusual for the imam to search him out because he knew of Hadi's desire to serve Allah. But this time, the words of the imam were different. Rather than speaking of Allah and the need to be subservient to him, the cleric spoke to Hadi about something more concrete. The imam knew Hadi was leaving to go to the United States for schooling. He explained to the younger man that this opportunity placed him in the rare position to help those working to bring about the caliphate, the area ruled by the chief Muslim ruler in the world.

Hadi was told that many people like himself were placed throughout the United States and were waiting to be called upon. The imam wanted to know if Hadi would like to join their ranks as soldiers for Allah. Hadi, excited at the prospect of serving Allah, immediately answered yes to the question. But rather than simply accepting Hadi's response, the imam asked him to think about it and said they would talk again.

That conversation took place four days later. When questioned by the imam, Hadi once again affirmed his desire to serve Allah. Almost immediately, the imam began training Hadi in earnest. By the time Hadi left for America, he was ready to serve both mentally and spiritually. He had been in the U.S. for some time before Ahmed approached him.

After the prickles of excitement he had felt during his conversation with Ahmed, doubts begin to creep into his mind. The Americans had treated him kindly during his entire stay in their country. Even though, as he had told Ahmed, the Americans seemed more interested in chasing money than in spiritual renewal, he had come to doubt some of his previous beliefs. Specifically, it was difficult for him to accept that anyone who was not a Muslim was not innocent. How could a small child not be innocent, he wondered?

These and other similar thoughts continued to play with his mind as he walked toward the mosque. Hadi had many questions that needed to be answered. Even though he had helped Ahmed by renting the warehouse and providing the addresses of the professors, he was torn as to whether this was the right or wrong thing to do. He needed to talk with someone about these doubts, someone who could help him sort out these inner conflicts. Hadi knew he could not discuss these issues with the imam at his mosque because he had lived in the United States for many years and did not believe in the radical ideas of other imams. Hadi was also concerned that many, if not most, of the other Saudi students were not radicalized in any way. Who could he talk to?

Hadi turned the corner and saw the mosque a block ahead. As he did, he heard someone call his name from behind. He turned and looked back to see Riaz hurrying across the street. They shook hands briefly and exchanged greetings. Riaz had become a good friend of his and was the one person he felt he knew. In a second, he made up his mind. "Riaz, I'm glad to see you today."

"Why is that, Hadi? You see me almost every day. You look troubled, my friend. What is it?"

"I am troubled, very much troubled. I need to talk to someone I can trust."

"If it is a religious question," Riaz stated, "then I think the imam would be the appropriate person. Have you thought about that?"

"Yes, I have," Hadi replied. "But I do not feel comfortable in discussing my troubles and concerns with him. Riaz, you're my good friend. I think maybe I should talk with you." Riaz remained quiet as he waited for Hadi to continue. "I'm in a situation I thought I wanted to be in, but now, I'm not so sure."

Hadi then explained to Riaz how he had been recruited in their home country and that he just recently had been contacted. He did not go into any detail concerning Ahmed. They continued to walk toward the mosque in silence. Hadi looked at Riaz waiting for answers but none were forthcoming.

"Tell me, Riaz, should I continue on the path that has been laid out before me or should I try to extricate myself and return to the teachings of my father? I just don't know what to do."

Riaz immediately knew he had to contact DJ. He was unsure on how to advise Hadi as to what course he should take. Riaz was clearly aware that, regardless of how good of friends he was with Hadi, he could not give himself away to the man standing beside him. It was clear that Hadi was simply too fragile in his faith and could easily give Riaz away.

Riaz spoke quietly. "It is difficult for me to advise you because it is such a personal matter of faith. I would urge you to talk to our imam. He is a wise man and surely knows of such things."

"As he finished, they arrived at the mosque. When they entered, Riaz nodded toward the imam. "Trust him, Hadi. He will help you."

When their worship at the mosque ended, Riaz left Hadi and headed for his apartment. He immediately phoned Professor Anderson.

I recognized Riaz's voice. "Hi, Riaz, how are you?" I did not speak another word for five minutes as I listened to Riaz's story. The words tumbled from his mouth and chilled me to the depth of my soul. After we hung up, I walked outside to where Ann, Mac, and Ty were standing. I related what I had learned from Riaz. For several seconds, the silence was deafening until Mac spoke.

"Now things are getting interesting."

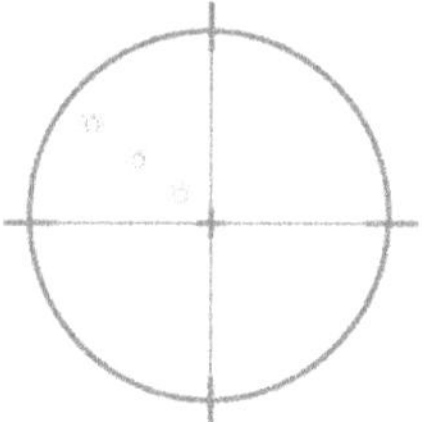

Chapter 55

Samir left the office in search of Omar, Saad, and Nasser. After locating them, he led them back to the office.

"You know that our attack begins tonight. There are certain steps you must take prior to initiating your part in the attack. Chuck will be taking you to your assigned hotels. Each of you should have the key cards for the three rooms in your assigned hotel. I assume your backpacks are ready, is that correct?"

The three men nodded in unison.

"Chuck will take Omar to his hotel, the Wynn. Omar, you will enter the room on the highest floor first. You will then use the newspapers left there when you registered, crumpling them and placing them in areas where it will help the fire spread. When you are finished and are preparing to leave, you have two important actions you must take. First, you must place your backpack under the bathroom sink. Second, when you leave the room, make sure you place the 'Do Not Disturb' sign on the outside of the door. Then proceed to the other two rooms and prepare them as you did the first. When you have finished, return to Chuck in the parking garage. Chuck will then take everyone to the second hotel, the Bellagio.

"Saad, you will prepare your three rooms in the same manner. Finally, you'll all go to the Venetian, where Nasser will prepare his rooms. Any questions?"

Omar spoke first. "If we place the paper as you've described, isn't it possible that it will be discovered?"

"Of course, that is a possibility," Samir explained. "That's why we are doing it so close to the attack. I would expect that housekeeping would already have cleaned your room, and if for some reason they have not, that is why you put the 'Do Not Disturb' sign on the outside of the door. That should stop them from entering the room and discovering how you set it up for tonight. Any other questions?"

Nasser spoke up next, "What happens if we're discovered before we return to the car?"

Samir smiled and answered, "I know that it is of some concern to you. However, you have done nothing that should attract attention. Just relax and talk your way through it. You could say, for instance, that you have a room here and are going to another casino. I doubt anyone will even take notice of you, given that this is New Year's Eve. With all that is going on today, I doubt that anyone will even give you a second look. Anything else?"

None of the three men indicated he had further questions. Samir looked at Chuck seated next to him. "Okay, Chuck, take them to the three hotels."

Chuck stood. "Let's go."

It took them 20 minutes to reach the Wynn. Chuck drove into the parking lot and found a space not too far from the elevator. He looked at Omar. "This is your hotel. We will wait for you here. Do you have any questions before you go to your rooms?"

Omar shook his head.

"Okay, get going." He watched Omar walk toward the elevator. It was half an hour before he returned. Chuck drove the men to the other two hotels to prepare those rooms.

The time for the attacks was drawing near and all of the men were excited.

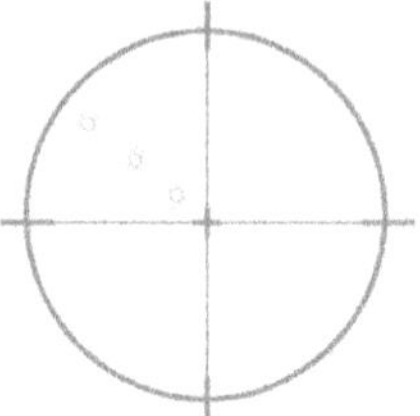

Chapter 56

Ahmed was jerked awake by sounds he did not recognize. He quietly got up from the air mattress he had been sleeping on, picked up his handgun, and slowly looked around the warehouse. Nothing came into view that seemed out of the ordinary. Ahmed approached the windows facing the street, cracked the blinds, and looked out. After looking both ways, he could see nothing that caused him to be alarmed. Ahmed went back to where he was sleeping and sat in the old lawn chair that had been purchased at a thrift store. He looked at his watch to discover that it was just after 5 AM.

He was certain that he had heard something, but maybe he had a little paranoia creeping into him. That would not be unusual, given the fact that he was in the midst of his sworn enemies and enemies of his faith. While this paranoia could keep him alert and watchful for threats to his life and his mission, he needed to take care that he is did not succumb to the stress.

Ahmed was not hungry enough to motivate himself to rise and fix something to eat. Instead, he pulled out his phone to scan the various news agencies. He started with CNN and was stunned to see the first story that appeared on the screen. There were three drawings of suspected terrorists and an accompanying story asking people to keep on the lookout for these men. The sketches were good enough for him to recognize Kamil, Samir, and himself. How could the police have come up with such incredible likenesses of him and his friends? He had no answer for that question, but the fact that these sketches were now being broadcast nationally did not bode well for his continued freedom.

Ahmed had previously removed his beard but had not shaved every day. Many days, he walked around with one to two days' growth on his face. He rose from his chair and walked into the bathroom and immediately lathered his face with shaving cream and proceeded to remove any remnants of hair on his face. When he looked in the mirror, Ahmed realized he needed to further change his appearance. He took his time and using a pair of small scissors, cut his hair as close to the scalp as he could. Ahmed then lathered up his head and proceeded to shave it.

When he finished, the mirror greeted him with an image of a person who did not resemble the sketches at all. He felt much better having made these changes to his appearance.

What Ahmed couldn't change was that the people of this country had been alerted to the fact that three Middle Eastern men needed to be found. He also believed that, unlike Samir and Kamil, who were in large cities, it would be more difficult for him to avoid detection in this small town.

Back in the main area of the warehouse, Ahmed let his eyes wander over the contents Hadi had obtained for him. Ten inflated air mattresses were stacked in the corner for the men who would be joining him. The spacious office refrigerator was stocked with enough food to feed the men for a short period of time. Two older pickup trucks were parked in the center; they would need the vehicles to carry out the assault on the professors. Ahmed still needed some additional materials, but there was time to acquire them before the other freedom fighters arrived.

He heard the sound of a vehicle pull up and stop outside the warehouse. He picked up his pistol, walked once again to the window, and looked out. Hadi was exiting his blue beater car and heading for the outside office door. Ahmed opened the door to let him in.

Hadi's eyes widened when he saw Ahmed. "What happened to you?"

"I needed to remove my hair so I could avoid detection. I'll tell you more later. I did not expect you this early. Why are you here now?"

"I was able to obtain more of the items you asked for last night. I thought I would bring them to you early so I would have more time during the day to find the other things you need. Is this a problem?"

"No, it is not a problem. What did you bring?"

"I found several more lawn chairs and quite a bit of canned food. I also brought a camping stove, propane, and some old cooking gear. I also purchased paper plates and utensils. It is all in my car."

Ahmed nodded. "I'll open the roll-up door. Drive your car in and then we will unload it in private."

Ahmed helped Hadi unload what turned out to be seven additional lawn chairs and several cases of canned food. He had Hadi set up the camp stove so it could be used later. Ahmed had come to appreciate the work Hadi had done for him. The fact that he did not need to go out in public certainly reduced the risk he faced of being discovered.

Hadi looked at Ahmed and shook his head. "You sure look different. Why did you decide to shave your head?"

Ahmed pulled out his phone and brought up the CNN story, showing it to Hadi. "I don't know how the officials got this sketch, but it is too close of a likeness of me. That's all I need is to have someone notify the police that I was in town based solely on that sketch. So I changed my appearance. I don't think I look like that person anymore. What do you think?"

"I think the sketch and you are two different people. I don't think you have to worry about it anymore."

"You see, Hadi, that is why it is so important that my being here or any connection that I have with you cannot get out. Even something very simple can turn deadly for me and result in the failure of my mission." A cloud crossed Hadi's face. Almost instantly, Ahmed noticed that the young man before him was deeply concerned. "What's the matter, Hadi?"

"Nothing, nothing at all."

"I know something is wrong, Hadi. So tell me now." Ahmed watched Hadi's body language and could see that the younger man was becoming defensive and nervous. "It's best you tell me now. Have you talked to someone about me?"

Hadi wiped the sweat from his forehead and fear clutched at his stomach. He knew that the weakness he felt yesterday was now coming back to haunt him. Hadi also realized that he feared the man seated next to him. He just wanted to get into his car and leave.

Ahmed sought to bring his attention into focus, and in a louder, harsher voice, spat. "Hadi! Answer me! Answer me now!"

Hadi muttered in response, "I...I don't know what you're talking about."

With a swift motion that surprised Hadi, Ahmed's hand shot to Hadi's throat. Ahmed rose and lifted Hadi by the neck off the floor. Hadi struggled and grabbed at the man's hand. As Ahmed stood there holding him, Hadi squeaked, "Okay, okay, I'll tell you."

Ahmed slowly brought Hadi down so that his feet touched the floor. The fingers around Hadi's throat loosened sufficiently so that he could speak. However, they remained there as a constant threat to the young man's life.

"I didn't want to say anything because it was so insignificant. Yesterday, I wondered whether what I was doing was right and I had to have someone help me get my head on straight. So I asked a friend of mine, whom I trust implicitly, for his advice. He said he couldn't advise me and I should talk to the local imam. That was all that happened, I promise you."

"You are less than a man when you need help to decide what to do," Ahmad growled. "Don't you realize the danger you put us in?"

"My friend would never say anything. You can trust him to be quiet."

"Like I trusted you to be quiet? What is your friend's name?"

"I'm not going to tell you. I don't want you to hurt him, he's my friend." Ahmed's fingers begin to close once again around his throat. "Stop, please stop, his name is Riaz."

"Living here in the United States has made you soft, Hadi. You are not capable of being a soldier in service to Allah." In what took just an instant, Ahmed slammed Hadi to the ground. The young man's throat was now encased by both of Ahmed's hands. Hadi squirmed, trying to get loose, and his hands clawed at Ahmed's face but to no avail.

Ahmed did not move for several minutes until he was absolutely certain that Hadi's life had left him. He felt no remorse for his actions. This unnecessary death rested solely with the young man who lay lifeless before him. He would dispose of the body later. Now, Ahmed realized, he would have to deal with the person named Riaz as well.

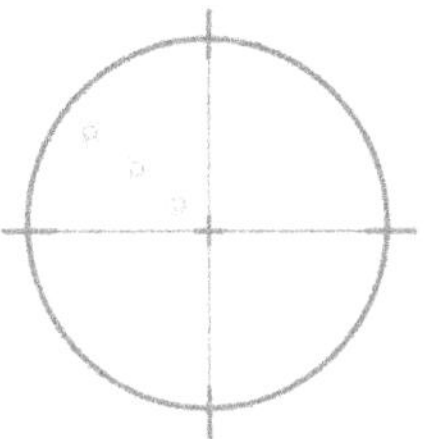

Chapter 57

The weather in San Francisco was cold and damp when Mohammed and his men awoke. Brianne made them an early breakfast, which they ate in the RV. The previous evening, Will had found an old pickup truck to buy. He was able to locate one nearby that would meet their needs. Both Mohammed and Will met the owner at a parking lot a mile from the warehouse. After a brief test drive, Will informed the owner that he would like to purchase the truck. Within minutes, they had negotiated a price that both agreed on. After the purchase, Mohammed drove the car and followed Will and the truck to the warehouse. They were now prepared to leave the warehouse and meet the sellers of the two boats.

Will was in the driver's seat of the truck as they pulled out of the warehouse, driving to the Turning Street boat ramp. Given the time of year, there was no traffic at the boat ramp. Within a few minutes of their arrival, the seller of the boat drove up. Will walked up and identified himself. Shortly thereafter, the boat was launched into the bay. Mohammed and Will joined the owner for a 15-minute test drive. All seemed in order.

Will asked the owner, "This boat is pretty old. Have you had any problems with it? Is there anything that I should know that needs to be done to keep it operational?"

The owner responded, "There's nothing I know of that needs to be fixed. I have maintained it as suggested by the manufacturer, which is why it is in such good shape. I don't expect there will be any problems for a while, but as you know, small things will creep up from time to time. As long as you keep it maintained properly, you will avoid any major problems. However, I have a question for you. Why are you buying a boat in the middle of winter?"

Will answered the man by stating, "Some friends and I want to go on the Bay tonight and watch the fireworks. I did that once a long time ago and it was spectacular."

"Well, all I can say is make sure you dress very warm. It gets pretty cold out there this time of year."

"Oh, I assure you, we will. Thanks for the advice."

After the three returned to the boat ramp, Will and Mohammed attached the boat trailer to their "new" truck. They backed down the ramp, loaded the boat onto it, and drove back to the warehouse. They repeated the process with the purchase of another boat at the Bayview boat club.

After arriving with the second boat, Will explained the operation of these specific boats to the three men who would be riding in them. Meanwhile, Mohammed and the two other members of his team finished the process of preparing the explosives in the trucks.

When that task had been completed, Mohammed took the two men, Fahd and Talib, who were scheduled to drive the rental trucks, into the office. "The time for our operation draws near. You have been chosen by Samir to martyr yourself in our battle against the Great Satan. You have known this for some time, but we have not discussed it at any length prior to today. When a man chooses to martyr himself, it is a very difficult decision. Unlike the Americans, who fear death, we embrace it in our service to Allah. Still, I must ask you if you are sure you can carry out your mission tonight. I want you to be honest with me. It is understandable that, now that the time is upon us, your conviction may waiver. So, if either of you have any concerns about your ability to finish this mission, I need to know now."

The first man sitting before Mohammed was Talib, 22, and full of confidence. He stated, "Fahd and I have discussed this many times since we left France and spoke of it again last night. We assure you that we are ready. Regardless of any concerns we may have, we are determined to carry out our mission successfully." Fahd nodded his agreement.

"Knowing each of you, your answer is what I expected. Now is the time for you to rest, eat, and prepare yourselves for tonight's attack. Allah is pleased with your determination to serve him."

The two men left the office and returned to the warehouse. Mohammed also stepped out of the office and walked to the window. He pulled back the covering and once again glanced out to see if anything suspicious was going on outside. He froze momentarily and then swiftly closed the covering. Waiting a moment, Mohammed slowly pulled the covering back once again.

Down the block, leaning against the wall of another warehouse, was a man who appeared to be about 50 years old. He was just standing there, looking at the warehouse in which Mohammed and his team had taken refuge. Within five minutes, another man joined him. They seemed to be carrying on an animated conversation, which Mohammed assumed was about the warehouse he was standing in. After about 15 minutes, the two men walked away out of Mohammed's line of sight.

He walked over to Will and explained what he had just observed. "Let's have one man keep watch out the window all the time. I hope that our mission has not been compromised. We only need a few more hours before we set out on our attack."

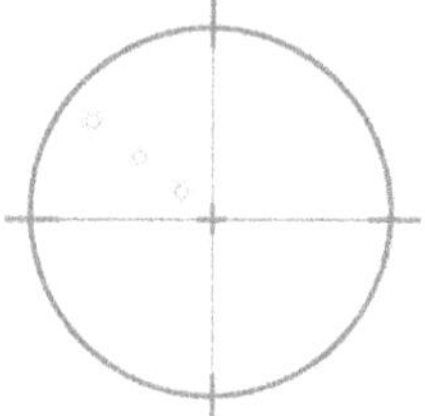

Chapter 58

Art Rheingold was surprised at how fast things were moving. He had expected that the release of the sketches would generate a large number of calls from across the country. He also knew that most of those would be bogus. What he had not expected was that some old-fashioned police work would bring them a lead. He had just got off the phone with Chief Martin, who told him what they learned from the hotel manager. Based on that information, Rheingold believed an attack on the professors was imminent. They now knew that at least one of the Paris attackers, and maybe all of them, were in the United States and were within striking distance of the professors.

Chief Martin had requested additional resources from the Bureau, which Art thought was appropriate. However, only Sam could authorize those resources. Rheingold had called the four agents Sam had sent to him, and then loaned them to the police chief for assistance. The FBI agents had found nothing since their arrival.

He pushed three on his speed dial and waited for Sam to pick up. Sam seemed distracted when he answered, "Hi Art, what's going on?"

"Well, those sketches have brought us some new information."

Art now had Sam's full attention. "Tell me what you know."

"The local police chief had his men check with all the hotels and B&Bs in the area to see if they could identify any of the men in the sketches. One hotel manager did. Evidently, the man only stayed at the hotel one night and had left by the time the officer arrived. The manager indicated that he left no forwarding address or information. The local police checked the license plate of the man's car. He obviously lied about that since it came back as a white minivan and had been described by the manager as a dark-colored sedan."

"So the terrorists are actually here, huh?"

"Well, we know that at least one of the terrorists is here, but it is certainly possible that all of them are. That's all we know. The team you sent here has not turned up anything either." Rheingold explained what happened at the drug house. "I have them helping the local police department. The professors have evidently decided on a new approach to their safety. Two of them, Anderson and Smith, who live in housing developments, have moved in with MacDonald, who owns a 100-acre ranch. From what we can see from afar, the professors are preparing to defend that location."

"Why don't they just leave the area?"

"They told me they want this to end so they are staying put. Do you have any information that would lead you to believe that other attacks may be imminent also?"

"You know, Art, we get information coming in here about that kind of thing all the time. I can tell you there is nothing serious enough that would lead us to take any special action."

"What concerns me the most is that the professors were pretty insistent in their belief that if Samir came to this country to go after them, that he would have planned other attacks also. The professors don't think that they are so important that a large well-coordinated attack on them would occur unless other acts of terrorism were planned. I think this is one of those times where we need to be extra vigilant."

"I couldn't agree more. Have the professors shared with you what they're doing, Art?"

"I haven't heard from them. I'm sure if I asked they would share, but I don't think they consider us the best of friends, since we haven't done a lot on their behalf. I also want to bring to your attention that the chief has specifically requested that we commit more manpower to the situation. I told him I would bring it to your attention."

"Do you have any recommendations?"

"Let me put it to you this way. If the terrorists come here with a lot of men and sufficient firepower, I don't think the professors will survive. Local police officers would not, in my opinion, be expected to respond in a manner like our guys would. It could turn into a public relations nightmare. I know how difficult it is to assign men for an indefinite period based solely on the information we have at this time, but I believe these guys could not stand up to a determined terrorist attack. If the word gets out, as I'm sure it would, that we knew of this potential attack and did nothing about it, the Bureau would be dragged through the mud and so would we. Therefore, my recommendation to you is that we need to have additional manpower and firepower available to destroy these terrorists should they attack."

Sam was silent for a couple of minutes as he pondered the advice and information Rheingold had provided him. "I'm more inclined to follow your recommendation at this point, Art. Please give me your recommendation on how we can approach this as soon as you can. I'll review it, add my own comments, and push it upstairs. Is there anything else we need to go over?"

"No, I don't think so, Sam. I will get that recommendation to you within an hour or two. Maybe luck will fall on our side this time."

"How are the four agents responding to the death of Turner?"

"It shook a couple of them to the core, but I think they'll be okay. They all want to take it out on the terrorists."

"I can understand that," replied Sam. "Hopefully they will have the opportunity to do just that before we have an attack on one of our cities. Keep me informed, Art."

"I'll talk to you soon, Sam." Rheingold clicked off and called his secretary. "Nancy, I need you to cancel my appointments for the rest of the day, and I don't want to talk to anybody unless it's absolutely critical. I need to put a recommendation together for Washington ASAP."

She responded immediately, "I'll take care of it. Do you need any help on anything else?"

"Not right now. If I do, I'll let you know. Thanks." Rheingold opened his desk drawer and pulled out a yellow legal pad. He started to jot down ideas that might help. Once the ideas started to flow, the pad was quickly full. He had decided that rather than go halfway, his recommendation would be for a full-court press, or in other words, he would ask for everything he could possibly need. If Sam or the higher-ups ruled against him, and if the shit hit the fan, at least he would be covered.

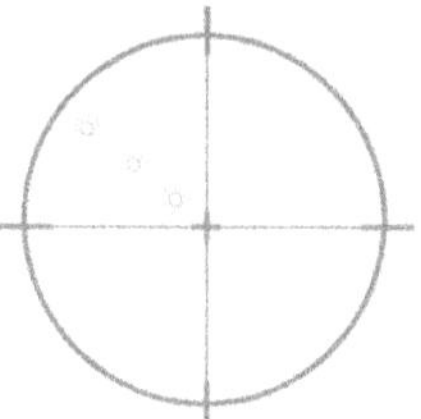

Chapter 59

Samantha pulled into the parking lot of Las Vegas Helicopter Charters. When she pushed open the door, the front office was smaller than she expected, with only five hardback chairs against one wall. She walked up to the counter. The uniformed man, somewhere in his mid-fifties, looked up at her and said, "Hi, how can I help you?"

Samantha smiled before answering. "Hi, I called a couple of days ago about renting two helicopters for this evening. I made a reservation." The man got up from behind the desk and walked to the counter. Samantha handed over her identification. "I wanted to come in and pay now if that's all right."

"Well, we never say no to a client who wants to pay." The man brought up the reservation on the computer at the counter. "Yes, here it is. It says that you want to rent two helicopters for this evening. Is that correct?"

"Yes, my family is here for New Year's. Some of them want to take photographs of the fireworks from the air. They're quite excited at that possibility. When I talked to the person on the phone, he told me this wouldn't be the first time a copter was chartered to take photos on New Year's Eve. The guy asked me how long I wanted to be flying and I told them just enough time to get the photos of the fireworks."

"I have here the amount they quoted you for both helicopters." He swiveled the computer so she could see the screen. "Is that what you understood the cost to be?"

She looked at the screen and noted the cost. "Yes, that's what I was told. Can I pay now?"

"Of course. I assume you're paying by credit card?" Samantha nodded and pulled a credit card not traceable to her from her purse. She passed it to him and he processed the payment. "Would you like a receipt?" The man saw her nod yes. He printed the receipt and handed it to her. "Now, as I understand it, six people will be flying tonight?"

"Yes, that's correct. What time would you like them to be here?"

"11 PM should be fine. Are you going to be one of the six?" He grinned at her.

"Oh, no, not me. I'm afraid of heights and if I went up, I would ruin the trip for everyone else."

"I understand. You'd be surprised how many people feel the same way. Just make sure one of the six who will be flying brings your receipt with them. That way, I will have confirmed that they are the appropriate ones to ride. Also, make sure they are wearing warm clothes. Winter desert nights are cold, and nothing ruins a flight like being cold."

Samantha smiled at the man and turned to leave. As she opened the door, she turned back and waved at him. He smiled and returned her wave. Samantha started the car and left the parking lot, heading back toward the warehouse. When she arrived, she went into the office to talk with Samir.

The terrorist leader looked up from his desk. "How did it go?"

"It went very smoothly," she responded. "There was no issue at all. He was glad that I came early to pay. He gave me a receipt and told me that whoever comes for the ride should bring it with them. You have to be there at 11 PM."

Samir listened carefully as Samantha spoke. "Did you detect any suspicion or concern on his part?"

"No, none at all. It seemed to be business as usual."

"Good. Let's hope it goes as smoothly tonight."

Entering the warehouse space, Samir and Samantha left the office. He called the five men who would be flying in the helicopters with him and escorted them back into the office. "I wanted to bring you up to speed on our plan of attack tonight. Samantha just returned from the helicopter charter company and there appears to be no problem with our charter. Make sure that the top of your bag has some camera equipment in it should they want to check your bag. Also, wear warm clothing. It is supposed to be cold in the air."

Samir then went over in detail what he expected them to accomplish that night. "Do you feel ready to take on this task for Allah?"

The men answered in unison, "We are!"

"We'll be leaving here around 10:30 PM. If you have any questions before then, just come and see me." Almost as one, the men stood and walked out of his office. His plan was coming to fruition and he knew in his heart that Allah would bless them in their strike against these Americans.

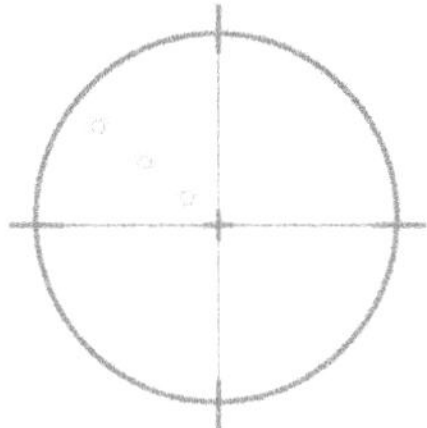

Chapter 60

It was late afternoon and Mac, Ty, and I were sitting on the deck having a beer. We had worked hard all day building our defenses and accomplished a lot. Derek walked up and stood in front of us with his hands on his hips. He smiled as he looked down on us. "You know, here I am working out in the cold, and you old guys are sitting down, relaxing, and drinking beer. What's wrong with this picture?"

Mac flipped him off and said, "If you want a beer, go and get one. You've been here more than two hours, which means you are no longer a guest and you can help yourself."

Derek looked at Ty and me and stated, "Did I say anything about beer?"

"So you don't want a beer, is that what you're saying?" Mac responded.

"I didn't say that."

"Oh, shit, I'll just go get one for you." With that, Mac stood and stomped off.

"He's a little touchy today, isn't he?" Derek commented.

I motioned for Derek sit down. "Derek, I'm not sure whether he is stressed because of the attack that may be coming, whether you criticized him for not working, or whether you alluded to his advancing age. In any event, I wouldn't worry about it."

Mac walked out the door and handed Derek a beer. "I hope that helps, Asshole."

I started laughing, as did Ty. I looked at Derek once again and said, "I think it is all about his old age. However, regardless of Mac's feebleness, let's talk about where we stand with our work. Derek, you start."

"I was able to find and buy all the electronic equipment we needed and have set up two cameras to watch the front and back gates. Mac and I also walked the ranchland and determined where additional cameras should be located. I just finished putting those in. All of these cameras will be linked to a central station in the house so they can be observed. I also thought it would probably be a good idea to record what the cameras show, so, I set that up also."

Mac spoke up next. "I used my front loader to dig out holes as bunkers to cover both gates and two bunkers to cover the ranchland. I've also dug four-foot-deep trenches that connect the bunkers to the house and to the barn. It ain't pretty, but I think it will do."

Ty continued the discussion. "DJ and I filled sandbags and finished the construction of the bunkers, which we hope will provide whoever is in them sufficient protection from any attacks. You know, I think this will surprise the hell out of Samir and his cronies. By the way, Mac, where did you go after you finished digging the trenches? We could have used help filling sandbags."

"There you go again, questioning my dedication to the task at hand. Let me tell you, I've been placing small surprises around the property for our honored guests."

"What kind of surprises?" I asked.

"I'm not going to tell you about most of them because it would ruin the surprise. However, I will tell you about one. I dug ten holes that are three feet deep, three feet wide, and six feet long around the property. I filled each one of them with about a foot of pig shit and covered them with sagebrush so they can't be seen."

Ty responded to his comments. "It seems to me like a waste of time. So someone falls into one of them and gets covered in pig shit. How's that going to help us?"

"Well, it's kind of fun and I think it will slow down their advance. It makes me smile just thinking about them crawling out of the hole stinking to high heaven. And you know how they feel about pigs."

"I'll be damned," Ty stated. "When do we get to hear about your other surprises? I will say this, you have a twisted mind, my friend."

Derek ended the conversation at that point. "You know, he did this kind of stuff in class. It made it a lot more fun, but I was kind of surprised he didn't get in trouble for it."

Mac smiled, "That's your problem, Derek. You need to learn to think out of the box. What were they going to do, fire me? To me, teaching was just a way to have fun and screw with you students. If the dean had called me in to talk about anything that I did like that, I would've shaken his hand and walked out the door."

Ann stepped out and sat beside Mac. "What are you dingdongs doing here sitting on your butts?"

Derek, without realizing it, fell into a trap. "Well, Ann, what have you been doing while we have been slaving out here today?"

"Well, I've been helping Mac set up his surprises. And before you ask, I'm not going to tell you about any of them. I will tell you one thing, though. I wouldn't want to be one of the terrorists who runs into one of those surprises. I can only hope one of you doesn't become involved in them either."

"Wait a minute," Derek said, "you mean one of us might get caught up in a trap?" Ann shrugged her shoulders. "Guys, I need you to speak up here," the young man said, peering at each of us in turn.

I smiled at him. "I'm old enough to know all of Mac's hidden surprises."

"Me, too," Ty responded.

Derek looked at the four of us sitting there. "This isn't funny anymore."

We all responded, "Yes, it is."

Before Derek could say anything else, Leanne opened the door and told us that dinner was ready. We all followed her into the house and sat at the table. As the soup was passed around, Ann leaned over and whispered to Derek, "I would be careful with that."

"Why?"

"Because I made that right after I finished preparing the pig shit for Mac."

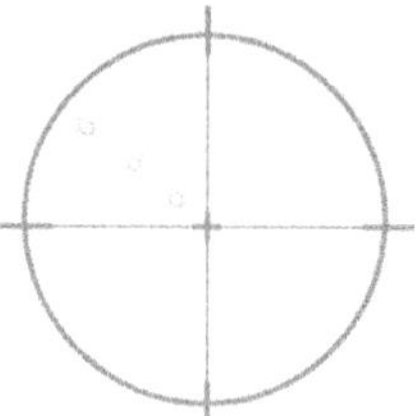

Chapter 61

Kamil woke with a start. He glanced around the RV to see if there was a reason for his abrupt awakening. Seeing nothing out of the ordinary, he got up off the couch and stepped out of the RV. He walked to the front of the warehouse and pulled back the black cloth covering one of the windows to look out. Many people had told him that Seattle's weather was dreary and now he understood why. Ever since they had arrived, he had not seen the sun peek through the heavy cloud layer that hung over the city. Seattle was known for its rain, but to Kamil's understanding, this was not rain, but rather a drizzle that never seemed to end. There was an oppressiveness in the gray that enveloped the city. He hoped that when this mission was concluded, he could head east over the Cascade Mountains and find the sun once again. Unrolling his rug, he was thankful for this time to pray to Allah.

After his men were up and moving about, he noticed a variety of emotions among them. Foremost was their desire to get on with their mission, but there also existed a definite hesitancy. Both were common feelings for those who were about to voluntarily give up their lives for their beliefs. The men had started to break up into two groups, those who were going to live to fight again, and those who were to be martyred on this mission. He also sensed a feeling of excitement. His men were truly excited to strike a blow against America. Too long, they believed, the U.S. had been left unharmed and free to kill those of Muslim faith. Kamil also believed he could sense fear within the warehouse. He was unsure about what the fear was based on. Was it fear of death, failure, or not measuring up to their peers? He would address each of these when he spoke with his men.

By 9 AM, Molly had prepared and served breakfast to the hungry men. This morning they enjoyed beef patties, eggs, and toast. He called for the men who were going to be martyred to join him in a corner of the warehouse. They sat in a circle on the floor. Kamil began, "As you know, we attack America tonight. During this attack, each of you will be martyred." Kamil, Ahmed, Mohammed, and Samir had agreed that this issue of approaching death must be discussed with each man. "We have talked about the actions that will result in your deaths for many months now. Up until today, you may have felt that this time may never come. But it has arrived. It is not easy to decide to give up your life in service to Allah, and it is natural to question your decision. Only you can make that choice for yourself, and I know it is not an easy one.

"I think it is appropriate that we discuss this openly among ourselves. I have a question I want you to think about and answer: Do any of you have doubts about whether you can take the necessary action to produce your martyrdom? I want you to think about this and give me your honest answer." Kamil waited, giving each man sufficient time to ponder his answer.

"Moiz, let's begin with you."

Even though Moiz was slight of stature and young, not yet 20, he had impressed Kamil with his determination to strike America. As a result of wounds he had suffered previously, he walked with a slight but noticeable limp. He was looking down at his small hands, which were folded in his lap. Moiz took a deep breath before he spoke. "Kamil, I have thought about this coming operation for many months now. I've wondered whether this action was the best way I could serve Allah. I've prayed on it long and hard. While I have a funny feeling in the pit of my stomach, my heart is strong and determined. I am ready for martyrdom. I'm ready to strike a blow against America. I'm ready to fulfill my destiny." Moiz then smiled at Kamil and said no more.

Kamil then pointed at Asad, who, since this operation began, had been the man Kamil was most concerned about. Asad looked Kamil in the eye and stated, "I, too, have given the subject great thought. At times, I found myself wavering in my determination to martyr myself. But as I have traveled through this country, I've been amazed at the grotesqueness of what Americans have. Their love of things continues to horrify me. No one needs all the possessions they have while others have nothing. I believe with all my heart that we must send a message to these people that will awaken in them the needs of others and the promise of Allah. I will have no problem executing my mission."

Kamil smiled at the young man, who was no more than 18. Then he looked at Majid. "Explain your heart to us, Majid."

Majid was taller and larger than the other two men. Like them, his hair and eyes were glossy black, his skin a dark brown that would be the envy of anyone lying on a beach. "I have no qualms with forfeiting my life in the service of Allah. I look forward to causing great harm to the Americans. I know that Allah is with me."

Kamil directed the same question to the other three of his charges. Each answered in a fashion similar to the first three. Kamil watched each of them closely as they responded and detected nothing that would cause him concern about their willingness to martyr themselves.

Kamil bowed to each of them in a sign of respect. "I'm proud to see before me soldiers of Allah. I'm proud of the important work you will do and I'm sure that you will carry it out to the best of your ability. I will inform your families of the actions that you have taken, which I know will also give them great pride. I want you to eat well and rest for the remainder of the day. We will strike a great blow against America tonight. The blessings of Allah be upon you."

He watched the men rise and return to their chosen places. Their training was complete and, Allah willing, tonight would bring great suffering to these Americans.

Kamil left the corner of the warehouse and walked to the RV. Once inside, he saw Ali and Jawad seated at the dinette, reading magazines. They smiled at him as he entered. He sat next to Ali. "Are you both ready for tonight?"

Ali answered, "Yes, everything is ready to go."

"I agree, we are ready. Do you have any questions as to whether we are justified in taking the actions we have planned? Are you feeling any concern for the people whose lives may be lost?"

Jawad responded first this time. "If you're asking me whether I have any hesitancy in striking the infidels, the answer is no. They have it coming to them. In fact, I'm full of fire to bring about their deaths."

Ali nodded, "I agree with Jawad. My heart is strong. I have no doubt that we are doing Allah's will. You need not be concerned about either of us. We are ready to strike."

Once again, Kamil felt pride swell in his chest. These were good and dedicated men who would do as he ordered. Once outside the RV, he looked through the draped window, dismayed by the drizzle and grayness. Truly, he would be glad to leave this city.

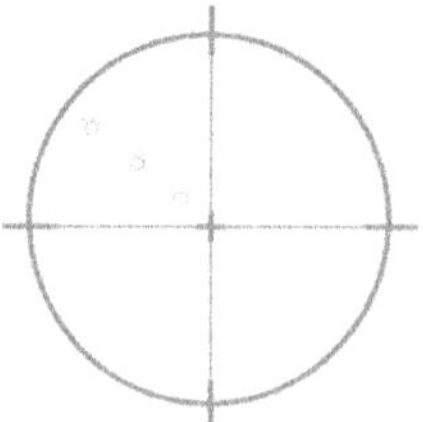

Chapter 62

It was cold enough outside for Ahmed to see his breath when he opened the door to the warehouse. He stepped out, looked both ways, and saw no one about. Ahmed opened the door of his car and climbed in. The Saudi turned the key, felt the engine come to life, and drove out the warehouse door, then shut the warehouse door behind him. He couldn't believe that people actually chose to live in an area this cold, and he would be glad to get back to Paris. Ahmed planned to take a trip to Saudi Arabia for a few weeks. If their mission here was as successful as each of them hoped, they would have earned some free time.

Ahmed had spent much of the previous day trying to find out where Riaz lived. Every computer search he initiated came up empty. He had called the university and explained he was Riaz's father; they were prohibited by law from giving out any personal information. Then it dawned on him. Probably the easiest way to determine where Riaz lived was to go to the mosque. However, when he arrived, the students he talked to were unaware of Riaz's address. Ahmed finally talked to the imam, who, after some brief questioning, provided the information he needed.

Driving down one of the side streets, Ahmed checked various house numbers until he reached Riaz's apartment building. He parked one block away so no one would tie the vehicle and his presence to Riaz. His watch read 2 AM. He now knew that Riaz lived on the third floor, in apartment 321.

None of the building's windows were lit; he expected that all the occupants were asleep. But to be extra careful, as he walked down the hallway toward number 321, he listened to see if he could hear anyone who might be up. He heard nothing coming from any of the other apartments. Ahmed had been told that Riaz shared the apartment with another man.

When he reached Riaz's apartment, Ahmed placed his ear against the door and again heard nothing. He easily picked the feeble lock and silently entered the apartment. There was little furniture, which to Ahmed confirmed the fact that students lived here. Even though it was dark, there was sufficient light coming from the street for Ahmed to make his way through the rooms. He approached the first bedroom door and opened it slowly, hoping that the hinges wouldn't give him away. Ahmed looked in and saw a man sleeping on a twin bed. Since he did not know what Riaz looked like, he would simply have to ask.

Ahmed walked over to where the man slept, turned him on his back, and placed his hand over the man's mouth. The man woke and tried to sit up, but Ahmed pushed him back down and looked into his eyes. He held up his knife in front of the student and saw the young man's eyes go wide.

Ahmed asked him, "Are you Riaz?" The young man shook his head from side to side. "I'm sorry for that," Ahmed whispered. He then brought the knife up to the man's throat and quickly made a deep slice. The man tried to scream but Ahmed only heard a bubbling sound. The young student struggled for just a few seconds before his life drained away. Ahmed stood and wiped the blood from his knife on the sheet before heading to the second bedroom.

Ahmed opened the second door and entered the bedroom. Another young man, who he hoped was Riaz, lay asleep in the bed. After Ahmed took only one step into the room, Riaz turned over and jumped up. "Who are you and what are you doing here?"

Without answering, Ahmed leapt at Riaz and wrestled him to the floor. Once he had control of the young man, Ahmed brought the knife up in front of Riaz's eyes. "I will not hurt you if you answer my questions. There's no need for violence here. If you understand, nod your head."

Riaz quickly nodded his head. "I understand that Hadi spoke to you about what he was doing. Is that correct?"

Riaz whispered, "Yes."

"Did he ask you for advice on what he should do?"

"Yes."

"What did you tell him?"

"I told him I couldn't give him any advice, but I suggested he talked with the imam," Riaz answered with a quavering voice.

"Did he tell you anything else?"

"No, it was a very short conversation."

"And who did you tell about the conversation you had with him?

"I told no one, I swear." Riaz answered.

Ahmed looked at him and stated, "I believe you, but unfortunately, this is going to end badly for you." Ahmed pushed the knife deeply into Riaz's chest. He died instantly.

Once again, Ahmed wiped off his knife. He made his way to the apartment door and walked into the hallway. In the dim hallway light, Ahmed noticed that he had someone's blood on his arm and shirt. As he walked down the stairs and arrived at the second floor, he looked down the hallway. He saw a young woman of maybe 20 standing outside her door.

She asked him, "I heard some noise coming from upstairs. Do you know what happened?"

Ahmed walked toward her smiling and stated, "One of the guys up there was drunk and fell down. He seemed to be okay." As he approached, she began to back up. He reached out, grabbed her long blonde hair, and easily snapped her neck.

Twenty minutes later, Ahmed was sound asleep in the warehouse.

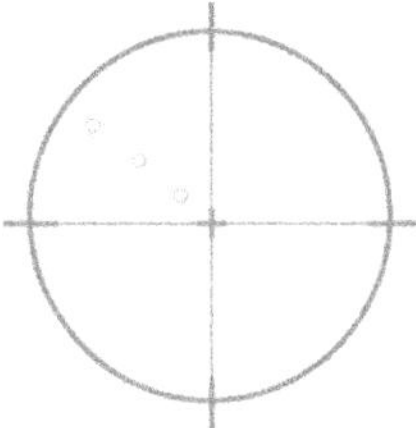

Chapter 63

For the first time in his career as a warrior for Allah, Samir's stomach was churning and causing him some distress. Previously, he had purchased some over-the-counter acid reducers. He continued chewing them, yet they brought little relief. Samir was surprised that he was having this reaction to the stress of the mission. During the Paris attacks, he had suffered no such problems. But today was different and he realized he would have to put this out of his mind and focus on the job at hand.

Looking at his watch once again, he decided to move up his review of plans with Omar, Saad, and Nasser. He stepped out of the office and called for the three of them to join him. Samir also asked Chuck to come in as well. When everybody was seated, he stated, "You understand that your part in our undertaking is critical in bringing fear to the Great Satan. You will have much glory by martyring yourself for Allah. Are each of you ready to go forward?"

Samir looked toward Omar first. "Not only am I ready, but I look forward to serving Allah this way."

Samir looked at all three men as he spoke again. "This is a very difficult task you've been asked to complete. Martyring oneself simply means giving your life in service to Allah, the greatest of all glories. Even so, it runs counter to one's natural inclinations. So, I ask you again, Omar, are there doubts of any kind in your heart?"

Omar responded quietly, "I understand the nature of your question and why you asked it. However, I want you to know that I have no doubts whatsoever. You need not worry about me completing my mission. I am ready and cannot wait for this mission to begin."

Samir looked at Saad. "I have the same question for you. Do you have any doubts in your heart?"

"I do not. I, too, am ready to carry on our battle against America. I know that my sacrifice will be just one of many, and I am fully prepared to go forward tonight. Please be assured, Samir, you need not be worried about my determination or dedication to our cause. Like Omar, I am anxious for this mission to begin."

Samir now looked at Nasser, who responded immediately. "I stand with my brothers. There is no doubt in my heart about what I'm going to do tonight. I do not fear death, I embrace it, for I know Allah will smile upon me and usher me into paradise."

Samir somehow felt humbled in the presence of these men. Unlike himself, they would not escape death tonight. He tried to look into his own heart to determine whether he could do what each of the three men before him would do this evening. He felt tremendous pride in his men. It was clear to him that he had chosen them well.

Samir continued, "Have each of you checked your explosive vest?" Each of the men indicated he had. "Do we need to go over the operation of those vests?"

Omar answered, "Samir, we know it is your responsibility to check to make sure we are ready. But I want you to know that the three of us have talked about this mission for many days now. We have checked and rechecked the vests. Each of us has explained to the other two how to operate these vests and we are ready. Again, there is nothing for you to be concerned about."

"Thank you for your dedication to our mission and your individual responsibilities. I see you are well prepared. May the blessings of Allah be upon you."

Samir turned to Chuck and asked, "What time do you think you need to leave to drop these men off at their hotels and be back in time to take us to the helicopter charter?"

"To be safe, we should leave here no later than 8 PM. I'm going to have to drop them off on a road off the Strip, which is also known as

Las Vegas Blvd. I understand that the Strip itself has been closed for tonight's celebration. That should give them plenty of time to reach their hotel. Furthermore, it should give me plenty of time to get back here and take you to the copters."

"Sounds good to me," Samir responded. Looking at his men, Samir stated, "Now leave and get ready to go with Chuck at 8 PM."

Turning back to Chuck, Samir said. "Bring in the rest of the team so we can review how we're going to proceed tonight?"

Chuck did as requested, and soon returned with the remaining five members of the team.

Samir looked at the men. "We are very close to launching our attack this evening. We have gone over what we're going to do many times, but I want to do it once more. At 10:30 PM, Chuck is going to take me and the two men of my unit to the helicopter company. He will then return here, pick up the remaining three, and bring you to the same location. Two from each unit will be bringing backpacks. As you know, the pilots of the helicopters will believe that we are going to be taking photographs of the fireworks. You will have them filled as we previously discussed and have at least one camera at the opening of the backpack. I will be in the front seat next to the pilot in my helicopter. Khalid will be in the second helicopter. I will lead the assault and the second helicopter will follow us. We will make two runs down the Strip and then fly to the place where we will meet Chuck and Samantha who will be waiting with the RV and car so we can leave as quickly as possible.

"Do any of you have any problem in following through with our plan?" The men shook their heads no. "Okay, I think we're ready. Wait in the warehouse until we leave."

Everything seemed to be going perfectly. Within a few short hours, he would know whether his plans worked as he hoped.

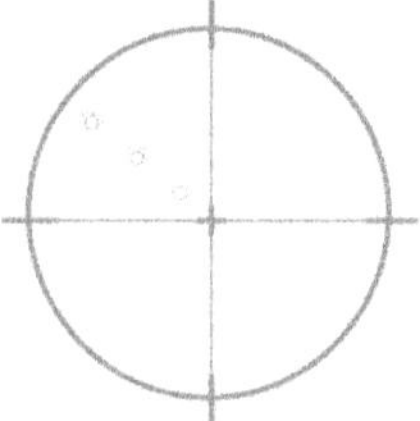

Chapter 64

Setting the explosives took some planning. George would take Ali in the truck and Molly would drive Jawad in the car. Kamil had closely reviewed the ferry schedule to find the best time. George and Ali would take the ferry Hyak, leaving Seattle for Bremerton at 4:20 PM and return to Seattle on the ferry Kaleetan, leaving Bremerton for Seattle at 6:45 PM. Molly and Jawad would leave Seattle heading to Bainbridge Island on the ferry *Wenatchee* at 4:40 PM and return on the ferry Tacoma, leaving for Seattle at 6:30 PM. Those return times would allow both men ample time to meet up and head for the locks.

The two vehicles left the warehouse at 2:30 PM for the ride to downtown Seattle. George pulled into line at the terminal after the ferry scheduled to leave at 3 PM had pulled away from the dock. Molly pulled into the line for her ferry after the 3:45 PM ferry departed. That allowed both vehicles to be near the head of the line, which would ensure that they would be one of the first cars on their respective ferries.

When given the go-ahead, George drove the truck onto the Hyak. After parking, he and Ali exited their vehicle and walked up the stairs to the concession stand. They purchased a cup of coffee and found seats. The ferry was only half full at this time of day. Ali placed his backpack under the table near his feet.

Once the ferry had pulled away from the dock, Ali grabbed his backpack and walked toward the stairs leading down to the truck. When he reached the next level, he quickly went to a door he knew led to the decks below. The sign on the door read Employees Only. Ali looked behind him, both to his right and left, and saw no one. Pushing open the heavy metal door, he stepped over the raised threshold, and quietly closed the door behind him. He waited a second but neither saw nor heard any ferry employees, which eased his mind.

Making his way to the right side of the vessel, he placed his hand on the steel hull in front of him and could feel the waves beating against the outside. He quickly placed one of the four charges from his backpack against the cold steel. It was hidden behind machinery in such a way that it could not be seen by anyone walking by. Thirty feet forward, Ali placed another hidden charge. Ali hustled back to the door, opened it, slipped through, and quickly made his way to the deck above. In a few moments, he had returned to where George's was seated and sat down.

In a subdued tone, George asked, "How did it go?"

"So far so good. No one was anywhere near me, and it was easier than I expected."

Once the ferry docked in Bremerton, George drove off the boat and parked on the street. When the Hyak left on the return trip to Seattle, George drove the vehicle onto the loading dock and was first in line.

Then the two men got out of the truck and took a walk to stretch their legs. They were back in their truck in plenty of time to board the Kaleetan. After the ferry left the dock for Seattle, Ali repeated the steps he had taken on the Hyak. Returning to George's table, Ali smiled and said, "This part of the mission was much easier than I expected. I have seen no security officers on either of the vessels. Have you?"

"I've only seen ship handlers and service people. These people obviously don't expect any trouble."

"Their lack of security is much appreciated," Ali laughed. "I hope it is as easy for Jawad as it has been for us."

***

Molly and Jawad's similar mission nearly started off in disaster. When Molly lined up on the ferry dock, she was in the line that ended up being the last to load. As their car moved forward to board the ferry, she worried that there wouldn't be enough room for her vehicle. Her car was the second to last vehicle allowed to load.

Like George and Ali, Molly and Jawad climbed the steep metal stairs to the deck where the concessions were located. They, too, waited for the ferry to depart. Once the boat had left the dock, Jawad made his way to the door leading below. Just as he was about to open the door, he heard someone say, "Hey, buddy, what are you doing?" The sound of the man's voice shook Jawad to his very core.

He looked at the man and responded, "I was going to get some coffee and bring it down to my car."

The man pointed at the sign that said Employees Only. "This is the wrong door for you." He then pointed toward the front of the boat and said, "The door to the stairs going up is that way."

"Sorry," replied Jawad, "thanks for your help." Once in the concession area, Jawad took a seat near Molly.

She smiled at him. "That was quick."

"I didn't get it done. Someone stopped me from going below deck. I'll wait for a few minutes and try again." The two sat in silence, lost in thought. Molly was now concerned that if he was caught, she might be found out. Jawad steeled himself for another try.

Five minutes later, he walked down to the same door, glanced around quickly and saw no one. He opened the door and descended the stairs. Jawad placed his charges as Ali had done.

A ferry employee, 30 feet from where Jawad was working, did not see him initially. That changed when Jawad stood to leave.

The man shouted at Jawad, "What the hell are you doing down here?" He ran toward where Jawad stood. He looked down and saw the charge that Jawad had placed. "Oh, my God, what is that?" He turned to face Jawad and was rewarded with a sharp pain in his stomach from Jawad's knife. The man collapsed to the floor. Jawad looked around and saw no one. He pulled the man to another door a few feet away, opened it, and saw a variety of cleaning equipment. Jawad pulled the man into the closet and covered him with a tarp that was lying nearby.

He quickly returned to the upper deck, where he found Molly waiting anxiously. She whispered to him, "Did everything go okay this time?" Jawad nodded but did not explain what just happened. The two returned to their vehicle and drove off after the ferry docked.

The time passed quickly as they waited for their next ferry for the return trip to Seattle. Jawad was able to place the charges on the second ferry without interruption. When they docked in Seattle and drove off the ferry, they were surprised to see Seattle Police Department cars with their lights flashing. The police vehicles had blocked off any approach to the ferry dock next to them. Molly looked at him and asked, "I wonder what's going on."

"I don't know and I don't care. We need to meet up with George so that we can carry out our next assignment." Molly said nothing further as they drove away.

***

Following Molly's car off the ferry were Dick Jensen, his wife Toni, and their two daughters, Michelle, 12, and Jordan, 8. They had decided to come to Seattle to watch the famous New Year's Eve fireworks display. Toni had initially been against coming to Seattle because she believed Jordan would fall asleep long before the fireworks went off at midnight. After a long discussion with Dick, Toni had finally agreed. They had decided to have dinner in the city and catch a movie before finding a place to observe the fireworks.

***

Molly pulled into a parking lot not too far from the ferry terminal. George had already arrived and was waiting with his lights off. Molly pulled up next to him, got out of her car, and went to the truck. George and Ali exited the truck and got into the car with Jawad. The three men drove off, heading for the Ballard Locks, while Molly drove the truck straight to the warehouse. She knew Kamil needed it later in the evening.

George looked at Jawad and asked, "Did you have any problems?"

"None at all. How did you guys do?"

"No problem, my brother." George gave a high five to both men. George and Ali both wore big smiles. Jawad, on the other hand, had a sick feeling in the pit of his stomach, hoping he had not disrupted the success of their plans.

* * *

At 9 PM, Kamil hooked Majid's boat to the truck. He and Majid drove to the Juanita Beach boat launch. It took just a few minutes for them to launch the boat and tie it to the dock. After Majid stepped into the boat, Kamil stated, "Stay with the boat until I get back with Asad. I will not be long."

Kamil quickly drove back to the warehouse. He returned with Asad, towing Asad's boat, and together, the two men launched it with no problem. Both he and Asad stepped into the boat. Since the keys were already in the ignition, he started the engine. "You're ready to go." He stepped back on the dock and walked up to Majid's boat. "Start it up." Majid turned the engine over and it came to life immediately. "It's going to take you a while to get there. Make sure you get close enough so that you can see Moiz when he stops. Allah be with you." Kamil waved them off and watched them move away from the dock.

* * *

After stopping for a quick bite to eat at Dicks, George and his two passengers arrived at the Ballard Locks at 11 PM. He parked near a chain link fence and the three men headed for the locks. All of a sudden, a man, obviously an employee of the locks in a dark uniform, confronted the three men. "What are you doing here? The locks are closed."

George pulled out a silenced Glock and pointed it at the man. "Unless you want to die, you will do exactly as I say. Do you understand?"

The man, whose throat suddenly was as dry as desert sand, croaked, "Yes, please don't hurt me. I'll do anything you want."

"Lead me to the control room. Now!"

"Yes, yes, this way, just follow me." The man turned and George followed behind with gun still in hand. Jawad and Ali split off and headed for the locks. The man led George to a building, used his key, and both men passed through the door. They walked up one flight of stairs and through another set of doors. "This is it," the man stated.

George looked at the man and stated, "Lie down on the floor, flat on your stomach. I don't want you to cause any problems, understand?"

"Yes, sir, I don't want to cause you any problems either," the man replied as he lay down on the floor. George walked up to him and fired one silenced round into the back of his head. The man did not move again. George took a small package of explosives out of his coat pocket and placed it under the control panel, the timer already set to blow at midnight.

Once George was outside again, he could see Jawad and Ali placing explosives on the gates to the locks. Fifteen minutes later, George saw them walking toward the car. "Did you have any problems?"

"None at all. When those charges go off, these locks are finished," Ali responded. "Let's get out of here before someone sees us and calls the police." George started the truck and they were soon headed for the warehouse.

* * *

When Kamil got back to the warehouse after dropping off the boats and their "skippers," he saw that Moiz Hossien, Yaser and Mohammad, who were to drive the explosive-filled trucks, were ready to leave. At 11:15 PM, the trucks left the warehouse. Kamil stood by the open roll-up door and watched the red taillights of the three trucks fade into the night. He walked back toward the RV.

"It's time for us to leave. We will know the success of our mission by simply listening to the radio. Let's go."

Everyone but Ali climbed into the RV, and George drove it out of the warehouse. Once it was clear of the door, Ali turned out the warehouse lights, pulled down the metal door, and got in the RV as well. The RV headed for Interstate 90, heading east toward the Cascade Mountains.

* * *

Dick and Toni were parked in a lot with a good view, waiting for the fireworks to begin. Dick looked into the backseat and saw that both of his daughters were sound asleep. He turned to his wife, "I guess you were right. It doesn't look like they're going to be able to stay awake to see the fireworks go off. Once again, you have proven me wrong."

"I don't think it's a matter of being right or wrong," she said. "At their age, it's hard to stay up this late. Do you want to stay here and watch the fireworks or should we head back?"

"I've seen these fireworks many times. If it's all right with you, let's go home."

"I think that's a good idea."

Dick turned the car on and headed for the ferry terminal. Soon they reached the road running along the waterfront. They could see the ferry terminal up ahead. Suddenly he heard his twelve-year-old daughter Michelle, pipe up. "Where are we going? I thought we were going to watch the fireworks."

"Honey, you were sound asleep, so we thought we would head home," Toni said. "I think it's best we do that."

"Mom, you promised we could watch the fireworks display. Why would we go home now when the show is about to begin?"

Little Jordan joined in. "This isn't fair! You promised! You have always said that I should never break a promise I made, but now you're doing what you told me not to do."

Toni looked at Dick and said, "Well, what should we do?"

Dick saw the turn into the ferry terminal just ahead. "I guess we shouldn't make a promise we can't keep." He turned the car away from the ferry and headed back to their lookout. Dick smiled when his daughters cheered and then winked at his wife.

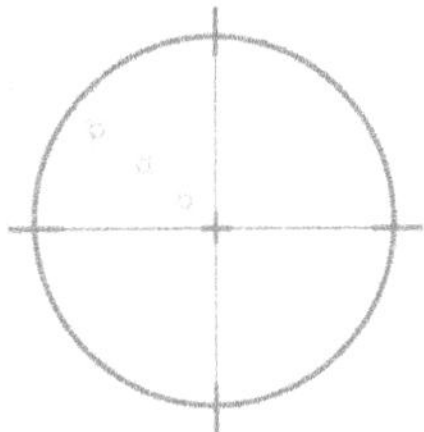

Chapter 65

Samir had not moved since Chuck had left his office. His stomach acid had subsided somewhat, giving him a bit of peace. He wondered how Kamil and Mohammed were doing. He occasionally brought up CNN on his phone, but there was no indication of either an attack beginning or failing. It was of no concern to him since each of the other attacks was scheduled to begin around midnight also.

His thoughts were disrupted by a sharp rap on the door. He looked up and saw Chuck leaning into the office. "What's going on, Chuck?"

"It's almost 8 PM and I should be getting these guys to their hotels. Do you have any other instructions?"

"No, there's nothing left to be said. Let me know how it goes when you get back."

"Will do." Chuck left Samir lost in his own thoughts. He walked up to Omar, Saad, and Nasser. "It's about time we leave. Are you guys ready to go?"

Omar responded, "We are, and before you ask, we have checked and rechecked our backpacks. We are ready for what the night brings."

"All right then. Let's get loaded up." Walking over to the vehicle, Omar climbed in the front passenger seat and held his backpack on his lap. The other two men got in the back seat. Chuck turned around and looked at the men in the back. "Let's buckle the seatbelts. If we get stopped by the police, we don't want to give them a reason to check us out." He nodded to Khalid, who was standing near the roll-up door. Khalid opened the door for them and they drove out. Chuck looked in the rearview mirror and saw the door was already being shut.

It took about an hour for Chuck to drop the three men off. Each had to walk about two blocks to reach their respective hotels. He had wished each of the men good luck as he got out of his car. He was glad he was not going to martyr himself like they were.

Chuck returned to the warehouse and parked in front of the door, got out, and entered the outer door leading to the office. Samir was not there so he walked into the warehouse and over to his RV. He poked his head in and stated, "Samantha, come with me. I'll open the door and you can drive the car in."

She had been cleaning up after having fixed dinner for the men. Samantha placed her dishtowel on the counter and walked out into the warehouse. Samantha followed Chuck to the door, watched him roll it up and then drove the car in. As she got out of the car, Chuck closed the door. "How did everything go?" she asked.

"A piece of cake. I can't believe how many people were roaming the Strip. Since it's closed off to cars, the nearest I could get to the hotels was about two blocks. The guys walked from there. It shouldn't be a problem for them though. We won't know for sure how they're doing until just after midnight. Are you sure you understand our part in this mission?"

"Yes, I think so. It doesn't seem to be very complicated. You're going to deliver the men to the helicopters. I'm going to drive the RV to where we are going to pick them up. You will join me as soon as you drop the last group off. Is there any more to it than that?"

"No, it's pretty simple." He and Samantha had driven to the rendezvous point the day before. It was to the east of Vegas where the residential areas stopped. It also had quick access to the highway heading for Boulder City.

Samantha spoke up again. "You'll finish dropping them off at about 11, isn't that right?"

"Yes, why?"

"How long do you think it will take before the helicopters land at the rendezvous point?"

"I can't say for sure, but they want to be over the city when the fireworks start at midnight. They will make one pass down the Strip from south to north, turn around and come back down the Strip, then head for the rendezvous point. I would expect they would be there by no later than 12:30 AM. Anyway, that's my best guess."

"How long will we wait for them to arrive? I mean, if something happens to them, I don't want to be sitting there all night. We want to make sure that we get away clean."

"Well," Chuck answered, "let's play that by ear. We won't hang around too long. I agree that we need to save ourselves."

At about 10:15 PM, Samir left his office and walked up to two of the men in his group, Abdullah and Karim, who would be in his helicopter. "Are you ready to leave?" Each nodded. Chuck was already seated in the driver's seat. Samir opened the door and stepped in; the two men got into the backseat. Samir looked back at the two men and said, "I want you to double check and make sure we have what is needed in your backpack." He watched the two men open their packs, take out the cameras, and then examine the remaining contents.

Abdullah said in an even voice, "Samir, we have what we need."

Samir tapped Chuck on the arm, "Let's go."

As they drove the 20 minutes to where the helicopter company was located, none of the men felt the need to talk. This was the time they had dreamed about. They were about to execute an attack that had started as a mere idea years before. When the car pulled up to the helicopter company's office, the three men exited the car and Chuck immediately drove off. Samir turned to Abdullah and Karim, "You stay out here while I go in and confirm our arrangements."

Samir walked into the office and saw two men seated behind the counter. He smiled at them and stated, "I believe we're scheduled for a ride with you." One of the men stood. Samir took out the receipt that Samantha had given him and handed it to the man.

The man looked at Samir quizzically and asked, "Are you the only one going? I was told there were going to be six and that we needed two helicopters."

"No, you're right, two of my friends are outside. They are as excited as little kids at Christmas. We only had one car and that has returned to get the remaining three guys. They should be here before 11. Is that all right?"

The man replied, "Yeah, that works. We'll take off at about 11:40, so we have plenty of time."

"Is there anything else you need from me? Samantha told me she took care of everything earlier."

"There's nothing left for you to do other than enjoy your flight." The man turned around and sat down again.

Samir walked outside and joined his two men. "Everything is ready to go. We're just waiting for the other three to get here."

They waited for what seemed like hours before Chuck returned with the other team. Khalid, Rashid, and Mustafa stepped out of the car. Samir walked into the office once again and stated, "Everyone's here now."

The man who had talked with Samir previously stated, "We'll be out in a minute to take you to the helicopters. We'll give you a short run down on the safety features and then we'll be on our way."

"Great," Samir responded and walked out to wait with his men. Five minutes later, the two men came out of the office and walked up to where Samir and his men were standing. The man who had talked with Samir stated, "My name is Frank Jordan," and pointing to the other man stated, "This is Blaine Jones. We'll be your pilots tonight. Just follow us."

It was a short five-minute walk to where the birds were located. Frank described the type of helicopter they were going to be flying in and the safety information he was required to give them. "That's about it. It's pretty straightforward and I think you will have a great time. Let's climb in and take off." Samir climbed into the front seat next to Frank. Frank turned and looked at the two men in the rear seat and pointed at their backpacks. "Why do you have those?"

Samir answered for them, "They are carrying their camera equipment. They want to take photos to take home. I, on the other hand, just want to experience the flight and the fireworks."

"Okay, then. Let's get this puppy fired up and on the way." Samir heard the engine wind up and soon felt the helicopter lift off. He looked to his right and saw the second helicopter rise off the ground.

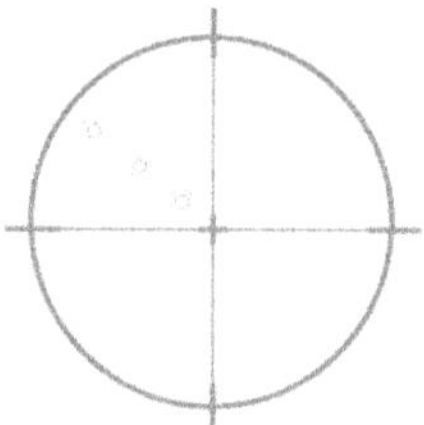

Chapter 66

Omar had spent the last hour and a half sitting on the bed waiting to begin his part of the operation. For the fifth time in the last half hour, he looked at his watch. It read 11:45 PM. He took out his cell phone and called both Saad and Nasser. "My friends, now is the time to begin."

Omar walked around his hotel room spraying lighter fluid on the bed, on his clothes and on the newspapers he had crumpled up and placed around the room. For good measure, he sprayed the carpet also. He then took out the long nosed lighter, pushed it on and proceeded to light each area where the lighter fluid had been sprayed. In seconds, the room was engulfed in flames. Omar opened the door to the room and shut it quickly. As he walked toward the stairwell, he sprayed lighter fluid on the carpet and walls. When he reached the stairwell, Omar lit the lighter fluid on the carpet, opened the door, and ran down two floors to his next room.

Since the young man had previously been to these rooms, he knew exactly where to go. Omar took the second key card of his pocket, slid it into the door, and saw the green light appear. In the second room, he proceeded to do the same as he had done in the first. That room also burst into flame.

As in the first room, the fire suppression system did not activate. Omar knew that none of the fire suppression equipment located in this hotel or the other hotels would activate. The arson investigators who would later examine all three hotels would learn that each hotel's fire suppression system had been compromised. They would eventually discover that the systems had been deactivated and destroyed in such a manner that it could not be reactivated easily. The $50,000 that Samir had paid to the man was money well spent.

As Omar left the room, smoke was already pouring out. He ran down the hall and turned the corner toward the stairwell. Suddenly the door to one of the rooms opened and out stepped a man and a woman. They appeared to be in their early 50s and dressed for a fun evening on New Year's Eve. The man could see smoke coming around the corner. He stepped in front of Omar and said, "What's going on here? What are you doing?"

Without even thinking, Omar sprayed both of the individuals with the lighter fluid and ignited the liquid. Both human torches ran screaming toward the stairwell as he followed. They collapsed in front of him. Omar stepped over the bodies and ran down the stairwell to where his last room was located.

Within five minutes, he had completed his tasks in the final room and headed for the lobby. In the other two hotels, the same act was being carried out by Saad and Nasser with similar results. Omar finally reached the lobby and stood there. No one seemed to realize what was occurring on the floors above. Soon, however, Omar heard calls coming into the front desk. He could hear the clerks talking about fire, making desperate calls to 911 and their own security team.

An announcement came over the hotel loudspeaker warning those in the casino and in the hotel that there was a fire in the building and that they should exit the hotel immediately.

In a matter of a moments, people were rushing by Omar in a panic while others were calm. When it seemed that no more people could possibly enter the lobby on their way to exiting the hotel, Omar made his way to the center of the lobby.

As busy as Michaela, the reservation clerk, was, she saw Omar standing against the wall, watching people hurrying to the exit. She could not take her eyes off him as he started moving. He seemed to be nervous. When Omar stopped in the middle of the lobby and looked up as if praying, she knew something was wrong. Immediately, she dropped to the floor.

Finishing his short prayer to Allah, Omar closed his eyes and pushed the button that activated the explosives contained in the vest he was wearing.

Immediately, Omar dissolved into a mist of red. Most of the people in the lobby did not hear the explosion nor realize that their lives had come to an end. The damage was extensive. The people outside the hotel who escaped injury were shocked not only at the explosion, but also at the fires coming out of the windows above. The people were stunned and speechless as they heard the two other explosions in the other hotels. For a moment there was silence and then the entire Las Vegas Strip erupted in screams.

Amidst the devastation, Michaela wondered whether she was dead. She was covered by dust and other debris. The young clerk realized she could not hear anything as a result of being so close to the explosion. Slowly, she got to her knees and stood up. What Michaela saw caused her to turn away and vomit on the floor. The center of the lobby was littered with the results of Omar's act. Various limbs not attached to their bodies were strewn about. Blood was everywhere from the dead and wounded. As she looked back again, it appeared to her that the wounded were screaming, though she heard nothing. The young woman collapsed in shock.

Hovering above the Strip, Frank, who was piloting Samir's helicopter, also saw the explosions. He exclaimed, "What the hell is going on?"

Samir was watching as well. Those explosions were the signal he was waiting for. Pulling a Glock out of a hidden holster, he pointed it at Frank's head. "I am now in control of this helicopter and you will do exactly as I say. If you do not follow my instructions to the letter, you will be killed, and I will fly this helicopter. Just so you understand, I have flown helicopters for the past five years. Do you understand what I'm saying?"

"Yes, but you can't do that."

"I am doing that. And if you get any ideas that you're going to try to take my weapon away, you should know that both men behind me are equally armed. This is what you're going to do." Pointing to his left, Samir continued, "You're going to fly to the south end of the Strip and level off at 75 feet. Then you are going to fly the entire length of the Strip at 50 miles an hour. Do you understand what I'm saying?"

"I can't do that. It's against the law. We have rules here about where you can fly and at what height. Don't you understand that?"

Samir stared at the man. "There are new rules operating tonight and I'm the one making them. I'm not going to warn you again. Either do what I say or die. Your choice."

Frank responded quickly, "Okay, okay, don't shoot me. I'll do what you ask." With that, he banked the helicopter to the left and flew toward the end of the Strip.

Khalid, who had taken control of the second helicopter, spoke to Blaine. "You will follow behind your friend, getting no closer than 200 feet to him." Khalid's gun rested against the side of the pilot's head. Blaine also banked to the left and followed the first helicopter.

Samir's helicopter was now 75 feet above the Strip. He looked at the pilot, "Okay, let's go. No more than 50 miles an hour." The helicopter began moving forward. The two men behind Samir had opened the windows next to them. Previously they had taken out their camera equipment and placed it on the floor of the helicopter. Now they reached in and felt the hard steel of the hand grenades. They pulled the pins and began dropping them on the unsuspecting partiers below.

Don Martin had not heard the thumping sound of helicopter blades since his time in Vietnam as a young Marine. Without conscious thought, he ducked down to avoid the low-flying helicopter. He looked up and saw it moving slowly over him. Don saw a hand emerge from the rear window and drop something. His only thought was that this pilot was in deep trouble for flying so low. He didn't realize they were grenades until it was too late. The grenade exploded near him, taking his life. This New Year's Eve celebration accomplished in a few seconds what the North Vietnamese Army was unable to do over five decades ago.

Frank did not see the grenades fall nor hear the screams of those injured by the blasts. From the second helicopter, the men were also dropping hand grenades. However, it was different for Blaine, the pilot of the second helicopter. He could see the explosions below him. He screamed, "What the hell are you guys doing?" Blaine was rewarded with the pistol pushing against his temple even harder.

As Samir's helicopter reached the end of the crowded Strip, Samir ordered, "Circle around; we're going back down the Strip. Once we finish that, you can set down and let us out." As Frank made the turn and began his second run, all he could see was fire—fire from the hotels and fire from the explosions on the Strip below. Frank applied more power so that they could end the madness quickly.

Blaine, a vet, could see what was happening in front of him. He saw the explosions and the people falling to the ground. He screamed, "I can't do this!" He banked the helicopter hard to the right and drove it toward the ground.

Khalid could see the ground rushing up at him. Khalid yelled, "You will do as..." His remaining words were left unsaid as the helicopter crashed and exploded on a side street.

When Samir's helicopter reached the end of the Strip, it banked and headed toward their take-off point. Samir looked back to find the second helicopter, but he saw nothing. Far away at the other end of the Strip, he could see a large, separate fire and had to presume that Khalid and his men were lost.

Frank looked at Samir frantically and said, "I'm heading back to my base."

Samir shook his head, "We're not going there." He then explained where he wanted the helicopter to land.

Five minutes later, Samir saw the headlights of the car and the RV. He pointed at the vehicles. "Land next to them." The helicopter descended, and Samir felt a slight bump as it touched down. "Shut down the engine. Stay here until my men and I have left. Do you understand?"

"Yes, yes, I understand. You're not going to hurt me, are you?"

"I will not harm you as long as you follow my instructions." Samir opened the door and stepped out, as did Abdullah, who had been sitting behind him. Without warning, Karim put his gun to the back of Frank's head and pulled the trigger. Frank flopped forward on the controls and did not move. His blood covered the Plexiglas and the instrument panel in front of his body.

As they walked to the RV, Karim asked Samir what he had said to the pilot. Samir responded, "I told him I would not harm him if he followed my instructions. I didn't say anything about you doing so, however, Karim." The shooter started laughing as they entered the RV. Samir walked up to Chuck and stated, "It is time for us to get out of here and make our escape."

"Where are the others?"

"For some reason, their helicopter crashed at the end of the first pass. I'm not sure what caused it, but I am sure they will not be joining us here." Chuck started the RV and began their escape from the city that was now in flames and filled with the screams of the living, the wounded, and those who would soon die.

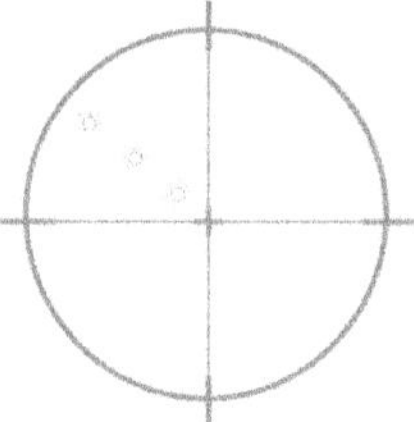

Chapter 67

Las Vegas Boulevard, known as the Strip by locals, was packed with people, and along with those people, were the medics, police officers, and other security personnel necessary to keep order. In every intersection, police and fire had set up emergency stations to deal with problems that came up in a New Year's Eve celebration. In usual years, this was limited to thefts and drunks.

Today was different because no one could've expected the kind of carnage that now surrounded them. People were bringing the wounded and dead to the medics to examine. It simply overwhelmed the number of medical personnel who were available.

Officers on the scene learned that the damage done by the exploding grenades might be the second largest cause of casualties in this disaster. The Strip was in absolute panic. As much as the police tried to arrange an orderly exit, it was simply impossible. Over half a million people were moving in a manner that could only be described as absolute chaos. If a person slipped and fell, he or she was trampled by those behind. If someone tried to stop and help the fallen, they too were knocked over and trampled. Soon the entire Strip was filled with blood of those killed or injured by the hand grenades and those trampled by people attempting to flee.

Those who remained in the middle of Las Vegas Boulevard were the lucky ones. Grenades were no longer falling and they were left alone by those who were seeking to escape. They did not escape unharmed, however, because the trauma of the event would remain with them the rest of their lives.

The medics tried to help those they could and to make comfortable the ones whose lives would soon end. While the medics continued to triage their patients, their work was simply doomed to fail. Medical vehicles were unable to come to the aid of the medics as the surrounding streets were full of panicked people, ambulances, and bodies. The medics, wherever they were, did yeomen's work that day.

One such medic, Jaron Reese, struggled to help those who were brought to him as well as he could. He quickly ran out of supplies and then, simply tried to make people comfortable. Finally, when no one was asking for his immediate help, he stood to look around. For as far as he could see, both up and down the Strip, the road was littered with bodies. Some, he could tell, had been slashed with the shrapnel from the grenades. Others had suffered from the trauma of being trampled by those trying to get away.

Jaron, as if in slow motion, collapsed to his knees. His hands covered his face as he tried to hold back the sobs that racked his body. At that point, he too, became one of the victims though his injuries were not visible.

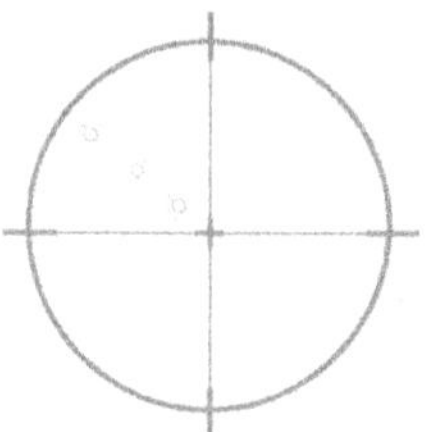

Chapter 68

The *Wenatchee* was still docked at the ferry terminal in Seattle as the police continued their investigation into the death of the ferry employee. Another ferry employee had found him in the closet where he had been dumped.

The captain of the *Wenatchee* was on the bridge when he heard two loud muffled explosions. The ferry began to list almost immediately. One of the seamen below called the bridge and informed the captain of the explosions and the resulting damage to the hull. He told the captain nothing could stop the ferry from capsizing. The captain immediately ordered everyone off the ship. Fortunately, no passengers had been allowed to board yet.

Two of the investigating detectives were unable to reach the dock before being thrown into the water. Fully dressed in the frigid water, they swam to a ladder attached to a piling and climbed up onto the dock. Later, when the captain gathered his crew on the dock, he found that a crewmember assigned to the engine room was missing. That man, Bobby Johansson, was found the next day by divers, having drowned in the engine room.

The crews of the other three ferries traveling back and forth across Puget Sound heard the same muffled sounds at the same time the explosives detonated on the *Wenatchee*. After quickly determining the scope of the damage, each captain ordered his crew and passengers to abandon ship, then radioed an S.O.S. to the Coast Guard that they were sinking. The listing caused by flooding hindered their crews' attempts at getting the passengers offloaded.

Within minutes of each other, the ferries had capsized, tossing crew and passengers alike into the frigid winter waters of Puget Sound. On two of the ferries, the crews were only able to launch a few of their life rafts. People who had been thrown into the waters tried to swim to the rafts. Those unable to swim simply disappeared into the waters of Puget Sound. Those who survived that night remember the sounds of the screaming of those who didn't.

The Coast Guard helicopter was flying over Lake Union as security for the boats that were there to watch the fireworks. The pilot had heard the distress call from the ferries and immediately headed to their location. The helicopter approached the ferry that had not been able to launch life rafts. The men in the helicopter were able to see the last moments of the ferry's life, its lights blazing as it slowly turned on its side and slid toward the bottom of Puget Sound. The helicopter pilot flew over and could see people struggling in the water; he dropped a life raft, which opened as soon as it struck the water. People began swimming toward it. The helicopter hovered over the raft, allowing one of the Coast Guardsman to jump into the raft.

Over the next 20 minutes, the man pulled into the raft as many people as he could. By the time additional helicopters arrived, there was no one left to save.

When rescue boats reached the spots where the ferries had gone down, the only sounds they heard were the waves and the quiet sobbing of those in the rafts. All the survivors could see were bodies floating in the water. The only thing the authorities knew was that each boat had radioed a distress signal and then nothing. It would take days, if not weeks, to come up with an accounting of the lives that were lost.

Once the State Department of Transportation officials realized the enormity of their loss, they activated an emergency closure of the floating bridges.

Trooper Ed Smith was a 12-year veteran of the Washington State Patrol. Like other troopers in the Seattle area, he had been briefed on the emergency plan that called for troopers to cordon off access to the bridges. He was traveling eastbound on I-90 at a high rate of speed when he passed a rental truck heading in the same direction. The emergency plan called for stopping traffic before it entered the tunnel before the bridge. Smith quickly realized he could not stop the truck before it entered the tunnel. He passed the truck and entered the tunnel with the intention of stopping it before it reached the bridge. He brought his vehicle to a sliding halt across both lanes of traffic.

Hossien, who was driving the truck, came to a stop a few feet before the trooper's car. He heard the trooper yell that the bridge was closed and knew he would not be able to carry out his mission. As the trooper approached the driver's side, Hossien detonated the explosives. The trooper and both vehicles disappeared in a flash of fire and dust.

While Hossien was unable to destroy the eastbound bridge, the explosion caused the collapse of a good portion of the tunnel leading to the bridge, making travel across that portion of the bridge impossible.

* * *

Mohammed and Yasser were traveling westbound on I-90 in their respective vehicles at the same time. Troopers who were speeding to block the westbound span of the bridge did not arrive in time to stop the two men. Driving side by side until they reached the middle of the bridge, Mohammed and Yasser looked at each other, nodded, and initiated the detonators in their trucks. The resulting explosions destroyed the center portion of the Mercer Island Bridge.

* * *

Majid and Asad were in their boats and approximately 100 yards from their target, the Evergreen Point Bridge. They both saw the fiery explosion to the south caused by Mohammed and Yaser on the Mercer Island Bridge. While troopers had stopped traffic heading westbound into Seattle on the Evergreen Point Bridge, traffic directly in front of them going eastbound still flowed freely. This was the direction they expected Moiz to come from.

As the two men sat there with their boats in idle, Moiz's truck with a red light on top traveled across the bridge. They immediately put the engines into gear and began speeding across the water toward the bridge. Majid had both men on a conference call so that they could coordinate their detonations. Within a minute or two, Majid and Asad brought their boats under the westbound lanes. Majid looked at Asad and nodded. He spoke into the phone, "5-4-3-2-1-0."

The three men simultaneously pressed their detonators, the explosions heavily damaging the westbound portion of the Evergreen Point Bridge and destroying the eastbound lanes.

As fireworks exploded all over Seattle celebrating the coming New Year, no one heard the muffled explosions that occurred at the Ballard Locks. While government emergency rescue crews went into action, no one seemed to notice that the water level in Lake Washington was quickly dropping. Though limited in scope, Kamil's attack had brought catastrophe to the Seattle area.

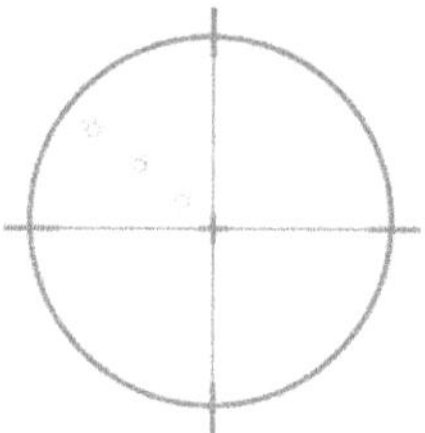

Chapter 69

Mohammed walked outside the warehouse and could feel a chill in the air that ran through his bones. It had taken a long time to adjust to the weather in Paris after he moved there from Saudi Arabia and he knew that the cold of San Francisco in late December was a climate he could probably never come to get used to. Mohammed looked at his watch and saw that it was nearing 8 PM. It was time for the operation to begin. He walked back into the warehouse and enjoyed the warmth that surrounded him.

Mohammed walked up to Abdul, the man who would join him on his boat, and asked him to come into the office. Abdul, at 35, was older than most of the men who traveled with Mohammed. He did not have the hellfire of youth in his eyes, but rather the calmness that comes with experience. Abdul gave off an air of quiet confidence that inspired the younger men.

Once they were seated, Mohammed initiated the conversation. "My friend, we're about to begin the mission we have dreamed about for so long. Will and I will take Bakir and Jalal to their boat ramp first. You'll remain here until I return. I want you to go through our boat very thoroughly one more time. The explosives we will use need to be checked once again. The last thing we want to happen is to have some issue with them. I hope to be back within an hour or so. At that time, we will leave for our launch point. Do you understand?"

"I do. Everything will be done as you have asked."

"Good. Let's go out into the warehouse and you can bid farewell to Bakir and Jalal." As they approached the two men, Mohammed thought that these men looked so much alike that they could be brothers. Each of them stood just short of 5 foot 10 and weighed just over 120 pounds. Both were deeply tanned with the same short black hair. He knew that Jalal was three years older than Bakir, but it was not evident as he looked at them. The only difference that Mohammed could detect between the two was that Bakir was serious, and Jalal had a smile that never left his face. Mohammed waved Will over to join them by their boat. "Bakir and Jalal, it is time for you to leave. Will and I will take you to your launch point and make sure your boat is in proper working order. As we discussed before, you will slowly make your way to the support tower. You should arrive there no earlier than 11:30 PM. You know what to do after that."

Bakir, the leader of this unit, responded. "We do. Both Jalal and I have studied the photographs and have discussed among ourselves how we intend to proceed. Once our mission is completed, we will drive the boat as quickly as possible to the location where Will is to pick us up. We will let the boat drift back into the bay so there's no connection to our departure point." With grim determination in his eyes, Bakir finished his thought. "Then we will join up with you to go after the professors."

"And we'll attack them just like we are attacking San Francisco tonight," Mohammed responded. He walked to the back of the truck and looked at the boat sitting on its trailer. "Will, did the men double-check the explosives on this boat?"

"They did. Everything appears to be in order. Are you ready to leave?"

"Yes. Let's get moving. We have a long night before us." Mohammed climbed into the front passenger seat and was joined in the truck by the three other men.

While it took some time to reach the launch point, the time seemed to pass quickly. As they pulled into the empty boat ramp, Mohammed, Bakir, and Jalal got out of the truck and helped guide Will as he backed the trailer into the water and then unloaded the boat. Will quickly pulled the trailer out of the water and waited for Mohammed to join him. Bakir and Jalal were in the boat and Mohammed was holding the line attached to the bow that kept the boat from drifting away. "Start the engine!"

Mohammed heard the engine turn over and engage. "Travel slowly and keep close to the shoreline until you are ready to make for the tower. We will meet up later tonight. May the grace of Allah shine upon you."

Jalal yelled, "Allah Akbar." Bakir shouted the same farewell. Slowly, the boat turned away and faded into the night.

Mohammed climbed back into the truck and looked at Will. "The attack has started. Now get me back to the warehouse so I can do my part." The return trip to the warehouse seemed to take longer than the outbound trip. In Mohammed's experience, return trips usually seemed shorter. He attributed these feelings to the fact his part of the mission had yet to start. When they pulled into the warehouse, Mohammed addressed Will. "Please get the other boat ready while I talk with Fahd and Talib, the men who will drive the rental trucks."

Mohammed walked over and entered the RV, where Fahd and Talib were sitting at the dinette. He stood before them and looked at each of them without speaking. Fahd stood over 6 foot 6 and was much stockier than most Saudis. A short and well-trimmed black beard covered his face and hid the scar that sliced across his lower jaw. Fahd, because of the scar, had not been required to be clean shaven. Mohammed had never seen a smile creep across his face, but the fire in his eyes matched the anger in his heart. At 30 years of age, he had been fighting on behalf of Allah for over a decade now. Fahd had lost too many friends to the weapons of his enemies.

Mohammed reached over and placed his hand on Fahd's shoulder, "You will have your revenge tonight, my friend." With coldness in his eyes, Fahd's head barely moved up and down in acknowledgment.

Talib did not notice Fahd's response because of the excitement he felt for his upcoming mission. This was his first action of any kind, and he knew that the time was drawing near. While Talib only stood 5 foot 6, he was well-built from the daily workouts he had become accustomed to. Though it was not evident when looking at him, Mohammed had seen the toughness in him during their training.

"Well, my friends, the time has come for us to part. I will be leaving with Abdul shortly to take our boat to the launch point. Both of you will leave the warehouse at 11 PM. That should put you at your target close to the time of our attack. Each of you has agreed to martyr yourself in this operation. Do you still feel you can do that?"

"You know me, Mohammed. I will not fail you or Allah," answered Fahd.

Mohammed shifted his gaze to Talib and observed some uncertainty cross his eyes. "And you, Talib, are you ready?"

Talib looked down at the table where his hands rested. His fingers were intertwined and seemed to be squeezing each other. "Mohammed, I must be honest with you. I do not want to die."

Mohammed felt a fist squeezing his heart and an emptiness in his stomach.

But before he could say anything, Talib continued. "I am a young man who has not enjoyed the fruits of my youth. I do not want to leave my parents or the woman who would become my bride. However, neither I nor my family can continue living with the oppression from the Great Satan, who does not understand the beauty of Allah. Because of that, I know that it is my duty and destiny to martyr myself tonight. You need not worry about me, for my heart is determined and strong. I go to my death willingly and understanding that I'm a mere minnow in the sea of our religion." He paused for a minute and looked at Mohammed. "You can count on me."

Mohammed stared at each man and stated, "You inspire me with your dedication to our cause. May your actions tonight bring great joy to Allah." With that, Mohammed left the RV and walked to the truck, to which the boat trailer was firmly attached and where Abdul and Will were waiting. "Let's go."

***

Pete Wilson was pissed as he paced back and forth in his girlfriend's apartment. Victoria was supposed to be ready to leave no later than 11:15 PM. However, she had spent too much time making herself look good for him and ended up making him angry instead. They were going to a New Year's Eve party which was supposed to start at 11 and go all night. With an edge to his voice, Pete said, "Victoria, if you don't hurry up, we won't be at the party before midnight. This is just bullshit that you are not ready."

"I'm sorry, Pete. Time just got away from me. I'll be ready in just a minute." A short time later, she walked out of the bathroom and saw Pete standing by the door to the apartment. "I'm ready now. Let's go."

Pete smiled in spite of himself. Victoria Walker was a truly beautiful woman with fair skin and long black hair that dropped below her shoulders. She walked up to him, wrapped her arms around his neck, and gave him a seductive kiss that took his breath away as well as his anger. Pete opened the door and they walked to his car. He opened the door for her and she got in. Soon, he was speeding down the road trying to make up lost time while the promise of the kiss lingered.

* * *

Will, Abdul, and Mohammed drove off and headed for the Bayview Beach club. When they arrived, they found no lights visible in the boat launch area. After the boat was launched, Mohammed approached Will, "After our attack, I will call you and tell you where we've come ashore. After you've picked up Bakir and Jalal, you can come to get us. If any questions come up, call me." Will nodded at him from his seat in the cab of the truck, and then headed back to the warehouse.

Mohammed and Abdul traveled in the boat for more than an hour along the coastline. The weather was foul as the boat pushed through the waves showering them with icy cold water. The wind was blowing and the rain crashed against their faces like so many needles. He and Abdul had taken turns out of the weather in the bow, but as they neared the target, they both stood next to each other, looking at the structure before them. Breaking the silence that existed on the boat despite the storm and waves, Mohammed heard the shrill ring of his phone. He adjusted the night goggles he was wearing and brought the phone to his ear, "Yes?"

Mohammed heard Will's voice, "Fahd and Talib have just left. They should be on the bridge within 30 minutes or so."

The bridge now loomed before him. Mohammed answered only, "Good."

Will heard the call disconnect.

***

The skipper of the United States Coast Guard Cutter Tern, LTJG Amanda Wakefield, was in radio contact with Chief Petty Officer Kyle Burke, who was the skipper of a 45-foot response boat that carried three other crewmen. The boat was equipped with two 50-caliber machine guns as armament. Wakefield began the conversation, "Chief, do you see anything unusual out there?"

"Not a thing, Lieutenant. Is your radar picking up anything?"

"Nothing out of the ordinary. Normal traffic coming in and out of the Bay, but other than that, not much else. Anything close to the shore would be difficult to pick up."

"How long are you going to keep us out here anyway? My lady is waiting for me, so we can celebrate the New Year."

"Since I have to be out here all night, chief, you know I'm feeling really sorry for you, right? But I'll tell you what, the powers that be believe that any terrorist attack would coincide with the New Year. If nothing has happened by 2 AM, I'll cut you loose."

"Thanks, Lieutenant, I appreciate that. You obviously have the makings of an admiral."

"And you, chief, are full of something I can't refer to on the radio."

While these conversations were going on, Lieutenant Wakefield did not know that one and a half miles ahead of them a small speedboat hugging the shore had a plan to do just what her ship was there to prevent. Likewise, Chief Burke did not realize that half a mile in front of him another speedboat was determined to place the explosives on the support tower he was about to pass as he crossed under the bridge.

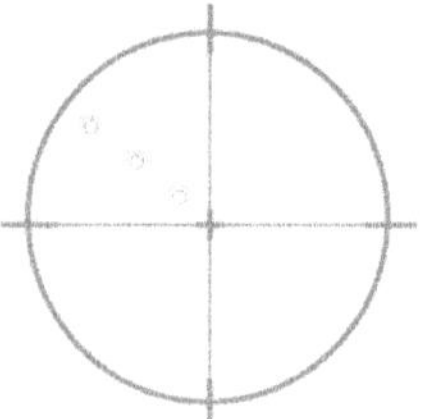

Chapter 70

Mohammed and Abdul approached the bridge quietly. The throttle was just out of neutral as they bumped into the concrete that surrounded the tower like a deck. Mohammed whispered to Abdul, who was standing next to him, "Go place the explosive. I will hold the boat here so that you can jump on and off to get what you need. We need to do this fast." Abdul jumped onto the concrete and then he was gone.

Wakefield's radio crackled to life and she heard Burke state, "Lieutenant, I have a small 18- to 19-foot vessel approaching the support tower of the bridge. It's going very slowly, but definitely heading for the tower. What do you want me to do, ma'am?"

"Go find out what's going on. Nobody should be around those towers and especially not in the middle of the night. Keep me informed of what you find. I'm heading for the other tower to check it out."

"Okay, I am powering up now and should reach them in a few minutes."

Wakefield turned to the coast guardsman standing next to her. "Jamison, get everybody up here to man the 50-calibers. We're heading for the other tower." She turned the cutter toward the second tower and increased speed. As the cutter approached, she activated the searchlight and aimed the beam toward the tower. She could see a small boat next to the tower and a man standing at the controls.

As soon as the searchlight switched on, Mohammed turned and observed the cutter bearing down on him. He screamed, "Abdul, let's go." Within seconds, Abdul jumped on the boat and Mohammed asked, "Did you finish and is the detonator set?" He could not hear Abdul's response but saw him nod. The cutter's loudspeaker was identifying itself and stated it was approaching and intended to board his vessel. He was instructed to remain where he was. Knowing that he would have no excuse for being where he was, Mohammed shoved the throttle forward and felt the prop dig into the water.

As they approached the tower, Wakefield looked at Jamison. "I'm going to drop you off at the tower so you can check it out. Then I'm going after this guy and will pick you up later. Make sure you have a radio with you." He grabbed a flashlight and headed for the bow. Wakefield brought the boat up to the concrete decking and Jamison jumped onto the tower deck.

She then charged after the slender boat, which had not stopped or slowed down. Wakefield issued two warnings to the boat on the radio and the loudspeaker. When the boat did not respond or slow down, she ordered the sailor manning the 50-caliber to put a shot across the bow. Watching the machine gun stitch the water in front of the boat, she grinned to herself and thought it was just like the movies. Once that warning shot was made, she saw the boat immediately slow down.

Jamison, after quickly looking at the foot of the tower, saw what appeared to be strings of explosives wrapped around it. He pulled the explosives from the tower and tossed each string into the bay. One string was left and he worked as quickly as he could to remove it.

Mohammed shouted at Abdul, "Get the AK-47s." Abdul grabbed two rifles and several magazines of ammunition from the bow. "When they pull up next to us, you fire at the machine guns and I'll fire at the bridge to stop it." As he finished the sentence, Mohammed heard firing coming from the direction of the other tower.

Wakefield ordered her men to stand ready as they approached the boat. The men standing behind the machine guns were more curious than watchful. They could see in the glare of the searchlight two men standing next to each other. One of the men smiled and held up a device that looked like a garage door opener. He pushed a button on the device and an explosion came from the tower they had just left.

Unknown to Wakefield, Jamison had removed the last string and was preparing to throw it into the bay when it exploded. While the bridge escaped serious damage, Jamison was torn apart and died instantly.

Suddenly, Mohammed and Abdul dropped to their knees. Both men brought their AK-47s up and opened fire. Tom Jayson, the coast guardsman behind the nearest 50-caliber, caught the full blast of Abdul's fire. Mohammed fired immediately into the bridge of the cutter, emptying an entire magazine. Two bullets struck Wakefield, one in the left arm and the other in the chest. As she fell to the deck, she turned the cutter away from the boat and it slowly moved in the opposite direction.

The Coast Guardsman manning the second machine gun immediately raked the small boat back and forth and did not stop firing until he realized there was no return fire coming from the boat. Had he been in the small boat, he would've seen that both Mohammed and Abdul had been shredded by the 50-caliber shells.

Petty Officer Jake Milam rushed to the bridge and found Wakefield lying on the deck. Milam turned the cutter back toward the boat and yelled at the machine gunner to take the boat in tow. Another Coast Guard man had arrived at the bridge and was kneeling over Wakefield. The deck was slippery with her blood and her face was pale. Before he could say anything, Wakefield asked, "How are we doing?"

The man answered, "We're going to be okay. The attackers are dead."

Wakefield then muttered, "What happened to Burke?" Before he could answer, he could see the distant, far-away look in her eyes. Amanda Wakefield's career in the United States Coast Guard had come to an end.

Milam radioed Burke, "Burke, this is Milam. What's happening over there?"

"Can you believe it, we had two Arabs open fire on us, but our gunners killed them immediately. Nobody here got hurt. What's going on there and why isn't Wakefield talking to me?"

"We weren't so lucky," he replied. "As we came up on the boat, they caught us by surprise. Wakefield, Jayson, and we think Jamison were killed. We're heading to check on Jamison and then into port. We will see you there. I'm just getting ready to notify the higher-ups about what happened."

***

Pete and Victoria were on the bridge and observed two U-Haul trucks ahead of them. They watched as one truck suddenly veered to the left and the other to the right. Each came to a halt. "What the hell are they doing?" asked Victoria.

"I don't know," replied Pete, "but I'm going to go between them."

"Maybe we should stop and see if they need help."

Pete responded, "We are late enough as it is. I'm not going to waste any more time." He hit the accelerator and sped up.

At that moment, the two trucks exploded in a brilliant flash of light.

***

Milam exclaimed, "Oh, my God. What just happened?" Milam and Burke watched and heard as the Golden Gate Bridge slowly came apart and fell into the Bay. It was not just the bridge that came down; several cars rolled off the bridge deck as well, including Pete's.

No one could hear Victoria's screams as she watched the water come closer. It was only when the car crashed into the water that her screams ended.

The sound of twisting, tearing metal was overwhelming. It would be years before either man could forget the sound of the bridge falling into the chilly waters of San Francisco Bay.

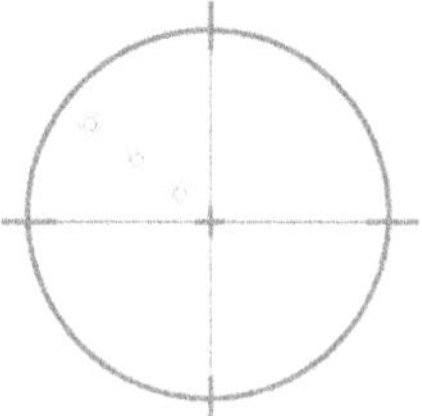

Chapter 71

Everybody had worked hard during the day to get the ranch defenses completed. We had decided to knock off by 6 PM so that we could get cleaned up and have a nice dinner. As we walked in the front door, the aroma of Ann's cooking found us immediately and tickled our noses. "What smells so delicious?" I exclaimed.

Ann poked her head around the corner. "You'll find out soon enough. Get yourself cleaned up and we'll have some drinks before the food is done."

Sandy and I went into our bedroom and closed the door. She asked me, "Do you want to shower first or do you want me to go?"

"You. I'm going to lie on the bed until you're out of the shower." I took off my dusty hiking books and stretched out on the bed. It had been a long day, and I was looking forward to a little rest. I could hear the sound of the shower pounding down and closed my eyes for just a moment. Then Sandy was shaking my shoulder. I had drifted off to sleep.

She kissed me on the forehead and said, "It's your turn, Big Boy. I'm going to help Ann in the kitchen." Still a bit groggy, I got up and soon felt the hot water warming my body. It did not take long for me to shower, dry off, and get dressed. When I walked out of the bedroom, I saw Ty exiting his room. "Did you get your shower already?"

"Yeah, I finished a little while ago. Leanne's getting cleaned up now." We walked into the family room and found Mac seated in front of the television watching a college bowl game. We joined him on the couch and Ty asked, "Who's playing?"

Mac chuckled as he answered, "I haven't a clue. But one has red uniforms and the other has white. If you can figure it out, please let me know. What would you guys like to drink?"

Ty saw Mac had a beer in front of him, pointed at it and said, "I'll take one of those, if you don't mind."

At that point, Derek had come up the stairs and stated, "I'll have a beer also, please."

Mac looked at me and I responded, "I'll have one, too." Both Ann and Sandy were once again drinking wine. "You know guys, the girls are showing a little class by having wine while we drink beer. That makes us look like nothing but a bunch of rednecks. You know what I mean?"

"Well, Mac is kind of a redneck," Derek stated, looking over at Mac directly. "I mean look, you live on a ranch with a bunch of cows and other animals. You drive a beat-up old pickup and have shit on your shoes when you come in the door."

"And since I have you guys as friends, I plead guilty. If it were only me, I would be considered a gentleman farmer. But when I add you three into the equation, being a redneck fits."

"Listen, Derek," I said, "he is too old and you are too young to get ahead of him. Now Ty and me, that's a different matter. We've been around his bullshit long enough to know better. We also know when to let it go as he slips into that dementia. Isn't that right, Ty?"

"Yep, and sometimes it's a sad sight to see, I'll tell you that."

Before Mac could respond, Sandy said, "Hey guys, it's time for dinner. Come on in and take a seat." We all took our normal seats and waited for Ann to bring in what had smelled so heavenly an hour ago.

Ann walked in carrying a large platter of meat. "Prime rib from one of our own cows. We also have horseradish if you like."

Leanne brought in baked potatoes and broccoli as Sandy walked back in the kitchen and returned with two bottles of a Columbia Valley Red Diamond Merlot, her favorite wine. "Those with a more refined taste can share in this wine." We all agreed to have our glasses filled with Merlot. I think Mac only had some to avoid being called unrefined.

Our dinner passed quickly as we dug into the food. None of us had realized how truly hungry we were. Ann received our proffers of praise with a smile. "When you're ready for dessert, I have some vanilla ice cream and Kahlua to be poured over it. Just let me know when you're ready." Everybody clambered for dessert right then. "Okay, give me a couple minutes and it will be served." Just a few moments later, the table filled with oohs and aahs as we finished the meal.

We men pitched in and helped clean up by clearing the table and doing the dishes. While the guys handled the domestic chores, the women relaxed in the family room. When we finished, the women humored us by letting us continue watching the game. It wasn't too long before both Ann and Mac got up to go to bed. They always seemed to go to bed before the rest of us and certainly got up way before the rest of us. Derek, Ty, and I watched part of the next game before Sandy and I got up from the sofa. "I think I'm too old to make it 'til midnight. You guys can bang some pans together; we're going to bed."

Derek also stood up. "I think I'll hit the sack too. Happy New Year to all of you and I'll see you in the morning." He headed down the stairs to his room.

As I went up the stairs, I saw Leanne switch channels on the TV until she found a movie she wanted to watch. She glanced at the clock and saw the time was 11:15 PM. Maybe she and Ty would make it to midnight. However, at about 11:40, she glanced at Ty and saw that he had fallen asleep next to her. She smiled at him and realized that New Year's Eve was for her to celebrate on her own.

Ty woke up and looked at his watch. 1:30 AM. He glanced over and saw that Leanne was sound asleep. She had left the television on. Something drew his attention to the TV and what he saw shocked him. He bolted upright, reached for the remote, and turned up the sound. Videos showing several hotels blazing in Las Vegas covered the screen. The announcer described the events as a terrorist attack. He ran to Mac and Ann's bedroom and pounded on the door.

A few seconds later, Mac opened the door, rubbing the sleep out of his eyes. "What's going on, Ty?"

"There's been a terrorist attack in Las Vegas! You may want to come out and watch this," Ty said in a tense voice.

Ty then came to my room and gave me the same information. We ran to the living room and called downstairs to Derek. Soon, all of us were seated in front of the television, watching the various newscasts of the evening's events. The news announcer recapped the hotel and helicopter attacks on Las Vegas. He described the three hotels that were on fire and the explosions that occurred at each, then the attacks by the helicopters and that one had crashed and burned.

I turned Ty and asked, "Didn't you get a room for Clint and his family at the Bellagio?"

"In fact, I did, but Clint decided to stay in a hotel off the Strip. Thank God for that!"

Mac spoke over the TV announcer. "It sounds like they were throwing hand grenades out on the crowd from those helicopters. They must've caused an incredible number of casualties. Have they given any estimates of the numbers killed or wounded?"

Ty responded, "I haven't heard any numbers as of yet. But as crowded as the Strip gets on New Year's Eve, it must've been a massacre."

Mac held his hand up to quiet Ty. The announcer went on to describe the attacks on both San Francisco and Seattle. The number of people killed or injured in San Francisco was less than in Las Vegas, but the economic havoc caused by the loss of the Golden Gate Bridge would be huge.

When we learned about the Seattle attack, we were stunned at how well coordinated the attack had been. Evidently, authorities had not yet released estimates of how many people had died on the ferries. Sandy, who had lived in Seattle for some time, told us that the loss of the two floating bridges would cause long-term economic disruption for the entire area.

At about 4 AM, we turned the television off. Mac looked at each one of us before stating, "I guess it's probably our turn next."

Book Five
Attack on the Professors

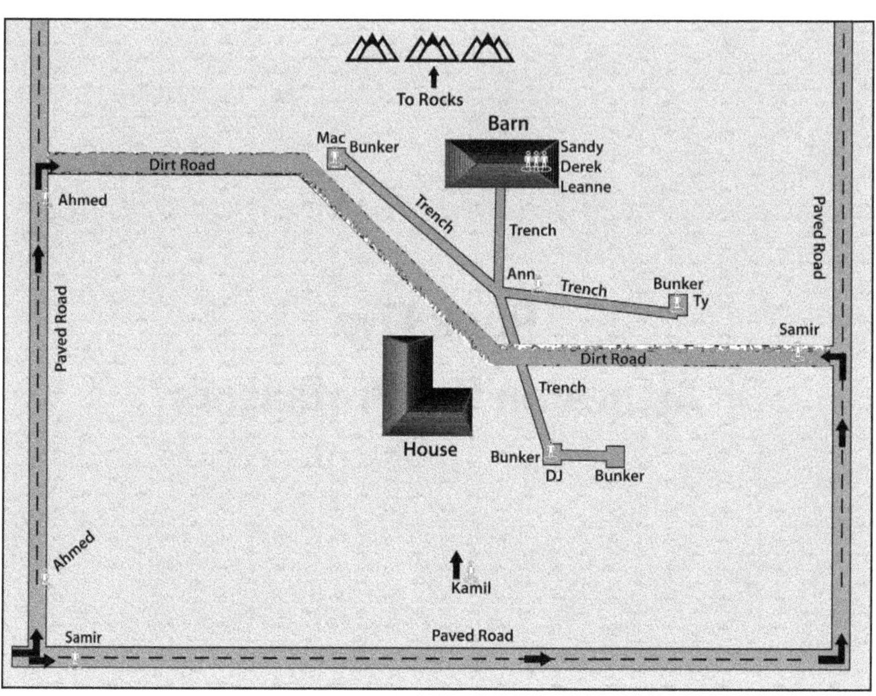

To Rocks
Barn
Mac
Bunker
Sandy
Derek
Leanne
Dirt Road
Ahmed
Trench
Trench
Paved Road
Ann
Trench
Bunker
Ty
Paved Road
Samir
Dirt Road
Trench
House
Bunker
DJ
Bunker
Ahmed
Kamil
Samir
Paved Road

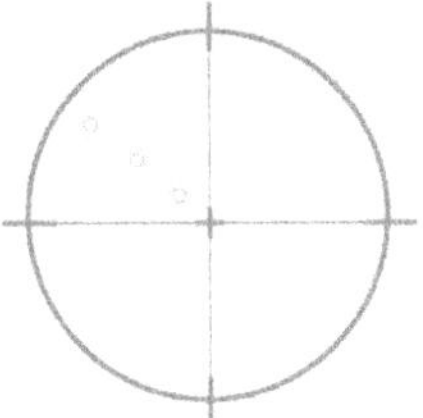

Chapter 72

As Samir was leaving Las Vegas, he called Ahmed. "Ahmed, we're just leaving now. You should expect us in four or five hours. When I'm within five minutes, I'll call you again."

Ahmed's response was terse. "I'll see you then."

Each man discarded their burner phones to avoid detection.

While he waited, Ahmed used his new phone to keep updated on the progress of the attacks. It was obvious to him the attacks on the three cities had been very successful. A little over four hours later, Ahmed received the call from Samir. He opened the door to the warehouse and watched Samir's RV drive in. He quickly pulled down the door and walked toward the RV. Samir stepped out.

Samir gave Ahmed a big bear hug and said, "We have done it, Ahmed! We have done it! Have you heard anything from Mohammed or Kamil?"

"I've heard nothing from Mohammed. Kamil called and indicated that he expected to arrive tomorrow. As you instructed, our conversation was short to avoid being detected. Do you have any knowledge of what happened to Mohammed?"

"No one has had any contact with him," replied Samir. "The only things I know is what has been reported on the various newscasts. They either have become casualties or are hiding and waiting for a chance to escape. We should continue to plan for our next attack without them. Tell me what you've accomplished here."

"I've had some problems that were unexpected. Our contact here was initially very valuable. He is the one who found this warehouse for us. However, his heart was not as strong as I would've hoped. He told me he weakened and needed to talk with another Saudi student to assure himself that he had chosen the right path. To maintain operational security, I killed both of them."

"Have the authorities connected you to those actions?"

"No, not at all."

"What have you done about the professors?" asked Samir.

"Having seen the ranch where the professors are staying, I came to the conclusion that we need some additional bodies to assist us in their extermination. Therefore, I've contacted six of our supporters here in the United States. I expect that all of them will be here by tomorrow afternoon. Depending on when you want to initiate the attack, we can be ready by tomorrow night or the next morning. Have you given any thought as to when we should attack?"

"Well," Samir responded, "since they know we are coming, there's no reason we should make their job easy by making ourselves visible during the day. Unless you have some other thoughts on the matter, I think we should attack tomorrow night," Samir said.

"That, too, would've been my choice. However, it would also make sense for us not to attack tomorrow night, but rather, wait one additional day. That would give us the opportunity to drive by their location to give you a sense of what we will be up against. Also, it will give the men a chance to catch up on their sleep and prepare for the next battle. It would also give Kamil time to arrive and rest. While I would like to finish our final attack as soon as possible, to go too early would create a substantial risk of failure."

"I think I may be too tired to see things correctly tonight. Let's wait on the attack as you suggested. Even though the longer we are here, the greater the risk of detection is, I think we need to take our time and do this right. Let us enjoy our success tonight and worry about the professors tomorrow," Samir stated.

Ahmed then went to greet the other arrivals in Samir's RV. He gave each one an air mattress and it did not take long before everyone was asleep either in the RV or on the floor of the warehouse. The adrenaline from the attack had dissipated; each man slept deeply. Chuck and Samantha had gone to their bedroom in the RV and had fallen asleep quickly.

While Samir was bone tired, he was also worried—worried about the fate of Mohammed and his men and about whether Kamil would arrive safely. Worried about whether they would be detected before they could attack the professors. His fury at the professors festered deep within him and he did not want anything to come between him and their pending deaths. Finally, having reviewed the many things that still needed to be accomplished, Samir drifted off into a troubled sleep.

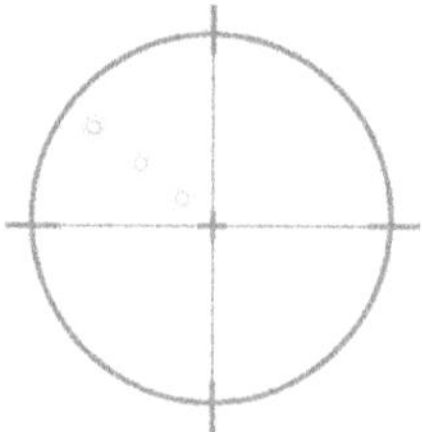

Chapter 73

Shortly after 8 AM, Agent Rheingold walked into his office and sat down at his desk. He had been watching the news accounts of the terrorist attacks in Las Vegas, San Francisco, and Seattle all morning. Initially, he thought that it was unlikely that such a coordinated attack had been carried out by one group. However, that is exactly what had happened in Paris—a broad, well-planned, well-coordinated attack. It was for that reason that Rheingold believed the terrorist named Samir was behind these latest terrorist incidents.

Rheingold picked up the phone and dialed Sam Wyman in Washington D.C. A moment later, Sam answered.

"Hi, Sam, are things going crazy there?"

"You have no idea. The city is up in arms over the safety of the country and people are already looking for someone to blame. I've already been called by the president and the director of the bureau. The only thing I could tell them at this time was that I had nothing to tell them."

"Do you have any new information for me that hasn't been carried on the news? We're in the dark out here."

"Here's what I know from talking with our agents in Las Vegas, San Francisco, and Seattle. First, in Vegas, it appears that three Middle Eastern men set fires in each of the hotels and blew themselves up in the hotel lobbies. At the same time, two helicopters from a local company flew down the Strip, dropping hand grenades on the people celebrating New Year's Eve. We're unsure why, but one of the helicopters crashed at the end of its flight. The other helicopter made a second run along the Strip, dropping more hand grenades."

Rheingold interrupted his friend, "Do you know how many casualties there were?"

"No, we can't be sure at this time. The three hotels were destroyed. We don't know why the hotels' fire suppression systems did not operate, but their systems were complete failures. There was no way to get firefighting resources to the hotels because of the masses of people in the streets. How many people lost their lives in the hotels, we simply have no idea at this time. The casualties suffered as a result of the grenade attacks were substantial. Because of the panic, there were as many, if not more, people killed in the stampede as people tried to get away.

"In San Francisco, the terrorists attacked the Golden Gate Bridge support towers. The Coast Guard stopped one boat from reaching the tower, but a second boat managed to reach the second tower and attach explosives to it. One Coast Guardsman was able to remove the explosives but was killed when the last string went off. There was minor damage to that tower. The second boat was engaged by a Coast Guard cutter and the two Middle Eastern men in it were killed. However, there were casualties on the cutter. The second attack on the bridge was by two trucks that exploded and severed the cables bearing the bridge weight, which caused the bridge to fail. At this point, we are unsure as to how many casualties occurred there either.

"In Seattle, the initial attack was against four Washington State car ferries used to connect Seattle with Bremerton and Bainbridge Island. Each of the ferries had explosives placed against the hulls below the waterline. When the explosives went off, the ferries flooded and capsized within minutes. There was one death on the boat that was tied up to the dock. The other three ferries were in Puget Sound when the explosives went off. Seattle authorities are unsure at this point how many people were on the ferries. The explosions were timed to go off about 11:30 PM. There may have been more people on those ferries than usual because it was New Year's Eve, but they were lucky this did not occur during rush hour when the ferries would have been filled to capacity. The second attack against Seattle involved the two floating bridges. One span was destroyed completely, the other partially. A third span was saved because an officer stopped the suicide truck before it reached the bridge. The truck was detonated by a terrorist and caused the collapse of the tunnel it was in at the time, as well as the death of the officer. That's about all I know, Art. It's a total cluster."

"Have you given any thought to the fact that these attacks may have been carried out by Samir, the terrorist going after the professors? I say this only because the likelihood of terrorist attacks was a major concern of theirs," said Rheingold.

"That certainly is a possibility, but I can't say for sure that all of this was carried out only by him. Whoever is responsible for these actions, the President wants them caught. You can't believe the heat that is coming down on me now."

Rheingold responded, "That's why I am bringing up Samir. In normal cases of terrorism, we would have no clue about what might happen, but it seems to me that we have a pretty good idea where they will strike next. I want to request that you send me additional resources so that I might stop this Samir from committing additional acts of terror. It may be our only chance of catching him and his followers."

It was several moments before Sam replied. "You may be right. I just don't know. I'll do what I can to send you additional agents. However, right now, every FBI office wants to keep their agents close in case they are the next target. While that is understandable, it may not be the best use of our resources. I'll talk to the director and recommend that we send you more help."

"Thanks, Sam. I can't ask anything more. If I can help you in any way, please just let me know."

"I will, Art. Let's just hope these bastards make a mistake."

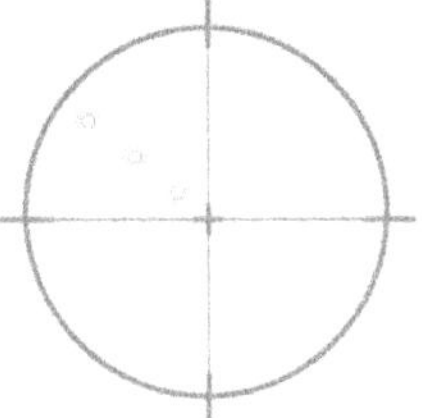

Chapter 74

President Bradford was in his office by 6:30 New Year's morning. After meeting with anyone in his cabinet who had any information about the attacks, he told his staff he wished to address the nation that evening. The press secretary indicated that he would contact the television networks to request that time be made available. Speechwriters were directed to provide him with the draft of a speech by 2 PM for the press secretary and the president to review.

Bradford was in the Oval Office when he was given the draft. It took him 20 minutes to carefully read it, and he decided that his speechwriters were not grasping what he wanted to say and how he wanted to say it. He asked his chief of staff to cancel all his appointments for the remainder of the day and told his secretary that he was not to be interrupted unless it was a dire emergency. With those instructions given, Bradford took out a legal pad, sat back with a heavy heart, and began to write.

The ideas began to flow more and more easily. He knew that his reaction to this incident would be the defining moment of his presidency.

Within two hours, he had finished the speech he intended to give. His staff was shocked when he explained how he was going to present this to the American people. They tried to get him to change his mind, but their arguments were in vain. He knew who he was and he knew the American people.

At 9 PM Eastern Time the President was ready to talk to the nation, and what would later be said to be the largest viewed broadcast of any political leader. Television sets and smartphones across the nation showed the President as he prepared to address his country. He was standing behind his desk in the Oval Office, dressed in jeans and a plaid shirt.

He began, "My fellow Americans, I am standing here in the Oval Office, a place where momentous decisions have been made by presidents of this great country. I know you're surprised that I am not wearing a suit, but sometimes I feel the trappings and formalities of this office come between you, the people of this country, and me, your President. So today, I want to talk to you not from behind the lectern or from behind the desk. I'm not going to read a speech from a Teleprompter. Tonight, it's going to be just you, me, and the notes I have scribbled on this pad.

"Last night and early this morning our country was struck a grievous blow in which we lost many of our fellow citizens. We have suffered serious damage to the economies of Las Vegas, San Francisco, Seattle, and, in fact, to our entire nation. Because of the nature of the attacks, I cannot give you an accurate number of the casualties we suffered. But each of those victims is held close to our hearts as we remember their families tonight. There'll be time in the coming days to mourn their loss, but tonight, our focus will be elsewhere.

"The men who carried out these attacks are not merely murderers, but they are cowards, because only a coward would kill innocent men, women, and children in the name of God."

The President walked over and sat down on the sofa. He leaned forward and looked directly at the camera, his voice rising. "Let me say directly to the terrorists, you are not heroes. You are cowards and a disgrace to your God. Let me also say, I promise you from the depth of my soul that you will be eradicated from the face of this earth. And I promise you not just on my own behalf but also on behalf of every citizen of this country. We will hunt you down and we will kill you."

From the look in his eyes, every American knew that he spoke the honest truth. This man, their leader, was not to be trifled with.

"And now, to you, the citizens of this great country, I make you this promise. While the government of the United States does not always do the right thing, the people of this country always want to do what is right. We have given the world the lives of our sons and daughters as members of our military and have asked nothing in return. We seek no one's land, no one's riches, or anything that is not ours. Our people do so because it is right to make such sacrifices. The people of America willfully give their national treasure to those who are in need. They do so not because they expect anything in return, but because it is right. The people of this country support those who seek freedom, not because we stand to gain, but because it is right. The goodness of the people of this country constitutes the soul of America. And yet, these evil cowards, who like snakes in the grass strike only from the shadows when they will not be challenged. These people, no, these animals run and hide when confronted."

Bradford stood once again. "You, my friends, should feel proud of who you are and what you have made of this country. I know I am."

The President returned to his desk, sat down and said, "Now, from behind this desk, I speak with the full force and power of the American presidency. Speaking once again to the terrorists who struck our country last night, your actions have not hurt America, but rather have strengthened it. We are now united in one cause. That cause is to find you and to eliminate you from the human race. You are no longer considered a member of the society of good men and women who stand for the right to love their families, to work hard to support those who depend on them and to raise their children in safety."

The President paused for a few short moments as his steely blue eyes peered into the camera. "When we have finished dealing with you, your name will only be spoken in hell.

Another pause. "My friends, there is nothing that will prevent us from achieving this goal. I ask that you join me in doing what needs to be done to remove this scourge not only from our country, but from the world itself. With the resolve that Americans throughout history have always shown, this is our time and this is our place to find justice. May God bless." The screens went dark.

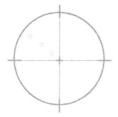

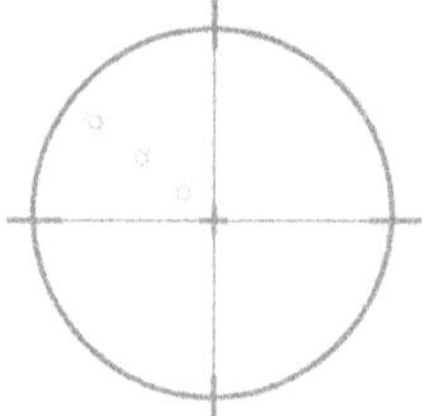

Chapter 75

I was working outside with Mac, putting some final touches on his little surprises, when my phone rang. I hit the answer button and said, "Hello."

"Hi, DJ, how are you doing?"

I immediately recognized Chief Martin's voice. "All right, given the circumstances. After what happened last night, I think we may be next. What's going on with you?"

"I wanted to know if you had heard anything from that Saudi student you spoke to me about."

"No, I haven't talked with him for a while. He said he would contact me by phone if he had any additional information. Why do you ask?"

"You never told me his name. What was it?"

"I promised him I wouldn't divulge his name because he was concerned for his safety."

"Let me ask you this then," the chief asked. "Was his name Riaz? I found your name in his phone."

"Yes, that's him. What do you mean you found my name in his phone?" My stomach clenched in fear.

"Riaz and his roommate were found murdered in their apartment this morning. One had been stabbed and the other's throat had been slashed. Also, a young woman in their building had her neck broken. We're not sure if these deaths are connected or not."

I sat there dumbfounded and could not help but believe that I was responsible for Riaz's death. I found myself going through a series of emotions in those few moments—sadness, fear that I had caused it, and tremendous rage at whomever killed him. "Do you have any leads on who may have done this, Chief?"

"Not at this time," he said. "The investigation hasn't been completed yet, but we hope something will come up. I'll let you know if we learn anything new."

Changing subjects to avoid further contemplating Riaz's death, I asked, "Do you think the terrorist attacks in Las Vegas, San Francisco, and Seattle were Samir's work?"

"It was the first thing that came to my mind when I heard about those this morning. Are you thinking the same way I am?" Chief Martin asked.

"I'm afraid I am. More importantly, I think we may be next. Have you talked with Rheingold about what he and the agency might be able to do?"

"No, I haven't," he answered. "I will be making that call this morning, however. I'll keep in touch."

"OK. Thanks for the call."

Mac came over to me. "I take it that was Martin. What's going on?"

I told Mac about Riaz and the other two people who had been murdered. "I bet it was that son of a bitch who was staying at the flea-bag motel. If we find him, he dies first."

"I'm with you on that, man. These guys obviously have no consider-ation for human life. That being the case, we should have no consider-ation for theirs. When the chance comes, we take no prisoners, and we eliminate all of them. We need to tell the others what has happened."

Mac and I walked back to the house. I gave our wives, Ty, and Derek a brief rundown on my conversation with the chief and what Mac and I had discussed.

Sandy raised the first question. "Do I understand that you want us to kill them even if they try to give up? Why would we do that?"

Mac answered both of her questions. "That's exactly what we mean. These people don't give a shit about human life. They kill innocent people in the name of their God. As long as they live, we are in danger.

If you don't kill them and they get away, I assure you they will kill you without thinking about it. They killed hundreds, if not thousands, of Americans yesterday. Why should we give them the benefit of the doubt about anything? The best thing we can do, no, the only thing we can do, is eliminate them if we can. They are not innocent civilians, they are soldiers whose sworn duty it is to kill us. If you can't do that, Sandy, we need to know that now."

Sandy, hands on hips, said, "I didn't say I couldn't do that. I wanted to make sure that you meant what I thought you did. I'm just not sure how I'm going to feel when it's all said and done."

The seven of us grabbed cups of coffee and sat around the dining room table to discuss the situation. There were concerns that if we killed someone who was trying to give up, we were as bad as they were. When the conversation ended, though, we unanimously decided that these men needed to be killed.

Mac and I left the house to continue what we had begun. He looked at me with concern. "I'm not sure Sandy can do this, DJ. If she can't, we might all be in trouble. What do you think?"

"I know she could do it, Mac. However, I'm not sure that she will. I'll talk to her again"

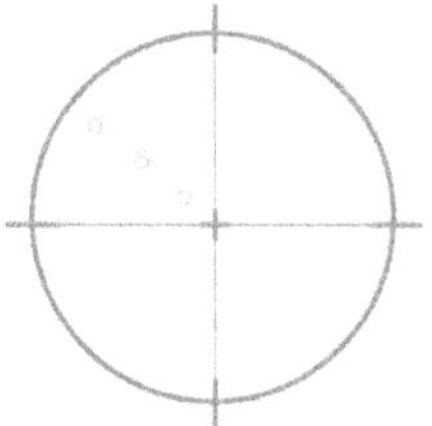

Chapter 76

Samir was walking through the warehouse when his phone rang, jerking him out of his thoughts. Kamil's name appeared on the phone. "My brother, how are you?"

"I'm good, Samir. We are within an hour of your location. Can you send me the address?"

"Of course. I look forward to seeing you soon." Samir disconnected the call without further conversation. He was eager to see Kamil and hear about the attack in Seattle. From the news reports he had been following, it was obvious that Kamil's attack had been successful. What he did not know, however, was the cost to his team.

The next hour seemed to drag into eternity. Once again, his phone rang and he answered. "Yes?"

"We are here." Samir asked one of the men to open the roll-up door, and Kamil and George drove the RV into the warehouse. Kamil stepped out and greeted Samir with a huge grin and a big hug. "Brother, we have done it. We have struck the Great Satan a blow that will not soon be forgotten. I want to hear all about your attack, too, Samir. Perhaps, Mohammed and Ahmed can join us so that I do not have to repeat my story a million times."

"Then Samir responded with a measured voice. "Ahmed can join us, but not Mohammed. We've not heard from him since his mission. From what we can decipher from the news accounts, it appears his entire team was destroyed."

Kamil looked puzzled. "From the news reports I saw, I thought that the attack on the bridge was successful. Am I incorrect?"

"No, you're correct. The damage to the bridge was caused by the truck bombs. It appears, however, that both boats that were to attack the towers were intercepted by the Coast Guard. There's been no word of any survivors from either of the two boats. News reports indicated that there were also casualties on the Coast Guard cutter. But I think it is very unlikely that we will hear from Mohammed. Also, we have no idea what happened to his drivers, Will and Brianne. There's been no mention of them in the news reports, nor have they contacted me. I would not be surprised if they were on their way back to their home."

Samir led Kamil to the RV in which Ahmed was sitting.

As they entered, Ahmed immediately stood and embraced his friend. "I'm glad to see that you have returned to us safely. Did you have any trouble on the way?"

"None at all. No one was interested in stopping our RV. How is everything here?"

The three men sat down at the U-shaped dinette. Ahmed spoke first, telling of the events that had occurred, from the death of the students to his preparations for the attack on the professors. When Ahmed finished, Samir recounted his attack in Las Vegas.

"It seems to me," continued Kamil, "that the attacks we planned were very successful. To top off our success, we need to eliminate the three professors. Where are we on the planning for that operation?"

Samir smiled at both men. "We are ready to carry out our final attack. The professors are staying at a ranch. We have had our American drivers conduct surveillance of that location by driving by at different times of the day and night. My guess is that they are waiting for us to come after them."

Kamil interrupted Samir and said, "What kind of protection do they have from local, state, or federal police agencies?"

"None that we've been able to detect." Ahmed continued, "There does not appear to be any increased police protection at the ranch nor have we detected any increase in police activity in the city itself. Either they have not told the government officials about our threat, or those officials are not giving it any credence. In any event, it certainly makes our job easier."

"Have you developed our plan of attack?" Kamil asked, looking at the other two men.

"I have developed a preliminary plan which I've shared with Samir." Ahmed responded. "However, we want to get your ideas on it before we finalize it."

"Explain it to me." For the next hour or so, the three men reviewed Ahmed's plan. Each questioned the assumptions that various parts of the plan were based on. After their exhaustive review, Kamil continued, "Ahmed, you made a wise decision to call in the new men. I think we will need as many soldiers as we can get. Do we have sufficient ammunition and weapons?"

"Yes," answered Samir. "We brought back a substantial amount of both from our warehouse. And, you, Kamil, were you able to bring back supplies also?" Kamil nodded his affirmative answer to Samir. "Good, then we have what we need to carry out our attack." Samir could see that Kamil had another question for them. "What is it, Kamil? You seem to have concerns. If so, tell us now."

"There is a potential problem that needs to be addressed. While we have Google Earth to help us look at the ranch, the only people who have seen it in person are our American drivers. They have no experience in this type of activity. I think it is very important that at least one of us drives by and looks at the ranch first hand. I would certainly volunteer to do so. While there may be a risk of discovery, there is a greater risk in initiating this action without having an experienced eye look at our target." He looked at the other two and waited for their response.

Ahmed answered first. "I agree with you. It has made me nervous not being able to personally observe the ranch. I would suggest that maybe two of us go and one remain here." Ahmed then looked at Samir. "Samir, do you agree with Kamil's suggestion and warning?"

"I understand his concern about not wanting to attack a target without proper observation. But I'm also concerned about the chance of us being discovered. If we do a personal reconnaissance of the ranch, I do believe we'll have a greater chance of being successful. On the other hand, if our reconnaissance is discovered, we may have no chance to attack." Samir pondered this conundrum for a few moments. "Given everything we know, I think our best chance for success is to do the kind of reconnaissance that Kamil has suggested. Ahmed, I want you to go with Chuck and see what you can learn about the target this afternoon. Kamil, I want you to do a similar trip to the ranch this evening after dark. We will finalize our plans tomorrow morning."

Kamil smiled at Samir and said, "When do we attack?"

"Soon."

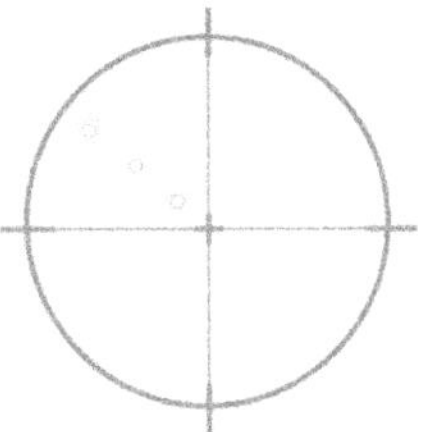

Chapter 77

Mac led the rest of us on a short walk around the property to point out all the surprises he had installed in the last week. He stated, "Just to be sure that none of you get hurt or stink up the place, I want you to know where my surprises are, so you can avoid them." As we walked, he occasionally stopped and pointed out an area we should avoid. It really didn't take that long as we traversed an area of about 100 yards out from the house. Regardless of how the attackers approached the house, they would run into one of the surprises. The danger for us is if we were forced into an area that had been booby-trapped.

After about an hour, he brought our slow walking tour to an end. "You know," he said, "I still have hope that none of this will be necessary and that we can look back on this whole adventure and laugh."

"From what we've seen of those guys in Paris, I don't expect this is going to end with laughter." Derek saw the pained looks on the women and said, "Just saying. What concerns me the most, it's the number of men he may have at his disposal. What we've heard on the news about the attacks in Vegas, Frisco, and Seattle, he obviously had enough people to do some serious damage."

Sandy was the first to respond. "Derek, as I've told you many times before, this is not your fight. You can leave at any time and no one will think anything ill of you. I can tell you that if I didn't have to be here, I wouldn't."

"I'm not complaining, mind you," Derek answered. "You see, I figure that I was a big part of our defense against these guys in Paris. I'm just as guilty, if that's the right word, as the professors are in bringing this attack here. My belief is we just have to end it here, once and for all. Am I nervous? You bet your ass I am, but that doesn't take away from what has to be done. I feel a little bit like I did before each football game. My stomach would get queasy and sometimes I'd dry-heave as I waited to go on. But once I took that first step onto the football field, it was ass-kicking time. Besides, if I hadn't been in Paris with these old farts, they probably wouldn't have survived."

Mac looked at me and stated, "Such a child, don't you think?"

Each of us were lost in our own thoughts after having listened to what Derek had to say. We headed back to the house for dinner. It was the guys' turn to cook and Mac decided we would barbecue. He went out and fired up the grill on the deck. I got some hamburger out of the fridge and began forming patties. Ty was gathering up all the condiments and Derek was slicing some tomatoes and onions. Once I had finished the patties, I headed out to the grill. Mac looked up at me as I came out the door. "Master Chef, I bring you the meat which we all expect will be cooked to perfection."

"Set it right here, my little minion."

"Of all the things I am," I replied, "I am not your little minion."

"Minion, it is only in your mind that you are not." Mac was laughing at this point and I joined him.

"The ladies are having cocktails while waiting for your skills to be put to use." I gazed out toward the road where the shot had come from. It seemed like a lifetime ago. "Do you ever think they may be out there watching us?"

Mac started placing the burgers on the grill and then answered my question. "If they're coming for us, they would have to do some kind of reconnaissance to determine how they would approach. Since I believe they're coming, I think they've already scoped us out."

"Do you feel like a little bit of a target standing out here? I mean, I do. It makes me uncomfortable to even think about it."

Mac pointed at the road across his property. "I've been watching the road pretty consistently. I don't expect them to shoot from there. At most, they would only hit one of us. If they're going to get all of us, I think they'll come to the house. You understand, if my house gets shot up, I'm going to hold you responsible for the repairs."

I smiled at Mac. "I guess you don't remember that I'm just a simple guest invited to spend the night here. However, I promise you that I will be here to help put patches on any bullet holes I can see."

"That's comforting. Without giving yourself away, look up at the road. Do you see that brown truck driving by?" Mac asked.

"Yeah, I see it. Why do you ask?"

"Because that's the second time I've seen it drive by in the past half hour. What do you say we go chase it down?"

I continued to watch the truck drive away. "Are you sure you're not getting a little paranoid over all of this?"

"Being paranoid is what kept me alive on the street. Oh well, if we left, Ty would probably burn the burgers and we cannot go to battle on an empty stomach."

"Mac, when do you think they'll come? If they come?"

"Well, DJ, it seems to me they've had sufficient time to get from Vegas, Frisco, and Seattle to here. If they don't have the equipment they need already, it will take some time getting that together. They'll need some time to figure out how they're going to attack the house. Who knows, they may not even realize we're all together at this house. They could be ready to attack tonight or tomorrow. It really doesn't matter. I think we need to be on 24-hour alert starting tonight. What do you think?"

"That's the first smart thing you've said today," I answered. "Let's tell everybody at dinner."

When the meat had been grilled to perfection, Mac and I walked back into the house and placed a platter of the juicy burgers on the counter. Everyone loaded up their plates and walked into the dining room. Mac gave a brief explanation of our conversation. "I'll put together a schedule for when each of us will watch the video feeds. I'll take the first watch at midnight. Whoever is on lookout duty will sound the alarm if they see anything that looks suspicious. Everyone should grab their go-bag and meet here. We will evaluate the threat and, if need be, go to our assigned locations. Now, the most important thing is that you must make sure to give the chef a thumbs-up for creating these incredible burgers just for you."

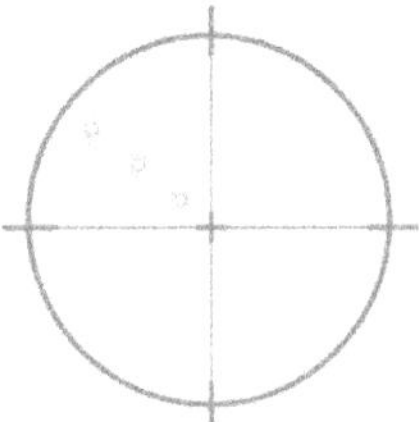

Chapter 78

It was a dark and moonless night when Chuck and Kamil drove out of the warehouse in the truck. Chuck and Ahmed had done a drive-by of the ranch earlier that afternoon. As they pulled out onto the street, Chuck explained, "I will be driving at the speed limit unless there is a need to do otherwise. We are too close to our objective to be stopped because of inattentive driving. If for some reason we are stopped, let me do all the talking."

"Okay, but if something happens that we don't expect, I'll take over from there. How far do we have to go, Chuck?"

"It will take us about 15 minutes to get to where I can let you out. I will slow down and you can jump out. I will park and wait for 30 minutes before I come back to pick you up. If you need more time, text me."

Chuck began the drive toward Mac's house; Kamil peered out the side window.

As they approached the house, Chuck said, "We're about a quarter mile away. Since we've disabled the interior light of the truck, that won't be a problem when you open the door. Are you ready?" Kamil nodded to him. When they were across from where the house stood, some 500 yards away, Chuck stated as he slowed down. "Okay, go now, go, go!"

Kamil opened the door and hopped out of the slow-moving vehicle. He ran to the side of the road and heard Chuck speed up and leave the area. Kamil saw the large house ahead of him and made his way toward it. There was sufficient moonlight for him to make his way forward unhindered.

After he had gone about 100 meters, he stopped and dropped to his knee. Kamil pulled out his binoculars. He scanned the area in front of him and around the house but saw nothing of concern. Then Kamil concentrated on the house itself. Even though it was several hundred yards away, he could see it clearly. There were lights still on in the house, which was not surprising since it was only 10 PM. He had an unobstructed view into the house; the large, floor-to-ceiling picture windows had not been covered with drapes. Kamil saw no one and settled in to watch.

Within a few minutes, several people entered the room. Two men and three women seated themselves in various chairs, talking with each other. Kamil thought that if he had a sniper's rifle, he could probably get one of the men before they could react. It was a long shot, but one he could make. However, the other two men would then be fully warned of his presence. As he continued watching, another man entered the room, walked to the window and was staring out the windows, looking directly at Kamil. Kamil dropped to his stomach and remained still. He started laughing at himself when he realized no lights would illuminate his location, and that it was virtually impossible for the man to see him. He rose once again and continued to watch any activity in the house.

Kamil considered moving closer to the house in order to get a better look. But as soon as he considered that action, he dropped it immediately. There was nothing further to be gained in moving forward. However, if by some chance he was observed, it created a risk that was not worth taking. Glancing at his watch, he saw that Chuck would be returning in about five minutes, so he started making his way back to the road. Once he felt the warm asphalt under his feet, he turned and looked at the house through his binoculars. Only one man remained in the room. It appeared that the others were going to sleep; the lights in the other windows were going out one by one. Then he saw a truck coming towards him. Its horn honked once to let Kamil know it was Chuck. A few seconds later, they were headed for the warehouse.

Chuck kept glancing in the rearview mirror to make sure they were not being followed. He looked at Kamil and asked, "How did it go?"

Kamil gave him a thumbs up and said, "I think I have the information I need. This should not be as difficult as one might expect."

A short time later, Chuck drove the truck into the warehouse. As the two men got out of the truck, Samir and Ahmed approached them. Samir was the first to speak. "Well, how did it go? Did you see any potential problems?"

"Everything went as planned. I only went in about 100 yards from the road, but I had a perfect view of the house and the surrounding area. I was able to observe six people altogether. They seemed to be just talking. By the time I left, five of the six had apparently gone to bed. The lone remaining man appeared to be reading. I also scanned the area around the house and there seemed to be no evidence of any kind of preparations for an attack. This may be a lot easier than we initially thought. After all, they are not professionals. In Paris, they were lucky. Their luck has run out."

"That would be a blessing," responded Ahmed. "Do you think we will be able to approach the house without being seen?"

"It is darker out there than the inside of a goat's stomach. There are no lights anywhere that I could see. If we attack when all the lights in the house are off, I think we can presume that everyone will be asleep. If that's the case, we should be able to enter the house quietly and go into each room and kill every person there. If we do this correctly, we'll be back in the warehouse in an hour or two. That would give us several hours to make our escape before anyone was even aware there was a problem."

Samir smiled at the two men. "Good work, Kamil. We attack tomorrow morning at 5 AM."

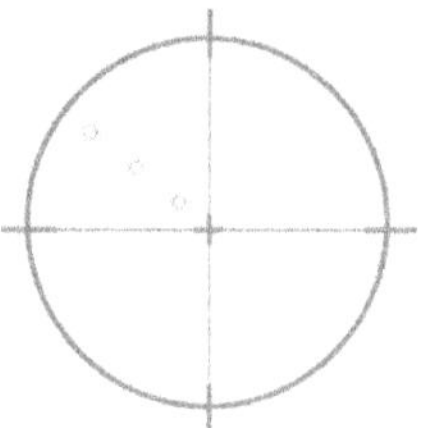

Chapter 79

Sam Wyman rode to the White House with the Director of the FBI, Richard Jackson. Jackson was a retired federal judge known for his determination to fight crime and his impeccable ethics. Over the years, he developed a slight paunch, which showed itself not only by his stomach drooping over his belt, but also in his 66-year-old jowly face. Both men would be joining the President and his national security team to review the progress of the investigation into the terrorist attacks.

They quickly passed through the entrance gate and were escorted into the White House Cabinet room. Already present were the secretaries of Homeland Security and Defense, as well as the Attorney General. Jackson and Wyman took seats next to the Attorney General and before they could speak, the President entered the room. Everyone stood and remained standing until he took a seat.

He looked around the table at those in attendance and stated, "Good morning, gentlemen. Thank you for coming. Let's get straight to business. Tell me what you know about the New Year's Eve attacks and the status of our investigation."

The Secretary of Homeland Security gave an overview of the attack in Las Vegas. "We do not have an accurate count of casualties. The number of dead from the hotels has almost reached 2500. The number of wounded is at least twice that many.

"As you know, Mr. President, two helicopters flew down the Strip, tossing hand grenades into the crowds below. One of the 'copters crashed at the end of the Strip. Four bodies were found, but they were burned beyond recognition. We cannot give you an accurate count on the number of dead and wounded from the helicopter grenade attacks because the injured were taken to several hospitals, which were overwhelmed by the number of people who were admitted. The numbers are fluid at best."

The secretary then briefed the President and the others on the attacks in San Francisco and Seattle. He finished by saying, "We have no accurate numbers of casualties in either city. In addition to the horrific loss of life from these three attacks, the economic damage to each city will probably reach billions of dollars. I will let Director Jackson detail what progress has been made in finding the terrorists who committed these attacks."

Jackson looked at the President and opened his remarks. "We are following every clue and lead that comes to our attention. But frankly, we have not made much progress simply because there is so little evidence to go on. We believe these men crossed the border from Mexico a week or so ago. That is primarily based on the fact that one of our border patrol agents was found murdered, along with another individual who was suspected of bringing illegal immigrants into this country. A few days later, a citizen reported to the local police that he was suspicious of an RV carrying what appeared to be Middle Eastern men. This information was passed on to the Nevada State Patrol, who checked all the RV parks near Las Vegas. Evidently, the RV in question had left one of the RV parks just before the state patrol arrived. We had another report about Middle Eastern men in a different RV in Oregon. However, the man who called in had been drinking heavily. Now I would like to turn the floor over to Sam Wyman, Director of Counterterrorism."

Bradford looked at Wyman and signaled for him to begin.

"Mr. President, I previously briefed you on the situation of the three professors who were involved in the terrorist attack in Paris and were recently threatened by a terrorist named Samir. I also indicated that the professors believed that Samir would carry out his threat but probably would accompany that with different terrorist attacks in this country. If the terrorist groups who carried out the attacks on the three cities are in fact coordinated by this Samir, then their next move may be toward the professors."

The President interrupted Wyman and stated, "If I understand you correctly, you believe that the terrorists will attack the professors next."

"I think it's a definite possibility, but there is no way at this time to confirm it."

"I assume then that you will send men to protect the professors and interrupt a potential attack."

"We can certainly do that and put the professors under our protection. However, if the terrorists see a protection detail assigned to the professors, they may simply back off and not act. We would lose any advantage we had. If we lay back in the weeds, so to speak, we may be able to capture the terrorists once they attack. Obviously, that leaves the professors in some danger, but that is my recommendation to Director Jackson, and to you, Mr. President."

"It sounds like you want to use the professors as bait to draw out the terrorists so we can capture or kill them."

"That's about the size of it, Mr. President," Sam nodded.

The President looked at the Secretary of Homeland Security. "Have we intercepted any electronic communications that would help us find these guys?"

"No, sir, we have not. Aside from the normal chatter we pick up, it's been as quiet as a church mouse. This is reminiscent of the attack in Paris where there was no breach in their operational security."

The President stood and looked at each of the men. "It appears we do not have any other choice than to continue as you suggest, Sam. Hopefully, it doesn't come to that. We must find these cowards as quickly as we can. Leave no stone unturned in your search and keep me advised of your progress."

The President turned and strode out of the room, leaving the others to work on details among them.

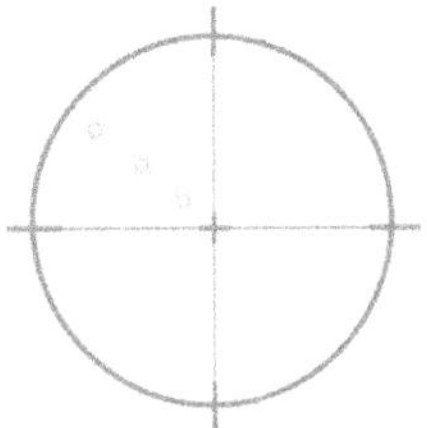

Chapter 80

At 7 PM, I looked into our surveillance room and saw Ann watching the video monitors. I stared at the screen over her shoulder for a few minutes. She was completely unaware of my presence. Finally, I asked, "Have you seen anything of interest?"

She jumped and looked up at me in surprise. "Damn. You scared me." She paused and then continued. "It doesn't get much more boring than this. I have seen absolutely nothing since I came on at 6 PM. This stuff is kinda cool, though. I have seen a wild turkey and a couple of deer. I never would've thought we would be able to see this much at night. If anyone comes onto the ranch by road or over the fields, we should be able to see them from here. The biggest danger is that whoever is on watch will fall asleep. I have to get up and walk around every once in a while to keep my eyes open. What's going on out there in the real world?"

"Not a whole lot really. Derek is reading and the rest of us are watching TV. Mac is in his shop, and I was just going to see what he's working on. I'll see you in a bit." I walked to the front door, opened it and headed for Mac's shop, which was in a separate building about 50 yards away. The lights were still on. I knocked quietly and walked in. Mac was feeling pretty proud of himself as he sat back in his chair with his feet up on his worktable.

"What are you working on, Mac?"

"I'm not working on anything. I've finished all my work, and I'm quite happy with it."

I looked around the shop and saw various pieces of metal on his worktable. They all appeared to be pipes of some kind. "Well, don't keep me in suspense. Does any of this have to do with our defense or are you just playing with your toys to pass the time?"

I was a bit concerned when Mac picked up his rifle and scowled at me. "Well, my old friend, and I use the word old in the most endearing way. I've been thinking about a way to give us an advantage over the assholes coming our way. We can use our rifles from a distance. The farther away our target is, the less chance they will hit us. However, these rifles make a lot of noise, which will bring attention to our locations." He picked up one of the metal pieces and started screwing it on to the end of his rifle barrel. "To avoid that problem, I have made silencers, or what we in the business call 'sound suppression systems,' for each of our rifles. Pretty cool, if I do say so myself."

"Well, I'll be damned! How did you ever learn to do that?"

"I went downstairs and started going through some of my storage boxes. I found this." He held up a black paperback book and tossed it to me. I looked at the title: The Anarchist Cookbook.

"That book was the bane of police officers in the early '70s. It tells you how to make all sorts of things, most of them illegal, like silencers. So I decided to put it to use."

I walked over and took the rifle from him. I held it up and examined it from every direction. "Does it work? Have you tried it out?"

"You have so little faith in me, my friend. Let's go outside and shoot a few rounds." We walked around to the back of his shop. Mac inserted a loaded magazine into the weapon. "Stand behind me. I don't want to make a mistake in the dark and shoot you. I can promise you with 100% certainty that this will work." He raised the rifle to his shoulder and pointed it at the ground. Immediately, he pulled the trigger and I heard a muted sound. Certainly nothing like I expected.

"DJ, my boy, you're free to get on your knees and bow to me and tell me I'm the smartest person you know." He started laughing as he saw my mouth wide open.

"How the hell did you know that was going to work? I would have bet you a hundred bucks it would not work the first time."

"It's quite simple really. I tested it about 10 minutes before you got here. So pay up. 100 bucks in my hand if you don't mind."

I smiled at Mac and stated, "I would gladly pay you if I had made that bet, but it was all in my mind. I will admit, however, that I'm truly impressed. What made you think of this?"

In the light from the window, I could see Mac's eyes twinkling. "We're going to be able to pick those suckers off without them having heard any rifle fire. At some point, they'll see the muzzle flash, but until then, they will be in a world of hurt. Hopefully, it will scare some of them and even the odds a bit." Mac led me back into his shop, where he picked up the remaining silencers.

"Let's go tell everybody about my cool invention and affix these to their rifles. Damn, DJ, this is actually kind of fun."

When we entered the house, Mac and I placed the silencers on the coffee table. Mac reached over and grabbed the remote to turn the TV off. Before Mac had a chance to speak, I stated, "Despite Mac's apparent mental decline, he has come up with an incredibly good idea. He is actually much smarter than he looks. Mac, show them the results of that weakened mind of yours."

Mac smiled at those sitting before him and said, "Despite DJ's advanced age, he was able, but just barely, to understand what I'm going to explain to you. I have designed and produced silencers for each of your rifles. We can shoot at those bastards and they won't hear a sound. It should allow us to take down a few of them before they realize what's happening. Go get your guns."

Then we all watched as he slowly attached the silencers to the barrels of our rifles. "Let's go outside and try them out." He led all of us out to the deck and watched as each of us fired a round into the ground below.

Ty reached out and shook Mac's hand. "I'm truly impressed, Mac, truly impressed. You are a man of many talents."

Derek fired a second round. "This is so awesome."

Even Leanne and Sandy jumped in to compliment Mac. I was enjoying this. It was like watching a bunch of children get candy on Halloween. It was getting chilly and I turned to go back into the house.

Mac yelled at me, "Why are you breaking up our party, DJ?"

"Sorry, Mac, it's my turn to go on watch. Do you want me to send Ann out so you can show her what you've done?"

"That won't be necessary, I told her about the silencers last night."

"Well, what did she think?"

A grin much too large spread across his face. "You have no idea, my friend, no idea."

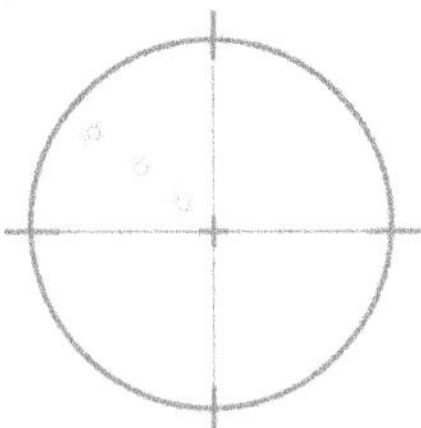

Chapter 81

Samir was in his RV, sitting on the couch. His eyes were closed as he thought of another time and day. In his mind's eye, he could see his good and longtime friend Salah. They had been together for so many years. He had never shared with any of his men that Salah had really been a brother and a member of his family. When Salah's parents were killed by Saudi intelligence agents, Samir's family had taken him in and made him a part of their family. He was the one man Samir would trust his life to without hesitation. The two of them made a formidable team in the battle against the West.

Now, Salah was dead as if by Samir's own hand. The more he thought of Salah, the more he was convinced that Salah's death rested solely on his own shoulders. The hurt to his soul was as deep today as the day Salah died.

That was the past and now was the present. He reminded himself that today was his day, his day for revenge. The only way he could possibly remove the scar from his heart was to take the lives of the three professors. One of them had fired the shot that snuffed out Salah's life. And today, it would be his shot that would snuff out their lives.

Samir had informed his men that if at all possible, the professors should be brought before him alive so that he could kill them himself. He knew this was highly improbable, but it was a dream that he had had many times. Samir pictured the three men kneeling before him, begging for their lives. He would not listen to their entreaties and would simply kill them slowly making them suffer like he had suffered. They would feel the pain he felt. And in the end, their lives would flicker out into nothingness.

Shaking his head to clear the reverie, Samir rose. From the door of the RV, he saw Ahmed talking with another man a few steps away. "Ahmed, would you gather the men here so I can speak with them?" When the men were gathered around, Samir stated, "Please be seated and make yourselves comfortable."

The men folded themselves into cross-legged positions or simply squatted on the floor.

Samir raised his voice. The poor acoustics in the warehouse made his words echo.

"Men, tonight, we will strike a great victory for our cause. We will eliminate the men who caused us the loss of many of our men in Paris. Not only will this rid us of an enemy, it will also be a signal to all Americans that there is no place they can hide to avoid the wrath of Allah.

"Before we leave this place, each of you must check all of your weapons and packs one last time. I do not want any mistakes because one of you did not do as I requested. When you have completed your review, go to your team leader, either Ahmed, Kamil or myself, to be briefed on the plan of attack, which will take place at 5 AM in the morning. You need to be in your truck prepared to leave at 4:45 AM. There is food in the refrigerator. Help yourselves and then try to get some rest. When we have completed this mission, we will execute our plan to escape.

"I want you each to know how proud I am of you and of what you've accomplished up until now. You are true soldiers of Allah and have carried yourself with great distinction. I believe that your names will be spoken with great reverence. Your family and your friends will know that you served Allah well as warriors on his behalf. Now go and prepare yourself."

As the men dispersed, Kamil came up to Samir. "And what about you, my brother. What are you going to do now?"

"I too, am going to prepare myself. Today is my day. This place is my place. I will have my revenge, Kamil."

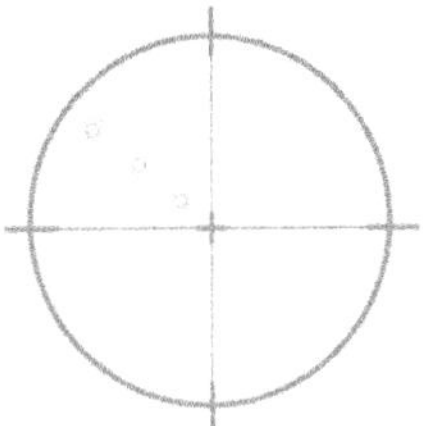

Chapter 82

Sandy had the 8 PM to 10 PM shift watching the monitors. Waiting for her to finish, I was sitting in the living room watching an NCIS rerun when I heard her walk into the room. "How did it go?"

"I didn't see anything for the entire two hours. Unlike our house, where the streets are busy, there's hardly anything out here." She walked over and sat next to me on the couch. She leaned into me as I put my arm around her. I could smell the floral scent of her shampoo. "We may want to rethink how long the shift is. I think it would be a lot easier if watching the monitors was in hourly increments. What have you been up to in the meantime, honey?"

"Just watching Gibbs kick a little ass. I love watching the show. Are you ready to go to bed?"

"Not just yet," she responded. "I have a lot of things running through my head. I don't think I could sleep even if I tried to. How about you? Are you tired?"

"No, I'm good now. I may not be so awake when I take my shift at 6 AM. I'll relieve Derek since he is taking the 4 AM to 6AM shift. Who took over for you?"

"It was Leanne's turn."

We sat there for a few moments saying nothing. Finally, Sandy looked up at me and said, "I'm really scared, DJ. I can't help it. I'm not like everyone else."

Tears flooded her beautiful green eyes and spilled over onto her face. I gave her a little hug and wiped the tears from her cheeks. "Honey, we're all scared. You haven't got a corner on that."

"I don't see that the three other guys are scared, and Leanne and Ann certainly don't look scared either. I know you're just trying to make me feel better and I appreciate that, but I know what I see."

"Well, I am trying to make you feel better, but not for the reason you think. Anyone with a brain would be worried about what the future holds for us. I was talking to Mac and Ty earlier and they each shared with me they were frightened to one degree or another."

She raised her head and looked at me as if I were crazy.

"I think they just know how to hide it better than others. It's an occupational requirement for being a police officer."

"Well, I can tell you one thing, DJ, I'm not brave, and I don't think I can hold up under the pressure that I feel is coming. You may want to take that into account when things get tougher. I mean, I can't believe how brave you were in Paris, but that's just not me."

"I wasn't brave in Paris. I was scared to death almost the entire time. The worst was waiting for the next attack. There were times when my hands were just shaking, and it wasn't only me. While we were waiting for the terrorists to strike again, I could see the fear in both Mac's and Ty's eyes."

"If you felt like that, how were you able to keep going? I just don't understand that at all. It makes no sense whatsoever. I mean, look at Ann. She's not scared. She's simply filled with determination to carry this thing through."

"Mac told me that Ann feels the same way you do. She's just able to hide it better. Also, as you know, she is a very determined and strong woman. But being determined and strong does not mean you're not scared at the same time. I know you have that same strength and determination. A friend of mine who served in Vietnam told me that being brave is not lacking in fear, but rather doing what is required in spite of the fear you feel."

Despite myself, I started chuckling and my dear wife looked at me like I was crazy. "You know, I should be a writer. That sounded pretty good to me."

She gently poked her elbow into my ribs, which brought my laughter to a quick end. "If we get through this and you write a book, I'll probably buy one. That's not a promise, mind you, but I will certainly consider it." She had a smile on her face now and was enjoying my discomfort. Her smile told me she was back with us again.

A short time later, we were in our bedroom getting ready to go to sleep. I set the alarm on my phone for 5:45 AM.

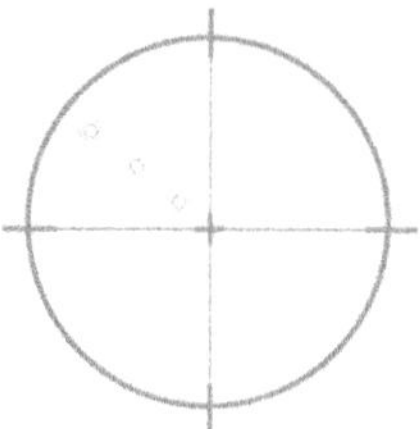

Chapter 83

Looking around the warehouse, Samir saw that his men were ready for the assault. It was 4:30 AM. The teams led by Kamil and Ahmed stood in their groups of four, talking among themselves. His own men stood around him, anxiously shifting their weight back and forth. He called to both Kamil and Ahmed to come over. "Are your teams ready to go?" The two nodded and smiled.

The drivers from the two remaining RVs, George and Molly and Chuck and Samantha, would wait in the warehouse for further instructions.

Samir spoke. "All right, men, we're about ready to leave. I want to go over our plan one more time. We will stop 1/2 mile from the ranch. I will do the final reconnaissance with Kamil and his men in my truck. If no activity seems to be happening at the ranch, I will drop Kamil and his men off. They will attack across the ranch land. I will return to Ahmed's truck and pick up my team. The teams in the two trucks will head for the roads taking them to their respective gates at the ranch. Remember, once we leave that location, all headlights will be turned off. When Kamil is 100 yards from the house, he will phone us, and we will converge on the house together.

"When all teams are in the vicinity of the house, one man from each team will act as security outside in case anyone escapes our assault. Two men will remain with each truck, the driver and one man to operate the machine gun. You are to kill anyone who leaves the house. The assault squad, consisting of the fourth man from each team, will meet at the back of the house. We will force the back door open, move from room to room as quietly as we can, and kill anyone we find. Are there any questions before we depart?"

Samir was pleased when no hands went up. His men were confident of their roles in this attack. "Let's go then. May Allah be with you."

As the men walked toward the trucks, Samir stopped and grabbed Ahmed by the shoulder. Pointing to the top of truck cabs, he said, "Very nice job, Ahmed. They will not be prepared for those." He gestured at the 30-caliber machine guns that had been welded to the top of each cab.

Ahmed had a big smile on his face. "It was a simple way to increase our firepower. It's just like the trucks ISIS uses. This is our mobile tank force."

Samir shook Ahmed's hand and climbed into the cab of his truck. Chuck opened the door of the warehouse and Samir drove out with Kamil and his men, followed closely by Ahmed. There was very little conversation in either truck as they made their way toward the ranch.

When they were about one half mile away, both trucks came to a stop. Samir stepped out and walked back to Ahmed's truck. "I'm going to check out the ranch and will be back in a minute." He stuck out his hand and Ahmed grabbed it. "See you shortly."

Samir hopped back into his truck, turned off the headlights off, and started forward. Kamil sat next to him and they both scanned the area around the ranch house. Samir pulled to a stop and looked at Kamil. "Good luck, my brother; may Allah be with you."

"And with you, my friend. I will call you when we're in position."

Kamil exited the cab and Samir heard Kamil's men jump out the back. He could barely make them out as they snuck through the field toward the ranch house. He turned around and drove back to where Ahmed was waiting. Samir's men quickly jumped out of Ahmed's truck and hopped into Samir's.

It was 30 long minutes before Kamil called to report that he was in position. Samir looked over at Ahmed and raised his thumb. "For the glory of Allah, my friend."

Both vehicles drove to the access roads that entered the ranch. When Samir reached his road, he conference-called Ahmed and Kamil. "Let's begin. I will see you at the back of the house." Both trucks started to move slowly along the dirt roads that would end at the ranch house.

Samir was surprised at the knot in his stomach and the tightness of his grip on the wheel. Earlier in his life, he had gone on many operations like this one. Because he was the leader of this organization, his recent activities had been more in the role of coordinator. Samir didn't have to participate in this attack, but his anger was simply too strong. He was going to kill the three professors if it was the last thing he would ever do. Samir could already taste the sweet revenge.

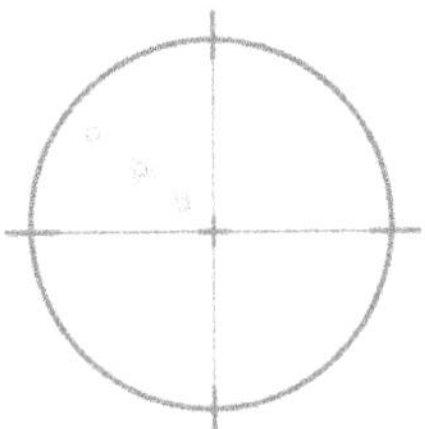

Chapter 84

Derek looked at his watch for the third time in the last 20 minutes. Time wasn't moving any faster. Standing watch and monitoring the video feeds was a pain in the butt. It was almost 5 AM and he was only halfway through his shift. Derek leaned forward to look at the monitors once again and rested his chin on his hands. The young man looked from monitor to monitor and saw the same old thing—nothing.

Derek stood and stretched, trying to get his blood moving. When he sat down, something caught his eye on one of the monitors. The young man leaned forward but couldn't make anything out. Something else happened on another monitor and he gave it his full attention. This was the one looking out over the field. Derek thought he saw some movement initially. He looked back at the first monitor and definitely saw something. It appeared to be a truck without its lights on. Derek glanced at the feed from the second road coming into the ranch and was able to make out another truck. He glanced back at the field camera and could make out people moving forward.

"Holy shit, holy shit!" Derek jumped up and ran to Mac's bedroom and opened the door without knocking. Mac sat up immediately. "They're coming, Mac. I could see them on the monitors. They're coming across the field and on the roads to the house." Without saying another word, he ran to the other bedrooms and gave everybody the same news. By the time Derek came back, Mac was dressed and heading to the monitors.

No lights were turned on and everyone converged on the camera room. After a quick glance at the monitors, Mac confirmed Derek's observations. "Get your weapons, go-packs and get to your assigned location immediately." Everyone vanished and returned within 15 seconds. "Make sure your radios are on and your ear buds are in. Let's go."

Sandy looked at me with fear in her eyes. I winked and said, "We're going to be okay and end this nonsense now. Let's go." Even so, the fear in my stomach nearly doubled me over.

With the farthest to go, Ty ran down the trench Mac had dug with his backhoe. It took him less than two minutes to reach his bunker, if it could be called that. It was a three-foot square, three-foot-deep hole covered by plywood. He entered the bunker from the back and looked down the road. His bunker was approximately 100 yards from where the road turned toward the house.

Ty took out his night-vision goggles and placed them on his head thankful that Chief Martin had supplied them, giving him a pale green view of the world. Coming toward him, having just turned off the road, was a truck with its lights out. He immediately keyed his radio and stated, "I have a pickup truck coming toward me with its lights out. I can't make out how many men are in it."

Mac, having run down a trench toward the other road, was in a similar bunker watching the other entrance to the ranch. He also saw a truck only 75 yards away advancing toward him. He keyed his radio. "This is Mac. I have a truck coming toward me. I can't make out the number of people in it either."

Derek, Ann, Leanne, and Sandy headed down the trench toward the barn. Ann stopped at the point where the three trenches from the bunkers came together. When Derek reached the barn, he quickly climbed a ladder to the roof where he had a 360-degree view of the ranch. He keyed his radio. "I'm on the roof and can see both trucks. I'm not sure I'm ready to take a shot because they're too far away for me to see clearly. Leanne and Sandy are set up in the barn."

I ran down the trench that led to a bunker facing the open field. Like the others, I had my night-vision goggles in place and started to search the field. A body hit the ground and screamed out an apparent curse. There was a sharp retort from another person, which quieted the first person down. I keyed my radio, "Mac, I think one of them just fell into your pig shit surprise."

Mac responded, "Well you probably won't need to see him. You should be able to smell him from a fair distance." I could imagine the smile on his face.

Ty interrupted them, "I have a better view now. Oh, shit."

"What is it, Ty?" Mac asked.

"It looks like they have a small machine gun set up on the roof of the cab. Boy, this could change everything."

I spoke next, "I can see four men in front of me. They have just turned and are heading for the house. I'm going to work my way back to where Ann is. If I don't, they could cut me off here."

Mac responded first. "Okay, but keep an eye on them to see if they head in any other direction."

"Will do."

Mac keyed his radio again. "Ty, any more information on the truck in front of you? I just saw two men jump off the truck in front of me and head for the house. My guess is this is their killing squad. They probably think we're asleep in our beds."

Ty answered, "The same thing just happened here. Two men dismounted and are heading for the house. What's our play, Mac?"

"Just a minute, Ty. Derek, has your situation improved any?"

"Yes, they're close enough that I think I have a decent shot at both trucks. What do you want to do?"

"Okay, guys. Here's the plan. Derek, I want you to shoot the guy in the truck in front of me standing behind the machine gun. When you're ready, count down from five. Ty, you and I should take out the men heading toward the house. Derek, after you fire your first shot, try to take out the gunner on the truck in front of Ty."

"Got it. Get ready, guys." Everyone could hear Derek slow his breathing through the radio. "5-4-3-2-1. Shit, I missed him."

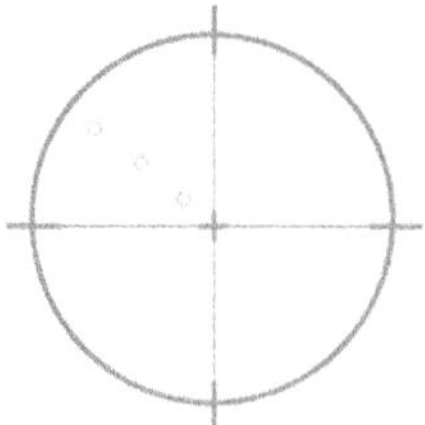

Chapter 85

After letting the two members of his assault squad out, Ahmed slowly drove his truck forward, eyes remaining focused on the house. The man standing in the truck bed manning the machine gun ducked down quickly. He pounded on the back window and yelled at Ahmed, "I think someone just shot at me."

"What the hell are you talking about? I didn't hear anything."

"I didn't hear a shot, but I heard the bullet whizz by my head. I've heard that many times in Afghanistan. I think we're under attack."

Mac slipped out from under his dugout and reached into his pocket, pulling out a long string of firecrackers wound together. He lit the fuse and threw it as far as he could. It landed between the truck and the house. He waited a moment and then the string started to explode.

In response, Ahmed let loose a full magazine toward where the firecrackers were exploding. The man operating the machine gun began firing as well. They waited to see if any further shots were being fired from that location.

Ahmed pulled out his cell phone and called Samir. "We're being fired on out here. Where are you?"

Samir answered, "We just cleared the house. No one is here. How many people are firing at you?"

"Only one, I think." There was a pause, followed by the sound of shattering of glass. "Damn! A shot just came through the windshield. I think these guys may be using silencers since I've not heard any shots. I have no idea where they are."

"I think I just saw muzzle flash in front of you about 50 meters. Have your machine gunner shoot ahead of you as you go. I'm heading back to my truck. Kamil will come out the front door and head toward the barn."

* * *

Mac saw the truck move forward toward him. He keyed his handheld radio, "They're moving toward my position. I'm going to fire a full magazine and then I'm heading for Ann's position." Mac raised his rifle over his head and pointed it toward the truck. With the rifle on full automatic, he emptied his entire magazine at the truck. He then ducked and took off at a full run down the trench toward where he knew Ann was positioned.

* * *

The machine gunner in Ahmed's truck saw where Mac's firing was coming from; he also saw the outlines of the bunker. He immediately unleashed a long burst in that direction. When no further firing occurred, he yelled at Ahmed, "I think I got him."

Ahmed responded, "Keep me covered, and I'll check it out." Ahmed got out of the truck, pointed his rifle toward Mac's bunker and crawled slowly toward it. When he reached it, Ahmed found that it empty. Even in the dim light, he noticed a trench running away from it in the direction of the house. Jumping to his feet, he ran back to his truck, jumped in, and called Samir. "There's a firing position in front of me, but it's empty now. There's also a ditch that runs toward the house."

Samir put his truck in gear, ready to move forward, when he heard a scream. He looked back and saw his machine gunner writhing on the bed of the pickup. Another man, who had returned from the house, jumped up to take his place at the machine gun. Samir yelled, "Get down. Someone is shooting at us!"

* * *

We all heard Derek come over the radio. "I think I got the machine gunner in front of Ty. I can't see anyone else, but I'll keep watching to see if I can get another shot."

Mac came running up and found Ann and me waiting for him. "Where's Ty?"

"I haven't seen him or heard from him for some time," said Ann. She keyed her radio "Ty, where are you?"

"I'm still in my bunker. The truck in front of me hasn't moved at all. I saw some people run toward the truck from the house, but they must be hiding behind it."

Suddenly there came a loud cursing from the direction of the house. I asked, "What the hell was that?"

"If I had to guess," Mac replied, "I'd bet it was my rake. I set it down in such a way that if someone stepped on it, it would bring the handle up and hopefully hit him in the head. Another one of my surprises."

"I think I can see the sonofabitch," said Ann. "He seems to be rubbing his forehead. Just a minute. I'll help relieve his pain." Ann slowly pulled the trigger of her rifle and sent a round into the man's forehead. He fell quietly without making a sound. "Yep, I don't think his head hurts anymore."

Over the radio, Ty interrupted her, "What do you guys want me to do? Stay here? I am beginning to feel a bit lonely out here all by myself."

I responded, "Some men are coming from the house. They will intersect your trench in about three minutes. Unless you want to be stuck out there, I suggest you get your ass back here immediately."

"I'm on my way!"

A minute later, two automatic rifles opened up where Ty would be running.

He appeared out of the darkness. After a couple of deep breaths, Ty said, "Have we killed many of them yet? I haven't even got a shot off and it's hard to tell if they're hit or have simply fallen to the ground looking for cover."

Mac answered, "I think we've killed two, maybe more; it's hard to tell. I'm not even sure about the two we think we got."

Derek interrupted our whispered conversation. "Both trucks are coming toward your location. It looks like they're following the trenches. Unless you want to get caught between the two of them, I suggest you move back toward the barn."

"Before we bug out, I have another surprise for them." Mac pulled out three more large rings of firecrackers, handing one each to Ty and me. "I'll light them, and then I will throw mine toward the truck coming my way. Ty, you throw it toward yours and DJ, throw yours toward the house. When the firecrackers go off, everybody be ready toget out." We nodded and he lit the three fuses. "Now."

Each of us stood and threw toward our assigned location. We waited about three seconds before the firecrackers started exploding. In response, the terrorists opened fire in the direction of the fireworks.

"Let's head for the barn," I yelled. Ann started off first, followed closely by Mac. "I've got the rear, Ty." He wasted no time and headed down the trench with me close behind. When all of us had entered the barn, we saw Sandy and Leanne covering our retreat. "Derek, what are they doing now?"

"They joined up where the trenches turned toward the barn. I'm going to try to get one of the machine-gunners." A moment later, we heard a scream. "Yep, I think I got him. They've all taken cover on the ground. Hey, guys, it looks like the sun is starting to come up. That means this has been going on for almost an hour. Why aren't the police here? Someone called them, didn't they?"

Mac realized that everyone had been too hyped up to actually think about calling for help. He took out his phone and dialed 911. When the dispatcher answered, he recognized Jolene's voice. He had talked with all of the dispatchers previously and informed them what was going on, so the call shouldn't be a surprise. "Jolene, it's Mac."

"Hi, Mac, are you doing your chores already this morning?"

"No, I haven't been doing chores. We've been fighting those damned terrorists I told you about. We could use some serious help, sooner than later, if you know what I mean."

"Why didn't you call me when they first attacked? I can't read your mind. Did you think you could just handle them all by yourself, Big Boy?"

"Jolene, if I survive this, I'm going to come down there and..."

"Oh, shut the hell up, Mac. You are getting awful sensitive in your old age. I've already put out the alarm. Seriously, be safe."

Mac was ready to respond to Jolene with a series of curse words that had never been used in the Marine Corps. Just then, automatic fire ripped through the barn. Everyone dropped to their stomachs.

Spitting dirt out of his mouth, Mac shouted, "Let's get the hell out of this bullet-infested place right now. Ann, go get them fired up."

"I'm on it," she replied and took off.

He then keyed his radio, "Derek, take two more shots and then get your ass down here."

"You got it, boss." A moment later Derek spoke again. "I'm on my way."

We all belly-crawled to the back of the barn, then crawled through the slightly opened barn's back door.

***

Kamil crawled over to Samir. "It's going to be light before long. What do you want to do now?"

Samir kept looking at the barn before he answered. "I don't want to get caught out here in the open during daylight. Let's spread out, charge them, and kill them all."

Word quickly spread to all the men of the action they were about to take. Samir looked around to see if the men were ready. "Now, let's go get them."

He and the others stood up and ran toward the barn, their guns firing on full automatic. They slowed briefly to change magazines and continued firing as they ran forward. Kamil reached the barn first and burst through the heavy wooden door, which had been shredded by the gunfire. He turned and sprayed the entire barn until his magazine was empty. Now dawn provided enough light to see that the people they were after were no longer in the barn.

The roar of engines suddenly filled the barn.

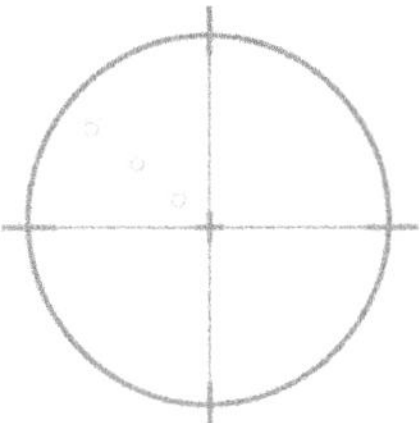

Chapter 86

Early on, we all understood that we would not be able to hold out very long at the ranch because they could attack us from different directions. As a result, we decided that it would be important for us to have an escape route. Mac recommended escaping by ATV to an area about one mile away covered with trees and large rock formations. Lucky for us, Mac and Ann owned two side-by-side ATVs that could carry four people each.

The vehicles were ready for us and Ann had them both up and running by the time we reached her. Mac's wife was waiting in the driver seat of one of the ATVs when we arrived. Sandy slid into the front passenger seat while Mac and I clambered over the sides into the back. Leanne scooted into the driver's seat of the second ATV; Ty and Derek jumped in behind her.

Ann shouted to Leanne over the roar of the engines. "Remember to keep your distance so they have to split their fire. Let's get out of here!" With that, both women hit the gas and the ATVs lunged forward.

Both Mac and I had our rifles and looked to the rear to see if we were being followed. I glanced over and saw Derek and Ty doing the same thing. Ann and Leanne drove over the open fields toward the rock formations where we intended to make our last, and hopefully successful, stand.

***

Samir ran toward the door of the barn and looked out. He could see the two ATVs heading across the open field. "They're trying to get away. Get the trucks and we will follow them. Hurry!"

Two of his men ran back to the trucks and drove to the back of the barn. The rest of the men loaded up and the trucks took off after the ATVs. Samir figured that the professors had at least a 200-yard lead. Samir, in the front passenger seat, yelled to the men in the back. "Use that machine gun to kill them now."

The machine gun opened up, sending its deadly rounds in the diverging directions of the ATVs. After a few seconds, it was clear to Samir that because the truck was bouncing across the open fields, the likelihood of a successful shot was minimal. However, he knew that he had more than enough ammunition to keep firing anyway. The machine guns continued to rattle off their deadly rounds.

***

Mac and I saw the machine guns open up at the same time. Mac yelled at me, "You try to hit the driver and I'll go for the machine gunner." I nodded at him and opened fire. The sound of our fire was still muted as we went through our magazines. Fortunately, we had packed extra magazines into both ATVs. Unfortunately, our shots were not striking home. Traveling over the open field and bouncing as we were made it nearly impossible to hit our targets, which were still over 200 yards away.

I looked toward the ATV carrying Derek and Ty. They were also shooting at the trucks. I hoped they were having better luck in hitting the terrorists than we were.

I glanced forward and saw that we were fast approaching the tree line, which would give us some cover. The trees were not close together, but rather irregularly scattered, with trails winding around them.

Even when we were among the trees, I could still hear the machine guns firing as the terrorists' trucks neared the tree line. Suddenly and without warning, there was a high-pitched scream, followed by the sound of a crash. I looked toward the second ATV and saw that it had turned toward us and rolled.

Ann stopped next to Leanne's ATV. I jumped out. Leanne was screaming and holding her left arm. It appeared that she had been shot, and it also looked like her leg had been broken in the crash. Except for some bumps and bruises, Ty and Derek seemed to be okay. I yelled at them, "Get Leanne on board this ATV."

Derek and Ty ran and picked up Leanne as gently as possible, then carried her to our ATV. She was still screaming from the pain. I picked up Derek and Ty's rifle and threw them in the ATV and grabbed as many magazines as I could carry. Derek and Ty had climbed aboard and were waiting for me. Ann screamed at me, "I'm leaving with or without you." Knowing that she meant it, I jumped on immediately and we bolted forward.

***

"We have them now!" screamed Samir. "Keep firing and don't let them get away!"

It seemed like every man on both trucks was firing his weapon. But as before, their aim was off, given that the trucks continued to bounce over the uneven terrain. Samir watched as the ATV wove in and out of the trees and appeared to be heading toward a large rock formation. The pick-up trucks had to slow down because of the narrow winding trails. Samir watched the ATV turn behind a rock formation. He yelled at both drivers, "Stop here for a minute."

As he studied the formation, it seemed to him that they planned to fight it out from behind the rocks. He leaned out the window and yelled at Ahmed in the other truck, "Go to the right and dismount about hundred yards from them. Have one of your men stay at the machine gun and the others get ready for an assault. We will go from one tree or place of cover to the next. I will be off to the left and do the same with my men."

"Let me know when you're ready to move forward," Ahmed responded.

"I will. It is our time to kill them."

***

The rock formation we had chosen for cover was divided into two parts. The first was a wall of broken rocks that stood up to six feet high that provided various points where we could fire and still be protected. The second part was six feet behind those rocks, a formation that stood close to 15 feet high. Through the middle of this wall of rocks was an opening through which a person could escape to the back portion of that formation. There was a natural trail we could follow from the six-foot-high rocks through to the back of the higher rock wall.

Ty carried Leanne behind the rocks and sat her against the taller rocks. That movement caused her extreme pain and, luckily, she passed out. Ty quickly looked at her injuries and wrapped her arm as well as he could with the supplies he had in his go bag. He straightened her leg out to hopefully ease the pain.

Derek went to the top of the second rock formation to use it as a sniper's perch. Ann went halfway up that same rock and selected her firing positions. Ty, Mac, and I would fire from behind the first rock formation. Sandy spoke up immediately, "I'll stay here and take care of Leanne."

Mac responded, "No, that won't work, Sandy. We need you at your firing position, especially since Leanne is down. The mere fact we are here does not mean we are safe. We cannot deviate from our plan at this point."

She looked at me, but before I could respond, Ty spoke up. "He's right, Sandy. You need to get up there. I'll look after Leanne down here."

"Okay, Ty, if you think that's best." She then followed Derek and Ann's path through the rock formation. Soon, they began climbing to find the best positions to fire from.

I looked at Ty, "How is she doing?"

"I think I got the bleeding from the gunshot wound to her arm taken care of. It's almost come to a stop. Her leg is definitely broken; we need to get her out of here and to a hospital. That is, if we get out of here."

Mac caught our attention by saying, "Hey, guys, we still have business to take care of here." He was standing in the middle of the rock formation looking out over the fields. Ty went to the left side and I went to the right side of the formation. "It looks like they've split up with the trucks going to either side. From what I can see, there's one guy manning the machine gun and the others have spread out. My guess is they're going to come at us using the machine guns as cover."

Just as he finished speaking, both machine guns started firing and I could hear the rounds pinging off the rocks in front of us. The three of us returned fire as well as we could while still remaining behind the safety of the rocks.

Occasionally, I could hear from behind us the muffled sound of Derek firing. We agreed that the women would not fire yet so as not to give away their positions. As Mac and I continued firing, it seemed that neither side was gaining an advantage. From my perspective, we were winning since none of us had been hurt since arriving at our current position. I adjusted my bulletproof vest and turned to Mac and asked, "Where in the hell is the chief and the help we're supposed to be getting?"

"I don't know, but he had better get here soon. I'm getting low on ammo."

Ty responded, "Same here. Pretty soon, the only people with ammunition will be the women."

***

Samir had not initiated his attack immediately because he wanted to observe the professors and see what they had planned. It soon became apparent that the professors were going to wait them out. He knew he could not fight a long battle, especially now that it was almost daylight and the police would soon come to assist the professors.

Just as he was signaling to move forward, Samir heard the distant *thump-thump-thump* of approaching helicopters. There was no time to waste. He signaled Ahmed and pointed forward. On cue, the machine-gunners threw up a wall of lead at the rock formations. His men ran at full speed toward the rocks.

***

Mac keyed his radio so he could be heard over the din of gunfire. "I hear the cavalry coming but it is going to be close. Be ready, here they come! Make every shot count."

The battle seemed to take on a life of its own as the terrorists came forward firing. Each of us fired at the terrorists as best we could.

Derek shouted over the radio, "I think I got two or three of them."

Mac asked, "Derek, how are you doing for ammunition?"

"I'm good."

Ty interjected, "I'm down to my last two mags."

"Me too," I responded.

"Ladies, you need to be ready," Mac shouted.

***

Samir turned around and could see men dismounting from the helicopters. He shouted to his men, "Everyone but Ahmed, Kamil, and me will turn and face the men coming from our rear. Don't let them get to us."

When Samir realized that the fire toward his men had slackened, he urged Kamil and Ahmed forward. They began running toward the rock formation.

Ahmed, who was to the far right of the rock formation, flopped down behind a tree. He could see one of the women lying on her side with her back against the rock wall.

***

Ty yelled at Mac and me. "Leanne has additional magazines in her go-pack. I'll get them from her." He turned and ran to where she was still lying unconscious, but now on her side. Picking up her go-bag, he took one step before he was hit in his left hip and fell to the ground. "Oh, God, I'm hit." He tried to drag himself along the ground to safety.

I looked at Mac and said, "I'll get him. Keep them off of us." Mac continued firing as I ran toward Ty.

Ty yelled at me as I approached him, "Get back or they'll get you too!"

"Shut up and I'll get you out of there." Running to where Ty was lying, I grabbed his shirt and started pulling him backwards to safety. Suddenly, it was like someone hit me with three baseball bats. I was knocked backwards and fell to the ground.

Derek keyed his radio. "I either hit the man who shot Ty or scared him off. He seems to be running away."

Mac, who was running to cover my spot on the right side of the formation, turned and looked up at Derek, "What did you say?"

Derek, who had been forced down behind the rock wall as a result of Kamil's firing from a position near Ahmed, did not respond.

Mac had just started to turn back toward the terrorists when Samir stepped from behind the rocks and slammed his rifle butt into Mac's forehead. Mac dropped to the ground without saying a word.

As Samir walked toward me, he stated, "So I've got all three of you here together. At least you get to die with each other. Which one of you killed Salah?" I smiled at him. "Then you get to die first." As he raised his rifle, I stared down the long dark barrel waiting for it to fire.

"I don't think so, Asshole!!"

Sandy had snuck through the pathway between the rocks. She stood with her handgun aimed at Samir. He spun quickly, raising his rifle. Two shots rang out. Samir stood with a shocked look on his face and then fell backwards.

Ann also walked into view and said, "Well, I'll be damned if you didn't shoot him. Good girl." Sandy and Ann walked up and stood over Samir. "Not bad for a beginner, Sandy, but you just hit his shoulder and his side. I don't think he'll die from those. Do you want me to shoot his balls off?"

Before Sandy could respond, Samir smiled at the two of them. "You don't want to do that; I'm a valued prisoner for your country. You see, they will want to talk to me to see what information I have to give them. And after that, they will put me on trial for murder. What they don't know is that I will use the trial as my platform to speak to the world about our cause."

Better late than never, Agent Rheingold came running around the rock formation and saw the Saudi lying on the ground. "Is that Samir?"

Sandy nodded in the affirmative. "You have a most important prisoner for us."

Sandy replied, "No, I don't." With her handgun, she fired two shots into the middle of Samir's forehead. "He was killed in the course of battle."

"You just killed him."

"There is not a jury in the United States that will convict me of anything regarding his death."

"You know, I think you're right about that."

Another muted shot was heard, ending Sandy and Agent Rheingold's conversation. They both looked at Ann, whose rifle was still smoking, and she responded, "That one won't be enjoying his 72 virgins either."

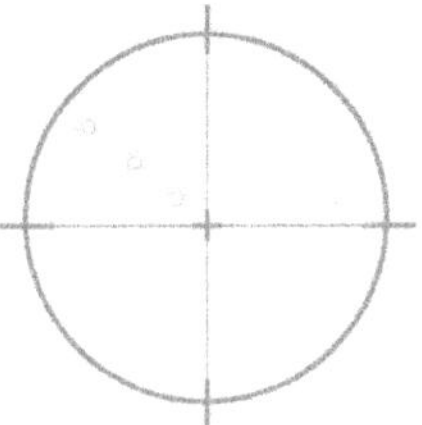

Chapter 87

Kamil had watched Samir knock out Mac and walk toward DJ. He continued to stay hidden because he knew the men behind him were closing in. Once he saw that Samir had been killed, he moved toward where Ahmed was hiding.

Ahmed had vacated his position when he began taking fire from Derek and made his way to a relatively small rock about four feet high. Kneeling behind it, he was shielded from both Derek and the men coming in from the helicopters. It was a very short fight between their men and the men who had landed. Even though their men had been well trained, they were no match for the FBI hostage rescue team who had been ordered in by Sam Wyman.

Ahmed watched Kamil move toward his position and slide in beside him. Ahmed then asked, "Now what?"

"Let's find a place we can hide until nightfall. I'll call Chuck and have him pick us up on a nearby road tonight. Then we'll get our asses out of this area. Any idea where we can find a place to hide?"

"Let's keep heading away from them," stated Ahmed. "There has to be something back here." Bent over and moving quickly, the two men searched for a place of refuge, making sure to keep the rock formation between them and the Americans. Suddenly, Ahmed held up his hand and stopped Kamil. "Look over there." He motioned to Kamil and pointed at a relatively small hole in the rock formation. He looked in and saw it was like a small tunnel. Ahmed took out his phone and switched on the flashlight app. The hole went back approximately 15 feet and would be wide enough for both of them.

Kamil got down and worked his way into the tunnel backwards so that he was facing the entry. Ahmed looked around to see if there was any indication of footprints or other evidence that might lead people to their location. Seeing nothing that would give them away, he found a large rock that fit the tunnel opening. He to crawled backwards into the hole and used the rock to block the entrance.

It turned out to be a nerve-wracking wait as the FBI searched for stragglers. Several men walked past their hiding place during the afternoon, but no one noticed their den. They heard helicopters taking off and returning several times. Kamil and Ahmad they assumed were taking live or dead bodies from the scene. In the early evening, they heard several men making one final search of the area.

They did not move from their hiding place for several hours. After sunset, when both men thought it was safe, Ahmed pushed the rock from the tunnel entrance and crawled out, followed by Kamil. In a hunched walk, they moved off slowly walking toward the road a few kilometers away. They called Chuck and arranged for him to pick them up. Ahmed told Chuck to change his lights from low beam to high beam when he believed he was close to their location.

As they walked, Kamil spoke. "I was afraid that Samir's obsession with the professors would get him killed. Just think of it, we carried out three major attacks in the US, which were successful beyond our wildest expectations. Now we've lost our leader because of three men." Thinking of the men who had been killed this day, Kamil stated, "Such a waste of good soldiers."

Ahmed continued the conversation. "At least Samir gave you the name and phone number of the person who is supporting us financially. When we get back, we should let him know what happened."

"Why wait until we get back? I'm going to call him right now."

When he disconnected the call, Kamil turned toward Ahmed. "He has someone he wants us to meet in Mexico. He'll text us the date and location." The two men continued walking until they came to the road where they would meet Chuck. Kamil dialed Chuck's number. "We are here."

"I'll be there in 15 minutes."

The time seemed to crawl by as they hid by the side of the road waiting. A vehicle turned toward them and flashed its lights. A few moments later, Chuck pulled up and stopped. They opened the door to the RV and stepped in. Chuck drove off into the night.

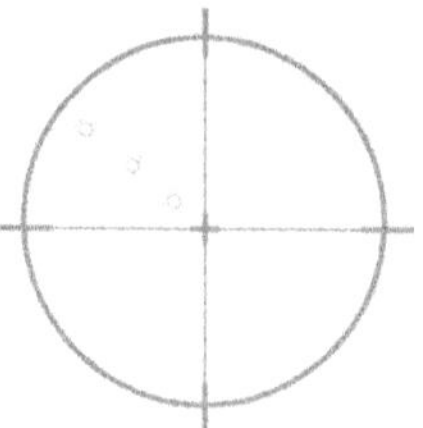

Chapter 88

The previous afternoon, Leanne, Ty and I had undergone surgery for our various injuries. None of them had been life-threatening, which was amazing in itself given the number of shots fired. Leanne's arm had been cleaned and bandaged, and her broken leg set. Ty, whose injuries were the worst, had to have hip surgery, which would require a long recovery. I had taken three shots to my chest. Two had hit my bulletproof vest and were stopped. The third had just missed the bottom of the vest, hit my lower abdomen, and exited through my upper leg without causing major damage. While all of us would be up and about soon, we knew how lucky we truly were.

At about 9 AM, Sandy walked into my room and greeted me with a big kiss. "How would you like to go for a little ride?"

Suspicious at once, I asked, "And where would you be taking me? You do know, don't you, that I was shot and need time to heal."

"You're such a baby. So just shut up and enjoy the ride." At that point, a nurse, Toni, so it said on her name tag, walked in and started unplugging the machines I was attached to.

I smiled at her and said, "I assume you're in on this. Should I expect that by unplugging all of those machines that my death has already been determined?"

She looked at my wife and responded, "You're right, he is a big baby."

"You're in cahoots with her, aren't you?"

She gave me a big smile, showing off her white teeth. "We women must always stick together."

They pushed my bed out of the room and down the hall. Shortly, we came to a halt in front of another room. Sandy opened the door and the nurse pushed me in. I realized we were in Leanne and Ty's room. Derek was there as well, with a large bruise on his forehead. It was good to see them again. I started the conversation. "They disconnected me from all my machines and brought me here. I think they need witnesses to my upcoming death."

The three of them responded at once. "You are so full of bullshit."

Toni responded immediately. "That's what his wife told me also."

All four of them were laughing at me. "I get no respect. None whatsoever. So why am I here? And, Derek, what happened to your head?"

"I ran into one of the Mac surprises. When Ann and I were walking toward the house yesterday, I stepped on a rake lying in the weeds. Damn near knocked me out." He turned red at the sound of our laughter.

Ty brought us back to the moment, "I think we're waiting for Ann and Mac." Ty looked at me, "How are you feeling, by the way?"

"The nurses were taking pretty good care of me before this morning," I said glancing at the nurse.

Toni walked over and lightly tapped me on the head with her finger. "Listen, Man-Baby, you're going to be here for a while. I suggest you discover a new attitude."

With a smile, I responded, "What? What did I say?"

As one, they all answered, "Oh, just shut the hell up."

The door opened and in walked Ann and Mac. Ann asked, "How is everybody doing this morning?" We all gave them a quick update on our respective conditions. Suddenly, there was knock on the door and Agent Rheingold walked in.

"Well, look who decided to join the party," Mac stated. "Late again, just like yesterday."

Rheingold smiled and walked up to Mac, shaking his hand. "Mac, why did you wait so long to call us yesterday?"

Knowing the direction the conversation was going, Mac responded, "Touché. What are you doing here today?"

"Well, I've got some great news for you. The President wants to talk to you."

"The President of the United States?" asked Leanne, her mouth open.

"The one and only," said Rheingold.

"Well, I'll be damned," responded Mac. "I wonder if he would be willing to waive my taxes for say the next ten years."

The door opened again and a tall man wearing a dark suit walked in the room. He nodded at Agent Rheingold and walked to the window. He looked outside for a minute or so and then placed his wrist next to his mouth.

The door opened once again and in walked another Secret Service man. Immediately following him, the President of the United States entered and smiled at us.

"Hello, ladies and gentlemen, I'm John Bradford, your President." The President, tall and distinguished, walked around shaking each of our hands and asking how we were doing.

Mac stated, "The President of what?" We all looked at him with our eyes wide and our palms raised toward the ceiling. He just smiled at us.

"Agent Rheingold, is this the one you warned me about?"

"Yes, sir, it is."

"I think we'll have the IRS take a look at his past tax returns."

"Oh, sir, I don't think that's really necessary. I'm sorry, but I always heard you had a great sense of humor." Mac tried to look contrite.

"I do, Mac. I think I can hear you sweating about your tax returns." The President continued after we all stopped laughing. "Seriously though, I wanted to take this time to thank you on behalf of a grateful nation. Without your grit and determination, we would not have been able to bring justice to the people who attacked us. I'm proud of what you have done and I know the people of this nation will feel the same when I explain it to them."

Rheingold interrupted the President by saying, "That might not be the best course of action, sir. I'll explain it to you later and then you can make up your mind."

After a few more moments of conversation, the President stated, "Ladies and gentlemen, I need to get going, but before I do, is there anything I can do for you?"

"Mister President," Mac responded, "is there any possibility you can help me with the damage the terrorists did to my home? It's not real pretty right now."

"I think we can help you out with that, Mac. I'll have someone call you. Anyone else?"

Derek had been quiet during the entire time of this conversation, stated, "Well, Mister President," Derek answered, "Is there any chance I might get some help with my student loans?" We all rolled our eyes at him.

"This is the other man I spoke to you about, Mister President," stated Rheingold.

"No, Derek, I can't do that. But what I can do and I'm willing to do is write a letter of recommendation in support of your application to become an FBI agent. We could use a man like you."

Derek stuttered his response, "Yes, sir. Thank you, sir."

The President ended the conversation by stating, "Just so you know, all your medical bills will be taken care of." With that, the President left the room.

Mac began walking around the room. "Did you see that? I can't believe that a politician can spend the people's money so quickly. No wonder the country is in such bad shape."

"You don't have to take the money, dear," Ann stated.

"Sometimes my mouth works before my mind does. Forget I said that."

Ty looked over at me. "Did you hear all that, DJ? Derek gets to become a junior G-man and Mac gets his house repaired. What do you and I get? A lengthy hospital stay."

"Well, Ty, Derek may deserve it. However, Mac is another story. You and I fight like crazy and what does Mac do? He lets himself get hit in the head with a rifle butt. Then he plays dead because both you and I know that his head is so hard it would never have knocked him out."

Mac spoke up immediately as he held his head with both hands. "Honey, I think we need to go. The doctors told me I had a very, very, very severe concussion and that this type of abuse would only make it worse." He looked around the room. When he had our attention, he winked, and walked out of the room.

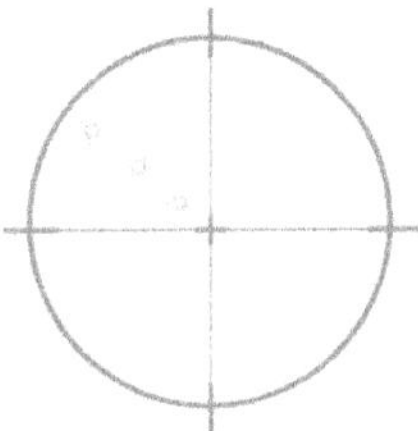

Chapter 89

Late that same afternoon, President Bradford arrived at the university where Ty and I taught. He walked onto the stage where just a few short months earlier, Ty, Mac, I and our students were warmly greeted by our family and friends on our return from Paris. He looked out at the basketball arena that was filled with more people than the fire marshal would approve of. As he stood at the lectern, Bradford smiled at the one camera at the back of the arena that was bringing the event to homes throughout America.

"To the people in this arena and to those Americans watching throughout this great country of ours, I'm happy to announce some very good news. The terrorists who committed the horrific acts in Las Vegas, San Francisco, and Seattle have been killed. They had the bad luck to try to kill four men who had disrupted their attack in Paris. These men, along with their wives, had a running gun battle with the terrorists yesterday. Along with members of the FBI and local law enforcement, these seven people brought the cowards to justice.

"Two of the men and one woman were seriously injured. I met all seven of them today in the hospital to thank them on behalf of all of us for their dedication and bravery in defeating these cowards. I told them they were heroes. They disagreed with my description. They told me that they weren't heroes, they were Americans. People who were thrust into a very difficult situation, and despite the fear each of them felt, continued to defend themselves and our country. We should be forever thankful for their actions on behalf of all of us."

The President sat down, and a young woman stood, beginning to sing Lee Greenwood's song, God Bless the USA. When she reached the verse, "And I gladly stand up," the entire audience rose to its feet. When the song ended, the applause was deafening.

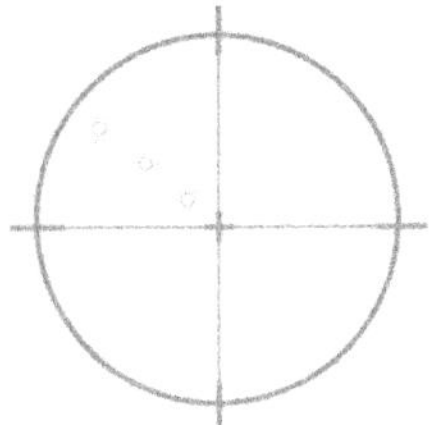

Epilogue

It was a cool, sunny January day in San Diego when Ahmed and Kamil left the hotel that catered to the downtrodden. The previous day, Chuck had purchased a 30-year-old Chevrolet Impala with way too many miles on it. Kamil climbed into the driver's seat and got on the highway heading toward Tijuana. When they arrived at the border crossing, they could see it wasn't a particularly long wait for passing through customs. As they had been instructed, they were wearing well-worn and dirty clothes. A custom official stepped out and asked, "What were you guys doing in the U.S.?"

Kamil responded, "We were visiting our families for Christmas, but now we're going home."

The official was tempted to ask him how they got into the country, but at this point, he knew it really made no difference. If they came in illegally, all the authorities could do was send them home, which was where they wanted to go now. Why waste the time and money, he thought. He looked at them and smiled, "Have a good day, gentlemen."

The two terrorists continued through customs and into Mexico.

A few days later, Ahmed and Kamil were in Mexico City. It was shortly before 2 PM when they entered the small park near their hotel. Samir's contact had arranged the hotel for them and then gave them the information for this meeting. As they walked through the park, they saw a short woman of Asian heritage seated on a blanket. Her black hair framed her rounded face. Both men approached her. Ahmed stated, "It is such a beautiful day today. May we sit on your blanket?"

She smiled at each one and pointed toward her blanket and said, "Yes, that would be wonderful. Please sit." With the code completed correctly, both men sat down.

She spoke in a low voice. "I understand you have just returned from the United States on business. Is that correct?"

Ahmed responded, "Yes, you are right. Why do you ask?"

"Because I think we will be doing business with each other in the United States."

Kamil looked at her closely, "Who are you anyway?"

"I am your Korean connection. Your North Korean connection."

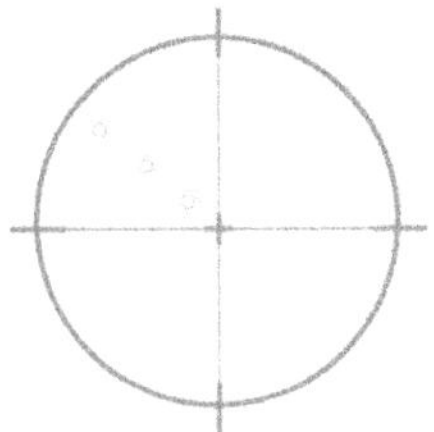

Acknowledgements

Many people are involved in the development and completion of a book such as this.

First, I want to thank Ron Flud and Dan Swanson for their thoughts and insights into police operations and the reactions of police officers. Their review and comments about Mac and Ty brought these characters to life.

Several individuals reviewed this manuscript and provided helpful advice in the development of the final product. Those individuals include Sharyl Admire, Beverly Flud and Madalyn Swanson. Pivotal to a good book are great editors. I had two of the best, as well as Kira Henschel and Katie Groves.

I also want to thank Ryan Allen for the exciting book cover he created.

Thanks to Sandi Lunt for the wonderful photographs.

I want to extend my gratitude to Kira Henschel and HenschelHaus Publishing, Inc. for believing in this book and bringing it to you.

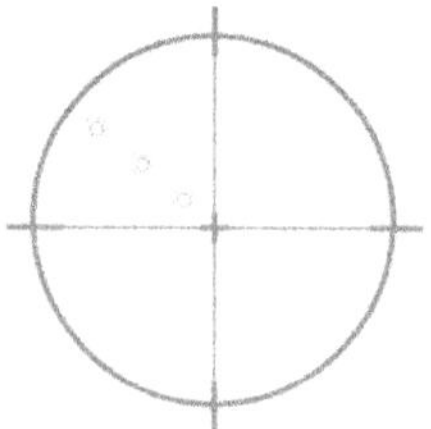

About the Author

Dave Admire received his law degree from the Catholic University of America. In his early career, he was both a prosecutor and defense attorney. At the age of 33, he was elected District Court Judge in the Seattle area. He served in this position for over 22 years. During his time of the bench, he developed a reputation for being creative and innovative in searching out alternatives to incarceration.

After retiring as a judge, Dave continued his work with young people by becoming a college professor. Before retiring, he was an adjunct professor at Seattle University for 20 years. He was chair of the Criminal Justice Department at Bethany College in Kansas. Subsequently, he became department chair of the Department of Political Science and Criminal Justice at Southern Utah University in Cedar City, Utah. In the summer of 2010, Dave served as a visiting professional at the International Criminal Court in The Hague, The Netherlands he acted as a legal advisor to Judge Christine Van den Wingaert of Belgium.

Dave resides with his wife Sharyl in Cedar City, Utah, working on his third novel, a sequel to *Samir's Revenge*, entitled: *The Korean Connection.*

Please visit his website for more information: www.daveadmire.com